NOT
my
type

OTHER BOOKS AND AUDIO BOOKS

BY MELANIE JACOBSON:

The List

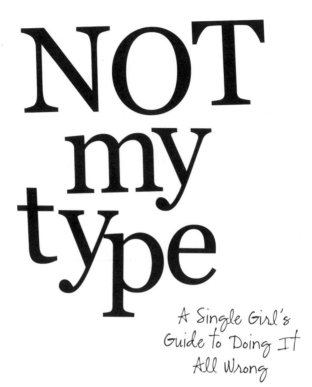

NOT my type

A Single Girl's Guide to Doing It All Wrong

a novel

Melanie Jacobson

Covenant Communications, Inc.

Cover images: *Colorful Socks* © 2009 Nika Fadul; Getty Images.

Cover design copyright © 2011 by Covenant Communications, Inc.

Published by Covenant Communications, Inc.
American Fork, Utah

Printed in the United States of America
First Printing: September 2011

17 16 15 14 13 12 11   10 9 8 7 6 5 4 3 2 1

ISBN 978-1-60861-467-7

To James
I am grateful for you every day

Acknowledgments

Always and first, I could never do this without my husband, Kenny, who supports me with his enthusiasm, his unwavering belief in me, and his willingness to overlook a messy house when I'm in the middle of storytelling. I also want to thank Amy Lou Bennett, sister and beta reader extraordinaire; my kindest critic, Aubrey Mace; my thoughtful and encouraging critique partner, Kristine Tate; and two other readers who are so generous with their time, Sue Marchant and Jaymee O'Rafferty. A special thank you to Josi Kilpack, Susan Auten, and Rachel Gillie for their honest and incisive feedback and for helping me grow as a writer by using the markup option generously. The same must be said for my editor, Samantha Van Walraven. Thank you to Joan Jacobson, who brags about me like I'm her own child, and to my father-in-law, Skip, for saying he's proud of me. Thank you to Jill Peterson and her magical camera for making me look good. Finally, thank you to the friends and family who continue to believe that I can do this.

Dear Ginger,

Thanks for the encouragement. Some people say it's wrong to kick someone when they're down—but not you. YOU march to the tune of your own demented drum. Don't let anyone tell you different.

Love always,
Your older, wiser, and far-better-looking sister

Chapter 1

A fistful of mayonnaise makes a decent projectile when you're in a pinch. If I'd been thinking more clearly, I would have grabbed a handful of jalapeños instead, but my vision did this red, blurry-anger thing, and when I ran after Brady Willardson's black Jeep, what I threw was . . . mayo. It's probably harder to clean up, and it's better that way, really. Less damage, bigger mess. Dumb kid. I owed him worse for the way he'd trashed Handy's.

I trudged back inside the sandwich shop, and the door swept aside approximately a thousand of the napkins Brady and his lame friends had strewn all over the floor. I scooped a few up and wiped the mayo off my hand. Katie and Tara huddled behind the sandwich bar like the sneeze guard was their last line of defense against me. Which it was.

I said nothing, just stared. Katie cracked first, like I knew she would.

"I'm so sorry, Pepper," she said, verging on a blubber. "I don't know what happened!"

I lifted one eyebrow slowly—the way my mom did when I was little, and I knew the longer it took to reach its full arch, the more trouble I was in. Even mouthy Tara shifted nervously now. I slowly scanned the wreckage inside Handy's Dandy Sandwiches and then eyeballed them again. "How do you not see this coming?"

A high-pitched seal bark escaped Katie. It was her nervous laugh, an involuntary reflex that I hoped, for the sake of her future social life, she would outgrow soon. Her laugh had summoned me from the back office to catch Brady Willardson's Band of Merry Teenage Idiots wreaking their usual havoc in the dining area.

A visit from Brady goes like this: He shows up, flanked by at least two of his wing men, and proceeds to put on a show to impress the girls. This involves flinging packets of condiments, punching each other, littering, and otherwise ignoring the counter girls they're there to impress. I guess not much has changed in the five years since I graduated from high school.

This afternoon's special performance reached new heights—make that lows—when one of Brady's atrophied brain synapses fired off what his underworked neural receptors interpreted as a "good idea." The ensuing napkin fight resulted in shrieking, giggling, and Katie's panicked seal barking. I walked out to discover her and Tara hiding behind the storage room door while one of the teenage terrorists lay pinned to the floor by a larger tribe mate, who was brandishing a squeeze bottle of ranch sauce over his head. All this while Brady tried to breach the storage room in search of . . . who knows what. More projectiles for lame teenage boys to throw when their hormones suffer a sun flare, I guess.

Don't judge me for chasing them out and lobbing a chunk of fatty mayo at their car. It was the least violent of all the impulses I entertained when I saw the napkins they had flung all over the floor. They didn't quite cover the few dozen smooshed mustard and ketchup packets that lay there as well. Worse, scads of busted salt and pepper packets formed a fine grit over the whole stupid mess. No, don't judge me. The only shock should be that Brady and his stupid lift-kitted Jeep didn't get what was coming to them months ago. Maybe I should keep an extra dozen eggs and a slingshot on hand as Brady repellent.

Tears formed in Katie's eyes. Knowing that a sobbing high school sophomore was not going to help my mood, I sighed. "All right. Here's the lecture. They can't eat here anymore. Call me out if they come back in. Clean up. If you want a paycheck next week, don't distract me again until payroll is finished."

The tears quivered and then rolled down Katie's cheeks, but she looked surprised and then thankful when she realized I was done.

"That's it?" she squeaked. Tara elbowed her, and Katie bit her lip while I glared once more for good measure then headed back toward the office. I could hear them scrambling behind me to clean up. Satisfied that they would have things righted within the hour, I settled down to make sense of the Payroll and Asset Manager program still open on the computer screen. Stupid PAM. I think she had it in worse for me than Brady and his army of condiment hurlers. *Awesome.* I still had a long afternoon to go at my dead-end sandwich job, with only a creeping tension headache to keep me company.

What a way to spend my birthday.

* * *

"Happy Birthday!"

A chorus of five chipper voices greeted me when I walked in the front door. I stopped short, sure that the small surprise party waiting for me was a figment of my imagination. It had to be because I had given my family strict orders to ignore my birthday. I planned to spend the evening wallowing in the room I shared with my seven-year-old sister, moping over the extreme loserdom I had achieved in my twenty-three years. I intended to bounce around my friends' Facebook pages and envy their cool trips and great jobs while I tried to figure out how my life had become an epic fail. My evening definitely did *not* involve a cheesy family birthday party that I'd forbidden several times. Loudly.

But no, when Rosemary detonated a party cracker near my ear and Ginger sprayed me down with enough silly string to soak up even the most aggressive BP oil spill, I had to concede that my family had, in fact, thrown me the world's weakest surprise party.

My mom's smile told me she knew they were on thin ice.

"What is this?" I asked, my head pounding worse than ever.

"A surprise party, duh." Ah, Ginger, an enemy of the obvious.

"Mom, I told you I don't want to do anything for my birthday."

"And I think that's ridiculous," she said. "Twenty-three is a big deal, and at the very least, you deserve cake with your family."

"Twenty-three is not a big deal," I said. "It's boring. There's no milestone. There's nothing I can do today that I couldn't do yesterday."

My brother Mace tore himself away from picking at the frosting long enough to say, "Twenty-three is a prime number. You can't even divide it by anything. It's totally lame."

I glared at him.

"What?" he said. "I'm backing you up."

"I'm with Mace," Ginger chimed in. She's halfway through her senior year and the resident pain in the neck. "I can totally see why you're depressed. I mean, your age is lame, your job is lame." She swiped her finger through some icing and took a little cake with it. "I'm sad for you," she said, her mouth full.

"Ginger!" Mom was struggling to hold on to her temper. Ginger has that effect on people.

"Forget it," I said. "She's right. There's nothing to celebrate, which is why I said I didn't want a cake or a party."

"But it's good!" Rosemary shouted. "I picked chocolate."

My jaw dropped, and my mom flushed. I like chocolate everything—except cake and ice cream.

"Rosemary really wanted it . . . and I got you butter pecan ice cream." My dad looked both sheepish and hopeful as he added the last part, as if it would compensate for once again indulging one of Rosemary's whims. She's hard to resist, and the fact that she's a surprise baby, eight years younger than fifteen-year-old Mace, doesn't make it easier.

"But it's *my* birthday cake!"

"That you didn't even want," Ginger pointed out. "You should chillax. You're getting older now. You could have a stroke or something."

That was it. Remembering the satisfaction of watching the mayo drip down Brady's car, I stalked to the counter where Mace had tugged the cake to the edge so he could sneak the frosting more easily. I reached out a finger like I was going to swipe some too, but instead, I flipped the whole thing over, pleased when it crashed to the floor and splattered chocolate chunks on Ginger's shoes.

"These are new!" she yelped. "I just got them! Mom!"

That got no reaction because Mom was busy trying to comfort a wailing Rosemary, and Mace was trying to get to the cake board to see what he could scavenge.

My dad stared at me, one eyebrow inching its way skyward, and then he pointed at Rosemary. "Apologize," he said, his voice calm.

I ignored the tiny pang of guilt somewhere around my appendix or some other useless organ and headed up the stairs. "I said I didn't want a party!" I yelled over my shoulder.

"You get back down here *right now*," my mom hollered up the stairs.

I slammed my bedroom door.

My room didn't improve my mood. A room shared with a seven-year-old rarely does. The Strawberry Shortcake on Rosemary's comforter mocked me with a serene, blank-eyed smile, and the bare walls on my side of the room didn't offer a better distraction.

Flinging myself onto my bed didn't help because I knew Rosemary would be crashing my pity party any minute. Seven-year-olds don't understand boundaries. I lay there for all of three minutes, staring at the opposite wall where her collection of American Girl dolls stared creepily back, before the door flew open. Rosemary stood there, fists on hips, looking cute, tear-streaked, and mad.

"You ruined my cake!"

The seed of guilt my dad's look had planted blossomed into an acknowledgment that I was possibly a horrible human being if I had it in me to make Rosemary cry. I clung to surliness to save me. "It was *my* cake," I said. "It's *my* birthday, remember?"

"But I picked my favorite flavor for you, and me and Olivia worked on it so hard this afternoon! She's going to think you're so mean," she said, as if I cared about her best friend's opinion.

Which, okay, I did. It's not like I plotted ways to hurt seven-year-olds' feelings. "Rosemary, I hate chocolate cake. Didn't Mom or Dad tell you that?" I asked instead, determined to rationalize my poor behavior.

"Yes, but I made yours special with chocolate chips. I even had to find them in the cabinet all by myself because they didn't come in the box, and you *ruined* it." More tears welled. I felt some of my own pricking my eyeballs. I hate being a sympathetic crier.

I pulled my pillow over my head, clinging to righteous indignation so she couldn't guilt me into feeling worse. Or crying. "Go away, Rosie."

"It's my room too. You can't make me leave."

"I need some time to myself," I said. "Why don't you go to Olivia's and complain about how awful I am?"

"You're rude!" she yelled, but the idea of relaying all the drama to Olivia must have appealed to her because I heard the door shut behind her. I enjoyed about thirty more seconds of blank-brained quiet before a sharp knock sounded. I peered from under my protective pillow to find my dad poking his head in.

He waved at the foot of my bed. "Is that seat taken?"

I shoved the pillow behind me then shook my head and stifled a sigh, knowing I was in for it.

He sat for a moment and studied me with a half smile. My dad has mad skills that are like Dr. Phil level. Except my dad is nice. Which makes it hard to kick him out of my pity parties. "So when you say you don't like chocolate cake, what you really mean is you hate chocolate cake's guts?"

I rolled my eyes.

"Hey," he said, giving my foot a gentle shake. "Where did your sense of humor go?"

"I don't know, Dad. Probably down the same black hole that sucked all the other good things out of my life."

He sighed. "Do you think that's an overstatement?"

Ah, the joys of having a marriage and family therapist for a dad. They're obnoxiously reasonable and hard to ruffle.

"No. I don't." I punched my pillow, trying to shove it into a more comfortable lump.

He didn't say anything else, just watched me with his patient therapist gaze.

I groaned. He still stared.

"Fine, I'll talk," I said, struggling to sit up straight.

"Resistance is futile," he intoned in his best robot voice.

"Let's start with the fact that I'm not overstating what a disaster my life is," I said. I crossed my arms tightly across my chest to communicate that I was totally not playing.

"Okay. That's as good a place as any."

"I have the worst job, I live at home and share a room with my kid sister, I have no social life, and I'm still nursing a broken heart."

"That's quite a list," my dad said. "Let's take them one at a time. The *worst* job? Really?"

"Yes. I have teenage customers all day long. I have teenage employees all day long. And even the nonteenage customers are cranky all the time. I have a college degree, for Pete's sake. Why am I managing a dumb sandwich shop?"

"Yes. Why are you managing a sandwich shop?" my dad echoed. His tone was neutral, but I wasn't fooled. He was using what he likes to call "reflective listening," a therapist term for spending an hour saying, "How do you feel about that?"

"Don't you do your counseling voodoo on me," I warned. "I'm on to your tricks."

He smiled. "This is dad voodoo. I'm in here right now because I love you and I'm worried about you. You flipped over the birthday cake that Rosemary worked on all afternoon. I thought I'd better find out if there was a good reason for that. It's not the action of a happy daughter."

"It was chocolate," I muttered under my breath.

Dad let that pass because he's smart. "So, your job. Maybe it's not the job you want, but it pays the bills, right?"

"Not fast enough," I said. "Otherwise I wouldn't still be living here and sharing a room with Rosemary. And before you say it—yes, I understand the law of natural consequences. It still stinks. "

"Natural consequences" was another one of his favorite expressions. He and my mom loved to throw that out anytime one of us kids was verging on or recovering from a disastrous choice—the perfect way to describe my broken engagement and the mountains of resulting debt. No doubt we'd be analyzing *that* soon. It was a perfect example of their mantra. "You're free to make your own choices, and you're free to pay the consequences."

The payment of my consequences turned out to be super literal when my ex-fiancé, Landon, forced me to call off our wedding a week before the date. I had paid for everything myself, and I had a massive credit card bill to prove it. That's because it was the second time in two years that we'd called our wedding off. The first time, my parents had footed the bill. They loved me, but not enough to do it twice. Even though my sandwich wages would (barely) cover rent in a borderline apartment somewhere in Salt Lake City, I'd had to move back home so I could pay my credit card off faster—a credit card my parents had advised me not to get in the first place. Right after they'd advised me not to marry Landon. In the gentlest terms, of course.

When I'd announced that the wedding was off (again) and I wouldn't be moving out, they didn't so much as hint at "I told you so." They did, however, inform me that they had promised Ginger her own room for the first time ever, and they weren't going to renege, which meant I had to swap places with her in the shared room with Rosemary. I guess my dad was absent from his family therapy class on the day they taught that family harmony depended totally and utterly on each child having their own room. That or my parents didn't want to pay for a six-bedroom house. Whatever.

"We've covered the bad job and sharing a room, which just leaves your social life and your broken heart. Might I guess that those two things are related?"

I shrugged. "Guess all you want. I'd rather not talk about this part."

"Then I will," he said with an easy smile. "How long do you think you're going to mourn the end of your engagement? It's been seven months."

"You of all people should understand that these things take time," I said. "You're supposed to be on my side."

He ducked down to stare me in the eyes. "I am always on your side, Pepper. Always. That's why I'm going to dish out a little tough love."

Aw, crud. Nothing good has ever followed those words.

"I have watched you climb out of depression and have cheered for you, but you've hit a plateau. I'm worried you'll backslide if you don't do something soon to fight this funk you're settling into. And you *are* settling. Almost everything you've mentioned as wrong with your life is something you have the ability to change. But you don't. Why is that?"

"I can't change any of it," I said. "I can't give up my job or else I can't pay off my debt. If I don't pay off my debt, I can't move out of the house. As long as I'm at home, my social life will continue to be severely limited. I definitely have grounds for a funk."

"I didn't say quit working, but there's no reason you can't find a different job." He tapped his finger on my knee. "You said it yourself; you're college educated. What do you want to be when you grow up?"

"It's an English degree, Dad. A bachelor's in English qualifies me to do exactly what I'm already doing: manage a sandwich shop."

"If only I had known that when I signed the tuition checks." He shook his head sadly. "I'd have made you switch to cosmetology school."

"What a waste. I'd have failed hair brushing 101 and been kicked out. You can write that check for Ginger."

"I will when it's her turn." Ginger had a five-year plan that involved opening her own salon, and a ten-year plan that included world domination via beauty spa. She already worked part time as a receptionist at the trendiest salon in town.

Even though I knew what was coming next, I couldn't resist a smile when he broke into the chorus of "Beauty School Drop Out" from *Grease*, his mellow tenor doing Frankie Avalon proud.

"It should have been you instead of Landon," I grumbled when he was done. "You have a way better voice."

He reached over to ruffle my hair. "I think I'm a little too old for *The It Factor*," he said, naming the show that had stolen my fiancé from me. "I'm happy with my adoring fans here at home."

"Dad, you're starting to make me feel better, and it's really annoying. Could you leave me to sulk in peace?"

"I would if I didn't love you. But the tough love is just beginning. I'm serious about you changing your job. This one isn't making you happy. What do you want to do instead?"

Before Landon and I broke up, I hadn't worried too much about my future career plans. I had toyed with the idea of journalism when I was in high school, but I met Landon as soon as I started BYU, and suddenly my goal was to marry, settle down, have babies, and support Landon in his career. There was no way I could work when he was going to be on the road touring all the time. I only got my degree because my parents had pushed me to get it, and I picked English because I could at least spend some time reading and discussing interesting literature. Once Landon and I married, I figured if things were tight at first, I could work as a freelance editor to pay the bills until Landon got his break. The only problem was Landon got his break way sooner than either of us expected, and it included a break from me. Permanently. I sighed. "I don't know what I want to do. Not make sandwiches. Beyond that, I haven't figured it out. It was hard enough to get this job with the economy as bad as it is."

"Really?" my dad asked, nudging my foot. "You really have no idea how you want to put that English degree of yours to use?"

I flushed. I knew he was hinting at my blog. "Blogging doesn't require an English degree," I said. "And it doesn't make any money unless you're crafty and have a billion followers to click on your sidebar ads. I'm not, and I don't."

"But you love writing," he said. "And people love reading you."

"A few," I said.

"A few hundred," he corrected me. "I've seen that people-counter thing on your blog page."

"My blog isn't going to make me enough money that I can quit my job," I said. "And I don't want to trade jobs to something for better pay but that I hate even worse."

"It sounds to me like you have all kinds of excuses for not moving your life to the next level," he said.

I shot him a wounded look. "What do you want me to do?"

"Find your bliss!" he said. "Find whatever it is that makes you happy, and do it because what you're doing right now isn't working."

True enough.

"Choose right now," he said. "If Handy's closed tomorrow and it freed you to find a different way to pay the bills, what would you do?"

I didn't actually have to think about it. A daydream had evolved over the last few months of sandwich assembly, my "if only" scenario I hadn't shared out loud with anyone. But my dad could read it in my face.

"What is it?" he prompted me.

"Writing," I said. "I want to be a reporter, do some slice-of-life stuff but for a bigger audience than my blog."

"Then do that," he said. "Dream big, Pepper."

I entertained the notion for half a second, the idea that I could be a famous writer and find a super-hot boyfriend, a cute apartment, and new friends to hang out with on Friday nights. I would write a fat check to pay for the last of my wedding debts and have money left over to buy a stack of new release books and a box of expensive chocolates to while away every Saturday afternoon. Maybe . . .

"No," I said out loud. "It wouldn't happen. No one is going to hire me when my only experience writing is from my blog and some old college term papers."

"Excuses, Pepper. We've let you make them for months, and it's not helping you or any of us." For the first time, I saw true frustration on my father's face. "I'm going to give you a writing assignment that I use with clients at work. Consider it practice. Every week for the next year, you are going to write a thank you note to someone." He held up his hand when I started to protest. "I mean it. You have spent so long feeling sorry for yourself that you are losing the ability to see the good things in your life. Maybe when you start recognizing the blessings you have, others will reveal themselves. You need an attitude of gratitude."

"Geez, Dad. You sound like a motivational poster in a guidance counselor's office. Can I get a 'Yay, team'?"

"I'm serious, Pepper. Your moping is unacceptable. And if you find your life unacceptable, then you need to change it. This has been a fantastic therapy for people with far worse problems than yours."

"I don't need therapy, and I'm not going to write a bunch of cheesy notes to people, Dad."

"That's your choice," he said. "But here's your consequence. We'd be pretty rotten parents if we stood by and did nothing while your life went off the rails. We will *not* be enablers. If you choose not to take this opportunity to grow by writing these thank you notes and looking for a new job, then we'll assume that living at home is holding you back because we're keeping you too comfortable."

My mom slipped in to hear the last part of my dad's speech, and the lack of surprise on her face told me they had discussed this well before the cake-tipping incident.

"You're okay with this?" I demanded, my voice rising in panic. "You would kick me out?"

She rolled her eyes. "Don't try to guilt trip us, Pepper. You can afford a room somewhere else, and you can still make your credit card minimums. We're not exactly dooming you to homelessness."

"But I'll never make a dent in that bill if I only make the minimums!"

She shrugged. "It's the law of natural consequences. You'll never make a dent in your self-pity if you stay here and keep doing what you're doing. Believe it or not, we're trying to help you."

My mom is a substitute teacher. She's immune to drama and far tougher in the tough-love department than my dad. My stomach flopped, knowing that things had just become *real*.

"So that's it?" I said. "I'm supposed to fill out a few job applications and write some thank you notes or I'm cut off?"

"See it for what it is," my dad counseled. "This is a growth opportunity. Use it."

My mom tugged on his arm. "Let's let her think it over, Grant. Think about your brothers and sisters too," my mom added. "You can be a good example or a horrible warning."

Ouch.

"Our imaginary maid has taken a permanent leave of absence, so I expect you downstairs within ten minutes to clean up the cake mess," she said on her way out.

My dad stopped at the door. "Before you do that, you owe both of your sisters big apologies, and I think Rosemary is really going to make you work. She's completely justified, by the way. Suck up like you mean it."

I let the door click shut behind them before flopping over on my stomach and pounding on my pillow for a while. I was okay with the apologies, but the rest was so unfair! Wasn't I proving that I was taking responsibility by trying to pay back my debt? Apparently, it wasn't enough though. I had to do it with a smile. Ugh.

I dug my beat-up laptop out from under my desk and logged into Facebook, scowling when a sidebar ad suggested that I "like" Landon Scott's fan page. Of course. "Being a grownup is overrated," I typed into my status bar. It took Ginger all of thirty seconds to comment. "Ur overrated." With a growl, I typed back a response, thanking her for her consideration.

Well, that was one note down. Only fifty-one to go.

Dear Mr. Graham:

Thank you for meeting with me yesterday to discuss my career path. I had no idea there was so much to learn, and I don't know if I ever would have figured it out if you hadn't pointed it all out to me. Repeatedly. That was the best part, so I want to give you an extra big thanks for that. I also appreciate you sharing your perceptions of my abilities, intellect, and integrity. Having those called into question is always food for thought. I can't understand for the life of me why people don't run around doing that kind of thing more. It's so . . . invigorating.

I truly hope, with every fiber of my "unqualified and time-wasting" being that you get everything that you so richly deserve. I really, really do.

Sincerely,
Pepper Spicer

Chapter 2

I rolled into church the next day in the middle of the opening hymn, as usual. I always have to wait on everyone else to get back from the family ward before I can use the car. I loan it to Ginger to bring Mace and Rosemary home so they don't have to wait for my parents to finish their meetings. It makes me late every Sunday. Not that it matters; half the ward pours in when the chapel doors open after the sacrament. Ten minutes late still gets me a cushy seat in a pew.

The sacrament program was pleasant and unobjectionable all the way until our high council member got up and spoke on good, better, and best. As he talked about growth and progress, I heard shades of my dad in his message. I stifled a groan, but by the time I got home, I had made a decision. I was six months away from paying off my debt if I budgeted like crazy. I couldn't afford to drop down to minimum payments on my credit card, which meant I couldn't afford to move out on my own. That meant accepting my parents' terms and writing their dumb thank you notes. What's more, I would take my dad's challenge to go after the job I wanted—if only to prove it wasn't as easy as he tried to paint it. Then I could get in my "I told you so," even as he made me write the notes.

I changed into some comfy sweats and pulled out my laptop. I had to figure out who I would grant the privilege of rejecting me first: the liberal *Salt Lake Advocate* or the staid *Bee News*. Thinking about how much it would chap my ultraconservative mother's hide, I grinned. The *Advocate* it would be.

One frustrating hour later, I sat back, perplexed. Forget needing a degree in journalism to break into the newspaper business; I would need a master's in computer engineering just to figure out who to contact from their website. The "Press Here for Your Dream Job" button wasn't on the home page. I tried Google Answers, and after wading through about twenty totally unhelpful question-and-answer sections, I had an idea of what to try next: pouting, followed by chocolate—of the noncake variety.

I wandered downstairs to sniff out the bag of M&Ms my mom had hidden somewhere.

"What are you doing?" she asked, looking up from the Sunday jigsaw when I crossed the family room.

I glanced at the puzzle. Ah, a devilishly difficult Jane Wooster Scott reproduction, where every piece looked like it had five possible placements on the board. "Nothing," I said, knowing she'd be way too distracted to follow up while I rooted around in her knitting basket. No M&Ms there, but years of experience led me to them on the fourth try. She'd shoved them behind the two-year-old frozen cod before. I'm no amateur.

I walked back through the family room with my hand in the two-pound bag, giving it a conspicuous shake as I passed her. She looked ready to hop up and rescue her candy when Rosemary hollered, "I did it! I finished the cottage!" Mom glared at me before turning back to Rosemary to help her fit in her patch of the puzzle. I love puzzle Sundays; it's the best way to keep everyone out of my hair for three hours.

A quarter pound of M&Ms later, I had a plan. First up, a movie marathon to inspire me. Surely a little Christian Bale in *Newsies* could only help me. I'd follow that up with some old seventies newspaper movie called *All the President's Men*—plus the rest of the M&Ms. Now that's what I call prepping for a week of job searching.

* * *

My mom poked her head around the door on her way to bed. I paused Robert Redford on my laptop and pulled my ear buds out. "You owe me M&Ms," she whispered, careful not to wake Rosemary.

"I needed them. They're helping me prep for my job search," I said.

"Does this mean you're taking our challenge?" she asked softly before coming all the way in.

I shrugged. "I don't have much of a choice."

"You always have a choice," she said. "This just happens to be the right one. So what's next? Are you quitting Handy's?"

"As soon as I find something to replace it," I said. "I'm applying for a job with the *Advocate*."

She tried not to wince. "What about the *Bee News*? It's a great paper."

"Are you invalidating my choices?" I asked, my eyebrows quirked at her.

"Of course not," she said. "The *Advocate* will be lucky to have you."

"Don't worry, Mom. They're not going to hire me. You guys will see that this whole idea of making my life happen however I want it to isn't so easy."

"It's impossible if you don't try," she said. "I'm proud of you for taking the first step. Even if it's the *Advocate*." She muttered the last part under her breath before slipping out the door with a small wave.

Back to my laptop. I had downloaded *All the President's Men* on a lark, a higher form of procrastination along the lines of shoving everything in the closet and calling your room clean. But . . . the story was compelling, sucking me in. And old-school Robert Redford was *cute*. Who knew? I pressed play and soaked up the last thirty minutes of the action, fascinated by this look into a slice of history too recent to have made it into my high school history curriculum in any detail. Told through the lens of the reporters who broke the story, suddenly a fancy-schmancy hotel in Washington DC and creepy Richard Nixon were riveting.

When the movie ended, I spent another hour researching more about Watergate and the guys who uncovered the scandal, my excitement brewing. This was good stuff, and eight thousand times more interesting than "The Human Tragedy of Sandwiches Gone Awry" or "The Drama of the Teenagers Who Made Them."

I'd almost majored in journalism, but I figured the demands of being a real-life reporter probably wouldn't gel with motherhood too well. English seemed like a smarter choice at the time. It didn't seem so smart now, unless I wanted to go to law school or grad school or something. But the idea of being able to write somewhere besides my blog, about something besides my own navel-gazing, to write about things and people that mattered . . . yeah, I wanted to do *that*.

I powered down the computer and snuggled under the covers, feeling the first tickle of enthusiasm for my dad's challenge. Maybe not the thank you note part, but pursuing an actual career, that sounded cool. And grownup. At twenty-three, it was about time.

* * *

The nice thing about managing a lunch place is sleeping in. The day starts at ten and ends at seven except the rare nights I have to close. This morning, though, there was no sleeping in. Today I would start my reporting career as the Bob Woodward of my generation. Carl Bernstein is a smart guy too, but given a choice between the Robert Redford and Dustin Hoffman characters, uh . . . yeah.

I started with the only journalism contact I had: Mrs. Mayers, my high school newspaper advisor. I called the school and found out that her conference period was during second period, leaving me two hours to get ready. I spent the first hour and a half doing quizzes on Facebook and the last thirty minutes running around like a wildly disorganized dervish, trying to get ready. I have short, dark hair, and people think that means it's easy to style. It's not. Taming it requires a blow dryer, pomades, and creams—and sometimes a flat iron. It's the curse of not-quite-curly hair. There's enough of a wave to be obnoxious, not pretty. Anyway, the Facebook time wasn't a lost cause. Thanks to six different poorly spelled and grammatically incorrect tests, I discovered that I'm destined to be a restaurant critic, my celebrity twin is Rooney Mara, and my "personality decade" is the eighties. So, you know . . . it was time well spent.

Mrs. Mayers looked the same as she did when I worked on the *North Valley Gazette* my junior and senior years at North Valley High. Except . . . she looked younger to me now than she did six years ago. That's probably because when I was sixteen, she was ten years older, and now that I'm twenty-three, thirty-three seems kind of young.

Anyway, everything else looked the same, down to the desks and posters on the walls. After wrapping me in a huge hug, she waved me into a seat and settled back in her chair. "What brings you in, Pepper?"

I leaned forward, feeling a little self-conscious. I overcompensated with enthusiasm. "I graduated from BYU—"

"Congratulations."

"Yeah, so. Um, I'm done at BYU, and it took me a few months after graduation, but now I know what I want to be when I grow up."

"Congratulations again," she said, amused. "Do tell."

"I want to be a reporter!" I felt stupid saying it out loud to someone else, but I hoped I'd said it cheerfully enough for her not to notice.

She didn't laugh, which was nice, but she did look confused. "That's great. You did an excellent job with features. But—"

"But you're wondering why I'm here, right?" I asked, and she nodded. "The thing is, I didn't major in journalism, so I don't really have any contacts. I was sort of hoping you might have some and that you could point me in the right direction."

Her brow smoothed, and she sighed. "I see. I wish I did, Pepper. My contacts are pretty limited though. I know the woman at the *Utah Valley Times* who coordinates our annual tour of their office, but that's about it. My only other 'connection'—and I use that term as loosely as possible— is the chair of the journalism program at the U. I'm sorry," she added when she saw my crestfallen face. "I wish I could help."

I nodded, unsurprised. Of course it wouldn't be that easy. If life were easy, I wouldn't be working my loser job at the sandwich shop.

"I feel bad," she said. "But most of the students who work on the *Gazette* aren't like you. It's something nice for their extracurricular activities, but they're not planning on careers in journalism. I don't really need contacts at the major papers."

"It's okay," I said. "I knew it was a long shot. Thanks for letting me drop in. It was nice to see you again." I slid out of the desk and turned toward the door, ready to leave, when she stopped me.

"Wait," she said. "This might be a total long shot too, and not at all what you're looking for, but one of my former students, Ellie Peters, has an online magazine she's starting up in Salt Lake. She graduated a few years ahead of you, so you may not know her, but she's pretty awesome. I could put in a good word for you."

"I know her name," I said. "Spencer Betham was obsessed with her and said she was ruining his legacy."

Mrs. Mayers laughed. Spencer had been the *Gazette* editor when I was on staff, and he was always claiming that Ellie had set an impossible standard for circulation during her tenure as editor-in-chief three years before because she had turned the paper into "a fashion bible with token sports reports."

"It might not have been the most insightful reporting," Mrs. Mayers admitted, "but Ellie had a knack for generating readers. Her magazine has potential, I think. Do you want her contact information?"

"Sure," I said. It wasn't exactly what I wanted to do, but it was a start. At worst, maybe Ellie could help me make some other journalism contacts.

She wrote down some information on a neon green sticky note and handed it to me. "Give me a few days to let her know you'll be getting in touch."

"I appreciate it, Mrs. Mayers."

"Call me Anna," she said. "You're not a student anymore. And good luck."

"Thanks . . . uh, Anna." It felt awkward, like I was a pretend adult talking to a pseudo-colleague, and I slipped out on her knowing smile.

My car was an unlovely green 1997 Camry, semi-affectionately nicknamed The Zuke—as in zucchini. I climbed in and stared at the sticky note with a grimace. I'm more "indie" than trendy. I doubted I would be hip enough to write for Ellie's magazine. I'd give her a call if I couldn't find anything more conventional, but I wanted to exhaust my other options. After all, the *Advocate* still deserved a chance to reject me first.

* * *

"Ta da!" I said, waving my fresh-off-the printer résumé under my dad's nose while he sat at the kitchen table reading the *Bee*. "I'm conforming to your ridiculous stipulations. Are you proud of yourself for stifling my natural evolution?" I ruffled his hair to show him I was teasing.

"Absolutely not," he said, deadpan. "I've been wracked with guilt over wrenching you out of your deep, deep trench of self-pity and wasted potential. How could I do that to you?"

My mom snorted from her post behind the kitchen counter, where she was kneading bread dough. She plucked the résumé from my hand with flour-coated fingers.

"Hey! You're going to get it all dirty!" I protested.

"Doesn't matter. You have to reprint it anyway," she said. "It smells like raw onions."

Ginger, drifting by on her way to the fridge, sniffed as she passed me. "So does your hair. Seriously, your job stinks." She laughed at her own joke while she foraged for an after-dinner snack.

I made a halfhearted lunge in her direction, but she danced out of reach and pawed through the crisper drawer. "I did this right after work. I didn't have time to shower," I said. I had endured another night of thankless sandwich making, plus a minidrama over who had let the avocados go bad, by mentally composing my résumé for the *Advocate*. The worse the night got, the greater the urge to work on my résumé grew until I could barely wait to draft it when I got home.

"We've been learning how to do résumés in my English class," Ginger said. "Let me look at it. I bet I can fix it."

"You don't even know if it needs fixing," I said but cut off the rest of my complaint when my mom shot me a warning look. A couple of adamant jerks of her head in Ginger's direction were enough to communicate that she wanted me to humor my sister's offer of "help." I rolled my eyes and nodded that I had gotten the message.

"All right, Ginger. Do your worst." I snatched the résumé back from my mom and thrust it at Ginger. "But you're going to have to quit stuffing your face if you want to see it." Ginger, like all the Spicer kids, eats nonstop because we inherited my skinny parents' super-high metabolisms. We burn calories as fast as we consume them, and we're always hungry. My mom says that's half the reason she had to start substitute teaching, to pay the grocery bill. I think it probably has more to do with my brother being out on a mission, but I don't know. I looked at the heaping bowl of edamame Ginger had grabbed for herself and considered that maybe my mom wasn't joking about the food budget.

"I'll look this over in *my* room while you take a shower. Because you stink," she added, in case I'd forgotten. Nice. A double dig.

I didn't bother answering, instead heading for the stairs. A shower sounded great. Thirty minutes later, I walked back into Ginger's room to find her curled up in an overstuffed beanbag in the corner where I used to keep my desk. I flopped onto her bed and stared at the ceiling where she had pinned up a poster of the *Glee* cast. "It doesn't bother you that these people stare at you while you sleep?"

"It's not your room anymore, so mind your own business," she muttered, absorbed in my résumé.

"I thought you were going to look that over while I showered," I said.

She didn't look up. "I had to do my nails first."

I amused myself while I waited by judging all the choices she had made in decorating "the room that used to be mine." A mirror sat atop my old pine dresser, now painted a soft pink. Ticket stubs and wallet-sized pictures of her friends were tucked into the mirror's frame, and a souvenir pompom in NVHS blue and white hung off the corner. A pleasant pastel jumble of nail polishes in light pink, medium pink, and every shade in between covered one edge of the dresser top, and the rest was covered with bottles of body sprays, hair products, half-used lipsticks, and several folded notes.

"I thought texting destroyed the art of passing notes," I said.

"It depends on whether your teacher will confiscate your cell phone if they catch you. Or if you have friends whose lame parents won't let them have cell phones." She didn't look up from my résumé.

"Ah." The wall the bed rested against used to host a collage of my snapshots from happier days, pre-breakup. Now it held two shelves of Ginger's dance trophies, plus a pair of battered, bedazzled jazz shoes.

I shook my head, wondering how we could be so different. I owned exactly three bottles of nail polish, all from the OPI Rocker Chick line. I figured a bar of Dove soap and a ninety-two-cent tube of Wet-n-Wild Cinnamon Spice lipstick, with a little mascara thrown on for special occasions, constituted a reasonable beauty routine. My guilty pleasure is funky jewelry. It used to clutter the space now full of Ginger's hair products. I can't resist handmade pieces, and the Circus Cookie box that holds mine runneth over on the much smaller dresser in my shared room.

The wall behind Ginger illustrated the biggest difference of all. When it was mine, it had held my growing collection of used paperbacks I'd picked up from secondhand bookstores and yard sales. But I'd boxed them up months ago and put them in the garage in anticipation of the post-marriage move that never happened. Ginger, who was amazing with anything involving her hands, had taken down my shelves and painted a really cool stylized mural of Rapunzel letting down locks of rich brown hair. As much as I missed seeing my old friends lined up, waiting to be read, I kind of loved the mural, a fact I would never, ever share with her. She already had an inflated ego.

"I'm done," she said.

"And? Do I pass?"

"You got all the formatting right," she admitted. I could tell she was bummed that she didn't have anything to criticize, but I can use a Word template with the best of them.

"Thanks. I know how to write a résumé," I said. "You can give it back now."

"You don't know how to write a *good* résumé," she corrected me.

"You just said yourself that I got it right." I stretched out on her bed and smacked her with my foot in the process. Accidentally, of course.

"I said you got the formatting right, but the stuff in it is pretty lame."

"Sorry I haven't lived a more fascinating life so I could write a more interesting résumé for you."

She thumped her head on the wall behind her. "You are so oblivious. You'd think an *English major* would be a little more creative and descriptive than this."

"I can only write down the stuff I've done, Ginger. What do you want me to do? Add my four years in the White House that never happened?"

She rose to her knees and shuffled over to the bed. "Look at this," she said, pointing at my entry for the two years I'd spent on the *North Valley*

Gazette. "You really think some big-shot Salt Lake paper is going to care that you wrote for a high school newspaper in Pleasant Grove? No, they're not."

"If I take that off, then I don't have anything journalism related."

"You don't have to take it off. You have to make it sound better." She held her hand out like a surgeon requesting a scalpel. "Pen!"

I slapped one from her nightstand into her outstretched palm. "You're ridiculous," I said.

"Shut up," she said. "I'm trying to prove to Mom that I really do have nice bonding moments with you."

"Nice bonding moments? Does she want me to mentor you to improve your attitude or something?" It sounded like something my parents would dream up.

"If she did, would she tell me that? No. I'm supposed to be, like, helping you or something so you're not a total recluse. It's lame, but you know how Mom is when she wants you to do something. It's easier to pretend you agree than to listen to the nagging." She grumbled the last part with an air of distraction as her pen scribbled furiously across the page. Geez. My one-page résumé was turning into a novel because I knew when she handed it back I'd be staring at some pretty spectacular fiction.

"Wait, Mom thinks *you* need to fix *me*?"

Ginger glanced up. "What? You don't think you need fixing?"

"I know I do, but why on earth would they think *you* could do it?" And I fell back on her bed, laughing.

Ginger glared at me and waved my résumé. "I have written proof of exactly how little you've accomplished in your life up to this point. Do you really think you have more going on than I do?"

I sighed. "No. But if I don't laugh that my seventeen-year-old sister has more going on than I do, I will cry. Big, fat, bitter tears." How lame is my life that my mom thinks Ginger has something to teach me? I decided not to digest that on account of how the idea would probably choke me.

"So you admit that I'm as qualified as anyone to help you with this sorry glimpse into your life?" She crumbled it, eyeing me defiantly. I said nothing until she was done and it rested in her palm, a pitiful white wad of paper.

"I can just reprint it, you know."

She chucked it at me. "I was being dramatic."

"No!"

"You could use a little more drama," she said. "Part of the reason your life is so lame is you're pouty all the time. Nobody likes a moper, Pepper." She scooted over and snatched the paper wad back. "Flipping the cake over was the most interesting thing you've done since Lan—"

"Don't say it!" I snapped.

"Whatever. But you should totally take my advice since I've pretty much got my whole future figured out and you don't."

The sad thing is that while anyone else who said that would sound like they were bragging, Ginger was right. She'd taken every business-related class North Valley High offers, not to mention her part-time job at the salon. Given her natural sense of style and unflappable self-confidence, she was well on her way to making her future happen sooner than later.

Which was nice for her but depressing for me.

"Fine. What do you suggest I do with this résumé, then?"

"You have to tweak it. I read your blog sometimes," she admitted grudgingly. "You can be creative when you want to. Like here," she pointed to the crumpled résumé where I had entered my experience as a features writer. "It doesn't have to say North Valley High School student newspaper. It can say you wrote for a Utah Valley regional newspaper."

"I'm not going to lie, Ginger. You better not be doing this kind of thing on your résumé either. Is that the kind of stuff your teacher has been instructing you to do?"

She stared at me, unmoved. "What's the lie? I'm just suggesting you be less specific than 'student newspaper.' Or you can be all uptight and precise and never get a job. I guess you have to decide how much you love Handy's."

Ouch. I cleared my throat. "Any suggestions for how to spin managing a sandwich shop?"

She grinned. "A few . . ."

Forty minutes later, I plucked a fresh copy of my résumé off the printer in my dad's office. The professional-looking document bordered on fiction, but it contained no actual lies, and in this job market, I knew I would need every edge I could get. Time to send it out and see whether my pessimism or my parents' optimism would triumph.

For once, I wouldn't mind being wrong.

* * *

I sat in my office at the back of the store and stared at the wall, willing the curling sticky notes left by managers past to rearrange themselves in a way that would suddenly clarify how to handle the food orders for Handy's. I had just spent a half hour placating a customer who was irate that there weren't any sprouts available for her sandwich. Who knew we'd have a run on sprouts during the lunch rush? I hated ordering for the store almost as much as I hated trying to figure out payroll. Maybe more since I couldn't ever get the food orders exactly right. Payroll eventually added up after much weeping and wailing and smacking the computer monitor. Ordering was more like playing darts blindfolded.

I desperately wanted to be done with Handy's, now more than ever, since all of this job searching had planted the seed of escape. I'd barely begun submitting my résumé three days ago, and I knew it would take time for it to get into the right hands, but as I agonized over how many tomatoes we really needed for the next week, I wondered how I could stand the wait. I'd sent it to every single paper I could Google in a fifty-mile radius, including the *Advocate* and the *Bee,* much to my mother's delight.

I stared down at the order sheet in front of me. How much mayonnaise did I need? Probably extra in case Brady and friends showed up again. What about bell peppers? And mustard packets? And toilet paper for the restroom?

Kill me now.

My cell phone rang in the middle of a desperate attempt to forecast our sliced turkey needs using the quadratic equation and a rain dance. I didn't recognize the phone number but would probably accept a collect call from the state prison if it got me out of ordering for a few minutes.

"This is Pepper," I said into the phone.

"Pepper, this is Tanner Graham from the *Bee.* I received your resumé and wondered if you would be available to come in for an interview this week."

I hopped up and did a three-second jig before I said calmly, "Sure. When should I come in?"

"I know it's short notice, but could you make it in tomorrow?"

"I can do that. When should I be there?"

He gave me the details, and I scrawled them down on a scrap piece of paper, my fingers tingling with excitement. It wasn't the *Advocate*, but it was light-years better than Handy's Dandy Sandwiches. When I hung up after the most professional good-bye I could muster, I squealed. It didn't matter that I sounded like a nine-year-old Justin Bieber groupie;

only the forlorn papers tacked haphazardly all over the office walls were there to witness my happy dance.

Then I began the freak out: what to wear, what to wear, what to wear?

* * *

"You don't have anything to wear."

Leave it to Ginger to cut to the chase.

I knew it was bad when instead of shushing her, my mom ordered her to help me find an outfit. Of course I have clothes to wear. I have a closet full of clothes that are great for going to a cool little dive and listening to live music. But to Ginger's point, I didn't have anything that screamed, "I'm a grownup journalist. Hire me." And I really, really needed clothes that said that.

In my room, she dug through the dresses crammed into my side of the closet. Rosemary bounced on her Strawberry Shortcake comforter and watched, beside herself with the joy of sister bonding. A dark purple dress flew over Ginger's shoulder.

"I like that one!" Rosemary said.

"Too funky," Ginger responded without turning around. My favorite denim skirt and a bright green sundress joined it.

"You're making a mess," I complained.

"So? I don't have to clean it up, and I need to make room in here," she said without turning around. She yanked out a plaid skirt and stared at it critically. It nearly joined the pile on the floor before I could snatch it from her.

"This is a great skirt," I said. "This could totally work."

Ginger snorted. "Maybe if you're going to work at *Emo Kid Weekly*. I thought you said the goal was to dress like a grownup."

"It is, but I don't want to dress like a creepy Stepford wife. I'd like to still look like me."

"There will be time for that later," she said. "Right now, you need to look like a reporter for the *Bee*. You keep picking stuff like you're interviewing at the *Advocate*. The *Bee* is going to have a much more conservative vibe." She pulled out a black pencil skirt. "This is a start. Put it on."

I did, pulling it on with the *Goonies* T-shirt I was already wearing. Ginger turned around with another blouse in her hand.

"Knowing you, you would probably wear it just like that," she said. I grinned, not arguing, and she rolled her eyes and thrust a shirt at me. "Try this. If we had one more day to go shopping, we could find something better for you, but this will have to do."

I stripped off my *Goonies* tee and slipped my arms into the button-down blouse she'd handed me. It was plain white and boring. "I'd rather wear all black," I said.

"No."

I saved my breath rather than argue.

"We have to work on shoes next," she said. "None of yours is going to do."

"They're going to have to," I said. "I can't borrow any before tomorrow." Ginger and my mom had ridiculous size-seven feet. I wear a nice, normal nine. Which is to say, I'm jealous of their small feet. At least we're pretty much the same size in everything else.

"You'd better borrow some because Converse are not going to cut it for this interview," she said.

"Please. I do wear something besides Converse. What about my church shoes?"

Instead of answering, she knelt down in front of the closet and sifted through the tangled mess of mine and Rosemary's footwear. She yanked a pair of black ballet flats out. "You mean these?" she asked.

"They're cute." They were the dressiest shoes I owned. That's not saying much.

"Yep, they are. Cute. Not grownup. Not big-girl-job appropriate. Just cute. If you'd like to roll into the *Bee* tomorrow looking like a high school sophomore, then yeah. Go ahead and wear your flats. Otherwise, follow me."

Ginger might be a pain, but she knows her fashion. I'd take her wardrobe advice—unless it involved pearls or flight-attendant scarves. Of course, Ginger was way too trendy for either, so while I might not like whatever she made me put on, she had a much better shot of getting an interview outfit right than I did. I sighed and trudged after her toward her room. I'd listen to her, even if it meant squeezing into a pair of her dumb, dainty shoes. Real women wear nines.

* * *

I pushed open the main entrance doors to the *Bee* office in downtown Salt Lake and limped through it. I cursed Ginger for the twentieth time since the Trax train had broken down a half mile south of my destination, forcing me to walk or be late. I knew showing up late would be the kiss of death for my chances, so I'd hoofed it in. Stupid Ginger had talked me into wearing tights because they're "on trend," so I didn't have the option to shuck off the shoes and run. Instead, I had to walk four city blocks in shoes two sizes too small.

I fought a grimace as I headed for the receptionist's desk, but her concerned expression told me I wasn't fooling anyone. Great. *Hire me. I don't have the sense to wear the right size shoes.* I pasted a smile on and stopped in front of her desk. "I'm Pepper Spicer. I have an interview with Tanner Graham."

"Pepper Spicer? What an adorable name," she said with a smile, but it wasn't a nice smile. I fought the tiniest urge to pinch her. Not a hard pinch—just a little pinch to say, "My feet hurt. Don't mess with me." I didn't do it because, despite the cake flipping and mayonnaise throwing, I'm not a violent person. Mostly.

"Have a seat," she said, tucking a strand of shiny brown hair behind her ear, the better to show off a delicate silver-star earring. "I'll call him."

She picked up the phone while I took a seat a few feet away in the waiting area and then pretended to ignore her conversation. "Hi, Tanner. Your interview is here." Giggle. "Aw . . ." Another giggle. "No, *you.*" More giggling. Oh, brother. After a final giggle, she hung up the phone reluctantly.

"Tanner will be down to get you in a few minutes," she said. "Feel free to read something while you wait."

There were a bunch of copies of the *Bee* on the table in front of me, and I picked one up and skimmed the front cover. I hoped I wouldn't get any current events questions in my interview since I usually got my news from Jon Stewart who was not . . . *Bee* compatible. I focused on anything local, although I didn't really want to report on that kind of stuff as much I wanted to do feature stories on interesting people and places. In a super perfect world, I wouldn't even do features. I'd get my own column where I could ramble about whatever I wanted and slay people with my wit and insight like I did for the few dozen people who read my blog. In a super perfect world, I'd also have size seven feet and my own apartment. Sometimes you just take what you can get, and I'd take any job the *Bee* offered me.

I inhaled the distinct scent of newspaper ink, a nostalgic smell that took me back to Sunday mornings from my childhood. My brother Cory and I would squabble over who got the comics while my dad read the city section to my mom, who fried up crisp bacon and flipped pancakes as she listened. Sometimes they got into a heated debate about whatever he read aloud. As I grew older, the articles became more interesting to me. In some ways, my view of the world was shaped by the lively discussions the *Bee* sparked at the weekend breakfast table.

I winced when I turned to a full-page ad for Landon's upcoming show at the E-Center. "Tickets on Sale Soon," the headline blared. Awesome. His face was everywhere lately: billboards, TV commercials, even stupid Facebook ads. They all conspired to confront me with *that* spectacular failure daily. I gritted my teeth and flipped to the next page, determined not to let Landon into my head.

A couple minutes later, I glanced up from an article on water rights, and my gaze landed on the dignified brass letters that spelled out the paper's name on the wall behind the receptionist's head. It felt like a full circle moment to be sitting with a copy of the *Bee* in my hands—oh, crud.

My hands.

I dropped the newspaper back onto the table and checked them. Sure enough, they were smudged with black news ink. I had no idea whether I had time to wash them off before Tanner Graham fetched me for my interview, and I didn't know where the restroom was anyway. I had a single, crumpled tissue in my small purse, and besides the fact that it would take more than that to do the job . . . ew. I needed to clean out my purse.

I glanced around the lobby, hoping for a solution. Everything was tasteful but worn, from the wood-trimmed brocade lounge furniture to the heavy mahogany reception desk, and a tinge of panic licked at my already nervous stomach. Maybe they were used to inky fingers around here, but I couldn't shake my potential employer's hand with my smudged one. Especially not after I limped up to him in Ginger's freakishly undersized black heels. Awesome first impression.

What to do? And then I saw the complementary hand sanitizer pump next to the front entrance. Thanking cold and flu season and the germaphobe who put the sanitizer out, I shuffled over and squirted some onto my palms. I rubbed them together and then on my skirt to get the ink off, but the gel evaporated too quickly. I stared at my hands, which were no cleaner and were now vaguely sticky to boot, realizing I would have to break down and ask Giggle Girl where the restroom was. I turned to do that when the door to the stairwell flew open and an utterly delicious boy—no, man—strode out. Thick

lashes ringed his gray-blue eyes. They reminded me of that Richard guy on
Lost, my Netflix obsession from a couple of years ago. His wavy brown hair
was as dark as my own and short enough to keep it neat. I guessed he was
probably near thirty. Too old for me, and I'd never date my boss anyway, but
checking out that gorgeous face at work every day? Excellent job perk.

"Pepper?" he asked, smiling. He stopped in front of me with his hand
outstretched.

I froze for a second and then decided that skipping the handshake
was the worst of all options. I took his hand but gave it the lightest,
quickest shake in the history of ever, hoping he wouldn't notice the
stickiness. I thought I saw a faint dip in his smile, but he started
speaking before I could worry about it too much. I pretended not to
notice when he wiped his hand on the side of his pants.

"Thanks for coming in on short notice," he said. "We're moving fast
to fill this position. Let's head up to the office."

I smiled back and followed him up the stairs, grateful he couldn't
see me struggling not to wince with each step. Protesting feet aside,
I appreciated the chance to check him out while he wasn't looking.
Although he was dressed far too conservatively for my taste in a gray
button-down shirt and black flat-front slacks, from my vantage point, I
could confirm that they fit his lean . . . *frame* . . . extremely well.

At the top of the stairs, he pushed the door open into the newsroom.
Nearly two dozen desks sat in clusters of three or four in the large,
undivided space. Glassed-in offices lined the perimeter of the room,
but they didn't disrupt the open-range feeling. Phones rang, desk mates
chattered, and several people zipped from one side of the room to the
other, couriering papers or gossip as they went. A middle-aged guy
walked past me with a fierce-looking camera slung over each shoulder,
like Uzis from one of my brother's video games, only scarier. He nodded
at Tanner as he passed us and scarfed down a Hot Pocket as he walked.

Just like that, I fell in love. With the hustle and bustle, with
reporters doing official-looking stuff, with photographers too busy to
eat real food while they chased a deadline. Even with grimy newsprint
on my fingers, I wanted it. It all looked so important and interesting.
And really, really cool. I loved the idea of being in the know, of putting
information out there before anyone else had it, of shaping words that
would shape people's opinions the way the newspaper had done for us
every Sunday morning of my childhood.

With the realization, I panicked. Since Tanner's call the day before, I'd spent all my time stressing about how to dress professionally and none of it figuring out what to say.

In some ways, that was better, right? I would probably be all stiff and freaked out if I had rehearsed my answers too much.

Right?

Tanner led me to an office on the far side of the newsroom. I willed myself not to limp now that several pairs of curious eyes were checking me out. He held open the door to one of the perimeter offices and waved me in. I guess after Tanner's conservative outfit, his office shouldn't have surprised me, but its lack of personality caught me off guard. Beige paint coated the walls, and the only pictures were framed photos of well-known Salt Lake landmarks, like the temple and the state capitol. Unobjectionable furniture—a dark wood desk and two inexpensive office chairs, ate up the small space.

He took the seat behind the desk and looked over my résumé, easily identifiable by my name in large type across the top. I took the only other chair in the small room.

"Those are nice pictures," I said, trying to make conversation. "Did you take them?"

"What?" he asked, glancing up for a moment. "Oh, those aren't mine. We're just using this office for interviews because it's a little more private. I have a desk out there with everyone else." He returned to the résumé, and I decided not to make any more small talk while he finished reading.

I caught myself drumming my fingers on the arm of the chair and quickly sat on my hands to still them. Then I realized that probably looked pretty juvenile, and I jerked them back out and rested them on the chair arms in the most casual pose I could think of. Tanner looked up again a few moments later, his expression much more focused. "I checked out your blog. You have a very strong point of view," he said and smiled.

"Um, thanks." Dang it. I was already flustered. I hadn't expected anyone to actually check out my piddly little personal blog, and I wracked my brains to think of any posts I should have taken down before putting the URL in my résumé. Maybe the one titled "Die, Boyfriend, Die." And I'd probably make a point of removing "I Need a Roommate Older Than Seven."

"Pepper?"

Realizing Tanner had said a whole bunch of stuff I'd missed while freaking out about my blog, I pasted on a smile, unsure if I was supposed to answer a question or comment on something.

"Do you agree?" he prompted me.

"Absolutely," I said, forcing my smile even wider.

One of his eyebrows quirked. He was on to me. "With what?"

I gave up. "I'm sorry. I missed what you said."

This time, he didn't smile. With a curt nod, he picked up my résumé. "It doesn't matter. Let's talk about the job and whether you would be a good fit."

I nodded too eagerly, hoping my bobble head communicated "I'm listening now!"

"I'm sure you know that traditional newspapers have been struggling for the last several years. The *Bee* still has strong circulation, but our editorial board recently agreed that we need to appeal to a younger demographic, one that currently uses newspapers as cheap wrapping paper and that's about it. We're looking for new perspectives in our reporting, and the board asked me to conduct the first round of interviews."

"I'm so glad you called," I said and wondered if it was my imagination that my voice sounded extra loud. "I'm definitely young and fresh." I winced, and Tanner looked slightly startled. *Young and fresh? What the what? Excellent. Surely the way to win this job would be to present myself as unripe produce.* "That's not to say I'm green, of course." *Aargh!*

"Of course," he said, sounding doubtful. No, highly doubtful.

My stomach sank. I was tanking, but the only thing I could think of to fix it was to shut up before I babbled something else colossally stupid. I snapped my mouth shut before I could add that green was good for the environment but bad for reporters. Biting off that particularly lame insight caused me to literally bite my tongue, and I couldn't stifle a tiny whimper as I waited to see if I would actually bleed.

A puzzled frown furrowed Tanner's forehead. Oh, boy. I was aging him before his time.

"We're trying to find the right balance of youth and experience," he said. "I'm impressed with your résumé"—Uh oh. —"and wondered if you could tell me more about your reporting experience with this Utah Valley regional paper. You didn't put the dates you worked there, but I assume, based on your age, that you did an internship at *The Valley Times*, right?"

"Um, not exactly. Our paper was a little smaller, and we focused more on north county news." I felt sweat pooling in my armpits and wondered how long I had before big old pit stains soaked my blouse.

"I thought I knew all the papers down there. What was it called?"

I cleared my throat. "It's called the *North Valley Gazette*." *Please don't ask me who—*

"Who publishes it?" he asked, suspicious.

Fake it 'til you make it, I admonished myself with advice I'd heard Tyra give on *America's Next Top Model*. "It's at North Valley High School," I said. His expression darkened. "It's an award-winning newspaper." I offered the last fact in a bright tone of voice, as if perkiness would somehow make everything better. An interesting choice, since I despise perkiness. Apparently, so did Tanner. His full-on scowl did not bode well.

"You padded your résumé." He said it as a statement of fact, which it was. I shifted and then stopped, knowing that fidgeting would make me look guilty. Which I was. "I don't have time for this," he said. "I still have deadlines to meet on top of doing these interviews, and I don't need this." He stabbed my résumé, the sound surprisingly loud, coming from one angry finger. At least he used Mr. Pointer. "Is any of this even true?"

"That's offensive," I said, going on the attack since I had nothing to lose. I wouldn't be getting this job. "Everything on there is the truth."

"I'm sure it's some version of the truth," he said. "This isn't a game. This a respected newspaper, where *grownups* work and report on real issues that affect real people. We don't deal in fiction."

That stung, especially since I'd thought of it in the same terms when Ginger had reworked it. My conscience pricked me, and I opened my mouth to apologize, but Tanner cut me off.

"You should be smart enough to figure that out. I can't believe you thought you could limp in here and bluff your way through this. That's pretty deluded."

I sat there, my mouth half open, too stunned to figure out where to start. Calling me deluded? Or making fun of my limp? How low is that? I was tempted to pull off one of Ginger's stupid shoes and chuck it at his head. As it turned out, I didn't need a comeback because Mr. Graham wasn't done.

"Just because you can write an entertaining blog doesn't mean you're ready to make the leap into real reporting. Journalism is serious business, and it takes training and paying your dues to succeed in this field. It's insulting that you would think you can show up here without any real experience and get the job done." He sat back and folded his arms across his chest, glaring at me.

I snapped my jaw shut and sat up straighter. "Dude, you need to get over yourself. You're not brokering world peace around here. You're writing a few inches of print a day on the who, what, when, where, and why of something that happens to someone else. It doesn't require any creativity, so you probably shouldn't be sitting there acting all superior." Tanner's fist clenched on the desktop, crumpling my résumé as it tightened, but I didn't care. "For the record, you're right. I shouldn't have padded my résumé, and I'm sorry I did that. But, hey, even though I played a little loose with the details, at least I'm not a hot head." With that, I shoved my seat back and stood up, ready to huff out. Unfortunately, a small tear in the chair's vinyl upholstery snagged my tights, and when I took a step toward the door, I could feel it tugging me back. I looked behind me to see a huge run forming from my knee down to my calf.

I backed up and unhooked the snag, pretending not to notice Tanner's smirk. "Good luck finding someone to work with you," I said over my shoulder. "Now *that* would be an accomplishment." Happy with my exit line, I stormed toward the door in three steps. By the fourth step, I was in so much pain, I slipped my shoes off my feet and marched toward the stairwell without a backward glance. Or even any sideways ones. I didn't want to know what the newsroom audience would make of the frazzled girl limp-stomping toward the door with shoes in hand.

I shoved the stairwell door open at the bottom, and Giggle Girl stared at me. I flashed her a blinding smile as I headed for the main exit. Her look of total confusion was the only good thing about the whole disastrous morning.

Dear Courtney:

I just wanted to let you know that you've made Sundays a little less stressful by always being kind to me. It's nice not having to worry about where I'm going to sit. Hiding on the back bench with you makes me feel less like the new kid in the cafeteria every single week. Thanks for always saving me a spot.

Sincerely,
Pepper

Chapter 3

Do crazy people know they're crazy?

A week ago, I would have sworn I was sane, but several hours after getting home from the interview and indulging in an angry cry in my bedroom, I moved out to the kitchen table and now sat waiting for my dad to come home and give me an official diagnosis. With all the mayonnaise throwing and cake flipping and angry storm-outs, I was beginning to wonder if I had any idea what was going on inside my own head. I needed the best therapist I knew, and luckily, my dad would work for ice cream and a scalp massage.

I texted him to come home and then snacked on Goldfish crackers, popping in one after the other without really thinking. My mind had chased itself in so many circles that I wanted it to be still, if only for a little while. So I counted Goldfish and shoved out any other intrusive thoughts. My dad walked in right after I'd killed number sixty-seven and plopped down in the chair across from me.

"Hi," he said.

I pushed the carton of Goldfish toward him. "Are you sure you don't mind coming home?"

"Of course not. I was only working on an article for the *Ensign*," he said. "It's not due for a while, and I don't have any clients again until after dinner."

"Okay. This isn't an emergency. It's okay if you need to go back to work."

He leaned his elbow on the table and propped his chin on his fist, giving me a long smile before he answered. "Maybe it's not an emergency, but it's way more important than anything I was doing. Is this about your interview today?"

I nodded, and then despite myself, two rebellious tears squeezed out. I dashed them away before they could trickle down my cheeks. My dad fished a clean handkerchief out of his pocket. That's the great thing about dads. They think of stuff like handkerchiefs. I dabbed at my eyes, not worried about getting anything on the cloth since I'd cried off all my eye makeup when I'd first come home.

"I didn't get the job," I said.

"I'm sorry," he said. "That must be really frustrating."

"More like humiliating," I grumbled, and when his eyebrow rose in question, I spilled the details. His expression reflected sympathy over my aching feet and proper outrage at Tanner Graham's jerkiness, but I caught him stifling a smile when I recounted my exit. "Dad! No laughing!"

"I'm not laughing at you," he reassured me. "But I love that you stopped and took your shoes off when anyone else would have kept limping. That's so . . . you. And I adore it," he added when he caught my grimace.

"I guess I'm worried that all this craziness really *is* me now." I crushed a Goldfish and then brushed his crumbled remains into my palm. "I kind of liked being in my funk better. At least I wasn't losing my temper every five minutes over something."

He smiled. "Do you find all your emotions a little unsettling right now?"

"Unsettling," I said, testing out the word. "Yeah. Good word for it."

"Therapist or counselor?" he asked. It was shorthand in our house for whether we wanted him to listen or advise us.

"Counselor, for sure." I was so tired of being in my own head.

"I think you went into an emotional cocoon after you and Landon broke up. It was your way of grieving the loss of the relationship and all the plans you'd had for your future. You're coming out of the cocoon and realizing that the world can be pretty exciting but also risky. I think your anger comes from two things: at first you were mad at anyone who tried to drag you out of your cocoon, and now you're reacting out of fear when you see risk in the world."

He sat back and studied my dubious expression then sighed. "Sorry, my last client was an eight-year-old. Let me try it again in adult terms. You liked being emotionally numb, but that can last only so long. You fought against joining the land of the living, hence some of your outbursts. Now you're kind of excited about moving on with your life, but you're reacting with fear when you sense obstacles. How does that sound?"

"It sounds about right," I admitted. "I don't like the cocoon analogy because I know you're going to follow it up with—"

"With how you're a beautiful butterfly ready to spread your wings? Nah," he said, a twinkle in his eye. "I know you better than that."

"Butterflies are nice and all, but I'm more of a . . ." I groped for the right metaphor.

"Sparrow?" he offered.

I wrinkled my brow. "What does that mean?"

"I don't know. Just seems right."

"Okay," I said, dragging the word out. "Then what's a sparrow to do? Suddenly, hiding in my room for months on end doesn't sound so good anymore."

"Let's eat and then talk about it," he suggested.

I climbed to my feet. "I'll make you a sandwich."

He stood and waved me back down. "Let me make the sandwiches. Seems like you do enough of that as it is."

By the time we polished off some PB&J, I was impatient. "I want to hear your ideas because all mine are bad. Help, please?"

He pushed his empty plate aside. "I'd love to. Let me ask you this. How did you feel today when you realized you weren't going to get the job?"

"Super bummed," I answered without hesitation.

"Because you're sick of the sandwich shop?"

I thought about it. "That's only part of it. I was mostly bummed because I realized how much I love the idea of getting into journalism. If I hadn't already been dating Landon when I started at BYU, I probably would have majored in it. Now I can't shake the idea."

"Then don't. Focusing on something you want and working toward it is going to make you happy. Just know that sometimes disappointments happen, and you have to work through them." He tugged my plate toward him to finish off my crusts, a familiar gesture that made me feel childish and loved all at once.

"I'm still worried I'm going to go ballistic again," I said. "It sneaks up on me."

"Awareness of the possibility will help more than anything else," he said. "But it will also help to keep inviting the Spirit into your life."

"Read my scriptures, pray, and go to church," I said, intoning the rote Primary answers.

"Of course," he said, unruffled. "And count your blessings. Or put another way, how are your thank you notes coming?"

"Great," I said. "Two weeks, two notes. Couldn't be better."

"Mm-hm. I saw the note you wrote to Ginger. Very letter of the law."

I flushed.

He leaned forward and made sure I held his gaze before he spoke again. "I think it's still part of your problem. If you can focus on the things you do have, the things that are going right for you, then maybe you won't worry so much about the things that sometimes don't." He reached over and punctuated each of his next words with a light tap of his finger on the back of my hand. "Write them like you mean them. See if it makes a difference."

I sighed but nodded. Wherever this path led, I didn't want to turn back now. If that meant following my dad's advice . . . the truth was he'd never been wrong about big stuff like this yet. "Anything else you think I should do?"

"Yeah. Keep going after your dream job. You don't like the *Bee* anyway, and they only put you one no closer to a yes."

* * *

Getting the *Bee* interview turned out to be a total fluke. My phone did *not* ring off the hook with calls from every newspaper I'd sent my résumé to. A tiny part of me was glad because I didn't want to embarrass myself again when they realized it was, um . . . a load of hooey.

What a difference a week makes. Last Sunday I'd researched newspaper jobs to prove to my dad that I couldn't get one. Now I wanted desperately to prove to myself, and maybe to stupid Tanner Graham, that I could.

I dressed for church and thought about my dilemma. Tanner was obnoxious but right, which made him more obnoxious. I didn't have the skills to write for a big paper, but how was I supposed to get them? And he was also right that big papers everywhere were fighting for the readers who were migrating to all the free news on the Internet. Which meant . . .

Maybe it was time to turn in a *real* résumé to Ellie Peters and her Internet project. And maybe it was time to put my dad's gratitude theory to the test. Tomorrow would be soon enough to tackle my career change and check out the Ellie Peters lead, but today I needed to start on something else, something perfect for a Sunday: writing a real thank you note.

When I slipped into the chapel, my Sunday friend Courtney smiled and moved her scriptures so I could sit down. Over the last several months, an unspoken tradition had evolved between us. She saves me a seat on the last bench, and then we share a hymn book. I don't know much about her beyond exchanging names after the first Sunday she shifted over for me, but it's nice not to sit alone or with strangers every week. She was only *mostly* a stranger. To tell the truth, I should be going to the Battle Creek ward, but I drive all the way to the Willow Canyon YSA ward in Alpine instead. Too many people from my childhood and adolescence attend Battle Creek ward, and I didn't feel like returning after a broken engagement so I could take the walk of shame. My parents kept doing their gentle nudge thing to get me to go to my assigned ward, but I hoped the Lord would be patient with me while I hid out for a while in Alpine. Since the wait for the car made me late every week, it was nice to have Courtney always save me a spot.

I shot her a quick sideways glance and wondered how I knew so little about her when we'd been sharing the same pew for months. I knew it was my fault. After breaking up with Landon, I hadn't quit wallowing long enough to make new friends. I'd been skipping Sunday School and Relief Society since I'd been in the ward, and as for the activities? Yeah, right.

But it was a little ridiculous that this girl had gone out of her way to do something thoughtful for me for months and I knew nothing more about her than that she owned cute shoes and had a pleasant singing voice. Chastened, I dug in my scripture tote and pulled out a blank thank you card, determined to meet my goal for the day. By the time the high councilman had droned out the last of his remarks, I had composed a friendly but not stalkery note. Now to figure out the delivery. Handing it to her would be dorky, and I didn't have a ward directory to find her address. I debated slipping it into her scriptures but imagined how awkward it would be if she saw me do it.

Gah! How could this be so hard? For my next thank you card, I would pick someone I could mail it to without all the fuss. I caught a lucky break when the closing prayer ended and the guy across the aisle jumped up and made a beeline for Courtney. She turned to talk to him, and I seized the chance to drop the card into her open purse. When I stood to scoot past her and make my escape, she smiled at me. "Good seeing you. Are you staying for Sunday School?"

It was the same thing she asked me every Sunday, and I gave her the same answer I always did. "No, I'm going to take off." But then I surprised myself by adding, "Maybe I will next week." And she smiled a little more.

"Cool."

I returned the smile and headed out of the chapel. Sacrament meeting always felt good, but in a young adult ward, the following two hours required more socializing than I had in me after my breakup. But it was definitely time to make more friends. Most of mine were paired off or married, and I had avoided their happy coupledom like they had a contagious cancer of their common sense. Courtney didn't seem to be tied down to anyone; maybe she wouldn't mind a new friend either.

* * *

Monday night I collapsed on my bed, exhausted. I'd spent all day making sandwiches and trying to think positive thoughts about my job. One of my part-timers had called in a half hour before his shift to say he couldn't work because he had to study for a history test. Now I lay staring at the ceiling after a double shift and eating a popcorn ball that was the only thing left of FHE when I got home. I was trying to focus on the extra cash I'd earned and not on the extra Advil I'd had to take to compensate for my tired legs. Even when I had to turn my lamp off at eight o'clock so Rosemary could sleep, I used the opportunity to hang out in my dad's office and revise my résumé in peace and quiet.

An hour later when Mace walked by and made a smart remark about my onion smell, I decided positive thoughts were overrated and chased him around downstairs until I tripped him and sat on him. I had his arm pinned behind his back and was insisting that he say, "Pepper is spicy goodness," when my mom found us in the hallway and, grinning, looked on.

"Mom! I want her off of me," Mace complained.

"I want a vacation to Bora Bora, but we can't always get what we want." She leaned against the wall and continued to watch us, amused. "Besides, I'm sure you deserve it. Pepper?"

"He totally does."

"That's what I thought," she said. "Continue."

Mace squirmed some more, trying to buck me off of his back, but I pulled his arm a teeny bit higher, and he quit. "You're really not going to make her stop?"

"Nope," Mom said. "Is this going to take awhile? Maybe I'll go stick some popcorn in the microwave and make it a real show."

I shrugged. "That's up to Mace. He knows what he has to do if he wants me to let him up."

"She's going to break my arm!"

Mom snorted. "Hardly. She's only leveling the playing field since you're bigger. Be thankful she's not yanking your leg hairs."

"Good idea!" I said. "I can't reach now but maybe next time."

Mace groaned. "I wish Cory were here. I hate being the only boy at home."

It was true that the brother right after me, Coriander, equaled the odds fast. "Too bad," I said. "I guess your only way out is to tell me what I want to hear."

He mumbled something into the carpet.

"What's that?" I demanded. "I can't hear you."

"I said, 'Pepper is spicy goodness.'"

I let go and hopped up quickly before he could retaliate. He climbed to his feet and glowered down at me, nearly a foot taller and on his way to passing my dad, who was six-foot-four. My mom shook her head. "Height is no match for strategy."

"We're calling that strategy? I thought it was plain old sneakiness."

"It's all in the eye of the beholder," I said. "And behold, you got whupped."

He stomped off toward the kitchen to inhale some food, and I eyeballed my mom. "Aren't you supposed to lecture me about acting my age?"

"Nah. It's good to see you having some fun."

"Have I been that difficult?" I picked some carpet threads off my jeans and waited for her answer.

"Yes," she said. "But I knew you'd snap out of it eventually."

"Sometimes I think I'm just going to snap—period," I confessed.

She gathered me in a hug. "Your dad told me, but we're not worried. We know you'll find your way."

I stepped out of the hug after a hard squeeze back. "Thanks, Mom. And now I need to finish revising my résumé. Do me a favor and don't ask Ginger to 'help' me with anything else." I smiled so she would know I wasn't mad. It was sad that for months, my family'd had reason to assume that peevish was my default setting.

"You got it," she said, and I headed back into the office to work on phase two of becoming a real, live journalist.

Dear Ellie,

It was great to meet you in person. Anna Mayers has nothing but great things to say about you, and I'm so glad she suggested that I contact you. I know I don't have a ton of experience, but I believe I have talent, and I know I have the drive to work hard. I'm blown away by what Real Salt Lake is doing, and the more I think about it, the more sure I am that I want to be a part of the team.

Thank you for taking the time to interview me. I look forward to getting started.

Sincerely,
Pepper Spicer

Chapter 4

Ginger poked her head around my door, and I threw a slipper at her. It bounced off the wall two feet away from her, and she stayed where she was, unperturbed. "Let me see," she begged.

"No. Your *help* is not so helpful."

"Not fair," she said. "Those shoes would have been fine if the train wouldn't have broken down. Blame Trax."

"Your résumé coaching was a disaster too," I reminded her. "And if I could find a reason to blame you for the snag in my tights, I would."

"Come on," she wheedled. "I won't comment. I just want to see what you're thinking about wearing tomorrow."

Knowing she wouldn't give up, I sighed and waved her in. She stood next to me and stared at the outfits laid out on my bed in anticipation of my interview with Ellie Peters the next day. She kept her word not to say anything, but I could tell she was about to choke with the effort. I ignored her for another minute or two while I debated between a black suit I found on the Target clearance rack for forty dollars and an outfit I had pulled from my closet. It was definitely funkier with skinny black pants, a soft gray tunic shirt, and a wide black belt. Ginger mumbled behind closed lips.

"Are you trying to say something?" I asked politely.

"I promised not to comment," she said, her face slightly pink from the effort of restraining herself.

"You don't have to," I said. "I know you want me to pick the suit."

"No, I don't." She looked pleased to have surprised me. "I checked out *Real Salt Lake* online, and I think wearing something more hip would work better. Wear the belt outfit."

"For real?" I was touched that she had bothered to check out the magazine.

"Yeah. It's got a young, urban feel. I bet it's not a suit kind of place," she said. "I'll give you my Steve Madden slides if you see anyone wearing a suit in there."

"Like I would want them," I said. "They won't fit."

"Your loss," she said with a grin. "But you should definitely go hipster. If anything, you might want to switch the shirt out for something bright. I bet their office is going to be one of those rule-breaking, creative-type places where people show up in ironic T-shirts."

"Go away now. I need to make a final decision on what to wear, and then I need to sit and think about the interview." Tanner Graham said I had a lot to learn, but I learn quickly. I would definitely be more prepared for this interview. I'd spent a lot of time researching the *Real Salt Lake* website, and I liked what I'd seen. It was designed for young, aspiring urbanites who wanted the big city experience, offering articles on all the cool places to eat, shop, and play. It had a youthful but sophisticated vibe, kind of like a weekly indie tabloid that grew up a few years and shaved off its pretentious goatee. If I didn't know Salt Lake from growing up forty miles south of it, I would look at *Real Salt Lake* and think the city fell a few points short of being Manhattan; the website's production was that slick. If this was all an outgrowth of Ellie's vision, then she definitely knew what she was doing.

Ellie had been expecting my phone call a few days before, thanks to Mrs. Mayers. Ellie explained that they were still a very small operation but that she had some possibilities to discuss with me. My meeting with her tomorrow had been the only thing that had kept me slogging through another week at Handy's. I clung to the hope that I would soon be able to shake sandwich purgatory forever.

After Ginger left, I tooled around the Internet for a while, reading articles like "How to Get the Job You Want" and "The Sure-Fire Guide to Acing an Interview." And I possibly spent a little extra time on Etsy looking at some cool retro jewelry designs. Maybe. When I slept that night, I dreamed I was waving a tiny digital voice recorder at the governor, who was a tomato, while standing on top of Tanner Graham, who had dream-morphed into a purple ottoman with a head and arms. I woke with that good omen fresh in my mind and set out to meet Ellie Peters and begin life as Pepper Spicer, sandwich shop refugee and girl reporter extraordinaire.

By the time I exited the freeway, I could tell that everything about this interview was already better than the *Bee* disaster. For one, the *Real*

Salt Lake offices were located in Sugarhouse, and I decided right away it would be my favorite part of Salt Lake. There was a relaxed vibe about it, and lots of young people lived in the area. The funky boutiques and quirky shops dotting the area made me feel right at home. As I drove down this section of 2100 South, I wondered how all this time I could not have realized what a cool area was waiting for me only a short drive up the freeway.

I found the address easily. It was a small office perched over a music shop advertising "Lessons from Accordion to Zither." That would make for some interesting ambient noise. I climbed the stairs to a glass door displaying the clean lines of the *Real Salt Lake* logo in its center. Taking a deep breath, I pushed it open and stepped into the crowded office. Like the newsroom at the *Bee*, everyone worked in one open space, but a much smaller one. Eight desks, all Ikea style, dotted the office in a configuration that allowed navigation through a narrow pathway running straight down the room. Four of the desks sat empty of people but full of loose papers, knickknacks, and oversized flat-panel computer monitors. Every other desk had someone at it. The lone male, a pasty-skinned guy in a Homestar Runner T-shirt, stared at his computer screen and clicked his mouse every few seconds. The three girls, none of whom looked more than five years older than me, were either talking on the phone in business-friendly voices or clicking around on their own fancy monitors.

One of them, a willowy brunette with a chic bob cut, stood and made her way over with a smile on her glossy lips. As I checked out her dark skinny jeans and gathered tee in an achingly cool retro print, I sent up a silent thank you to Ginger for suggesting I skip the suit.

"Ellie Peters?" I asked, my hand outstretched.

"And you're Pepper," she said, assessing me even as she shook my hand and smiled. I hoped I looked like a good fit. *Love me*, I silently begged. *Love me so much that you offer me a job on the spot.*

"Yes. I'm so glad to meet you. I love what you're doing with *Real Salt Lake.*"

"Thanks," she said, her smile bright. "We work hard at it. Why don't you follow me to the break room, and we can talk more about it." She scooped up her laptop as she walked.

I trailed after her, trying to look as hip and cool as the other girls in the office, although I was feeling very Old Navy in an Anthropologie world. I didn't have a lot of time to study the office before following Ellie out, but besides the modern desks and furniture, earthy terracotta-color paint warmed the walls, and a few abstract paintings in thick oils and a couple collages with a slightly vintage feel caught my eye. The space looked like the love child of Ikea and a Moroccan bordello. Weird but cool.

The break room was far more generic. A worn fridge hunkered in a corner, and a coffee maker and microwave crowded the cheap Formica countertop. Ellie waved me into a seat at the folding table in the center of the room and pulled out the chair opposite me.

"Sorry about the ghetto fabulous décor in here," she said. "As a start up, we try to keep our money invested only in things that affect the public's perception of us. We need the front to look nice for investors. By the time we can afford a break room makeover, we should be graduating to bigger, nicer digs."

"That makes perfect sense." I nodded and then caught myself, not wanting to go down the same crazy head-bobbing path I'd taken with Tanner Graham. "Thanks again for seeing me."

"I'm glad you called," she said. "What do you know about *Real Salt Lake?*"

I did a mental fist pump, glad I had spent time studying the webzine. "I love the design of it. You've created the look and feel of an expensive glossy magazine online. The writing is excellent, the topics are interesting, and I will definitely be checking it out in the future, regardless of what happens today."

She beamed. "I love hearing that. This is all I've eaten, breathed, and slept for more than a year. I like to refer to us as small but mighty. We only have eight full-time people on staff right now, but it's a high concentration of talent."

"That's definitely fair to say," I agreed, meaning it. They had a really good thing going. "I'm honestly shocked I haven't heard of it before."

Her face fell for a moment, but then she mustered another winning smile. "That's our biggest headache right now, figuring out how to get our name out there. That's part of what drove the choice in our name. It's a play on Real Salt Lake, the soccer team, to get us more hits when people do Internet searches. Get it? It's real, but it's also *real,*" she said, giving the last word the proper Spanish pronunciation.

"Nice," I said. Ellie Peters was a very smart girl. Er, woman. Young lady?

"We're looking at new ways to draw reader interest and create some buzz. We get high traffic before the weekend when people are Googling searches for places to eat or stuff to do. We want to convert more of that traffic to click throughs for other articles, not just our restaurant and theater reviews. We sell a fair number of ads to restaurants, but if we could attract more readers to our other content, we could charge more for what we already sell, plus attract whole new categories of advertisers."

I nodded. It sounded like pretty straightforward common sense.

"That's where you come in," she said. "We want new, fresh voices to uncover the quirks and secrets of the city for our readers, someone that our target demographic can relate to. I think that's you."

"Me?" Remembering Tanner's diatribe the week before, I cleared my throat and took a stab at total transparency. "I'm inexperienced, but I learn fast. You won't find anyone willing to work harder, and I'm full of ideas."

She smiled. "We're not worried about your experience. I know you can write. I read through your blog archives—" and here again, I experienced a rush of relief that I had taken down the posts not fit for potential employer consumption— "and you have a great voice. I also asked Anna to send me copies of the features you wrote for *North Valley Gazette*. You have a good sense of story and a subtle sense of humor."

"Wow, uh, thanks," I stammered and then felt like I was about fourteen and Ellie was the senior cheer captain deigning to sit with me at lunch. *Pull yourself together,* I scolded.

"You're welcome, but I'm stating the facts. I think your style is a good fit for us, and we can polish you in editing where you're still green."

Holy cow. It sounded like she was on the verge of whipping out a contract for me to sign on the spot. Maybe I was more awesome than I realized . . .

"We've got a special assignment we'd like to start you out with," she said.

Yes!

"Are you single?"

Wha . . . ? I nodded, stupidly.

"Perfect. Then you're definitely the right girl for this assignment," she said.

"Great?" I said, but I was so confused that it came out sounding like a question.

Ellie laughed and tucked her hair behind one ear, better exposing the hand-worked silver curlicue earrings dangling from her lobe. This girl had an impeccable sense of style. "Based on the hits different articles and search terms get within the website, we think we could grab another huge chunk of Internet traffic if we added a *Sex in the City*–type feature, and we want you to be our Carrie Bradshaw."

My jaw dropped. I couldn't find the presence of mind to do more than stare, slightly horrified. *Sex in the City*? Had she seen on my totally sanitized, painfully accurate résumé that I was a BYU graduate? What kind of craziness was this?

The look on my face sent her into another peal of laughter, and she took a minute to pull herself back together.

"I'll clarify," she said when she had calmed down, although she grinned broadly. "This is a highly modified, no-sex version. It would be more like *Love in the City* than *Sex in the City*."

I was less alarmed but still confused. "I don't understand where you're going with this," I said, careful to keep my voice neutral so I didn't sound negative.

"Forget *Sex and the City*," she said. "Bad comparison. I'll pitch it a different way. A significant number of the visitors to our magazine are drawn by search terms related to dating, especially Internet dating. Anytime we run a feature about the do's and don'ts of Internet dating, it lights up with page hits. We want to tie it more closely to the Salt Lake experience, not just generic Internet dating tips. We're going to launch a weekly column about the online dating experience in the Salt Lake area."

"How do I fit into this?" I didn't like where this was going.

"You'll take the LDS point of view in your column, since that's half our readership anyway. The hot site everyone uses right now is LDS Lookup. We'll pay for your account and ask you to set up one date a week. We want it to be safe, so we'll always know when you have a date and where you'll be going. You'll write the column under a pen name so your dates won't guess who you are, although we'll leave it up to you whether you want to tell them that you'll be writing about the date. You'll need to disguise their identities." She'd been typing as she talked, and now she turned her laptop to face me. The LDS Lookup site was on the screen, looking sleek in tones of sage green and slate blue. She gestured for me to click around on it and then continued her spiel.

"Whenever possible, we want you to leave it to your date to plan the activity. We think it will better reflect what the experience is like for other women doing the online dating thing. Your column will be your take on the experience, and we'll run it every Tuesday, giving you a couple days to write it. What do you think?"

She was offering me a job. Right? I didn't know what to think. This was so far off from what I thought I'd be doing. "Why me?" I asked, realizing I shouldn't let the silence drag on too long. "Why not one of the other people on staff?"

She shrugged. "Several reasons. We only have one writer who isn't in a relationship or married, and she flatly refuses to do it. I can't make her. I can only find someone who is looking to get their foot in the door, and that's you."

"That's blunt," I said.

"Yes. But true, and it's an amazing opportunity for you." She pushed the laptop to the side and leaned forward, her eyes bright. "Think about it. It's your chance to start at the ground level of something new and exciting. You can be a part of taking *Real Salt Lake* to the next level. You get to stamp this column with your personality, and if your blog is anything to go by, that's where your writing will shine. Besides, you'll have a date every week."

I shook my head. I wanted to find a way to break into journalism, but the idea of Internet dating sounded awful. I had no interest in a relationship, so why would I suffer through weeks of awkward dates just so I could write stories that would force me to relive them online? I could play in interstate traffic every Saturday and then report on it every Tuesday and feel more excited about the notion.

Ellie must have sensed that I was about to reject the offer because she rushed to keep me on the hook. "I'll sweeten the pot," she said. "If getting a break in the news business and starting off with your own column aren't enough for you, consider the potential. We can't pay you a salary at first—"

Hold the phone. I wouldn't even get paid for this?

"—but we can offer you excellent exposure and experience."

"I'm sorry," I said, unable to believe what I was hearing. "You want me to go on a date every week with a complete stranger, write about it, and then not get paid for it?" I felt like I had landed in the offices of Crazy Town.

"Of course we'll pay you for it," she said. "We just can't offer you a full-time position. You'd be the equivalent of a stringer at a large paper."

I made a mental note to look up *stringer*. "How many hours a week should I expect to work?"

"Right now, it would be the time you spent on the dates and then writing about them, but we wouldn't be paying you hourly anyway."

This was getting weirder and weirder. In the dozen or so "How to Interview" articles I had read, every single one said to save salary negotiations until the employer offered the job, but I couldn't help it. This was all so bizarre that I had to ask. "Then how will you be paying me?"

"Based on page views," she said. "We'll offer you a cent for every page view your column receives up to $150 per column."

I struggled to do the math in my head and determined that $150 was about half of what I could earn working full-time somewhere at minimum wage. And that's assuming I got the maximum number of page views. I shook my head.

"I'm sorry, Ellie. I don't think this is the right fit for me. The idea of dating gives me a headache. Besides, I'm looking for something more full time, something more news driven."

"Don't say no yet," Ellie said, leaning back and looking relaxed. "Look at the potential here. I know you want to break into journalism, but you're not coming in with any real credentials, via your schooling or your work experience. To be honest, if I weren't in a pinch, I'd look around some more before hiring someone to do this. And no, we can't afford to hire you full-time now, but we will. As we add more features like your dating column, we'll draw more readers, and that means we'll sell more advertising. Your position could become full time soon if we can build our readership fast enough. Which we totally can. We have great stuff brewing."

It still didn't feel like the right fit. Ellie, probably reading that in my face, sighed. "If we sent you on news-related assignments periodically, would it change your mind?"

"Can you be more specific?"

She studied me for a long moment, and her shrewd gaze sized me up as she tried to make a deal I couldn't pass up. "We're spread pretty thin. What if we used you from time to time when we're short staffed to go cover breaking news? We'd pay you per article only on what we assign you, but it would give you a chance to build your résumé, and it would mean a slightly larger paycheck. As it is, you have the chance to make up to six hundred dollars a month just with the dating column."

My eyes widened. I hadn't done the math that far, and suddenly that sounded like a pleasant number. I couldn't quit Handy's on that, but I could put myself months ahead paying off my wedding debt. Maybe . . .

No. "That's a better offer," I admitted. "But I still don't know about the dating thing. I'm not a typical Mormon girl. There's no guarantee that anyone would even want to date me."

At that, Ellie burst out laughing. "You're kidding me, right?"

I shook my head, confused about what was so funny.

She calmed down enough to say, "You're so stinkin' perfect for this I can't stand it. If you were a cookie-cutter LDS girl, you couldn't do this gig. But you've got sass that shows up in everything from your haircut to your writing. If you can fill out your dating profile to reflect the personality that comes through on your blog, you'll be in good shape. If you post a picture on your profile, you'll have dates lined up for weeks."

I flushed. It had been so long since I had been on a first date that I didn't even have a good perception of my fair-market value. How sad. Ellie was a stylish, business-savvy girl. She wouldn't be pushing for me to do the column if she didn't think it would succeed. I weighed my options. Working with *Real Salt Lake* wouldn't happen on the terms I'd imagined. I'd still have to work at Handy's, but I would have a foot in the door—and a shot at turning it into something full time and permanent. If I didn't take the job, I had . . . no other options.

But I hated the idea of Internet dating. *Hated* it.

I sighed. "I have to think about this, Ellie. When do you need an answer?"

"Take the weekend," she said. "But I'll need to know by Monday. I do have someone else I can use, but you're my first choice."

I nodded in understanding, and she stood and offered me another handshake. "I really hope you'll consider it, Pepper. I know you don't love the whole online dating thing, but it's a great opportunity for you to develop your writing voice. I'll walk you out, and I hope it isn't for the last time."

I stood and followed her, returning the smiles of the salesgirls on the way out. The guy in the Homestar Runner shirt offered me a brief nod and turned back to his digital wizardry.

All the way home, I ran the offer through my mind, trying to decide what to do. I really wanted to quit Handy's, but considering that only two weeks before I'd been convinced that any type of newspaper job was impossible, this was a pretty good place to start. If I couldn't convince myself to love the idea of online dating, maybe I could approach it as a chance to mine for comic gold and it wouldn't be so bad. Far more people had done far worse things when getting started. Probably.

At least these dates would be a free meal every week. I hoped.

By the time I pulled into the driveway at home, I had my mind made up. I rushed in to change into my Handy's Dandy Sandwiches

T-shirt and rushed out again before either of my parents could come home and ask me about the interview. I needed time to figure out a way to break the news of my impending online dating adventures. They would hate the idea more than I did.

Oh well. At least Ginger would love it, if only because she'd have one more reason to make fun of me.

Dear Coach Sweeney,

Thank you for teaching us first aid and CPR in tenth grade. I realize that we were inattentive, rowdy, and obnoxious, but some of it stuck. If I had known then that I would actually need that stuff, I would have paid way more attention. Still, enough stuck that I could use it when I really needed it. Also, I'm really sorry I named the CPR dummy Cootie Carol. I was trying to get a laugh, not deter almost the entire class from refusing to give her mouth-to-mouth. But hey, the Red Cross says straight compressions are better anyway, so really, in the long run, it all worked out fine, right?

Finally, I thought I'd pass along a small lesson from my real-life first-aid experience. I think you should warn future classes that even though you can do the Heimlich maneuver on someone much larger than you, it's hard. And also embarrassing. But it will work, thank goodness. It just puts the kibosh on a second date is all.

Sincerely,
Pepper Spicer

Chapter 5

Fridays were becoming action packed by Pepper Spicer standards. Then again, up until my dad's thank you challenge, leaving the house to visit Redbox and grab a bag of Funyuns would have counted as a big night. By those standards, tonight was epic.

I had a date.

Aaagh!

"I can't believe you're doing this," Ginger said. She and Rosemary watched from Rosemary's bed as I got ready for my first *Real Salt Lake* gig. My mother was downstairs, probably trying to figure out how to lock me up without violating any laws. I'm sure my dad was waiting at the foot of the stairs with an argument designed to make me change my mind while convincing me that it was my idea to stay home.

"I can't decide if it's cool or lame," Ginger added.

"Definitely lame," I said. "But I have to do it if I want the job." My stomach churned with equal parts of panic and dread. Even before Landon, I hadn't done much dating. I'd met him in a summer class at BYU before I started my official freshman year, and we'd dated until the week after I graduated, a measly week before our (second) wedding date. Of course, there had been a short breakup somewhere in the middle when he called our first wedding off because it conflicted with the South by Southwest Music Festival and he'd scored a gig fronting a local band that made it into the semifinal competition.

After that, I had this crazy idea that our relationship wasn't going anywhere. But I think he must have shown up at my apartment after they'd bombed at the competition and batted his eyelashes at me and I took him back. "Yeah, don't worry about the thousands of dollars your parents dropped on the wedding." He maybe didn't use that exact argument, but it was close. *And I went along with it.* Because I didn't know how not to be "Landon-and-Pepper."

Clearly, I didn't have the necessary life experience to know what to expect from casual dating. Most of my "dating" had been in high school, and that was more like a bunch of girls and guys hanging out. Anyone holding hands was classified as "going out."

This LDS Lookup thing was big-girl dating, involving getting-to-know-you conversations and possibly table manners. In a way, I was glad this first date had happened so quickly because I had little time to stress out about it. Tonight, I was going out with Brent, better known as Snow_Junkie on LDS Lookup. I had set up my account Monday afternoon after a call from Ellie, who welcomed me onboard. I had no idea what I was supposed to put in my profile, even after reading through all the Internet dating how-tos in the *Real Salt Lake* archives, but I did pay extra close attention to the advice for staying safe when meeting someone that you've only known online. Not that it was going to make my mom feel any better . . .

"Don't take this wrong, but I'm surprised you got a date so quick," Ginger said. "Did you see a picture of this guy? Is he ugly or something?"

I turned away from the closet to face her. "Geez, Ginger. Is there a right way to take that?"

"Not nice," Rosemary said, wagging a finger at Ginger. "Anyone would want to go out with Pepper. She's pretty and sweet."

Ah, seven-year-olds. So clueless, and yet I still loved my littlest sister's fierce loyalty. "Thanks, peanut," I said.

"I'm just saying, it can't be normal to join a dating website on a Monday and have a date in five days." Ginger hopped up and whisked the Mumford and Sons concert T-shirt out of my hand. "You can't wear this. Band T-shirts are tacky for a first date."

I snatched it back. "I know that. I meant to grab the shirt next to it." I pulled out a smoky blue knit top with a cool flower appliqué winding from one shoulder down across the chest. "This will work for a casual first date, right?" I asked, thrusting it toward Ginger.

She held it up to study it, her head cocked. "For a soccer game? Yes. Shoes?"

In answer, I dug out a pair of black canvas ballet flats. She nodded.

Satisfied, I changed into the outfit, glad I could wear jeans. A blind date would be miserable enough without having to dress up in something uncomfortable.

I sifted through my jewelry in search of a pair of beaded earrings I had picked up last year at the Park City Arts Festival and responded to Ginger's earlier doubt. "I have no idea if it's normal to get a date online so fast. All I know is that I posted my picture on Tuesday and I got three e-mails by the next day. Maybe that's a lot, or maybe it's pathetic. I don't know." I also didn't know how normal it was to go from first e-mail to first date in less than a week, but since my goal wasn't to form a long-term relationship, there was no reason to have a big buildup before a first date. Why not go out early in the whole process? Actually, there wouldn't be a process. Just first dates. A whole string of first dates.

Gah.

I had no idea how many of these I would have to go through before I could move on to writing other stuff for the magazine, and it depressed me to think about it. So I didn't.

I fastened the second earring and turned around for inspection. Rosemary clapped. "Pretty!"

"You'll do," Ginger said, like it was painful to admit. Seventeen-year-olds are way more of a pain than seven-year-olds. "Besides, this guy is ugly, right? I'm sure he's happy to even have a date at all."

I rolled my eyes and grabbed my laptop to click open his LDS Lookup profile. "He's not ugly." I plopped it on her lap while I scrounged for my favorite tinted lip gloss. Brent was my age, from Sandy, and was finishing up a degree in biology at the University of Utah. He sent me a message on Wednesday saying he liked most of my tastes in sports teams and wondered if I wanted to catch the Real Salt Lake soccer opener with him because he had an extra ticket. Granted, I had only listed the Jazz and the Cougars as my favorite teams, so I'm pretty sure we only had half of my favorite teams in common. And it was a fairly underwhelming offer as dates go. "Wanna use my extra ticket and maybe share some nachos?" Which, okay, was not *exactly* how he had put it, but it's more or less what he meant. Still, it was a date, and that's what I needed for my column. Besides, he was reasonably cute. His picture showed him posing with his mom, and he had nice hazel eyes and neatly cut sandy blond hair.

"He's okay," Ginger said. "Maybe you'll find some hotter guys later."

"Hotness isn't everything," I said and took the laptop back. Landon had schooled me on that one.

"Really? So you have an amazing spiritual connection with this guy, huh?"

I shot her a withering look.

Rosemary, bored, slid off the bed. "I'm going to get cookies," she said.

"Me too." Ginger followed her toward the door. "That way I can see the Mom drama unfold."

Five minutes later, I followed them down. They both sat on the living room sofa with a bag of Oreos between them, watching the door instead of the TV. I sighed. "Mom, I'm leaving!" I nearly made it to the front door, but she was too fast. She charged out of the kitchen with my dad right on her heels.

"Don't go," she said.

"You can't make me stay," I pointed out reasonably.

"But I can prey on your guilt. I'm going to worry about you the whole night. Do you really want to put me through that?"

"Teresa, we can't interfere with her decisions," my dad said, resting a hand on her shoulder. "If Pepper thinks it's worth a calculated risk to her safety and our mental well-being, we can't interfere." He looked at me hopefully.

"Good try," I said, halfway through the door. "We're meeting in a public place, I'll text you every hour, and I'll call you as soon as I'm on the road home. Let me be a grownup, please."

My mom looked like she wanted to argue, but Dad squeezed her shoulder. "Every hour," he said.

I flashed him a thankful grin, needing to escape before any more of my mom's paranoia rubbed off on me. Tugging the door closed behind me, I took a deep breath and headed for The Zuke and the soccer game. And Brent, my date for the evening.

* * *

An hour later, I wished I'd let my mom talk me into staying home. I wasn't in any danger, unless it was death by boredom. I texted a quick update and then watched the field again. Brent shifted in his seat next to me, which meant I had to shift too, since every time he moved he encroached on my personal space. His build was tall and athletic, as advertised on his profile, but "tall" didn't really do him justice. We had met at the entrance gate, where I had told him to look for a confused-looking girl with short hair and a yellow purse. I figured my cute, twelve-dollar Old Navy bag was a better way to identify me than me standing around with a rose pinned to my shirt or something dumb like that.

He'd told me to look for a tall guy in a maroon shirt. He found me a few minutes before game time, and I knew I had the right guy because he was six-foot-seven. I'm average height, exactly halfway between five and six feet, but standing next to him, I looked like I had drunk Alice in Wonderland's shrinking potion. He wasn't twiggy, basketball tall either. He was solid, more like football tall, which is why it felt like he had been in my space for the last hour. He couldn't help it. Freakish height aside, he was unobjectionable. He didn't have much to say besides occasional comments on the game. At one point, he turned to me and asked if I wanted anything from the concession stand, and I requested a pretzel.

"Is that it?" he asked. "I'd be glad to buy you some dinner."

Considering that a rubbery hamburger and a soda here would cost roughly as much as filet mignon at La Caille, it was a generous offer.

"No thanks. I'm not that hungry." It was true. My nerves had squashed my appetite.

He nodded and left, and I sighed in relief at having a little room to move. Just because I could, I stretched my arms to either side and enjoyed the open space for a full thirty seconds. I watched the field, but I couldn't focus on the game, distracted by a raging internal debate. Should I tell Brent I would be writing about our date for the magazine? On the one hand, I like to be upfront about everything. Disaster strikes when I'm not. I offer the padded résumé debacle as Exhibit A.

On the other hand, I knew I would be looking for the funny in the whole night, and even without being mean, some of it would come at his expense. It would be kind of a double whammy to get a laugh and then point him to the website and rub his nose in it, even if names were changed to protect the boring.

By the time he showed up with a pretzel, giant soda, and two hot dogs, I had made my mind up. I wouldn't say anything to him. I had no intention of leading him on by going on another date or keeping up an e-mail exchange, so my conscience felt okay.

I eyed the second hot dog and reached for it to be polite. "Thank you," I said. "You didn't have to get me one too."

Startled, he jerked it away and then flushed. "Sorry," he said. "That's a reflex from growing up with three brothers. You learn to defend your food or lose it. It's, uh, it's actually for me. I eat a lot."

It was my turn to blush. It's not attractive when I do it. I'm fair, super fair, maybe even borderline Cullen-ish. Instead of this delicate pink stain on my cheeks like you read about in romance novels, I turn dull red. Tomato-y. Painfully not cute. "Right. I knew that."

"Sorry," he stammered again, thrusting the pretzel and one hot dog at me. "You can have this one. I'll go get another one."

I warded it off. "The pretzel is enough, I promise." I settled it in my lap and broke off a piece then chewed it with relish to show how much I was enjoying it. "Yum."

His expression was still uncertain, but he took his seat, crowding me and my ultra-dry pretzel, and started into his hot dog while he watched the game. Up to that point, RSL had been down a point after an early goal from the other team, but suddenly, one of their midfielders stole the ball and went streaking toward the net. Brent threw his hands in the air and yelled encouragement, stringing together the most words I'd heard him say besides his hot dog speech. His arms flailed, and I didn't duck fast enough, my upper arm paying the price for my slow reflexes. I gauged his elbow and wondered how big my bruise would be. Roughly the size of West Virginia, I guessed, and then I made a mental note to put that line in my article.

Everyone around me was now on their feet, and the energy was hard to resist as our forward surged toward the goal. I jumped up to see better as he sent the ball sailing into the net with a lightning-fast strike.

"Goooooooaaaaaaaaal!" I screamed with everyone around me. I cheered, ducking from my date's waving arms so he didn't add Ohio and Kentucky to my bruise collection. As the excitement died down a bit, his arms kept flailing. Man, he took his sports seriously. I stayed standing to be polite, but now his flailing looked . . . not right. And he wasn't cheering, he was . . . choking! He turned toward me, his eyes wide and watering, his face redder than mine had been when I'd tried to take his hot dog. He couldn't even draw a breath to wheeze, and I froze before a memory of tenth-grade health class flashed through my head, and I knew I had to give him the Heimlich.

I stared at him for two seconds, since I came up to his sternum at best, and I had no idea how to get any leverage. It would take too long to find someone taller and explain the problem, especially since I had no idea how long he'd been choking. I did the only thing I could think of and jumped up on the seat behind him. I executed the Heimlich the best I could remember, wrapping my arms around him and clasping my hands together, but I could barely reach, he was so big. I jerked as hard as I could, twice, three times, and finally on the fourth time, he made a weird hacking noise and a chunk of slimy hot dog and bun flew out of his mouth and sailed five rows in front of us, hitting the back of some kid's head. I jumped down, and the poor kid jerked around to see what hit him, but he couldn't figure it out. Oh well. Someone would eventually point out the small patch of mustard in his hair.

"Are you okay?" I asked, adrenaline making my voice shaky.

Brent rubbed his throat and sat down. "Yeah." He took several long swigs from his soda. "Thank you."

"No problem. Sorry it took me so long to figure out the problem."

He shook his head. "I swallowed the wrong way when we scored."

"I hate when that happens."

He didn't say anything, just rubbed his throat and drank some more. I didn't know how long we were supposed to discuss his near-death experience, and since he wasn't say anything, I thought maybe I should watch the game instead. After couple of minutes, Brent cleared his throat. "Um, would it be bad if we ended the night early? I think I might want to go home and lie down or something." He looked chagrined, and I tried to school my face to show a socially acceptable level of disappointment, but even my liver exhaled with relief.

"That sounds like the smart thing to do," I said.

He stood, and I followed him out to the same gate we had met at before the game. "Thanks for coming," he said after a short but awkward silence.

"Thanks for inviting me." And here was the moment I knew I could dread on every one of these stupid dates I went on: the good-bye. Do I shake? Offer a hug? Stiff-arm anyone who tries to kiss me?

Brent moved slowly toward a different gate. "Thanks," he said again and then stopped and added, "I'm really glad you know the Heimlich, but that was the strangest good night hug I've ever gotten." And then with a small smile and a wave, he picked up his pace and headed out.

I laughed, but the flash of humor was a little too late to save the date for me. On the plus side, he'd handed me the perfect ending line for my Tuesday column. It was definitely the strangest good night hug I'd ever given.

Dear Marian,

It's just too delicious that you're a librarian named Marian, first of all. Imagine me singing that song from The Music Man. How often does that happen to you, I wonder?

Anyway, that has nothing to do with the point of this note, which is to say thank you. Thanks for the dozen or so book suggestions you've made over the last several months for me. You've pointed me toward some really great novels. They got me through some tough times when I needed a little space from the rest of the world and a book was the only place I could find it.

You have excellent taste, and I'm grateful you shared it.

Sincerely,
Pepper, your most loyal patron

Chapter 6

On Sunday, for the first time in a long time, I didn't have to drag myself to church. I looked forward to it. I had five weeks down in my dad's challenge. This could be my first opportunity to see if my notes were having an effect on anyone. Would I get a different vibe from Courtney? Would she think I was weird and be hiding in a different part of the chapel? Or would it be exactly the same as always?

I threw on a black shirt dress, some gray tights, and a pair of two-inch-heel Mary Janes. I'm not much for super-tall heels. I feel like I'm playing dress up when I wear them, like I'll get busted for being a fake grownup, but I wanted to throw them on today to change things up.

When I slipped into sacrament meeting, Courtney was saving my usual spot. She smiled, and that was that. All righty, then. Business as usual was better than her avoiding me.

After the closing prayer, she turned to me and smiled again. "Thanks for your note."

I shrugged. "No problem. Thanks for always saving me a seat."

"Are you coming to Sunday School today?"

I opened my mouth to decline on the grounds that skipping it was now a habit, but Courtney must have seen my answer written on my face because she jumped in to preempt me. "You have to. And if you won't come because I asked you, then I'll have to guilt trip you into it."

The twinkle in her eye undermined her threat.

"Take your best shot," I said.

"I've been saving you a seat for months and rescuing you from the hinterlands," she said, pointing toward the metal folding chairs in the overflow. "Now you owe me. You need to come sit with me during Sunday School so that Bow Tie Boy can't."

"Bow Tie Boy? Is wearing it some kind of ironic hipster statement?" I asked.

"No."

I shuddered. "Yeah, you deserve better." A shadow dimmed her face so fleetingly that I wondered if I'd imagined it because she was already smiling again. "I'll go with you to Sunday School," I said, "if only to save you from Bow Tie Guy."

That night when I collapsed on my bed and considered the week behind me, I smiled. A new job, a date, and a new friend. Each one represented some kind of baby step toward . . . the future? I didn't even know. But I guessed it was toward something good.

The only downside was the article due in two days. I might rather be reporting on Salt Lake current events or writing about local heroes, but I would write the best column I could on the world's most boring date. It would take every bit of storytelling talent I had to turn that into six hundred and fifty interesting words, but hey, that's what I was getting paid a penny a click for.

I got up early the next morning, like seminary-early if I lived in one of those mission-field states, and drafted my first attempt at the article. I read through it and decided that I was a two-time victim of my Friday night date because reading it was boring me as much as the actual date had. I would earn a whopping two dollars out of this experience with all the clicks this piece would generate. Oh, who was I kidding? Fifteen cents, tops. For a moment, I wished that instead of working at the kitchen table on my laptop, I had an old-school typewriter so I could rip the paper out of the machine for the satisfaction of crumpling it. Instead, I hit the delete key and manually erased my lame article one letter at a time, watching the cursor race backward, eating everything in its path. Good-bye, unnecessary description of the arena. Good-bye, reference to Brent as "tall." So poetic, that.

I sighed and dropped my head on my keyboard, which hurt. Then I picked it up and stared at the screen that now read, "yu7y767t." It was better than what I had written the first time. A half hour and another four deleted paragraphs later, Mace stumbled in and grabbed a gallon jug of orange juice from the fridge. He stared at me blankly while he chugged, but at some point, his stomach registered the presence of fuel, and his eyes focused.

"What are you doing?" he asked, rubbing his hand across his mouth to scrub away his juice 'stache.

"Trying to write my new column. It's not going so well."

"You have that writer's block thing?"

"No. I can think of lots of stuff to say. It's just not good."

He put the orange juice jug, now empty, back on the shelf and pulled out a gallon of milk.

"If you swig out of that, I might throw something at you."

He eyed the jug and then me. "Like what?"

"Like my laptop. It's not really doing me any good right now anyway."

He reached into the cabinet for a cup. "You gotta find the funny. Like on your blog. Isn't that why they hired you?"

"This is different. It's *reporting.*"

He snorted. "I know I'm a math guy and not a writer, but I don't think telling about your dates is journalism. It's supposed to be entertainment." He grabbed his glass of milk and a banana and headed out of the room. "Find the funny," he called over his shoulder.

I turned back to my laptop. Since I had failed at my first two attempts, it couldn't hurt to treat it more like a blog post. Switching gears a little bit, I tapped out a new open. "You know all those articles that warn you about how everyone misrepresents themselves on their Internet dating profiles? If a girl says she's slender, maybe add twenty pounds. Or if a guy says he's six foot, you should subtract a couple inches—or maybe a whole ruler's worth of them. Those articles don't warn you about what to do when a guy who says he's tall really means it—to the point that he's always in a different weather pattern. *That's* tall."

Ahhhh . . . now it was going somewhere.

Two hours later, I had drafted, revised, and polished it to perfection. It was like something I would write on my blog, only . . . better. I hoped. I attached it to an e-mail for Ellie and hit send, crossing my fingers that she'd like it. I had an hour before work, and wanting to spend it at the library, I hurried to get dressed and out of the house. My favorite librarian had promised to snag any Meg Cabot books that came in over the weekend.

* * *

"What do you mean you want 'more'?" I asked, not for the first time that day. I had asked two teenage boys that question when they'd tried to finagle extra pastrami on their sandwiches. This time, I was asking

Ellie, who had called to say she liked what I'd sent her, but she wanted "more."

"How much longer do you need it to be?" I'd hit the word count she'd originally given me. Maybe it was so good they wanted my column to be longer.

"No, the length is fine," she said. Oh. "It's a little tame. We need it to have more bite."

I switched the phone to my other ear and chewed on a hangnail that had been driving me nuts for an hour. "Bite doesn't sound nice," I said.

"It doesn't need to be mean," she said. "Just funny, with a little more edge."

"You want me to be snarky," I said, not loving the idea.

"If that's what you want to call it, yes."

"That's not what I do," I said. "Maybe I can make it funnier without any edginess."

"Snark is the currency of modern lifestyle humor," she said. "We're giving you prime placement on the home page tomorrow, which guarantees you at least five thousand hits. But if you don't think you can handle it . . ."

"No," I said, hurrying to reassure her. "I can handle it. I'll work on it when I get home. You'll have it by midnight." I winced, thinking of the long evening I had ahead of me if I wanted to meet that deadline. And I really, really did. At least *five thousand* people reading my words. Mine. Possibly more, if the column took off. It beat the heck out of fifty people eating my sandwiches every day.

"Good," she said, her voice pleased. "I'll expect it then."

I pushed end and sighed. My job rarely ever had my undivided attention, but it would be getting even less for the next three hours while I mentally revised my article. I might as well start with the title. Maybe "When Hot Dogs Kill."

Or maybe not.

I grabbed a mop and headed for the dining area. Maybe a little focused manual labor would clear my mind. Three hours later, I hated my job so much I was ready to do whatever Ellie asked if it would put me one step closer to quitting Handy's permanently. Mrs. Lehman, the bean sprout police, had returned for another tour of duty. Seriously, how anyone could be so passionate about a lack of bean sprouts was beyond me. Boo hiss, Mrs. Lehman.

At home, I found everyone in the kitchen finishing up dinner. My mom rushed up and flung her arms around me, pretending to weep on my neck. "You're home, you're home! Hallelujah!"

I disentangled her. "Ha ha." She'd been doing the same thing every night since my Friday night date.

She swerved around me to the sink to scrape off a stack of dishes. "You know how to make me stop."

"I'm not quitting my job, Mom."

"Then I'll continue to express my deep, deep joy every time I realize you haven't been kidnapped by an Internet stalker." She scrubbed furiously at the plate in her hand. My parents still weren't thrilled about this Internet dating experiment, but my dad had backed off a little. My mom wasn't going to quit worrying until she found a way to break the Internet so I couldn't set up any more dates.

"Want to play Super Mario?" Mace asked as I crossed the kitchen.

"No thanks. I gotta go find the funny."

"Cool," he said.

"Dad, can I work in your office?"

"Sure," he said. "Your mother and I are watching *Dancing with the Stars* anyway."

I dragged myself up the stairs, but after a quick shower and a change into my BYU sweats, I was excited to tackle my article. I knew just where to go with it.

* * *

"'When Dating is a Near-Death Experience'?" my dad read aloud when I came down the stairs the next morning.

"It's up?" I rushed over to the laptop in front of him and looked over his shoulder. Sure enough, there it was, my column on the home page with the byline "Indie Girl." It was the same screen name I used on the LDS Lookup site, at Ellie's suggestion. She said it "captured my essence." Whatever. It was better than "Here Under Duress," "I Hate Cupid," or "Just Say No to Romeo"—my suggestions. It was after nine, and everyone should have been gone, but Ginger sat at the table with my dad. I skimmed through the article. It looked like Ellie had run it with very little editing, which made me feel good. I hoped it meant I had a strong voice already.

"What do you think?" I asked, grinning. I'd been up well past midnight tweaking it, "punching it up," as Ellie had requested, and I knew I had nailed it.

"It's funny," my dad said, his voice neutral.

"That's what I was going for." I headed toward the pantry to scrounge up some steel cut oats. I needed a bowl of something hot and hearty to refuel after my late night.

"Yeah, it was pretty good," Ginger added. "I like the part where you put 'Imagine Milhouse stretched an extra nine feet taller and capable of conversation revolving only around food or useless sports trivia,'" she read from the computer screen. "I already sent the link to some of my friends."

"Wow. Thanks." That's as ringing an endorsement as you can get from Ginger.

My dad cleared his throat. "So is this the kind of writing you'll be doing for the magazine?"

I paused in my oatmeal making. "For now. Why?"

"I'm a little concerned about the tone," he said carefully.

"Meaning?"

"Meaning, you weren't very nice to this Giant Milhouse young man. It's funny but at someone else's expense."

"How is that different from usual for her?" Ginger asked.

"Why are you even here?" I asked. "Go to school."

"Major cramps," she said, suddenly clutching her stomach and looking pained.

Dad shot her a knowing look, but he never argues about "women's stuff." She must have complained about cramps after my mom left for work, or she wouldn't have gotten away with it. After staring at her long enough for her to decide she should go lie down, he turned his steady gaze on me. I ignored him and stirred my oats, but the weight of his stare made the back of my neck hot.

"Yes?" I sighed, turning around to face him.

"Are you comfortable with the work you did?" he asked.

"Yeah. It's not a big deal. No one knows my name or his. He doesn't know I wrote about the date, so he's not going to stumble across it and get his feelings hurt. Presto, there you have it: it's a totally harmless article." I scooped up a blob of oats and let it plop back into the pot, suddenly angry that steel cut oats take way longer than stupid Quaker Instant.

My dad was silent for a long moment, and when he spoke, all he said was, "Okay." More Spicer shorthand, this time for "I'll let you figure this out on your own."

But I wasn't falling for that. I had worked too long to get the tone just right, and I had produced something funny—maybe even hilarious in spots. If I thought for a second that there was a chance Brent would read it, I would never have sent it in. Even if he did find it and see himself in the article, the only two people who knew it was him were Brent and me, and I wasn't going to tell anyone.

I ignored the little voice informing me that I was justifying myself. That voice is such a nag. I ran upstairs to get dressed while I waited out the oatmeal. I had a Handy's T-shirt half over my head when my cell phone went off. I scrambled to pull the shirt down and answer the phone. It was Ellie.

"Hello, rising star!" she greeted me.

"Hi," I said. "I saw the column. It looks like you were happy with it."

"Loved it," she said. "I made some minor tweaks, but I barely had to touch it. Good stuff, girl. I love the line about how the piece of hot dog hurtled out of Giant Milhouse's mouth like it would rather leap to its death than hang out with him one second longer."

"Thanks," I said. My dad was being sensitive. Anyone could see that was hyperbole, not meanness.

"Do you have your next date lined up?" she asked.

"I will soon, I think. Two different guys have been e-mailing me, and I think I can set something up by Friday."

"Awesome. So far, we've had the normal level of traffic, but I'll keep you posted on how your column does as the week goes on."

"Thanks," I said. "And don't forget, if you have any news stories you need covered . . ."

"I haven't forgotten," she said, sounding amused. "Give it time, Pepper. I'm still figuring out your writing style and observing how you handle deadlines. I'll kick stuff your way soon."

It amazed me that even though she'd only graduated three years ahead of me, I felt like I was ten years younger. Or better put, ten years less mature.

I finished dressing in my jeans and Converse. Today I would interview candidates for an assistant manager, someone with flexible hours who could come in on short notice if I got the call to cover something cool for *Real Salt Lake*—and someone who could potentially take over my job if I ever managed to get myself hired on permanently at the magazine.

Dear Sister Nelson,

Thanks for being my Mia Maid advisor. I know it's such a dramatic age that it was hard to know if anything was getting through to us, especially when we seemed to be more worried about freshman gossip and boy drama. But you did get through, and I can't believe how often the lesson you made your husband give us on how to change a tire has come in handy.

That's just one example. You're a really neat lady. I'm glad you were patient with us even when we were crazy with hormones and sure that what we wore and who we hung out with was the end all, be all of everything. I'm learning that it's true, but not the way I thought it was.

Anyway, I just wanted to thank you for doing a hard job.

Sincerely,
Pepper Spicer

Chapter 7

I checked the dashboard clock, eying it nervously as the new minute flicked past. Great. I was running almost fifteen minutes late for my date. I didn't give out my cell phone number, so I didn't have his either. Calling or texting was out. I had to hope Justin, screen name Hat_is_ Back, was still waiting at the Salt Lake Public Library when I got there.

I wasn't super optimistic about the evening ahead. On screen, it all sounded good. We were going to meet at a poetry reading and then eat at a nearby café. Something about this Justin guy came off as self-consciously hipster, like the coolness was forced. I had about twelve miles and who knows how many minutes before I'd see whether my suspicion was right. The flash of red taillights flared in a ripple effect in front of me, and I tapped my brakes, stifling a groan. If I hadn't taken Oprah's pledge a few years ago not to text and drive, I would have shot off a blistering message to Ginger. "Thanks for getting back The Zuke so late, ruining my night, and making me look like a jerk before this date even starts." I swore, like I always did, that I'd never let her borrow it again. Until my parents made me. Again.

I contented myself with pretending the gearshift was her head and banged my fist on it a few times to vent my frustration. The slowdown turned out to be mercifully short while all the cars in my lane dodged a helium balloon drifting near the center divider. It was pretty freaky that in the half-light of dusk, a Cookie Monster made of Mylar could look like a small child trying to dodge traffic.

I pulled into the library parking lot and made some minor adjustments in the visor mirror. Ginger convinced me to do a subtle cat-eye thing with some eyeliner to fit the evening's beatnik vibe. It looked pretty cool, and I felt better knowing that despite showing up way later than I wanted to, at least I didn't look like a traffic-battered Muppet.

I hurried out of the car and went looking for Justin, whose message this afternoon had told me he would be wearing a hat. Hm. I guess that was fine as long as it wasn't a backwards baseball cap. Or a beret. His profile picture was pretty clear, and I spotted him as soon as I pushed through the entrance doors. He was standing in front of a glass display case. I thought he was studying the art inside it, but then he raised a hand and smoothed his eyebrow. Not satisfied with his reflection, he played with the porkpie hat he wore, trying a couple different angles and facial expressions.

Great. This was going to be another lonnnnnnnng night.

* * *

Poems, in general, are often short. Ish. And I like them. I have even written a few earnest but awful ones myself. The fact that the one hour we sat listening to some pretty good poetry could feel like ten could only be credited to one Mr. Justin Cool Hat. Unlike Brent, the Fortress of Solitude, Justin did *not* shut up. Ever. He commented on *everything*. He threw out things like "That's a clear reference to Richard Brautigan's Gen X opus," and "Hah. Ginsberg-lite."

Considering that the poet was reading a series of pieces reflecting on her relief work in Haiti, Justin's comments were in poor taste. At best.

When my cell phone vibrated, I thanked whoever it was for the temporary reprieve. I would have been delighted to hear from my credit card company with a new and exciting offer at that point. I shot Justin an apologetic smile when he looked miffed that I was taking the call and then fled into the main foyer. It was Ellie.

"Pepper! How's the date?" she asked.

"Um . . ." I tried to think of how to sum it up.

"Never mind. I'll read about it when you turn your column in." She laughed, but I wasn't sure what the joke was. "I hope it's great, though, because I need you to spend some more time with this guy."

"What? No! I was already trying to figure out how to get out of dinner!" As soon as I said it, I wanted to kick myself. Arguing with the boss: bad idea. I thought of Handy's and shut up.

"Sorry. Chantelle called in, and she can't make it to the concert she was supposed to cover tonight. Something about Cookie Monster and a fender bender. I need you to go cover it."

I groaned.

"What's the problem?" She sounded a touch cranky. "This is what you wanted, right? Something besides your dates to write about?"

I didn't bother clarifying that I was hoping for something more along the lines of . . . news. But the groan wasn't about the assignment. It was about doing the assignment with Justin in tow. Blech.

"Tell me what I need to do," I said.

"That's what I like to hear," Ellie said, pleased. I rolled my eyes. *She* wasn't stuck with Justin. "There's an indie group called Sonic Machine performing at Spackle tonight. See? Indie group for an Indie Girl." She laughed again. At least this time I knew what the joke was.

"Okay. Tell me how to get in, I guess."

She filled me in on what to tell the door guy, and we hung up. I texted my parents to let them know I hadn't been kidnapped yet and I would be later than expected because of my new assignment. If not for my date, I'd have been stoked. I love live bands, but not when I'd have to endure Justin's commentary through the entire show.

Yay.

I checked myself, determined to find the positive. That used to be my go-to response. I'd have to practice making it automatic again. On the upside, I might get to hear a cool band. And yeah, I'd have Justin with me, but maybe the band would be so loud it would drown even him out. Okay, that's mean. At some level, I recognized that I was witnessing an image he had constructed for himself and not the true Justin. I hoped. But the idea of trying to figure out the real him exhausted me. I sighed. Maybe he would relax as the night went on. At worst, I'd definitely have more material for my column.

I headed back into the poetry reading, glad that we were sitting in the back. The poet wrapped up her last poem and bowed her head as the audience applauded. Justin rolled his eyes at me and then clapped as if he were doing her a favor. Lovely. I wondered what he would do if I reached up and tipped his hat off of his head. He probably had a massive bald spot.

While people stood to mill around and congratulate each other for being culturally evolved, I leaned over to Justin. "I know we talked about grabbing dinner, but what about a change of plans?"

"Like what?" Suddenly he looked guarded, as if he were waiting for me to give him the slip. How shocking that it wouldn't be the first time. Not.

I paused, realizing I needed to be careful about the way I phrased this. If I told him I was covering the Spackle show on assignment, he might check out *Real Salt Lake* and land on my review of our date. That would be bad. I chose an explanation that let me sidestep the problem. "A friend of mine has some tickets she can't use to the Sonic Machine show. Want to go?"

"Sonic Machine? They're a little derivative, but, hey, free tickets. Why not?"

Squashing my retort with the half-dozen reasons of why not *him*, I smiled and led him out of the room. We agreed to drive separately since we'd be going opposite directions at the end of the night, and I refrained from pounding my head against the steering wheel when I got in the car. "Think positive," I muttered.

At least the same clothes you wear to a poetry reading will work for going to see an indie band.

* * *

I loved them. They weren't particularly good, but they were extremely loud. I couldn't make out a single one of their mumbled lyrics over the noise of their dissonant wannabe Radiohead sound, but I didn't care. As far as I could tell, Justin's lips had been flapping most of the night, but even when he leaned in to shout-talk in my ear, I couldn't make out a tenth of his criticism. I nodded a lot like I understood, or sometimes I pointed at the band and smiled apologetically that I couldn't hear his pearls of wisdom.

When they broke for a rest between sets, the house deejay replaced them, spinning some trance music. Sadly, he wasn't as loud, and I could hear Justin again.

"Even though they're trying to do ironic Swedish synth pop and even though I know the lyrics are pretty pedestrian, I like the beat," he said. "Do you think less of me?"

Was he kidding? Was that supposed to be his effort to show that he was human like the rest of us? That he was a sucker for the beats of a mediocre band? Ah, Justin . . . so many more questions than answers with that one. Very frustrating questions with unimportant answers too.

I changed the subject to avoid answering him. "Man, I'm thirsty."

"Want a soda or something?" he asked.

"Sure," I said, glad my ploy to get a breather from him had worked.

"Cool," he said near my ear. He held out his hand like he was waiting for something, and I stared at him blankly. "I don't want to offend you by assuming you can't pay your own way. I know it's all about the independent woman."

What a tool. I stared at him for a few seconds, but of course, he wasn't joking. The guy took everything, most of all himself, way too seriously. I dug into my yellow handbag and handed him two dollars. It was worth it if it meant he would go away for a little while.

He wove his way toward the bar, and I turned my attention to the crowd, liking the mellow lull of the trance music after the Sonic Machine ear assault. The crowd grooved and pulsed. I thought about joining them since I was the only one standing on the fringes and watching, but then I saw someone else standing off to the side. Someone who looked very out of place in relaxed jeans and a golf shirt. Someone who wasn't pasty-skinned and slightly grungy. Someone who looked all ruggedly handsome in a room of broody artsy types.

No way. Tanner Graham.

I thought fast. This was totally not his scene, which meant he must be covering it for the *Bee*. He seemed like an odd choice for the job, but then, I didn't know what his beat was for the paper. I assumed it was news or maybe even sports, but I had boycotted the *Bee* since our interview, and I had no idea. His gaze flickered over the crowd, observing, and I knew he would spot me in a matter of moments. Panicking, I squeezed into the mix with everyone else and tried to figure out what to do next.

Unfortunately, my name on the door list, courtesy of Ellie, also granted me backstage access so I could interview the band. That meant Tanner had press access too. The only thing I could do was be glad my shoes fit right and bluff it out if we ended up face to face.

Justin found me several minutes later, where I was still bouncing in gentle rhythm with the deejay's hypnotic set. He handed me a half-full glass of Coke, not the Sprite I had asked for, and I wondered if part of my two dollars had paid for Justin to enjoy some liquid refreshment. Wow. This guy came with an extra helping of awesome sauce. Whatever. I wasn't going to drink it anyway. Rule number one of Internet dating: always meet in a public place. Rule number two: never leave your drink unattended.

Sonic Machine shambled out again, three mousy guys who looked in desperate need of showers and hugs, and played their second set.

Justin bobbed, and I wondered what his equation was. I knew he had one that involved striking the correct hipster balance of acknowledging the beat without acting like he was having a good time. I spent the rest of the set ignoring him and trying to brace for a run-in with Tanner, all while making mental notes for my review of the band.

When they finished and the deejay came back out, I turned to Justin. "I'm going backstage to talk to the band," I said.

"Cool," he said. "I have some questions I'd like to ask them too."

Oh boy. I didn't want to tip him off that I was connected to *Real Salt Lake*, and as I scrambled for a way around it, a blissed-out girl dancing next to us flung her arms wide to . . . embrace the music, maybe? . . . and knocked his hat off.

He had a giant bald spot, all right. Right at the back of his head—and a thinning front too. Even in the dim light, I could see his scalp turning a deep shade of red as he froze, humiliation darkening his eyes.

For the first time, I caught a glimpse of the vulnerable guy who hid beneath the stupid hat and intellectual bluster. I felt bad for him and reached down to pick up his hat. He beat me to it and shoved it on his head, his face still flushed. I started to say something, but he cut me off. "Actually, I see someone I know over there," he said, pointing to the opposite side of the club. "Why don't you go chat with the band, and I'll meet you outside in a few?"

I nodded, understanding that he needed the time to compose himself and feeling grateful that I wouldn't have to explain my magazine connection after all. I made my way to the backstage door and gave my name to the bouncer there. It was a small venue and an unknown band, so security wasn't exactly tight. On the other side of the door, a short hallway led to a back alley exit where I could see a roadie, or maybe one of the club employees, loading sound equipment into the back of a van. An open door with people spilling out of it told me where I needed to be.

I had no idea how I was supposed to do this, but since winging it was my only choice anyway, I took a deep breath and weaved through the crowd. Once inside the room, I realized there weren't a ton of people so much as it was just a really small room. Unfortunately, it meant Tanner spotted me right away. I saw the recognition in his lifted eyebrow and sardonic nod. I lifted my chin and offered a cool nod in return then tried to figure out what was going on around me. It looked like a few newspapers had sent people to cover the show. Someone in front asked a question I missed, and the lead singer, a guy named Foley, expounded about disaffected youth and politicians stealing our hope, all in the same monotone he used for singing. Someone else asked a question about musical influences, and everyone around me either scribbled in palm-sized spiral tablets or held out recorders to capture his answer.

I had neither, since I hadn't planned on doing any reporting when I left my house. I could feel Tanner's eyes on me while I scrounged through my purse, trying to find something usable. Darn those incredible eyes. I didn't dare sneak a look at him because somehow I *knew* I would catch him laughing at me. Determined not to give him anything else to ridicule me for, I snatched my cell phone out and slid open the keyboard. There was no way I could type fast enough to keep up with Foley, even though he spoke in a slow drawl, like it was too much effort to get worked up about his theme. But Tanner didn't know that. Maybe he would assume I was using an extra-special reporting app.

Yeah, right. But it was better than standing around looking dopey.

Someone else called out a question about their tour experiences, another guy asked about how the band had formed, and the ball kept rolling. I felt stupid, not asking anything myself. I didn't know the etiquette on using the answers from other people's questions, but Tanner stood there, smug in his golf shirt, and scribbled without asking anything either. Maybe this was like a presidential press conference where everyone got to use the same information. An intense dislike of Tanner's shirt seized me. It mocked me by saying, "I'm not trying to fit in with you band groupie people because I'm above you." I wished I still had my Coke to spill on him.

The questions continued to fly. "How did you get your band name?" "How long have you been together?" "Where do you get your inspiration?"

Some of the questions surprised me. I could easily find most of the answers by standing there and Googling while they waited for their turn to ask. I wish I'd had enough notice to research them so I knew what I wanted to ask too, but my next best choice was to listen to everyone else. Eventually, Foley's drawl slowed and then stopped altogether, and people trickled out of the room. Not knowing what else to do, I followed them and headed to the door that led out back. It would be much faster to dart around front from there than to thread my way through the crowd still dancing inside. A human traffic jam at the exit slowed me down as two guys loaded a large speaker into the van.

"Did you like the show?" an uncomfortably familiar voice asked behind me.

I composed myself before glancing over my shoulder at Tanner. "It was fine." He stood barely a foot behind me, close enough that I could sense his body heat. I struggled not to squirm.

"How did you score a backstage pass?" he asked.

I turned around with reluctance, sure to let my body language show that it was inconvenient for me to do so. "My editor asked me to cover the show at the last minute, so she called in and cleared me."

"Your editor?" He shook his head. "I guess I shouldn't be so surprised. You wrote the Wonderbra of résumés. Who wouldn't want to hire you?"

My hands flew to my hips. "I apologized for that already. My new editor, unlike you, knows talent when she sees it. I turned in a completely accurate résumé to her, and she saw my potential."

"Potential for *what*? Disaster?"

I glared at him and whirled back around.

"So who is it? Your new editor?"

I ignored him.

"How very mature," he said. "Maybe you should stick your fingers in your ears and sing so I get the hint."

I turned back around. "It's Ellie Peters at *Real Salt Lake*."

His eyebrows shot up. "You work for *Ellie*?"

I had no idea what to make of his emphasis, but I was learning with Tanner that when in doubt, I should take everything as an insult.

"Yes, I work for Ellie. Is that so hard to believe?"

His brow furrowed, and he hesitated before answering. "Yes."

I scowled and felt the short line to the door moving. "Any other questions? I need to find my date."

"You brought a date with you on an assignment?" His incredulous tone was the last straw.

"I told you this was a last-minute gig. I'm sorry if my existence bothers you, but I'm not going anywhere. I don't care if you like how I do things, and I don't care if you like my writing. I plan to be a key player for *Real Salt Lake*, and I'm going to make it my mission in life to steal every single one of the young readers your paper is trying to win back." A lock of hair flopped over my eye, and I shoved it out of the way, furious at it and at Tanner. "I don't need your opinion or your approval, thank you very much."

"You already said that."

"Said what?" I spat, wishing the band's van would back up and run him over now that we'd reached the alley.

Instead, he leaned against the wall, his hands in his pockets, a smile playing around his lips.

"You already said thank you. I got your note, remember?"

I had been wishing for a week now that I had never sent it. My ears burned. Trying to rein my temper back in, I smiled sweetly. "It was totally heartfelt." Then I turned and headed out toward the street and Justin while Tanner's soft laugh sounded in my ears.

To my relief, I saw Justin as soon as I rounded the corner, his hat safely on his head and his bravado back in place. "There you are," he said. I didn't respond. I wasn't a big fan of stating the obvious. It probably came from passing the winter in Handy's with dozens of people coming in all day and proclaiming, "It's cold out there!" like I couldn't see the snow on the ground through the storefront.

"Are you ready to go?" I asked.

"Sure. I'll walk you to your car," he said.

I shrugged. Whatever. This date was already over as far as I was concerned.

I shoved my hands deep inside my coat pockets to protect them from the chilly night air. Even in early March, winter hadn't loosened its grasp completely. It was two blocks to the parking garage, and Justin filled the walk with opinions about the deejay's choices, the band's lack of authenticity, and the quality of the street lighting we passed. Realizing that it came from a place of deep insecurity made me far more patient with him, but relief washed over me at the sight of our cars.

We stopped by The Zuke, and I tried to figure out how to navigate the awkward good night.

"Thanks for the evening," I said.

"Yeah," he smiled. "It's been real." And the tiny hint of irony in his tone made me smile back. He tugged at his hat brim. "So, uh, I should get your num—"

I shook my head. Better to nip it in the bud.

"No?" he asked. And before I could answer, he did. "You're right. No. Want to hug it out?"

I smiled again. If I'd been hanging out with *this* guy all night, it would have been a much better date. I accepted his hug and then unlocked my car door while he walked three slots down to his. I was messing with the radio, trying to get my favorite alternative rock station to come in, when a knock sounded on my window and startled a scream out of me.

It was Justin, looking sheepish. I rolled the window down. "I have a flat," he said. "Do you have AAA?"

I did, but I'd have to stay with him until AAA sent someone out so I could show them my card, and I was an hour past exhausted. I opened the door and climbed out. "It'll be faster if I change it. Do you have a donut or a full spare?"

"You can't change my tire," he said, confused.

"Why? I can buy my own sodas."

He flushed. "All right. Point taken. But I don't have a spare."

"Let me check." I held out my hand for his keys and headed for his car. Sure enough, under the carpeting in the trunk of what I was fairly sure was his mom's Buick, he had a spare. I wrestled it out while Justin shifted from foot to foot, fluttering his arms for a few seconds like he wanted to help but didn't know what to do. Next to the spare, I found a jack—a pretty old-school one, but it would work. I hauled out the lug nut wrench and set to work, spinning the lug nuts off as fast as I could. The sooner I got this tire changed, the sooner I could go home.

I braced myself to tug the flat tire off and then pulled. A vehicle turning the corner toward the exit flashed me with its headlights, causing me to lose my balance and land on my butt, the tire in my lap. I glared at the car, only to see Tanner behind the wheel, his expression surprised. Well, that figured. I'd been wondering how this night could get any worse, but I hadn't been humiliated yet, so why not add that to the mix? Why not have Tanner Graham drive by and catch me changing my date's tire? Justin reached down and attempted to pull me up, yanking me by the armpits. I batted him away. "I'm fine," I said, still sprawled with the tire on my legs. I was so thankful I had on jeans and not a skirt. "Can you go turn on the hazard lights?" Trying to find the button should keep him busy.

Tanner slowed to a stop and rolled the window down. "You need any help?"

I was already up and wrestling the spare in place. "Nope. I know what I'm doing." Justin stayed blessedly silent as he poked around on the dashboard.

"Are you sure?" Tanner asked, sounding concerned.

"I'm really fine," I said. *I'd be even better if you'd leave.*

He hesitated, and I picked my head up long enough to pin him with a steady, unflinching gaze before he nodded and lifted his foot off the brake to roll away.

It took about ten more minutes of wrestling, but I secured the spare and stood up. Justin didn't say much as I worked, just jumped to hand me things as I asked for them. Now he thrust some crumpled but clean fast-food napkins at me. I accepted them but doubted they would do much for the tire grease all over my fingers. Oh well. I could wrap the napkins around the steering wheel so I didn't dirty it on the drive home.

This time, the good-bye was too short to be awkward. He said thanks, and I said see ya, and I hurried to my car before either of us had to think of something else to say. Once I hit the wide-open lanes of the freeway, I navigated on autopilot and thought about my next article. I focused on the concert review, heeding Ellie's directive to write with a strong point of view. I played with an opening hook. *If you like your music loud and lacking any real emotion, then Sonic Machine's Friday night show was a must-see. The band compensated for lack of talent with volume, serving up self-consciously political lyrics that criticized anyone or anything that did not embrace veganism, legalizing marijuana, or environmental activism. If front man Foley Helm's bored explanation of their lyrics is anything to go by, their embrace of liberal policies is limp at best.*

It was a start.

Dear Sister Miller,

Remember when I threw a huge fit several years ago during a Laurel activity because you made us learn proper table manners? How could you forget, right? I bet no one has ever offered a louder opinion about the pointlessness of a salad fork than I did.

Now imagine me cringing and begging your forgiveness.

I want to thank you for having more wisdom than your short-sighted Laurels. Specifically, me. Just the other night, when I needed it most, that long-ago lesson saved me from making an idiot of myself—although, I would have deserved it.

If they ever convince you to work in Young Women's again, tell the girls that Pepper Spicer says knowing their salad fork from their entrée fork will one day help them out as much as all their scripture mastery memorization put together.

Of course, what I learned from you goes far beyond silverware usage, but hopefully I didn't give you as much grief about the rest of it. Thanks for serving with us even when we were a total pain.

Sincerely,
Pepper Spicer

Chapter 8

"Ginger, when you sent the link of my article to all your friends last week, you didn't tell them it was me writing the column, did you?"

She favored me with an irritated stare. "You said not to. I didn't." She turned back to flip her pancakes on the griddle.

I breathed a sigh of relief and downed another spoonful of oatmeal. This week's column on Justin would make the Boring Brent date look downright benign by comparison. I didn't want to risk exposing my identity because although I knew I'd sent Ellie a hilarious recap of my night, I'd feel the teensiest bit awful if someone figured out who my date was. I'd renamed him Tragically Hip and had no reason to think that Justin would see my article, but the fewer people who knew it was me behind the column, the fewer clues they would have in identifying my hapless subjects. I even omitted the tire-changing story because Tanner might decide to check the website, and that would give me away.

I'd definitely checked *him* out. Tanner. Online, I mean. I'd prowled through the *Bee* archives on Saturday afternoon, looking for Tanner's byline. Close to a hundred articles popped up. Working from the oldest ones, they dated back about a year, and most of them focused on local Salt Lake news. Over the last month, though, several of them took more of an arts and entertainment slant. I wondered if his bosses were making Tanner cover the "young guy" angle until they found someone they wanted to hire. Like I told him in the interview, good luck. He was so condescending and thorny, it would be a miracle if he could find someone to work with him. Or even near him. Unless his hotness blinded them. I thought about his attitude problem for a moment. Nope, even good looks couldn't lure someone in.

I had to admit that he wrote well though. His news pieces were straight to the point, while managing to include enough details that my curiosity was satisfied by the end of the article. I doubted the wisdom of sending someone who wore a golf shirt to a trendy venue to cover the local band scene, but he surprised me. In his write-up, he made intelligent comparisons, and his review showed thoughtful analysis.

I pictured him standing in Spackles, his hands in his pockets as he observed everything from the fringe of the crowd and brooded. However professional his reporting was, he wanted to get back to serious news.

Well, me too. Maybe not the hard news, but I'd kill for a shot to do some feature writing. Instead of reviewing Sonic Machine, I would have loved a chance to sit down with their manager or one of the roadies to find out what life was like on the road for them. The life-of-the-band angle had been done to death. What about the guys who played support roles without any of the glory? Maybe they had some insight on the band, a perspective that could add texture and interest to the dull interview Foley had given.

Ginger glanced over at me. "What are you doing anyway? You don't have to be at church for a bazillion more hours." She was already dressed and grumpy about it, not being a fan of nine o'clock church.

"I'm double-checking my article before I send it," I said.

"It's good, but Dad's going to hate it."

I jerked up. "You read it?"

"Don't leave your laptop open when you're in the bathroom if you don't want anyone snooping." She shrugged, clearly deeming it my fault that she had looked.

It didn't really matter, I guess. If Ellie liked it, Ginger would see it the next day anyway. I skimmed it one more time then sent it off. "Dad's not really my target audience," I said, responding to her earlier observation.

"I know that. And the people who read it are going to think it's hilarious. But Dad's going to give you a sad frowny face."

Since I hated the feeling that she might be right, I decided to do the mature thing and shift the attention to her shortcomings.

"Those are my earrings," I said. "I don't remember loaning them to you."

"Do you remember cake-bombing my new shoes? Letting me borrow these earrings is one of the cheapest ways you can pay me back."

"That's the fourth time you've used that argument."

She got up and took her dish to the sink. "Yeah. And I'll keep using it forever until you buy me new shoes."

I studied her. "You don't want me to buy you new shoes. You want unlimited access to my jewelry."

She lifted her eyebrows in a "So what?" acknowledgment, and I gave up, scooping my laptop up and heading for my room. At least when Rosemary was at church, I could pretend our room was all mine, as long as I ignored the giant pink Strawberry Shortcake staring up from her blanket in an eerily flat gaze. I dropped a pillow on her face and felt better.

Car doors slammed as everyone else left for church. I loved having a quiet house to myself. I considered my options. Blog? Spider Solitaire? Sleep? And before I could think too hard about it, I pulled up Tanner's *Bee* archives, telling myself I was just scoping out the competition . . .

* * *

"You survived last week," Courtney teased me a few hours later. "Think you can stand Sunday School again?"

"What the heck. I'll stick it out all the way through Relief Society."

"Pace yourself," she said, grinning. "You might need to build up a tolerance."

I laughed, something Courtney made me do every Sunday now. "I used to be a pro. I think I can handle it."

I followed her to the cultural hall, where everyone met in one combined Sunday School class. We grabbed a pair of seats, and while we waited for the teacher to get her visual aids all situated, Courtney turned to me with another smile. "I wondered if you maybe wanted to come over for Sunday dinner."

The invitation caught me off guard, but not in a bad way. Despite all her jokes, there was a sense of reserve about Courtney that I couldn't quite figure out. I caught an occasional flash of sadness in her eyes during certain hymns, and once, she had excused herself from the chapel during "Where Can I Turn for Peace?" Maybe I was nosy, or maybe I was just destined to be a journalist, but I sniffed a story. Not one for the magazine but a whole tale that explained the sweet and melancholy air that sometimes hung about her. However, when I smiled and accepted her invitation, it wasn't because I was on the trail of a story; it's because I needed a new friend, and it looked like Courtney wanted to make friends too.

The rest of church was all right. Good, even. I'd sort of forgotten that I like Relief Society. Afterward, Courtney gave me her address and a warning. "There's no telling who will show up for dinner. My parents tend to do things kind of freestyle. Or maybe free-for-all is a better way to put it. But it's fun."

"No problem," I said. "It's like that at our house too." But it occurred to me as I drove home to change my clothes that I had no idea what her family was even like. For all I knew, she had ten siblings and two dozen nieces and nephews. I guess I'd find out in an hour. I let my mom know where I was going. I knew she wouldn't mind because she would be so relieved I was doing something social. I popped my head into the den to tell my dad and found him crashed out on the sofa, with Mace and Rosemary on either side of him, watching *Planet Earth*. "I'm going to a friend's house for dinner," I said.

Rosemary's head popped up over the back of the sofa. "A *boy* friend?"

"No. Just a friend."

There was no story in *that* to run next door and tell Olivia. She sniffed and slipped down, tucking herself back under my dad's arm.

"You're going tonight?" Mace asked.

"Yeah."

"That's messed up," he objected. "I cooked dinner tonight."

That had been a deciding factor in accepting Courtney's invitation, to be honest. Mace's slow cooker attempts were almost legendary, but more along the lines of the Hindenburg or Three Mile Island. My mom made us all take turns doing Sunday dinner, and Mace insisted on improvising, which resulted in one failed experiment after another. A month ago, he dumped a jar of strawberry jelly in with a bunch of chicken and then charred it into a glutinous mass in the Crockpot. That ended up being a mac and cheese night.

My dad turned his head and mouthed, "Run like the wind."

I grinned and headed for my room to change. "Don't smother Strawberry Shortcake," Rosemary called after me.

I threw on some dark jeans and a blue-and-gray striped v-neck sweater. I slid into my ballet flats and headed back out. Ten minutes later, I pulled up to Courtney's house and stared. Our house is solidly middle class. My parents bought it when I was ten so there would be room for four kids. Even when we added Rosemary, it worked out okay. It wasn't a fancy house, but it was comfortable. While we weren't rich, my dad's practice had always thrived, and we got everything we needed plus a little extra. Looking at Courtney's house, I decided that even though I had no idea how much money my dad actually made, her parents made at least five times as much. The house was bigger than ours, definitely, but the whole street was full of manicured lawns and custom-built homes that told me this was the extra nice part of Highland. I pulled up behind a sporty Mazda and made my way to the front door. Courtney opened it within moments of my knock and ushered me in with a big smile.

I followed her through a front room that looked like it had been ripped from a Pottery Barn catalog to the kitchen, a gorgeous room in warm neutral tones with marble countertops and copper pots dangling over an elaborate stove. She introduced me to everyone seated around the breakfast bar as they continued to snack on pita chips and hummus. "These are my parents, Glen and Donna, and my brother and his wife, Rhett and Emily." Her parents stood, and I shook hands with everyone except her mom, who gave me a warm hug. Courtney belonged to a good-looking bunch of people. Her parents were a bit older than mine but had youthful faces. Her mom's delicate features were soft and pretty, without any of the weird stiffness of plastic surgery. Courtney definitely took after her. Her dad was nearly as tall as mine, his dark hair brushed with silver at the temples, but instead of feeling intimidated by his dignified appearance, I returned his kind smile and felt totally at ease. Her brother looked my age, maybe a little older, and he kept a protective arm around his cute wife, Emily, who looked like she had a beach ball shoved under her shirt.

"When are you due?" I asked.

"What?" Rhett asked, confused.

"Your baby? When are you due?"

He stared at me blankly. "What are you talking about?"

I flushed, mortified. Emily was so thin it seemed obvious she was pregnant, but my mother had told me a million times never to bring up someone's pregnancy unless they mentioned it first. "I'm so sorry," I said. "I thought—"

Emily slugged her husband affectionately. "Stop it, Rhett." She smiled at me. "Ignore him. The Grahams have a twisted sense of humor."

"If you think I'm bad, wait until Tanner gets here," Rhett added.

Tanner? Graham?

Oh no. Oh please, nonononono.

But my plea to the guardian angel of disgruntled twenty-three-year-olds went unanswered as the front door opened and I heard *that* Tanner Graham's voice call out, "Mom? I'm hungry. Feed me!"

No one else registered the shock on my face when he swept into the room and scooped his mother up in a hug. By the time he had exchanged a hearty back-thumping embrace with his father, I had schooled my expression into something neutral, verging on amused. I hoped. He was reaching for Courtney to hug her when he caught sight of me and froze.

"You gotta be kidding me," he said.

I didn't answer, other than to offer a small smile. I did my best to make it mysterious, hoping it would come off as serene and Mona Lisa. And also not creepy. It occurred to me that he might assume I had stalked him and wormed my way into his parents' house. Oh man. Despite my best effort, panic crept into my smile and tugged it downward into a grimace. Even with the delicious smell wafting from the kitchen behind him, I suddenly longed to be at home sawing through another one of Mace's dinner attempts and playing guess-the-meat.

Courtney's glance bounced between the two of us. "You know each other?"

I nodded, waiting for him to explain, totally at his mercy. If Tanner exposed me as the incompetent—maybe even dishonest—loser he had rejected for a job, it would be a long, uncomfortable dinner. If he accused me of stalking, I would hurl pita chips at his head then storm out and dissolve into a puddle of embarrassment.

Tanner hesitated for the tiniest second, and then he smiled. "Sure, we know each other. Pepper interviewed for a job at the *Bee*, but she went with a different option." He leaned against the counter opposite Rhett and Emily, his posture relaxed.

Apparently, he was opting for a comfortable family dinner. I stifled a sigh of relief.

"Cool," Courtney said. "I can't believe I didn't know you're a reporter too, Pepper. Which paper do you work for?"

I cleared my throat. "It's actually a digital magazine called *Real Salt Lake*." Several blank faces confronted me, so I explained. "It's sort of an online lifestyle look at Salt Lake City."

"That sounds interesting," Sister Graham said, her tone encouraging. "What sort of things do you write about?"

I'd pretty much die before explaining my Internet dating assignment in front of Tanner, so I stuck to the best answer I could give, considering I'd written exactly one nondating story for them so far. "Right now, I'm part-time, and I catch assignments when there's no one else to do it. It's a good experience. Dues-paying and all that," I added for Tanner's benefit.

"Have you gotten to cover anything cool yet?" Rhett asked.

"I reviewed a concert on Friday," I said. "It wasn't cool though."

"I saw your write-up," Tanner said, but he didn't offer an opinion on it. I wanted to know if he thought it was any good, but I'd drive American Fork Canyon blindfolded before I'd ask him.

"You did a concert on Friday too, didn't you, Tanner?" asked his dad.

"Yeah. The same one."

"It seems like they're having you do more and more of that kind of thing lately," Sister Graham said.

"*Making* him do it is more like it," Rhett said. "When are they going to hire someone to handle all the arts and entertainment stuff so you can get back to real news?"

I tried not to wince, both at the knowledge that I was part of the *Bee's* unsuccessful attempt to bring in young blood to cover that beat and at Rhett's unintentional diss. Emily kicked him under the table, and he winced and scrambled to correct himself. "Sorry, Pepper. That came out wrong. I didn't mean to sound like the arts and entertainment stuff isn't cool. Tanner likes to deal with the hard news, is all. If it were up to me, he'd be covering sports and getting me a press pass to everything."

"It's okay," I said. "I know what you meant. I'm very . . . aware . . . of Tanner's opinions."

I saw a smile threaten to escape Tanner at that phrasing, but his mom shooed everyone toward the dining room before I could verify whether he or the smile got the upper hand.

From the minute I'd pulled up to the house, I had felt a touch of awe, but the dining room downright intimidated me. Deep burgundy walls surrounded a long linen-covered table set with sparkly water goblets and beautiful cream-colored china. I followed Courtney's lead and took the seat next to her, shaking my linen napkin out and draping it across my lap. This was a far cry from the boisterous dinners we had at the kitchen table in our house.

Sister Graham bustled back and forth to the kitchen, bearing one great-smelling platter or bowl after another. She set them each on a sideboard against the wall. Wanting to help, I pushed back my chair, but

Emily leaned slightly across the table and shook her head. "I know that look in your eye," she said. "Don't worry about helping Donna. She says Sunday is the only time she gets to fuss over her family all together, and she won't let anyone help, especially not guests. My advice to you is to sit back and enjoy it. She's an amazing cook."

I contented myself with studying the table, from the gold-trimmed dishes to the gorgeous centerpiece of white early spring tulips. The place settings unnerved me. I counted three forks, two knives, and a spoon. All of our plates had bowls sitting on top of them, so I guessed that meant we were starting with soup first. That solved the mystery of the spoon, but I hoped I could figure out the rest of the utensils as Sister Graham served each dish.

I wanted to ask Courtney which fork to use when, but Tanner sat across the table and one seat down from me, and I didn't want to give him the satisfaction of knowing that the tableware was throwing me for a loop. I flipped through my memory files at hyperspeed, searching them for anything on fork etiquette. I vaguely recalled a Laurel activity where we had learned proper table manners. There was something about using the utensils from the outside in, with a new one for each course. I'd go with that and keep a sharp eye out to figure out if I was doing it wrong.

While the soup circulated, Tanner caught my eye. "I didn't catch how you and Courtney know each other."

As much as I didn't want to do the small-talk thing with him, I was glad he had asked. I could dispel any notion that I was there to stalk him. As I returned his gaze, I noticed once again how light the gray of his irises was against the dark gray ring around them. I suspected he'd probably earned himself a stalker or two in his time simply by batting the lashes that framed them. I realized he was waiting for an answer, and I blinked. His eyes glinted in return. Somehow, what felt like half a minute had evaporated in that stare down. I cleared my throat. "We met at the singles ward. She saves me a seat every Sunday." And then, because I couldn't look away, I saw his gaze sharpen. He started to say something, but the soup made its way to me, and I dished it up to break the moment.

From the first taste of butternut squash bisque to the last bite of cherry cheesecake, the food was divine—as in, I think Courtney's mom stirred everything with angel feathers. It tasted that incredible. I knew I was probably embarrassing myself with my exclamations of amazement after every course, but I couldn't help it. Sister Graham looked pleased, and I didn't really care what Tanner thought. He said little during dinner, just ate and watched everyone, including me, with a thoughtful expression on his face. It was a nice change from the pruney grimace he usually treated me to, but I still ignored him as much as I could without being rude. The fork situation worked out okay. Starting from the outside in solved the problem.

Sister Graham hopped up after the cherry cheesecake rounded the table to head for the kitchen again, and I looked at Courtney in panic. "Is she getting more food? I can't eat anything else. I'll blow up."

Courtney smiled. "She's going for hot chocolate. She makes it from scratch. You don't have to drink it. Just hold the saucer up to your mouth every so often and be like, 'Mmmmm.'"

"We should have warned you to pace yourself," Tanner added.

"Thanks for humoring her," Courtney said. "She lives for these Sunday dinners."

"Are you kidding? I need a thesaurus to find more synonyms for *delicious*," I said. Lowering my voice, I added, "We're never this fancy at our house."

Emily heard me and smiled. "If it were anyone else, I would think using the good china and real silverware was pretentious, but not Donna. She says she should be pulling out that stuff for her most important dinner guests. For her, it's family."

"That's cool," I said. That's the way my mom would see it if we had fancy china. My grandmother has a set in her front cupboard that I've never seen used. She dusts it religiously, but I'm pretty sure no one important enough has come for her to pull it out. It gave my mother a disdain for things like fancy dishes, but staring down at the gorgeous hand-painted flowers visible through the crumbs of my dessert, I could see the appeal of eating from beautiful plates every night.

Sister Graham returned with a teapot full of hot chocolate. She poured a bit in the teacups for each of us and sat down, looking relaxed and satisfied that everyone had been taken care of. I considered how tight my jeans felt and swallowed a groan. My super-high metabolism had failed me for the first time, but I doubted anyone could be a match for a five-course meal like this one.

Eventually, Rhett and Emily rose, saying they needed to get on the road for their drive to Springville. I wondered how far Tanner had to go. I stared at him over the brim of my cup while I savored more hot chocolate.

He had moved down the table near his father and sat listening intently to whatever his dad was telling him in a low voice. Tanner was definitely the oldest, but now, after observing him relaxed and laughing with his family, his face seemed younger. It helped that he had on a pretty cool retro-style black sweater with a funky purple stripe across the chest. Much better than Dockers and golf shirts. Maybe he wasn't pushing thirty like I had thought when he'd interviewed me.

I amused myself with some investigative journalism, compiling facts and making inferences. He'd driven here, which meant he didn't live at home. I bet he lived in Salt Lake so he could be near the paper and closer to breaking news. I wanted to snoop around the family pictures and see what else I could dig up to figure him out. He'd done such a thorough job of analyzing my character with a limited set of facts during our interview that it entertained me to draw all kinds of wild conclusions about him now.

I decided he lived in a tiny studio apartment and that the reason he wasn't married was he was such a workaholic; no one would put up with him. In fact, I bet his last girlfriend dumped him when she realized he had a deeper commitment to his Blackb—

"They're talking politics," Courtney sighed. "They could take awhile. Want a tour of the house?"

"Definitely," I said.

She led me back to the kitchen and into the family room dominated by a completely tricked out entertainment center. "This is my dad's hobby. He loves tinkering with his television and speakers and all that."

I heard the clink of dishes from the kitchen and frowned when I saw her mom at the sink rinsing off a plate. I started over. "Let me do that," I offered. "You should definitely not have to clean up after cooking such an awesome dinner."

She waved me off. "You're sweet," she said, "but this is only my dessert plate. Don't worry. Tanner and Glen will handle the dishes. They do them every Sunday."

"I get out of it by setting the table," Courtney said. "The china has to be washed by hand, and I'd much rather iron the tablecloth every week than deal with that."

"Deal with what?" Tanner said, coming in from the dining room.

"The dishes," she said. "You're a saint."

He shrugged. "I like doing them." He pushed up the sleeves of his sweater and ran the water again.

I followed Courtney to their library and decided on the spot that I had to have one when I grew up. The book-lined room was cozy, with heavy leather furniture, thick carpets, and a window seat that I wanted to crawl into with one of the novels from the shelves. Several photos perched on the fireplace mantel, and I wandered over to check them out. Mostly, they were family snapshots of Courtney and her brothers at different ages. One in an ornate silver frame caught my eye. It showed Courtney and a really good-looking guy about Rhett's age in a formal pose, like an engagement picture. Courtney didn't look much different than she did now, so it had to be fairly recent. "Who is this?" I asked. "He's cute."

That odd shadow I'd seen flicker over her face a few times returned and settled there. "That's Grayson. He was my fiancé."

I wondered why someone who spoke in the past tense about her fiancé would still have a picture of him on her fireplace mantel, but I didn't like that it made her sad, so I dropped the subject, choosing friendship over nosiness. I grabbed the next framed photo in an effort to change the subject. "Wow," I said, staring down at Tanner's senior photo. "Tanner took this photo very seriously." He stared out of the picture without the hint of a smile, giving the camera his best Blue Steel.

She mustered a small smile. "Sometimes he takes *himself* too seriously, but if you scratch a little under the surface, there's a pretty good sense of humor."

I stared at the picture doubtfully. "This is not the face of someone who laughs a lot." Hoping to cheer her up, I held the picture up next to my face and did my best to imitate Tanner's serious expression, which is how he found me when he walked in a second later. His eyebrows shot up in surprise, and then he scowled when he realized why Courtney was laughing so hard. I set the picture back on the mantel, nearly knocking over the photo of Courtney and her ex-fiancé in my hurry.

I turned around and clasped my hands behind my back. "Done with the dishes already?" I asked, offering no explanation for my mugging.

"The pans are soaking." He stared back and forth between Courtney, who was still grinning, and me, with my innocent face. "Mom sent me in to see if you guys want to play cards."

"No!" Courtney shouted at the same time I said, "Sure."

"No way," she said again. "Trust me. You do not want to play any kind of card game with this family. They turn into crazy people."

"No one's crazier than my family," I reassured her. "My sister Ginger has psychotic breaks every time Uno doesn't go her way."

"Ginger?" Tanner repeated. "Pepper. Ginger. Do you have a brother named Basil?" he asked, giving it the British pronunciation.

"No, but I do have one named Coriander and another one named Mace."

He laughed and then stopped when he realized I wasn't joking. "Seriously?"

I nodded. "And there's one more sister named—"

"Don't tell me!" he said. "I want to guess. Turmeric? Parsley?"

I refused to take the bait. This was not the first time someone had poked fun at me for my parents' ridiculous idea to name all of their Spicer children after actual spices.

"Cayenne? It can be a Porsche. Why not a kid?" Tanner was on a roll now.

I shook my head at Courtney. "Why don't you take me to the cards?"

We formed a single file line out of the library as Tanner followed me, rattling off guesses. "Marjoram? That's a nice name for a girl. Oh, or how about Anise?"

I ignored him. Ignoring annoying males was a job skill at Handy's.

"Cumin? Oregano?" Tanner persisted. When he saw I wasn't going to crack, he relented. "I give up. What's your sister's name?"

"Cardamom. We call her Cardy for short," I said with a tone that dared him to comment.

He cleared his throat. "Cardamom? Oh. That's, um . . ."

I laughed. "It's Rosemary."

His face cleared. "That's pretty," he said.

"So is she, so it works out, I guess."

"Did your parents predict your personalities when they named you, or do you all just live up to your names?"

I stared at him. "You think I have a pepper personality? What does that mean?" This was also not the first time I'd heard this theory, but I liked putting him on the spot. Most people tripped over their explanation or gave me lame answers like, "You're really spicy." Ugh.

Leave it to a word guy to have an answer ready. "You're black pepper, definitely. The kind that comes from peppercorn."

I arched an eyebrow, waiting for the rest of his metaphor. After eating a meal at his mom's table, I had no trouble believing he knew what a peppercorn was.

He picked up his pace a bit until he was right on my heels before he leaned forward and said so only I could hear, "You can't do much with a peppercorn . . . unless you grind it down, of course."

I shot him a sharp glance, but his eye was on his mom. He didn't want her to catch him picking on me.

I took a stool beside Courtney at the breakfast bar. "Anyone with a little talent in the kitchen knows what to do with a whole peppercorn," I said in a normal tone. "It's the cooks with no imagination who think it has to be cracked."

Courtney followed this exchange in puzzlement. Without knowing about our previous run-in, I suppose my annoyed expression and his satisfied smile didn't make much sense. Clearly trying to dial down the tension, she turned to Tanner. "Do you mind getting the cards?"

"Yeah, I'll snag them," he said and wandered over to the antique hutch in the giant television's lair to find some.

"Sorry about my brother," Courtney said loudly, meaning for Tanner to hear. "His sense of humor is as bizarre as Rhett warned you it is."

"Don't worry about Pepper," he said, digging through a stack of games. "I don't think she needs any protection."

"Protection?" Sister Graham echoed, walking out from the giant pantry she had disappeared into moments before, her hair now mussed. Brother Graham followed, looking pleased. Courtney's face flushed pink. "You guys are so embarrassing," she said. "Sorry, Pepper."

"Everyone's parents are embarrassing," I said. "Don't worry about it."

"Do yours make out in the pantry when you have company over?"

"No," I admitted. "But my mom has chased me around and wrestled me to the ground to steal back some M&Ms when I had company."

"We weren't making out," Sister Graham said with a sniff. "We were—"

"We were definitely making out," Brother Graham said. "You're just so cute in an apron."

"My dad is a marriage and family therapist," I said. "Even though it embarrasses you, Courtney, I've listened to him long enough to know that you should probably just slap your parents a high five and not worry about it."

"Thank you, Pepper," Sister Graham said, arranging her hair and smoothing her apron in an attempt to restore her equanimity.

"No problem, Sister Graham."

"Call us Donna and Glen," she said as she passed me to help Tanner at the cabinet, where he was growling over a lack of cards. She paused for a moment to give me a quick squeeze and to whisper, "We owe you."

Confused, I watched her reach around Tanner and pull out a Phase 10 deck.

"I hope you're better at dealing cards than you are at finding them," Courtney teased Tanner.

"I can't stay," he said, stopping behind her chair to drop a kiss on her head. "I need to go. Deadline tomorrow."

Donna sighed, and I could tell it wasn't the first time Tanner had cut an evening short with them. "At least you made it to dinner. Drive home safely, okay?"

He hugged her and his dad good-bye and then paused in the doorway. "Bye, Pepper. I'll see you around."

"See you," I said. I breathed a little easier when I heard the door close behind him, glad once more that he hadn't exposed me or my pathetic job interview to his family. He was still a jerk professionally, but tonight, I had to admit . . . Tanner Graham wasn't all bad.

Dear Josh,

I know you were only doing your job when you came out and fixed the fridge yesterday, but I have to thank you for saving my bacon, both literally and figuratively. A free meal isn't enough of a thank you for jumping us ahead of other customers every time the Rust Bucket breaks down, but I hope this note communicates to you how grateful we are for making us a priority when you have no real reason to, except that you're so nice. I know five times to repair that dumb freezer in six months must be a new record for you, but until I can convince Mr. Handy that a new one is worth the investment, I'm glad we've got you to take care of us.

Sincerely,
Pepper Spicer

P.S. Come in for a free lunch anytime, not just broken-down-freezer days. You're awesome!

Chapter 9

The next week flew by in a blur. Ellie liked the reader feedback on my Sonic Machine review. The article didn't get a ton of hits, but the dozen or so comments that people posted backed up my opinion. One reader went so far as to write, "Finally! An honest critic that sees past the Emperor's lame new clothes with this group. It would take them playing naked to make them halfway interesting!" As a result, Ellie had asked me to cover another band on Thursday night.

Elsewhere in *Real Salt Lake*, my second "Single in the City" column about Justin received a mixed review. Ellie loved it, as did the handful of readers who commented on it, but my dad hated it again. Of course, he would never say "hate." It came out more like, "I don't think you needed to describe him as having 'a solar panel for a kitsch machine.' People can't help having bald spots."

I had an argument for that. "I don't care that he was bald. I care that he was so pretentious about it that he hid it under his stupid hipster hat and checked his reflection all night."

It didn't appease my dad, but he said nothing else, and once again, readers pointed to that line as a favorite. Mixing my blog voice with a little more snark was turning into a winning formula. Only four days after the column posted, it had a few hundred more hits than the one the week before. That was a whopping three dollars and fifty-nine cents. Shoot, at this rate, I could buy myself a Happy Meal and make change. If I ate Happy Meals. Which I don't. I find them more depressing than happy.

Still, it was growth. And for the first time, I crossed my fingers that my date on Saturday would be a total disaster. I needed Wade, aka Mountain_(Bike)_Man, to be a letdown. The worse the date, the better. It made my column much easier to write. Even if Wade turned out to be okay, I could at least hope that I was a terrible mountain biker. I needed *something* for column fodder. I'd rather make fun of myself anyway. At least I wouldn't get a guilt trip from my dad.

At the moment, I didn't have the brain cells to spend on worrying or planning for the date and column because I had a concert to get to. Hiring a new assistant opened up room in my schedule, but he couldn't make it in early because he had a class on Thursday nights. I almost never work nights anyway, so I couldn't complain, but it meant I would have to stick around the store until eight and then do a speed change in the office to get to the club in Sugarhouse by nine. It was a local group called the Krunk Lunkers. This time I had done a little Internet research so I could ask semi-intelligent questions afterward and had a fresh palm-sized notebook nestled in my purse so I could take notes and not just work from memory. Maybe I'd work up to buying myself a cool little voice recorder gadget, but I would kick it old school for the time being with a trusty Bic pen.

The clock ticked toward closing time. Katie, looking bored during the slow dinner shift, had already taken it upon herself to organize the condiments and paper goods, and each table now had a flower-shaped collection of mustard packets on top. Taking pity on her, I sent her home. Only a half hour remained until closing time anyway. I puttered around, restocking the supplies under the sandwich bar, but it didn't keep me too busy to wonder if the *Bee* would send Tanner to cover tonight's concert. Everything with his byline this week had been straight news again, no arts stuff, but it didn't stop me from taking extra care with my outfit for later—not because I wanted to impress him. I wanted to look like I had as much business reporting on the show as he did. You know, if he happened to be there. Not that I cared if he was.

The bell tinkled over the front door to announce a customer. I popped up and almost fell over when I saw Tanner on the other side of the sandwich bar, Courtney by his side, both of them waiting to order. He looked startled. Courtney's expression reflected pleasant surprise.

Ah, how silly of me to think my humiliation at his hands had been complete when I'd limped out of the *Bee* three weeks before. No, *now* it was complete as I stood there in my mustard-stained shirt and Handy's baseball cap.

"I didn't know you work here," Courtney said. "I thought you wrote for that website."

"Only part time," I said, feeling the flames in my cheeks burn brighter by the second. "This pays the bills."

"We come here all the time," she said. "I've never seen you here before."

"I rarely work the dinner shift." I willed my stupid cheeks to cool down, but they didn't oblige. Lovely. How could I go from never laying eyes on Tanner to not being able to escape him? I stole a glance at him, bracing myself for his mockery, maybe even a snide remark about how this must be the "artisanal café" I had referenced on my blasted résumé.

Instead, his expression was neutral. "We only come in on Thursdays," he said. "My dad has stake meetings, and my mom has a card-making class, so I come down and hang out with Courtney."

She flushed. "He's babysitting me," she said. "They all do."

"I'm not babysitting you," he said. "I like hanging out with you. Thursday night fits my schedule, that's all."

Behind them, the clock crept closer to eight. I needed to get their sandwiches made and send them on their way if I wanted to clean up and make it to see the Krunk Lunkers in time. "It's good to see you guys," I said, and by "guys," I meant Courtney. I could tell by the glimmer of amusement in Tanner's eyes that he knew it too. "What can I get for you?"

They gave me their orders, and I flew through the sandwich bar. When I rang them up, it embarrassed me to take Tanner's money. I don't know why. Maybe because it reinforced that this was my job, and I couldn't pretend we were all hanging out in a sandwich shop by choice. Only two of us were.

"Can you sit with us, or do you have to sit back there?" Courtney asked.

"I can sit with you," I said. Part of the massive perks package at Handy's was soda whenever we wanted, so I poured myself a Coke and took a seat, feeling more uncomfortable than ever. Now I could sit in my nifty food-stained work shirt and watch them eat. Oh joy.

"How long have you worked here?" Courtney asked.

"Since last August," I said.

"Do you like it?"

I shrugged. "It pays the bills. I've been able to cut back my hours a little since I started writing for *Real Salt Lake*. I'm hoping I can quit here soon."

Tanner nodded and finished his bite of pastrami. Such a guy sandwich. "If Ellie is smart, she'll start sending you out on more stories."

I stared at him, surprised. "You've been reading my work?"

"I read everything I can find that's reported in Salt Lake. Part of my job."

Oh. Right. He didn't stalk my articles like I stalked his. I cleared my throat. "She's sending me to cover another band tonight."

"Which one?" Courtney asked.

"Krunk Lunkers," I answered. "They're from Salt Lake."

"That sounds fun," she said. "Tanner always complains when they make him cover arts and culture because he's the youngest guy on staff, but I think it's cool because he gets into all kinds of stuff for free."

I was about to drop a casual hint about how the show started in a little more than an hour, maybe help nudge them on their way, when the front door bell tinkled again. I turned around to find Josh, our fridge repairman, standing there. He had been in on Monday to repair the commercial refrigerator we dubbed the Rust Bucket. I'd seen him at least once a month for repairs on that thing since I was hired, and I couldn't believe it wasn't just cheaper to buy a new fridge. He was a quiet guy in his mid-twenties, and I was so used to seeing him in his service uniform that it took me a second to realize it was him.

He wore a Western-cut shirt and Wranglers. His Nelson and Sons baseball cap was gone, and his slightly damp hair showed fresh comb marks. He held a small bouquet of red roses and shifted uncomfortably from foot to foot.

"Hi, Josh," I said, heading toward the sandwich bar. "Are you here to take me up on my free-sandwiches-for-life offer?" It was the least I could do for all the times he'd put us first on his repair route when he had much bigger clients to service. I had told him as much in my thank you note earlier in the week.

He shot a nervous glance at Tanner and Courtney seated at the table nearest the counter before making his way over. "Hi, Pepper." He watched me reach for the honey wheat bread he usually requested before he gave himself a little shake. "Uh, I'm not here for a sandwich."

"Oh." Puzzled, I put the bread back. "Did I forget to sign something?"

I heard a muffled choke and glanced up to catch Tanner stifling a laugh with his napkin. What was wrong with him?

"No, ma'am. I mean, no, Pepper," Josh said, even more flustered. Wait. Was he trying to—

"I came to see you," he stammered and thrust the roses at me over the top of the glass sneeze guard that shielded the sandwich fixings. Bewildered, I took them and stared down at them, then back at him.

"Thanks?" I said, unsure how to react. What had brought this on? And why did I have to have witnesses? I made a point of ignoring Tanner.

"I wondered if you might like to go do something?" he asked.

"Right now?"

His cheeks pinkened. "Oh, sorry. No, I mean sometime. Like any time that's good for you."

"Oh." I had never given any thought to Josh as a date, mainly because I'd sworn off guys indefinitely after Landon and I broke up. Even without his cowboy clothes, I would have guessed he wasn't my type. I go for outgoing guys, guys with a little bit of edge and maybe the teensiest bit of broodiness about them. Josh was not . . . that. He was cute but shy and simple, and he deserved someone much, much nicer than me. Time to let him down easy. "I know we've only seen each other in here, so it's probably hard to tell, but I have a feeling I'm not really your type. I like weird bands and wear strange jewelry, and I don't listen to country music."

"Do you like heavy metal?" he asked hopefully, and I heard choking again. I was about to scowl at Tanner when I caught the slight smile on Josh's face. He was teasing me about the heavy metal. Well, well. Maybe he had hidden depths.

"I hate it," I said, smiling back.

"Then I guess we can find something nonmuscial to do. And nonsandwich," he added with another smile.

"All right," I said. "I'd love to. Do you text?"

He pulled a cell phone from his back pocket. "I'm a hick, not a caveman."

Laughing, I gave him my number. "Weekends are bad," I warned, "but another night would be fun."

He nodded and headed toward the door with a quiet good night.

I had a date. *Another* date, I amended, thinking about my Saturday plans to cheat death on my first mountain-biking trip with Mountain_ (Biking)_Man. And although I knew with instinctive certainty that Josh and I weren't a good long-term fit, at least I didn't dread the idea of a date with him like I did my online matches. If worse came to worst and the date with Josh tanked, I'd have to switch our refrigerator repair service to a different company. I suspected with his mellow nature that, second date or not, it wouldn't be an issue. Still, I made a mental note to be more careful about the thank you notes I wrote to single guys. Apparently, while my average looks were not enough to make men fall at my feet, my notes had the power to move them to heroic acts, like bringing me flowers and randomly asking me out.

Ha.

When the door closed behind him, I checked the clock. Tanner was on his phone, and Courtney shoved the last bite of her sandwich into her mouth. Good. It was five minutes past closing, but when did a rock-and-roll band ever take the stage on time? If I rushed, I could make it.

I hurried around to their table. "Thanks for coming in, you guys. I'll walk you out. I have to change for the show."

"We're not leaving," Tanner said, done with his phone call.

I scowled at him. Was this some sort of distraction technique to keep the competition from doing her reporting job? Courtney caught my expression and laughed. "Yeah, we're going to the concert with you."

"I called my editor, and he switched the assignment to me," Tanner said in confirmation.

"Isn't that kind of rude to whoever was supposed to be covering it?" I asked.

"No. It was Linda from the city desk, and she's glad to hand it off. Not her scene."

"So why are you picking up work when you're supposed to be off?"

"Because it will be fun," Courtney said. "This is what I mean about him using his press credentials to get into cool stuff. This is way better than letting him beat me at Mario Kart forty times tonight."

I stared at him. Buttoned up Tanner played Mario Kart? It didn't compute.

"Concert reviews are easy," he said. "If Courtney wants to go, it's no big deal to get us in, and it'll take me all of thirty minutes to write it up. If you don't mind, could you give her a ride back?"

"I can do that," I said.

"Cool," she said. "Go change. I'll wipe down everything out here."

I shook my head but handed her the bleach-soaked rag so she could disinfect their table and headed to the office where my clothes waited. Courtney wasn't the reserved girl I'd assumed her to be for the last several months at church, and I liked her fun personality. I could put up with Tanner if it meant having Courtney to hang out with at the show instead of standing around bored like Tanner had done at Spackles.

Fewer than ten minutes later, I was out of the office in a pair of skinny jeans, purple ballet flats, and a couple of layered T-shirts under my favorite black fitted pea coat.

I pulled the cash register drawer out and walked it back to my office, where I locked it in the supply closet and secured it with a chain and padlock. That's what passed for high-tech around here. I'd come in early to count it out and deposit it in the morning. Tanner and Courtney waited for me at the front door, and I locked up behind us then turned to face the parking lot. The Zuke sat on the far side, waiting for me, and a newer-looking Accord occupied the space directly in front of Handy's. I guess someone driving a Camry couldn't make fun of a Honda driver for his conservative choice of car . . . even if I didn't exactly have a choice in mine.

"I'll ride up with Tanner and back with you. Does that sound okay?" Courtney asked.

I nodded and headed out to my car. Tanner watched me climb in before he got in his Accord and started it. It was thoughtful—and surprising—coming from him. I'd seen him do several things in our last two encounters that didn't jibe with the perception I had of him after The World's Worst Interview. It was harder and harder to think of him as a jerk, and I really wanted to. *Needed* to, if I wanted to keep a safe distance. I didn't know what to think about him, actually, and that was a problem.

A big one.

Dear Dad,
Thanks for teaching me to listen.

Love,
Pepper

Chapter 10

Nothing qualified me to review music besides having two working ears—and a former fiancé on the verge of hitting it big in the pop music scene. But Ellie didn't know about Landon, and I wasn't telling. I had no problem going to shows and then putting my opinion out there. If every night was like tonight, I could officially count doing music reviews as my best job ever.

The Krunk Lunkers tore up the joint with fast-paced ska-influenced funk grooves that were downright irresistible. At least, Courtney and I found it impossible to resist. We bounced along to the band's infectious beats, but Tanner looked immune to the contagion. His impassive expression made me want to poke him, if only to check for signs of life.

I made my way over to him, the happy music thrumming through my system. I smiled, and a return smile peeked back at me. Rather than yell over the loud horns and drums, I pointed to the crowd rising and falling in energetic unison and gestured for him to join us. I did it to tease him, knowing he never would. Instead, he reached out and snagged my hand, pulling me closer as he bent toward me. My stomach flipped, but then a spark of mischief in his eyes clued me in, and I knew he was trying to mess with me. I took the dare and didn't pull away. "No thanks," he said. His warm breath so near my neck made goose bumps break out on my arms, and I fought a threatening shiver. We stood frozen that way for the longest five seconds of my life before I tugged my hand free and took a step back. I slid my hands into my back pockets, hiding the small tremor in the one I had liberated from him, and offered him a bright smile.

"Too bad," I said. "It's way more fun where we are." I thought I caught a nod from him as I turned to rejoin Courtney.

We didn't need press passes to talk to the band after the show. We wandered backstage with Courtney in tow and found them easily enough. I felt self-conscious, with my hair a sweaty mess and my makeup all smudged, but no one in the band minded. I felt better when I whipped out my pristine, new notebook, although . . . Tanner had to loan me a pen when I couldn't find one in my purse.

I hustled home to write my review after I dropped Courtney off. If Tanner could do it in thirty minutes, I'd make it happen in twenty-nine. When I finished an hour later, I decided Tanner had exaggerated when he'd said he could knock something like that out in half an hour, but I figured I hadn't done too badly. Besides, it was about quality, not speed.

The next morning, I refreshed my Internet browser window obsessively, like I was watching a closing bid on some eBay treasure. I was looking for my Krunk Lunker write-up—and for Tanner's. At last, right before I headed out the door to work, I checked the *Bee* online and found Tanner's review. It was short but descriptive, labeling the band as a fun party group with energy to spare. He didn't think they would set the music world on fire but termed the performance "a great way to pass an evening." I guess he'd been paying attention, after all. It was so hard to tell with him.

I kept tabs on my own review at work with my phone. Once it posted, my write-up of the Krunk Lunkers garnered even more reader viewer responses than my first one. Ellie called at about five o' clock, sounding pleased. "Great job on the review," she said. "How do you feel about picking up another regular feature?"

"Doing music reviews?"

"Yes."

"Yes!"

Ellie laughed. "You have a knack for them, and the reader response is good."

"Great," I said. "Is Chantelle going to be okay with this?"

"Chantelle is relieved to get them off her desk. She wants to focus more on the arts."

"I'm thrilled to do it," I said. "Thanks for the vote of confidence."

"It was an easy judgment call, Pepper. The readers are voting for your writing with their responses in every comment trail. Speaking of which . . ." She paused, and I could hear the tap of her nails against a keyboard. "The numbers today show that your second 'Single in the City' column drew a thousand readers last week. Keep it up. I'll be looking for something golden after your mountain-bike outing."

Another thousand hits? Well, there was another ten dollars I could count on. That would pay off five of the See's wrapped truffles I'd eaten in my post-breakup depression instead of using them as wedding favors. That left a little less than two hundred to pay for. Whatever. It was progress. Note to self: big weddings are overrated.

"The page views on your Krunk Lunkers write-up is outpacing the Sonic Machine review," she continued, "probably because they've got local friends and family reading the link. I'd like to shift toward covering more local bands or bands with local people who hit it big, like The Used."

"Sounds great," I said. "How many shows a month do you expect me to watch?"

"At least one a week, but two is better."

I hated to say no to a new boss, but I knew my limits. "That'll be tough. A lot of shows are on the weekend, and now I've got at least one date for the column every weekend too." Stress over how to fit two shows a week on top of my tight schedule caused a throbbing behind my left eye.

"We haven't talked about the pay," she said. "It's a little different since these reports will be paid on a freelance basis." She named a figure for each article that would let me knock four hours off of my Handy's schedule and still come out slightly ahead on my bills.

Take that, See's charge! I'd be decimating truffle debt in no time. Or at least a month ahead of schedule.

After work, I headed home, but for once I didn't retreat into my room and mope at my computer. Courtney was picking me up for a movie. When I answered her knock at the door, instead of seeing her cute Mazda in the driveway, I saw Tanner's Accord, complete with him behind the wheel.

"Ready?" she asked.

"Yeah," I said, grabbing a light spring sweater jacket off the coat rack. "Is Tanner driving us?"

"Is that okay? He didn't have any assignments tonight, so I said he should come check out the movie."

Courtney idolized her brother—that was clear—and I didn't want my wariness of him to get in the way of our growing friendship. I smiled and nodded. "Sounds great."

At the car, Courtney slid into the backseat. Was I supposed to climb in front or join her? The idea of making Tanner drive us around chauffeur style amused me, so I got in next to Courtney. Tanner turned to stare at us. "Really, girls?"

I tapped his headrest. "Could you put up the privacy glass, please?"

Courtney giggled. "I meant for you to get shotgun. I didn't want to make you sit back here by yourself."

"Now no one is by themselves," I said.

"Do I not count?" Tanner asked.

I let my silence answer him. Courtney giggled again, nervously this time, and Tanner put the car in gear and backed out. I asked Courtney if she'd heard anything about the movie, a light romantic comedy that just came out. I listened to her chatter, but part of my mind wondered what motivated Tanner's presence. Granted, I didn't have a ton of dating experience, even with two LDS Lookup dates to my credit, but I wasn't too naive to miss the undercurrent running between us. The moment between us on the dance floor the night before had been so electric I'd had to have been dead not to feel it. It confused me. Even though he hadn't outed me for my awful interview to his family, I knew he didn't like me. He'd made his opinion of me clear at our interview, and he hadn't said anything to suggest he'd changed his mind. My opinion of him had budged marginally—but it was a pretty small margin.

Courtney sat between us during the movie, and I did my best to ignore him and watch the film, but the fact that the male romantic interest wasn't nearly as good-looking as Tanner didn't help. Grr.

When they dropped me off at home after we again made Tanner play chauffeur, I bolted from the car, glad to leave the weird energy behind. Courtney rolled down her window and called, "I need new boots. Wanna go shopping tomorrow afternoon?"

"Can't," I answered from the porch, my hand already on the front doorknob. "Got a date."

She flashed me a thumbs up, and I slipped inside before Tanner pulled away. I could hear a bunch of teenage voices in the family room, so I skirted it and headed upstairs. With all my writing for *Real Salt Lake,* my blog had been neglected, and it was time to write just for the fun of it. I wanted to hammer out my feelings on re-entry to the land of the living via loving parental coercion. My blog was a great place to think out loud, especially since I could expect my dad to weigh in with a long and thoughtful comment. It was a face-saving way for me to say, "Maybe you were right."

* * *

There's no way to prepare for the experience of hurtling down a mountain on a bike at breakneck speed. I thought there was. I Googled a little. I posted a request on Facebook for people to tell me what it was like. Words like *fun, challenging,* and *awesome* don't help, FYI. They fail to fully capture the experience. Words like *insane, terrifying,* and *life-threatening* work better.

I didn't think anything would be worse than the pure torture of trying to power uphill, but trying not to die on the way down was infinitely more awful. Someone told me to look at wherever I wanted to go. "If you look at a rock, you hit a rock. Don't look at rocks. Look at the trail." I tried very, very hard to unsee all the rocks. But there were a lot.

Wade, who was an extra crunchy granola type, yelled encouragement over his shoulder all afternoon. I learned about the breadth and depth of his motivational vocabulary, but riding ten yards behind him for two hours did nothing to help us get otherwise acquainted.

It was too bad because Wade was pretty hot. I don't think I could handle his intense personality for long periods though. I bet he was the kind of guy who got bumped up to AP on his mission in his third week out. I respected his positivity, but it wore me out the tiniest bit. That—and the grueling climb on the bike. And the almost dying on the way back down.

I knew my "Single in the City" column would be all about me this week because whatever Wade hoped he was getting in a date, I was pretty sure I wasn't it. Even in early spring, he had a healthy outdoor tan. Me? Still Cullen-ish. Wade had a bounce in his step from the moment we met at a soup and sandwich café until he hopped off his bike after our second downhill—which I begged to make our last. He reassured me that it was hard because I was riding a borrowed bike and that mountain biking was truly fun. I nodded and smiled, but I knew the truth: the bike was fine. I was the problem. I lacked the gene for sports of any kind.

When I limped back to my car in the café parking lot, I consoled myself with the knowledge that my dad couldn't object to this week's column. Instead of feeling sorry for Wade because I was poking fun at him, my dad would be pitying the poor guy for having to go out with me.

By the time I pulled into my driveway, I already had the opening hook for my mountain-bike disaster figured out. *I bought myself a new shirt last night. It says,* Warning: This Date Will Be Hazardous to Someone's Health. *It seems only fair to warn these poor guys up front. It's going to be them or me, but there's no doubt that first aid will be involved at some point during the date. Maybe I should focus exclusively on dating paramedics? That's it. I think I'm a genius. I should bag this whole Internet dating thing and lurk around ambulance bays because THAT'S not completely creepy.*

I collapsed into bed early, too worn out to do more than click my mouse and surf the Internet. I checked out *Real Salt Lake* and saw that my "Tragically Hip" recap had almost double the number of comments than the first column the week before. There was no way to know how that would translate into page views, but generally, the greater the number of comments, the higher the number of readers.

I checked out the *Bee* too. Or rather, Tanner's articles this week. Other than The Krunk Lunkers, he'd written straight news stories. I read through them, wondering if I still wanted to do the regular news. I liked the chance to stamp my personality on the pieces I'd written so far, and I wouldn't have the same leeway with news reporting. Maybe I wouldn't even be any good at it.

I drifted off to sleep with a vision of myself as a premiere celebrity journalist, writing lifestyle pieces for something like *Vanity Fair*. Nah. Not me. But maybe I could write about single-girl issues for one of the big magazines like *Marie Claire*. Except their models looked like they were two seconds away from leaping through the pages of the magazine to scratch your eyeballs out. Now *there* was a group of people who could use more sandwiches. Hunger probably made them look that cranky.

Ginger woke me up the next morning when she rattled the hangers in my closet. I cracked an eyelid and stared at her ransacking my semi-color-coded organization. "For someone who hates the way I dress, you sure do borrow a lot of my clothes."

"There's nothing wrong with most of the pieces," she said and then wrinkled her nose at a thrift shop peasant blouse. "Except maybe this one. The issue is how you put them together."

I shooed her out of my room and helped Rosemary pick an outfit for church. In the peace and quiet of the house after everyone else left, I sprawled on the living room floor and read one of my favorite novels, *The Book Thief,* until it was time for me to get ready too. I dressed carefully in case Tanner was there. He hung around with Courtney a lot. Had he always done that or just lately? Was it because of me? Maybe he did it to make sure none of my crazy wore off on her. I hoped that was the reason. My brain circuits wouldn't handle the alternative.

Courtney needed some crazy, I thought. More and more, I saw little snatches of carefree laughter or mischief glint in her eye, but the faint shadow of sorrow always lurked too. I wondered if she would ever feel comfortable enough to tell me her story. I knew it had to do with the guy in the picture sitting on her mantel, but I had no idea what might have gone wrong.

When I slid in beside her, she was Tanner-less. That was good. And then I annoyed myself by feeling a pang. I didn't want to think about Tanner. Right away, Courtney's demeanor distracted me anyway. Her face had little color besides the bluish circles under her eyes, and I could tell she hadn't taken much effort with her appearance for church. Her hair hung in a low ponytail, and she wore little makeup, only a touch of mascara and sheer lip gloss. She offered me a limp smile, and I understood why her family babysat her; the sight of her looking wan bothered me so much I wanted to drag her out and demand to know what was wrong so I could fix it.

Halfway through the closing hymn, "Each Life That Touches Ours for Good," I saw tears pooling in her eyes, and she stood and slipped out of the chapel. I had a sinking feeling I knew exactly what was wrong now. I scooped up my purse and hurried after her. She was halfway down the hall to the back exit. "Courtney!"

She stopped. She didn't turn around, but she let me catch up and then started walking again, her eyes on the floor, a curtain of her hair hanging between us so I couldn't see her face. I heard her sniff, though. "Sorry," she whispered, her voice thick with tears.

I touched her arm lightly. "Let's go to the mother's room," I said. The family wards were done for the day. It would be quiet and, more importantly for Courtney, private. I urged her into one of the comfy armchairs and nipped some tissue from the bathroom before settling into the seat across from her. She took the tissue with a quiet thank you, and I smiled but said nothing, one of the best skills my dad had ever taught me.

After a few minutes and a few more silent tears, a short laugh escaped her. "I'm having a bad day. Can you tell?"

I shrugged. "I figured it was allergies. I think the guy behind us was trying to chloroform everyone with his cologne."

This got a real smile. She dabbed at her eyes with the tissue and took a deep breath. "Today is an anniversary for me." Her eyes clouded again. "That picture you saw on the mantel? The guy I said was my fiancé?"

I nodded to show I remembered.

"It's been a year since his funeral." She stared down at her lap.

Even though I knew it was coming, it stopped my breath for a moment. There was something very wrong with the universe when a guy didn't live to see twenty-five. "How did he die?" I asked, stepping carefully. My dad says most people appreciate the chance to talk about people they've lost, but I didn't want to assume.

"Afghanistan," she said. "He was a Marine reservist, and his unit got called up. He was shot in a firefight with the Taliban six months into his tour." She swallowed and fought for control of her emotions. "We sang that song at his funeral. I can't believe I heard it again today of all days."

"Will you tell me about him?" I asked.

She looked up, maybe to see if I was just being polite. "You really want to hear about some guy you never knew?"

"I really do."

She hesitated. "I know you love Sunday School and all, but do you want to skip it today? I don't have two more hours in me. If you want to hear about Alex, I could bore you with a bunch of pictures. It'll be like a vacation slide show, only sadder."

I smiled. "That sounds great, actually."

I followed her to her house and offered a silent prayer that I could be the friend she needed me to be. An hour later, we sat laughing in her room over a picture of her and Alex with a giant stuffed panda between them. Donna tapped on the door and walked in.

"Hi, Pepper. I thought I recognized your car. You're home really early, Courtney." She wandered over to our spot on the floor, and tension radiated in her body language. "What are you guys doing?"

"I'm showing her pictures of Alex," Courtney said.

I could read worry in her mom's expression, so I gave her a tiny smile and nod to reassure her. She looked torn, like she wanted to say something. She cleared her throat. "Do you girls want some soup?"

I knew it wasn't what she wanted to ask, but I answered like it was. "Sounds awesome," I said. Courtney said yes too, and Donna slipped back out.

Courtney released a sigh. "I love her, but she hovers."

"Better too much parenting than not enough," I said.

"Maybe. But I need a little space sometimes. I feel so loved that I can't breathe." She dropped her head back against the bed behind her.

I thought about my mom's anxiety over my "Single in the City" column and grinned. "I hear that."

She climbed to her feet. "Potty break."

"I'll go help your mom with the soup." I briefly coveted the luxury of a bathroom attached to my bedroom, one that I didn't share with mirror-obsessed Ginger, toothpaste-flicking Rosemary, and AXE-abusing Mace. Then I got over myself and bounced down the stairs to help Donna. I found her in the kitchen, stirring something delicious smelling.

She smiled when I walked in. "Corn chowder. Would you mind getting some crackers from the pantry?"

I didn't mind and fetched them for her. I set the box down on the countertop, and when she looked up, I smiled. "I think Courtney's okay," I said.

A crease appeared between her eyebrows. "I hope so. Is it obvious that I'm worried?"

"She told me why today is rough. Any mom would be worried."

She sighed. "It's been a hard few days for her. The funeral is when Alex's death became real for her. She's asked me not to crowd her, but I can't help it. She was broken for a long time. It's only been in the last couple months that I've seen the old Courtney trying to break through the fog." She stirred the whole time she talked, but she did it on autopilot. I guessed she was inside a memory, recalling the aftermath when Courtney learned of Alex's death.

I kept quiet, trying to let her work through it. After a moment, she snapped out of it and reached for a bowl. "I wish I could do more than feed you to thank you," she said as she ladled chowder into it.

"You've said that before, but I don't know what you mean," I confessed, eager to try the soup.

"Your thank you note. The one you wrote to her a few weeks ago? She showed it to us, and I'm not sure why, but it caused some kind of . . . breakthrough, I guess. She's been more present, more here."

The praise embarrassed me. "I just told the truth."

She handed me a second bowl of chowder. "Not everyone takes the time to do that. I'm glad Courtney has you for a friend. Now, why don't you take both of these up so my daughter doesn't think I'm hovering again." With that, she tucked the cracker box into the crook of my arm and sent me on my way.

I found Courtney on the floor, but her scrapbook was gone. I handed her a bowl.

"Did we look at all the pictures already?" I asked, surprised.

"No," she said. "But the ones that are left are from his deployment and clippings from the newspaper about his . . ." She waved a hand, the words escaping her. "I don't want to go through those today. It's been good remembering the other stuff. Thanks for putting up with it."

"Are you kidding? That was such a cute love story." They had met when Courtney was sixteen and Alex had come to speak in her family ward when he was fresh off his mission to Poland. In the throes of a mad high school crush, she had chased him and he had stayed out of reach, sure she was too young. He joined the Marine Reserves to pay for schooling, and the night Courtney graduated from high school, he stood waiting on her porch with a bouquet of flowers in hand, ready to beg for a date. It was very Jake Ryan a la *Sixteen Candles*, she assured me. When he got his orders for deployment, he proposed, and the wedding was set for when he came back. Only that never happened.

Even though Courtney didn't go into a lot of description about her emotional state when she heard the news, I could put the pieces together and see that it had cut deep. If her family's protectiveness was anything to go by, things must have gotten scary bad. And yet, the Courtney I was getting to know was someone with quiet strength.

A knock sounded at the door. "Is everything okay in there?" Donna called.

"Fine!" we called back in unison. Courtney shook her head ruefully, and I grinned. "So much for not hovering, huh?"

"I know they mean well, but it's like they need me to have a backbone of steel. I don't," she said. "And they get all worried."

I whipped out my phone and blessed my 4G connection.

"What are you doing?" Courtney asked.

"Looking something up," I said. A minute later, I found it. "You do not have a backbone of steel. You have a 'multi-walled carbon nanotube' where the rest of us mere mortals have spines."

"A what?" she asked, her brow wrinkled.

I waved the phone at her. "I Googled it. It's the material with the most tensile strength. That means it can take stress. Tons of it."

She checked out my phone and lifted an eyebrow. "Thank you, Wikipedia." She handed it back. "Your turn, Pepper. Spill your guts."

I flopped back into the beanbag. "Whatever do you mean?" I asked.

"I'm on to you," she said. "You have a 'boys are evil' vibe sticking to you. Who was it?"

"Seriously, that would be the most boring story in the world. Want to watch paint dry instead?"

"No, I want to bond with my new friend. After you tell me about your boy, we'll braid each other's hair and make friendship bracelets."

"Cool. What about magic jeans? Are we getting any magic jeans outta this deal?"

"We're kind of built the same, so I don't think it would be very magical if the same pair of pants fit us both."

"True." She had an inch on me, but she was thin too. She had more going on in the bra department, but the jeans thing was pretty much even. I stared up at the ceiling. "What am I doing to put out an evil-boy vibe? I've gone on three dates in the last three weeks."

"Dates I didn't hear anything about, so you must not have enjoyed yourself." She propped herself up on her elbows and stared me down. "Besides, you're not into Tanner. All girls are into Tanner, so if you don't like Tanner, then you probably don't like guys."

"I like guys!" I said. "Just not at the moment."

"Because of . . ."

I grumbled. "Landon."

"Here's where you spill it, friend."

I hated talking about that failed relationship, but Courtney looked lively for the first time all day, and I knew I'd have to tell her the story at some point. "I'm only doing this in the name of bonding because there is nothing I want to discuss less," I said.

"Okay. Bond."

"I was engaged too. My fiancé called the wedding off a week before the date, and I went into hibernation for seven months. The end."

"Boo! That's bad storytelling for a reporter. Do over!"

"My ex-fiancé is Landon Scott."

Her jaw dropped. "*The* Landon Scott?"

I nodded, and she digested the information before speaking again. "He's an idiot for breaking up with you."

"Oh, he didn't breakup with me." I gave her credit for not jumping right to questions about what Landon is like or if I could get tickets to his next show—the usual response to the revelation that we used to date.

"But you said—"

"That he called the wedding off. He still wanted a relationship, but I'm the one who ended it completely." I waited for the look that always came next, the look that showed the listener was trying to fathom why anyone would breakup with a celebrity like Landon. She surprised me again by thinning her lips and saying, "He must have deserved it."

I sighed. "He did." I felt more comfortable telling her the whole story since she wasn't starting from the assumption that I was crazy for walking away from him. "I met him during my first summer term at the Y, before the full fall semester even started. We clicked right away."

"I can see that," she said. "You both have this kind of independent spirit thing going. Or at least, he seems to." She shot me a questioning glance, but I could only shrug.

"I'm not sure how well I ever really knew him, which is sad, considering he's the only guy I dated the whole time I was in college." I picked at a loose stitch on the beanbag, a bit startled that dredging it up hurt less than it used to. "We set a wedding date once, and he canceled it for some music festival competition. When that didn't go anywhere, he showed up again, and I took him back. We dated for two more years and then got engaged again last spring and set the wedding date for the end of the summer, a week after my graduation. The idea was that having a degree would make it easier for me to find a job when we moved down to LA so he could pursue his music."

"Making it big as a pop star was the plan all along?" she asked. I nodded, and she looked vaguely disgusted. "In all *The It Factor* interviews, he always made it sound like auditioning for the show was a whim, like he had no idea how good he was."

"He knew," I said, "but he thought he needed a compelling back story."

A look of understanding crossed her face. "So his story is that he had no idea he had this amazing voice and now he's going to be an 'accidental' star."

"That's about it," I said. I had never liked his idea of fabricating a backstory. Landon always intended to break into music, and it seemed pointless to cover that up. He worked hard to cultivate a soulful singer-songwriter vibe, but it hid a deeply rooted narcissism that finally revealed itself toward the end of our relationship. He wasn't into music because he couldn't imagine himself doing anything else; he was into it because he thought it was the fastest path to stardom.

I looked up at Courtney. "I figured most of this stuff out after we broke up. I couldn't have stuck with him if I had known how shallow he was."

"Why do you think he was able to hide that part of his personality from you for so long?" she asked.

I sighed. "Part of it was because I was young and dumb. I got caught up in the fact that he's super hot and he was interested in me. I was always the quirky girl, not the prom princess all the guys in high school drooled over, so to have him coming after me . . . it scrambled my brains, I guess."

Courtney's understanding smile encouraged me. I shoved my hand through my hair as I searched for the easiest way to explain what I had realized with time and distance after the breakup. "I'm not super high maintenance, so even a little attention from Landon was enough to keep me happy. We started talking marriage by spring of my freshman year, but I knew my parents would flip if I wasn't done with my schooling yet. Landon was cool about it. We talked about his future plans in the music industry, and suddenly, I went from wanting to be a journalist to thinking about how I should get a job that would support us in the short-term until he broke through, and then I could stay home with our future babies."

I hated that part, the part where I had so easily given up on what I wanted because I was blinded by Landon's conviction of his own talent and my belief that it was more important to nurture his than mine. It took little persuasion on his part to talk me into changing my major to a field that *he* viewed as more flexible and less career driven than journalism. "You should major in English," he had said. "You'll still get to write, you'll get to read a ton, and it'll be a great undergrad degree to have under your belt if you decide to go to grad school later."

Ha. Like he *ever* would have supported that. He wanted me biddable and available to him, to pander to his ego and make him the center of my everything. Worst of all, I had done it. I thought being a dutiful Mormon young woman meant putting everything I wanted aside so I could support my husband and raise kids. It's like I hadn't been paying any attention to the stellar examples I had in my parents, in the way they did everything as a partnership and each looked for ways to support and encourage the other in whatever they did. It was Landon's sea blue eyes and perfect white teeth and heart-stopping dimple that did me in . . . and my amazement that he picked me when other girls flirted their brains out trying to capture his attention the whole four years we were together.

In hindsight, the reason was obvious. I was impressionable when we met and easy to mold. I didn't listen to anyone who warned me that maybe Landon was trying to control me by granting and withholding affection to keep me dancing on an invisible string. That string bound me to him as surely as a steel chain would have.

"What did your parents think about all this?" Courtney asked.

"When we announced our engagement again, they confronted me because they were concerned about his influence. They begged me to rethink things."

"Let me guess," Courtney said. "You clung to him tighter."

I laughed. "I cast myself as a star-crossed lover, defying everything to be with my man. It was ridiculous. I announced my independence and said that I didn't need their full support because MasterCard would be happy to sponsor the wedding. Which was how I ended up with a nearly ten-thousand-dollar credit card debt."

Courtney winced.

"Yeah," I said. "Turns out credit card companies will offer you obscene lines of credit for a shot at all your future earnings." The tops of my ears burned as I told Courtney the rest of it, about how Landon scored a spot in the semifinal round of *The It Factor* Hollywood auditions and suddenly felt that it would be best to postpone the wedding so he could "focus on the competition." I insisted that I couldn't do that. I could imagine the expressions on my friends' faces if I mentioned a postponement. First of all, I didn't want anyone assuming we were delaying the wedding because of worthiness issues. There were no issues, and I didn't want anyone judging me, which they would have. It's human nature. I also felt Landon slipping away from me emotionally. His focus on the show and making the top ten drove everything else out.

As I argued with him about keeping our date or pushing it back, a distinct thought sliced through all the noise in my brain. It was simple but shone a giant light on a situation I'd been examining through half-closed eyes: if Landon loved me, there is no way he would have waited for four years to marry me and then postpone it a little longer until it was convenient.

"It's so obvious now," I concluded to Courtney, "but I'd been able to sustain a really phenomenal piece of fiction by telling myself that he was fine waiting on a wedding because he wanted to respect my parents' wishes. But he only wanted me on the hook until he lined up something better."

"Right now, I think viral videos might be my favorite thing ever," she said.

I smiled. She was referring to a half dozen YouTube clips that had surfaced showing Landon doing several pre-*It Factor* performances. They belied his manufactured back story that he'd been unaware of his own talent. It called into question his authenticity for the viewers, and entertainment and gossip blogs flogged the story to death. He was voted off before he could get past a sixth-place finish.

"Was that you?" she asked, watching me closely.

"No! My revenge was never speaking to him again. I know, I'm really mature."

"Still, I bet you were happy to see him miss out on the big prize. Justice is served, right?"

I shook my head. "Not really. He got the exposure he wanted, and girls really do fall for his looks. Someone is going to snap him up. Several misguided friends like to send me links to articles about what he's up to, and I think after *The It Factor* tour ends this summer, he'll go right to work on an album. He came out of this exactly where he wanted to be. Look for his future celebrity scandals coming to a grocery store tabloid near you."

"I've got your back," she said. "If I ever see his face on a magazine cover, I'll flip it around on the rack and then glare at anyone who tries to buy one."

"Excellent," I said. "We should be able to completely undo the national exposure he's gotten within a matter of weeks if we stick with your plan."

She grinned and flexed an arm. "Small but mighty."

I laughed and ate the rest of my soup before it got too cold. Courtney did the same, and we sat in companionable silence for a while. When my spoon clinked against the bottom of my empty bowl, I set it down and leaned back with a happy groan. "Your mom is the best cook ever."

"Stay for dinner," she said.

"Thanks, but I should probably head home soon."

A thoughtful gleam lit her hazel irises. "This is about Tanner. You don't want to see him."

"Not really."

"Why not? For years, girls have befriended me to get to him. I don't mind that you aren't interested, but why not? Does it have something to do with Landon?"

"Only in the sense that I don't feel like dating anyone," I said. "That's not specific to your brother."

She looked confused. "So why are you going on dates every weekend?"

I flopped back on the beanbag and stared at the ceiling. "Keep a secret?"

"Of course."

"I'm writing a column for *Real Salt Lake*, and that's why I have to go on dates every weekend."

"No way! You're Indie Girl?"

I sat up again at her amused gasp. "You've read 'Single in the City'?"

"Both of them. I'm waiting for more. They're hilarious," she said.

"Thanks."

"You don't think there's a chance you could find the guy to make you forget Landon?"

I shrugged. "I'm not looking for that guy. I make it clear on my dating profile that I don't want a relationship. If someone who contacted me had a needy 'love me' vibe, I wouldn't go on a date with him."

"But do you think the online thing could work for you if you *were* interested?" There was a forced casual tone to her voice.

"Courtney Graham, are you considering online dating?"

She flushed. "Is that a stupid thing to figure out on the anniversary of my fiancé's funeral?"

Her eyes reddened, and I hurried to reassure her. "No, I think it's healthy. It makes sense that you would pick a day like this to kind of mark your progress and figure out that things change. You look back at how things were, and you wonder how things are going to be. In fact, it would probably be kind of weird if you didn't."

"I guess." She was quiet for a moment. "I'm not ready yet. Just thinking about it."

"It's better than not being ready and having to do it for your job," I grumbled.

"Tons of girls would love that job."

"Believe me, I'd love to give it to them, but I have to stick it out until they promote me to write the kind of stories I'm really interested in. They want me to do regular concert reviews, which is awesome, but I hope they let me sink my teeth into even more soon."

"Like the stuff Tanner does?"

It was my turn to flush. "I guess I better spill another secret. I know Tanner mentioned that he interviewed me for a job a few weeks ago, but he didn't mention that it was a disaster. I stormed out of his office before the interview was even finished, which is why I don't like the idea of hanging out with him so much."

"I knew it!" she crowed. "I knew there was some kind of weird vibe between you." She tilted her head. "That explains your part, but now Tanner has some 'splaining to do too."

"What are you talking about?" I asked, disturbed by the mischief lurking in her smile.

"Sorry to tell you, but Tanner drops in all the time now, specifically when he thinks there's a chance you're going to be here."

I shifted. "Did he say that?"

"No. I just know him. He wants himself a dash of pepper."

I groaned. "Do you have any idea how many times I've heard lame jokes like that?"

"Blame your parents," she said, grinning.

"I don't think Tanner is coming around because of me," I said, not buying it, mainly because I didn't want to. "I understated the situation when I said our interview was a disaster. Besides, he's way older than me."

She stared at me strangely. "How old do you think he is?"

"He's got to be almost thirty, right?"

She laughed. "No. He's only twenty-six. It's his old soul thing he's got going on."

"That and his Dockers," I said. "He dresses more like a dad than a brother."

"I get on him all the time about it," she said. "He started writing for the paper so young that he overcompensated for his age by dressing and acting older. Now it's kind of a habit."

"How did he get to be a senior reporter already? You'd think someone who started out early themselves would have been more sympathetic to someone like me trying to do the same thing."

"Have you read his articles?" she asked.

I nodded. "He's good."

"He's really good." Her defense of her brother was sweet. Of course, Ginger was a total pill, but I'd never let anyone else say that about her. It's what sisters do. "It's a pretty interesting story how he got on with the *Bee*," she said. "He started as a guest columnist in high school, and it went from there. You should ask him to tell you about it sometime. Like tonight, after dinner."

"As much as I'm tempted to stick around and eat more of your mom's food, I'd better get going."

"Hurry. Tanner will be here any minute on the off-chance he gets to see you."

"I think you're reading into stuff," I said. "I'm sure he's got lots of other dates to keep him busy enough not to worry about me." I hesitated before letting curiosity get the better of me. "I know he's young and all, but how come he's still single?"

Courtney shrugged. "He's slightly a workaholic. He's had a couple of serious relationships, but they didn't survive the bad starting reporter pay or his crazy hours." She grinned at me. "He's been a lot better about dating since the prophet told the guys in priesthood session to quit goofing off and put a ring on it."

I snorted. "Too bad Landon didn't get that talk a year earlier." I hauled myself out of the beanbag. "I still have to go. My mom did Sunday dinner this week, and she makes a pretty mean pot roast."

She stood and led the way to the door. "My brother loves a challenge," she said, a teasing warning in her voice.

"I'm not a challenge," I said. "I'm not even a mystery."

"Tanner won't see it that way."

"Then Tanner's wrong."

She opened the front door for me. "Not usually. Good luck."

I shook my head and climbed into The Zuke. So what if there was chemistry between us? It didn't mean doing anything about it was a smart idea. I wanted Tanner at a safe arm's length, maybe even two arms' lengths, while I focused on getting my new career off the ground. I was done being someone else's shadow.

It was time to break through in my own right.

Dear Nathan,

Thanks for teaching me all those swear words back in second grade. Even though my mom grounded me for two weeks when she found the list under my pillow, they came in handy this past week. Without your crash course in profanity, I never would have understood half the insults that were hurled at me the other day.

Also, I'm sorry I released your frog back into the wild that one time. I was still mad at being grounded for harboring your bad word list. I tried explaining to my mom your argument that they couldn't be that bad if you can find them in the dictionary, but she didn't go for it. That was still no reason for me to steal Hoppy the Hulk and liberate him.

I hope you'll forgive me. Tell your mom I say hello. She still makes the world's best oatmeal cookies.

Sincerely,
Pepper

Chapter 11

Seven thousand five hundred.

There are a lot of contexts in which that would be considered a great number. Like, for example, if that were the number of dollars showing on your paycheck due to a payroll error and the owner was like, "Eh, keep it as a bonus." Or if it were the winning jackpot when you hit bingo while hanging with your grandma at the senior center. Or if that's how many readers your article pulled in, once again an increase of almost a thousand page views over the previous week. That was a trend I could get behind.

Something had clicked for me in my conversation with Courtney. The list of ways in which I let my circumstances swallow me up instead of working to shape them was long and embarrassing.

No more.

The same stubbornness that caused me to finance my own wedding without any help from my parents drove me to think about how to make journalism a real deal, full-time gig. I'd figured out quickly that Ellie was right. The snarkier I was in my "Single in the City" column, the more readers it drew. I didn't go out of my way to find things I hated about my dates, but I was so, so grateful when I found them anyway. It made the columns much easier to write.

I sat at the kitchen table, waiting for my dad to come down. My laptop was open and ready for him with the column titled "The Bowels of Misery" already on the screen. When he ambled in with his hair still wet from his post-run morning shower, I pointed to his chair. "Sit. Read."

He lifted an eyebrow but did as commanded, and I leaned back, enjoying the mellow tenor of his voice. "I love breakfast cereal as much as anyone, but that doesn't mean I want to marry it," he read. "Frankenberry, my last date, credits the power of some South American berry with righting his gastrointestinal system. In fact, he is so convinced of the power of this berry that he spent the whole evening describing the change in the frequency of his bathroom visits and the improvement in the quality of time he now spends there. Best of all, I got to hear his pitch off and on through two hours of miniature golf about why I should buy some for myself ('Do it for your bowels!') and then become a distributor and sign up all my friends ('Do it for *their* bowels!'). To be fair, I don't think he asked me out solely to sell me on this miracle berry, but really? There's a time and a place. First date, no matter where it is, is not that time or place. It's monstrous, really. Frankenberry, you so earned your name."

A few times my dad struggled to keep a straight face. When he finished the rest of the article, he lifted his eyes to meet mine. "Did you exaggerate any of this?" he asked.

"Nope."

He leaned back against his chair. "All right. This guy totally deserved it."

I grinned. "I know." Lewis, Frankenberry's real name, had made this my easiest column so far.

"I still don't think this is a great idea," he said.

"I'm smart. I keep myself safe. I meet these guys at a busy location, and I make sure we're always around other people. Haven't I proven I have some common sense yet?"

"That's not what I meant. I think someone is going to find out who Indie Girl is and then it's going to get uncomfortable for you. And I still don't think you need to go the sarcastic route so much."

I pointed to the laptop again. "I couldn't have made that up if I tried, and there's nothing Frankenberry could refute in there. It all happened exactly how I said it did."

"Yes, but would you have shared your feelings about the evening to his face the way you spilled it in your column?"

I squirmed.

"That's my point," he said. "When you put it in writing like this, it's worse than if you outright told him and hurt his feelings when it was only the two of you. Now it's between you, Frankenberry, and a few thousand people by the end of the week."

"You're assuming he's going to read it. This column is way under the radar," I said. "And it would have to blow up pretty big before I would even start to worry about the extremely tiny chance that one of my dates would see it."

"But if they did?" he asked.

"Then I go back to my other argument that it doesn't do them any good to spread the word that it's me. For every single person they tell, it's like them advertising, 'Hey, I'm a bad date. Here's the proof in print!'" I drummed my fingers against the table, not loving where the conversation was going.

He sighed. "How long do you think you'll be writing this column?"

"I don't know," I shrugged, stung that he wanted it to be over so soon. I understood that he didn't like the humor in the column coming at someone else's expense, but my readership was increasing every single week, which meant so was my paycheck, and it was absolutely not hurting anyone. "I want to move on to news, but Ellie likes me on music reviews for the time being. I have to hope one of the other staffers quits or can't take a story and I get a shot at covering it."

Ginger had made it down by this time, dressed and ready for school, with my mom right behind her. "You shouldn't change the column," she said. "My friends are all addicted to it now."

"You still haven't told anyone it's me, right?"

She rolled her eyes. I wondered if it was possible for her to even speak a sentence without rolling them first. "No, I haven't told anyone."

"I don't think it's a problem for you to write up your dates," my mom said, surprising me. She and my dad were generally a united front. "But I question the dates you're picking."

"They're picking me," I said.

"So you don't do anything. They all send you messages saying they want to go out and you don't do a thing to encourage them except sit and look cute in your profile picture?" she asked.

"Not exactly. Sometimes I send them a smile icon or something if no one contacts me for a day or two."

She stared at me, her gaze knowing. "And how are you picking the guys you send these smiles to?"

I shrugged, not wanting to answer.

"Are you trying to find guys that you would legitimately enjoy getting to know or are you choosing guys that you think have the greatest train wreck potential?" She thumped a nearly full carton of milk down on the counter.

I cleared my throat. "I plead the fifth."

"Thought so." She poured herself a glass and watched me as she drained it in one go. My mother, milk chugger extraordinaire. "That's my issue with all of this. You're looking for people to mock, so it isn't fair to act like you don't have any responsibility for it when they turn out to be goofy in person. You're looking for easy marks for your column. I dare you to find someone on that site you genuinely find interesting and see what you can do with it."

"Good point," my dad said. "Your readers aren't going to believe that every single person on the website is as cartoon-ish as you make them out to be. You're risking your credibility with them if you don't add more variety."

He had me there. A few comments to that effect had popped up after the last two columns, either complaining that I was way too harsh on my dates or it wasn't possible to go on so many bad dates in a row unless I was trying not to have good ones. Which I wasn't.

"Okay," I said. "But the odd guys are much easier to get a date with. I don't know how much luck I'll have with the normal ones."

"Quit your crazy talk," my dad said, leaning over to ruffle my hair as if I were Rosemary's age. "Anyone would love to go out with you. You'll see."

Finding the positive was suddenly harder because I knew my dad's love for me was blinding him to the fact that I wasn't everyone's cup of bleached blond tea. Most guys wanted a nice chamomile, and I was more of a . . . well, I'd have to be a tea drinker to make that analogy work. The point was, guys I might have an interest in weren't usually looking for a girl like me. They were looking for Barbie, not her bony, wisecracking sidekick. "Isn't it enough that I'm putting myself out there at all? You've been bugging me to do this for forever."

"But you're not putting yourself out there," my mom argued. "You're taking the easy route."

"And you're taking easy shots," my dad added. "I'm going to issue you a challenge"— I groaned. —"to find a guy on the site you could realistically be interested in. Maybe it will add a whole new level to your writing."

He and my mother stared at me expectantly. It was a look that said, "We're waiting to hear you make the right decision."

Resistance was futile. "Fine," I said.

"Let me help you pick!" Ginger said.

I shuddered. "Heck no! I'd end up with a string of guys who have deep and abiding testimonies of hair gel and Quicksilver shirts."

She stared at me blankly. "Yeah. So?"

My mom laughed. "Time for school," she said. "Mace!"

He tore through the kitchen, not even pausing when he snagged a banana on his way out to the car.

The door closed behind them, and my dad pushed back from the table. "I'd better go take care of Rosemary." She started school a half hour later than Mace and Ginger.

When I had the kitchen to myself, I opened LDS Lookup and started a new search. My parents' observations needled me. I would look for a date with real potential, but it was a sure bet none of the guys I found interesting would return the interest. At least I could say I tried. Salve for the conscience and all that.

I spent an hour checking out profiles and narrowed the possibilities to three choices. Feeling like an idiot, I sent each of them the smile icon that LDS Lookup provided. I could have sent a winking eye or puckered lips. I *could* have. But never would in a million years. That done, I pushed my laptop away and sighed, looking around the kitchen and soaking up the rare silence.

I had a day off. Usually, I worked every weekday, but I swapped one of my shifts out with my new assistant, Austin, because I had a show to see tonight and didn't want a forever long day at work leading up to it. The band, Empires of Solace, had sent me an e-mail over the weekend that verged on begging me to come see them. I don't know why they wanted me in particular, but they were local, which pleased Ellie, who approved the assignment.

What to do with all the time yawning in front of me? A few weeks before, I would probably have crawled back into bed with a tub of Red Vines and watched YouTube clips for hours on end, but that didn't sound fun anymore. I'd save that for the inevitable rejections from Lookup.

Restless, I skimmed through the *Bee* to see what Tanner had covered in the last day or so. He'd written one article on a city councilman who wanted to install a solar energy system to power the city park lights at night, but that was it. Nothing told me how he had spent the weekend, no reviews of anything musical or otherwise. I chided myself for even wondering. I needed to get all of Courtney's insinuations out of my head.

As if thinking of Courtney summoned her somehow, she sent me a text.

Love the Frankenberry column this morning. If you don't want to go out with him again, can I have a shot?

I snorted. *He's all yours,* I texted back.

I clicked around the *Bee* website to see if I had missed anything else with Tanner's byline. I didn't see any more of his work, but a linked article in their Style sidebar caught my eye. It was a press release from a local clothing company announcing a preview of their new line titled "Love and Rockets." I recognized the reference to one of my dad's favorite eighties bands. An idea niggled at me, and I did a little more digging on the company. Just as I thought: they incorporated a rock-and-roll aesthetic in their design, and the few images I could find on the Internet showed some pretty cool pieces.

I jumped up and headed for the shower. It was time to start making my breaks, and I would begin by finding and writing my own story for *Real Salt Lake*. I would prove to Ellie that I was good for more than snarky opinions.

* * *

Two hours after lunch, I collapsed on a park bench in Hidden Hollow, a little gem of a park I had stumbled across in Sugar House. The Urban Grit headquarters was not far from *Real Salt Lake*'s office. It was one of the few businesses still holding on in the Granite Block. They must be doing all right if they had survived all the redevelopment in the area with their lease still intact.

According to the owner, Kirbi Dawn, Urban Grit was doing extraordinarily well, even in a down economy. She explained it in terms of smart marketing and business sense, but I could see that she was the heart and soul of the company. She designed the clothes and then worked with her business partner to make sure customers found them. Her concept was Prada for an H&M budget, styles with great lines and a little bit of edge.

I was the only reporter to show up for the press conference. Kirbi smiled and told me that was normal in the Salt Lake market. The company's sales were almost exclusively online or through specialized boutiques in cities like LA and New York. I got to preview the collection all by myself, and I knew I could do a great write up on it. I stared out over the park and thought it through, including what angle to take. I didn't want to turn it into another opinion piece like my music reviews. I wanted to go with the human interest angle, uncover the story of a woman making waves in the national fashion market out of a tiny little shop in Sugar House.

I dug into my purse and pulled out my palm-sized notebook, jotting down impressions and lines I could use in the article. I already had some great quotes from Kirbi about her creative process and dreams for the company's future. I dumped out everything in my head to sort through later. With that done, I had time to kill. I didn't want to drive to Pleasant Grove and back twice in one day, so I'd brought clothes to change into for the show later tonight, plus my laptop to keep me busy. Maybe I could drop in on *Real Salt Lake* and see what was going on.

I made the five-minute drive and climbed the stairs to the office. When I pushed the door open, six heads shot up to stare at me, including Ellie's. "Pepper!" she said, surprised. "What are you doing here?"

"I was in the area and thought I'd pop in," I said. I hovered near the door with a death grip on my purse strap, unsure if popping in was okay. "I've got some writing to do. Would it be cool if I set up in here to do it?"

"Uh, sure. Is it something for us?"

"If you want it. It's not a big deal if you don't," I said.

"I'm intrigued. What's it about?"

"A clothing line called Urban Grit. Did you guys already cover that?"

Her brow furrowed. "That doesn't sound familiar. Tessa?" she called to a girl on the other side of the room. "Did you cover a company called Urban Grit?"

Tessa rolled her eyes. "They're a little flash-in-the-pan start-up business, so no. I didn't think there was a story there."

Ellie quirked her eyebrows at me. "But you do?"

Tessa's dismissive tone eroded some of my excitement, but I didn't let it show. I nodded at Ellie. "I do." Maybe I was wrong, but Kirbi's story fascinated me, and I wanted to take a stab at telling it.

She shrugged. "Take Denny's desk. He's working from home today." She pointed to the seat the pasty-skinned lone male had occupied on my previous visit.

I sat down and accessed the Wi-Fi connection then did some more research on Urban Grit and its owner, letting my thoughts coalesce as I worked. I paid attention to the chatter around me. Ellie schmoozed on the phone almost nonstop with advertisers. A couple of the other girls sounded like they were working on advertising too. The other three all clacked away at their keyboards. None of them came over to talk to me, and I felt the tiniest bit like an interloper, but I rationalized that they were probably busy with deadlines too. Only theirs were real, not self-imposed. About a half hour after I got there, the door opened and Chantelle walked in. I remembered her from my last visit. I'd taken concert reviews from her.

She stopped short when she saw me. "You're Pepper, right?"

Hoping this was a good thing, I tacked on a smile and nodded.

"I liked your take on Sonic Machine. I hate that band."

My smile turned real. "*Hate* is a strong word. I'm more on the could-do-without-them side."

"I'm glad you're on band duty now," she said. "Music isn't really my thing. I like it, but I don't follow the industry enough to write credible reviews. And I'm getting too old to hang out at clubs in the evening. I've got two kids. I feel like an idiot backstage."

"I'm relieved you're okay with it," I said. "Ellie said you were, but it's nice to hear it from you."

She skirted around a couple of other desks to take the one next to mine and dropped her cute handbag into the bottom file drawer underneath it. "If you start covering art galleries and new museum exhibitions, we'll have a problem, but the bands are all yours."

She powered on her computer and set about checking her e-mails. One of the girls who had been on the phone since I'd walked in pushed back from her chair and walked over. "I'm Janie," she said. "I wanted you to know I love you."

Startled, I stared up at her while another of the ad girls hooted. "Thanks?" I said, not sure how to respond to that.

"Seriously, 'Single in the City' is blowing up for us," she said. "Don't take this personally, but I hope you never have a good date. Your Tuesday posts are turning into advertising gold."

I smiled and said thank you, but as I turned back to my laptop, I caught a scowl on Ellie's face, which smoothed out when our eyes met. She rose and headed over to me. "I'm going to grab myself a soda from the break room," she said. "Want to come with?"

Since it wasn't really a request, I said, "Sure," and followed her back. She grabbed a diet Dr. Pepper from the fridge and handed me one then waved me into one of the plastic folding chairs at the dinky table while she took the other one. "I've been meaning to talk to you about 'Single in the City,'" she said then paused for a drink. "It's coming along well. I'm happy with it."

"Good," I said. "It's only costing me my sanity."

She grinned. "Hold on to enough that you can still write coherent articles, okay?"

I laughed. "Yeah, yeah. So Janie said something about my columns being advertising gold?"

"Yes. I meant to call and tell you that we're logging more and more hits on your previous articles. We've picked up a couple new advertisers as a result."

"That's great, right?" I asked. "What does that mean for me?" *Please say more money.*

"Right now, it means that I want you to know we're thrilled with what you're doing. We're not in a position to pay you more for it yet, but I definitely want to acknowledge the response it's getting. Thank you again for stepping up to do it."

"You're welcome," I said, feeling deflated. I wanted to be much closer to getting out of Handy's.

She stood, satisfied with our conversation, I guess. Definitely more satisfied than I was. "I'm looking forward to your review tomorrow."

Did she really have to drag me back to the break room just to say thanks for still working for practically free? I took a swig of my drink. I guess the pat on the head and the soda were supposed to be enough reward for my column "blowing up."

I followed her back out into the main office and took up my place at my laptop again. Chantelle shot me a curious look but said nothing, only typed until Ellie disappeared to the back to take another call. Then she tapped my arm and nodded at her computer screen. Clearly, I was meant to read it on the sly. *There's the Ellie version of events and then there's what actually happens.*

I squinched my forehead at her to show that I didn't understand. She typed some more, her fingers flying over the keys, and then I read, *Ellie has incredible ideas, and the magazine will do well, but she does it on her own terms.*

I took to my own keyboard and typed, *I know you're literally spelling this out for me, but spell it out even more. What are you trying to say?*

She shook her head at me and typed, *She poached me from the* Bee. *She got most of us there. Real Salt Lake pays well, so I don't leave. But she's underpaying you and a couple other people to meet my salary. She can afford to pay more. I'm only telling you because your dating column is driving more traffic than she's letting on. In a couple of weeks, you'll be able to bargain from a position of strength.*

When she was sure I had read it, she erased the paragraph and went back to working on a story about a local artist. I stared at my screen while

I processed Chantelle's revelation. Now I had a . . . I checked an online thesaurus for the word I wanted. A *quandary.* A *dilemma.* A *briar patch.* If Ellie was underreporting the number of page views my article got so she could cut me a smaller check, how was I supposed to find the true number and get the money I deserved? I couldn't think of a way to ask for actual documentation on my page hits that wouldn't imply a lack of trust.

My mom had once covered a long-term sub assignment for a first-year teacher who raised such a stink about everything that she was fired midyear. While the teacher had been incompetent, my mom said it was the teacher's complaints that made the principal unwilling to wait for her contract to expire at the end of the year. I remembered my mom's advice at the time: let them pour cement around your shoes before you rock the boat. Same rule applied here. Ellie could replace me with another anonymous Indie Girl if I made too much of a stink. I needed to become indispensable.

How to do that? I wondered. I drummed my fingers on the desktop, blindly rereading my last sentence over and over. "Urban Grit is as much about Kirbi Dawn's grit and determination as it is about a fresh and edgy aesthetic." Then it hit me that I was staring at the answer. I had to create more opportunities for myself like I had today. I would throw so many good articles at Ellie that she would have no choice but to keep printing them. I'd have to go after smaller news stories or find other human interest profiles that weren't on the magazine's radar. Then I'd have to write them so well she couldn't resist them. When I became an integral part of their reporting team, I could ask for the truth on how many page hits my columns were getting.

The early May sunlight filtered through the front windows of the office, the angle telling me that it was close to the end of the work day. Within minutes, Janie and the other salesgirl began gathering up their stuff, sticking things in desk drawers, and rummaging in their handbags for car keys. It made sense that the ad people would go home first. I guess they could only sell advertising during business hours.

By five-thirty, only Chantelle, Ellie, and I were left. Ellie hung up the phone with what sounded like someone in a local congressman's office. She scooped up her chic black trench coat and a shiny red bag with not-so-discreet Coach tags hanging from it. Maybe that's where my extra pay went.

"Can you lock up, Chantelle?" she asked.

"Sure."

Ellie looked at me. "You're welcome to stay as long as Chantelle is here, but you'll have to leave when she does because she has the keys."

"I figured," I said. My tone was pleasant, but I had experienced a paradigm shift during the course of the afternoon. I'd gone from desperately wanting to please Ellie to realizing I had more leverage with her than I thought.

When the door closed behind her, I turned to Chantelle. "Thanks for the heads up."

She shrugged. "Ellie's smart. She can write, she can edit, she has business sense and a good instinct for what readers want."

"You don't sound impressed," I said, wondering how long I could keep Chantelle talking as I figured out the dynamics at the magazine.

"She lacks a little something," Chantelle said. "Probably a soul." She fell quiet for a moment and then sighed. "I'm only saying this because it's the end of a long day. But watch your back with Ellie. She feels more beholden to the investors than she does to her employees. She doesn't see her people as being as important as her investment capital."

I studied Chantelle, trying to figure out her motivation for helping me. She was around thirty, maybe just barely past. She wore a wedding ring and a trendy outfit I'd seen in one of the upscale boutique windows at the mall. Her hair was perfectly styled in long, honey layers around her face, but the side-swept fringe of her bangs framed tired eyes. "Did you say you used to work for the *Bee*?"

She nodded. "I was on the city desk there."

"Why did you leave?"

She shook her head slowly, like she wasn't sure of the answer herself. "I'd been angling for the life and style section for months, but the *Bee* is kind of an institution, and institutions aren't always open to change. The same old dried up prune of a little man that has covered their arts and entertainment for almost twenty years will not retire, I think specifically to spite me. And he more or less threw a fit every time the editor tapped me to cover something in his little hemisphere of the newsroom, like new artist exhibitions. When Ellie came calling with a job offer that increased my pay and let me write about the stuff I found interesting . . ."

"You couldn't resist," I finished for her, and she nodded. "Yeah, I've noticed she can be pretty convincing. Obviously, you're not happy with the change."

"I don't hate it here," she said. "We all work together pretty well, but I wish I hadn't left the *Bee*. Ellie demands a lot for the paychecks she signs and I have two little kids at home. I think I'm ready to dial back on the journalism career, but then I look at our budget, and I have no idea how to do that. So I'm stuck covering all kinds of events at night, and I miss tucking in my little guys several times a week because Ellie calls last minute and wants me to check out a concert or a play or a dozen other things. And I have to do it."

"Why not go back to the *Bee*?" I asked.

"I can't," she said. "I burned my bridge royally when I left. My editor told me he was working on making some changes and asked me to be patient, but I'd been hearing that for a year. I thought I was so cool because I already had a job offer lined up so I was totally snotty when I turned in my resignation." She fidgeted with her mouse. "The *Bee* won't want me."

"Oh." I didn't know what else to say.

Chantelle shrugged and packed up her workspace. I took my cue to do the same. "Do you mind if I run back and change?" I asked her. "I have a show to go to tonight. I'll finish writing at a Starbucks or something, but I'd rather not have to change in a public restroom."

"Knock yourself out," she said.

I grabbed my laptop bag where I had managed to squeeze in a thin, teal, graphic T-shirt and my faded black skinny jeans. I had Converse in the car, making it a passable outfit for going to hear Empires of Solace do their thing. A few minutes later, I was back out front, hustling to gather my other belongings so Chantelle could leave. When we reached the parking lot, I turned to face her. "I'm not sure why you're helping me, but I can't thank you enough."

"Ellie is borderline ruthless when it comes to the business side of journalism. Everyone and everything around her is either a stepping stone or a pawn. You're not totally caught in Ellie's web yet," she said. "I figure you should know that she's trying to spin it around you." She waved good-bye and climbed into her car. I threw my stuff into the back seat of The Zuke and pulled out after her, not sure where I wanted to go next. I drove aimlessly for a while, exploring more of the area while I tried to puzzle out the Ellie Peters problem. So far, I didn't have much to go on. I knew Tanner seemed surprised that I was working for Ellie, and it could be because of her reputation as a poacher at the *Bee*. Janie had said my Indie Girl stuff was a hit with advertisers, but I didn't have any actual numbers. And I had Chantelle's suggestion that Ellie wasn't on the up-and-up but no corroborating evidence.

My gut said that Chantelle had no reason to lie, yet I still didn't have a reason to rock the boat. If anything, I needed to sit tight with *Real Salt Lake* and build up a great portfolio of work as fast as possible so I could jump ship to somewhere like the *Advocate*. With that in mind, I parked in front of a little café advertising free Wi-Fi access and pulled my laptop out of the car. I would grab a salad and a corner table and spend the next two hours until the show polishing my Urban Grit story.

Panicking over vague insinuations about my boss wouldn't get me anywhere.

* * *

I'm not a morning person, but even so, there are definitely ways I prefer to start my day over others. Waking up to the smell of my mom making chocolate chip waffles is pretty good. Logging onto my e-mail and finding a profanity-laced diatribe about my musical tastes and parentage is not so great.

I had e-mailed my review of Empires of Solace in the wee hours of the morning, writing it up fairly quickly after mentally composing it on the drive home from Salt Lake. Ellie must have posted it as soon as she got it. The band bordered on terrible with unoriginal music and lyrics that tried too hard to be highbrow. I had written, "Every song is a soundalike to other, better bands. Empires of Solace is a post-punk derivative of Joy Division without a tenth of the talent." It was true, but it sparked a minor firestorm in my inbox.

The message that greeted me was sent to the e-mail assigned to me by Ellie, a *Real Salt Lake* address she had given me. The sender, a guy named Liam Black, had objected to my review of Empires of Solace with the most original combination of curse words I had ever seen. I knew from my preshow research that the angry Liam was the band's bassist and sometimes lyricist.

By the time my mom walked in, I was laughing.

"What's funny?" she asked.

"Listen to this e-mail. 'You are a soulless cretin with no depth of musical heritage if you confuse simply paying tribute to our musical influences with being derivative.'" I scrolled down a bit farther, skipping the profanity. "My review of the band last night did not go over so well. He has a bunch of other beefs with my critique, not to mention my personal hygiene and my mental faculties."

"And this makes you happy?" she asked.

"No, I'm laughing because it's hard to take someone with these kind of rage issues seriously."

She shook her head while I tapped out my response. "Dear Liam, if only you had shown this level of creativity in your lyrics, I could have written a much better review. Have a great afternoon!" It was petty, but if he wanted to start my day off with a string of obscenities and questions about my intelligence, a gentle poke back was the least he deserved.

I checked out the other local papers while I polished off my oatmeal. Neither the *Bee* nor the *Advocate* had sent anyone to cover the show. No problem. I could corner the market. Tanner had a story in the *Bee* about a health inspector accused of racketeering. He was charging restaurants an under-the-table fee to keep him from issuing citations, but the kicker was that there weren't any violations; he threatened to make them up to score hush money. It was a tricky piece of writing because Tanner wasn't tracking an ongoing official investigation. He actually broke the story and found one source willing to go on the record about the inspector's antics.

If anything, an investigation would result *because* of his reporting. I read through it, fascinated by the threads Tanner had pulled together to weave the heart of the story, amazed by the sources he had found. One disgruntled woman, the mistress of the corrupt inspector, revealed how he would play his game at high-end restaurants and then tell them that he would turn in a satisfactory inspection report if they would comp his dinner that night. He'd take his mistress, and they'd dine on salmon, while the owner probably stewed in the kitchen, praying the inspector choked on a bone.

It was an extremely good piece with every allegation backed by corroborating statements. Tanner let the reader draw the conclusion about the inspector's character. Even though he wrote it as an investigative news story, it gripped me like a great feature or human interest story would. On a whim, I added a comment at the end under my initials, P.S. "Props, T.G. I'm learning." He may not have any idea who PS was or what I was learning, but it was the right thing to do. Tanner had been correct about my résumé, and the more of his work I read, the more I realized he had been fair to call me out on my inexperience. I followed two writers at the *Advocate* closely too, analyzing the way they presented their information and how they used their sources. I used them as models I wanted to emulate in my own writing. My sophomore critical theory professor would have called this "developing voice," but I thought of it as simply finding out what I wanted to say and how I wanted to say it.

Tanner's health inspector piece exemplified the kind of article I wanted to write. He had found the story inside the facts and the people inside the story. It showed insight and discernment, yet another set of layers to him I hadn't expected.

I clicked around some more, looking for press releases and story ideas, trying to figure out where my next self-assigned freelance piece would come from. I would finish my profile on Kirbi Dawn and send it in after work tonight, but I already wanted a new project queued up and ready to go. I landed on the City Events calendar and perused upcoming activities. One in particular caught my eye, an announcement for a Latin Heritage Festival in Pioneer Park. I had Saturday morning free; I would drop in and see if I could sniff out any stories, maybe about the immigrant experience. In a celebration full of people with diverse ethnic backgrounds, I was bound to find a feature. But I wanted to do what Tanner did and find the person inside that story.

I was ready to take my writing to the next level. In fact, I was ready to take a lot of things to a new level. Like LDS Lookup. I needed to see if any of the three guys I'd pinged had returned my attention. Someone interesting on there eventually had to find me interesting too.

Right?

Dear Rhys,

Don't worry, I'm not stalking you. I just wanted to say I'm sorry again for the black eye. I don't know what happened. I'm not a huge athlete or anything, but usually I have some coordination. I think maybe my body was temporarily inhabited by a fish out of water, what with the flopping and the waving about of extremities.

Thanks for being so nice about everything. And thanks for a great afternoon until The Incident. It was just bad luck that I was your first LDS Lookup experience. Don't give up on the website. I have a feeling you'll have no problem finding what you're looking for—and soon.

Sincerely,
Pepper Spicer

Chapter 12

To my surprise, an e-mail from one of my three LDS Lookup smile recipients showed up an hour before the end of my shift at Handy's. I love, love, love having the Internet on my phone. It's one of the few luxuries, besides my ridiculous jewelry obsession, that I've allowed myself on my pay-off-the-wedding plan. Without access to the Internet at work, the dull moments would do me in. And not because I might lose it and try to cram my head in the toaster oven. No, I'd be in far more danger of suffering a psychotic break and plastering the dining wall with pepperoncini murals depicting the rise and fall of Jeep-driving adolescent tyrants.

Anyway, the e-mail was from RJby25, a really cute guy whose profile had caught my eye more than once. In his picture, he had dark hair and a great smile, but even more interesting were his listed hobbies and interests. We shared a lot of things in common, like a love of eating at hole-in-the-wall dives and watching Wes Anderson films. Like most of the guys on the site, he included an interest in sports, both watching and playing, which are take-it-or-leave-it activities to me. I like watching sports live, and if I'm going to play a sport, I do it just for fun. I'm not all cutthroat and life and death-y. His book list hooked me. The fact that his list was long said he read way more than ninety-nine percent of the guys on Lookup. But the titles told me even more about him. They ranged from travel accounts to literary mysteries.

There was only one customer, and Katie could handle him, so I stepped into my office and pulled up the e-mail. "Thanks for the smile," it read. "I see we like a lot of the same stuff. I just barely joined this site, so please excuse me for being clueless. What do we do next? E-mail for a while?"

I smiled. A few weeks longer on the site than RJby25, and I already felt like a pro by comparison. I tapped out a reply. "Next is a matter of personality.

We can trade e-mails for a while if you want." I wrote a few more things about some of the bands he liked. The back-and-forth with someone I had an interest in versus the column fodder I usually dated made it more fun. If this RJ guy wanted to take things easy, I'd have to figure out a date with someone else by the weekend pretty quickly or come up with a new idea for my column. I still owed Josh, the fridge guy, a date. He'd called twice to invite me to something, but I had genuine conflicts with magazine duties each time. If worse came to worst, maybe I could set something up with him and use it to compare and contrast online and conventional dating.

That night before I collapsed into bed, I read through my Kirbi Dawn piece one last time, then offering a silent prayer, I hit send and hoped for the best. I knew it was the strongest piece of writing I'd done for Ellie so far, and I loved that it had a clear point of view without being an opinion piece.

Ellie's e-mail the next morning confirmed it. "It's good. We'll run it." An e-mail from RJby25 cheered me even more. He wanted to know if it was too forward to get together sometime that weekend for a low-key hang out.

His message made me laugh. On purpose—a welcome change from some of the guys I had dealt with on the site. "If I have my mom and/or my bishop write a note vouching for me that I'm a nice, stable guy, could we skip some of the e-mails?" he wrote. "At some point, I'm going to make a grammar mistake, and I can see from your info that you majored in English. It's only a matter of time before I screw up and sound like I never made it past fifth-grade spelling." He suggested meeting up to play Ultimate Frisbee if the weather was good on Saturday afternoon.

That coincided perfectly with my plans to drive into Salt Lake the same morning for the heritage festival. I'd already be there so it would be easy to swing over and meet him at the . . . Ultimate Frisbee grounds? I didn't even know how the game was played, much less where. I sent him an e-mail accepting the invitation and asking for the note from his mom. I figured the Frisbee details would work themselves out.

I planned to spend my free time until Saturday morning researching the Hispanic population in Salt Lake. I needed an angle that would both inform and appeal to the hipster sensibilities of *Real Salt Lake*'s readers. Hipsters are defined by their ability to suss out and embrace a new trend before regular middle America has any idea it's out there. I would prowl the festival to find something that fit the bill.

Friday morning, my Kirbi Dawn piece ran. My dad called me at work to congratulate me. "This is your best work so far," he said. "I know I give you a lot of grief over the dating column, but it's because I was hoping to see more of this, more using the power of your pen for good things. Great job, honey." Even though I know I can always count on that kind of support from my dad, his praise warmed me. While I debated which of my five work T-shirts to wear, a text popped up from Courtney, congratulating me on the piece. *Read it, love it, you rock*, it said. My mom left a congratulatory voice mail during the lunch rush at Handy's, and Mace stopped by to buy a sandwich and tell me he didn't know much about writing articles but mine seemed pretty good. That might have been my favorite compliment out of the bunch.

Late afternoon fell, and when Brady, the target of my mayo-hurling, slinked in looking both sullen and nervous, I rolled my eyes and waved him up to the order sign. I could tolerate even him today. Katie giggled at his lame jokes while she made his sandwich, and I eyeballed the whole transaction to make sure she charged him for the extra pastrami he requested. When the end of my shift rolled around, I was feeling pretty good about life, the universe, and everything in it.

I grabbed my stuff out of the office and got halfway to the front door before Josh walked in. I stopped, the tiniest bit of guilt pricking me. I wasn't avoiding him, but I didn't know where to fit one more thing into my schedule. Truthfully, he was a nice enough guy, but it was hard to be motivated to make a date happen when I knew we weren't a long-term reality.

He wore his service uniform and looked tired, but he mustered a smile. "Should I move out of the way so I can't block the exit when you make a run for it?"

I laughed. "I'm not trying to get away from you. Sit. I'll make you a sandwich."

He picked a table, and I dropped my stuff in the seat opposite him then nipped behind the counter and rustled up a French dip sandwich. I didn't have to ask what he wanted because he ordered the same thing every time. Most people do. When I brought it to him and took a seat, he smiled but didn't say anything until he'd downed a couple of bites. Josh wasn't much for small talk and even less for chatter.

When he set the sandwich down, he heaved a pleased sigh before he caught my eye. "I came to let you off the hook," he said.

"What hook? I'm not on a hook." But I knew what he meant.

"It's all right," he said. "Don't feel bad. I just don't want you to think you can't call the next time the Rust Bucket breaks down because you're afraid I'll bother you."

My guilt blossomed into a full-blown prickly thistle. "I promise I haven't been avoiding you. I work two jobs, and my schedule is crazy right now. It's an issue of time, that's all."

He took another bite of his sandwich and chewed, his expression thoughtful. "You're getting off work?"

"Yes."

"Then how about we go do something right now?"

I glanced down at my clothes. "Because I'm wearing a mustard-stained shirt and I reek of onions."

He shrugged. "I'll stay in my uniform too, and we'll go bowling. People are always dressing up in themes to go bowling. Maybe they'll think we're dressed for a blue collar theme."

I wanted to protest, but I didn't have any reason not to go. I found Josh easy to be around, and the alternative to his invitation was to sit at home and do some research before the festival in the morning. Since I already had a ton of information and I'd grown much less fond of my own company over the past few weeks, I grinned. "You're on. Prepare to feel awesome when you beat me by a million."

He shook his head, his face sad. "If only the score went that high."

I laughed. "How high does it go?"

"Three hundred."

"Then prepare to beat me by two-fifty."

I followed him to his work truck and once I climbed in, he peeled the magnetic sign off my door that announced that he worked for "Nelson and Sons HVAC Repair." After he did the same thing to his side, he tossed the signs in the back and climbed in.

"You get to drive this even when you're not at work?" I asked. The interior of the truck was far nicer and cleaner than the utilitarian white exterior would have led me to expect. "That's a pretty good perk."

"It comes with being the owner's son, I guess."

I glanced at him in surprise. How had I not known he was the "and sons" part of that equation? Just more evidence of my total self-absorption over the previous months. "How many sons are there?"

"Me and my brother, but he's on a mission right now," he said. "And he doesn't really want to go into the family business when he gets back. He's more interested in architecture, I think."

"What about you?" I asked, curious. "Do you like working for the family business?"

"It's okay, but it'll get better when I'm done with my MBA. It's hard working part time and going to school, but I'm almost finished."

Well, well, well. Mr. Josh was full of surprises, as the rest of the night proved. I was ashamed that I had assumed because he wore a repairman's shirt that he was simple and uneducated. Josh was definitely simple but in the best sense of the word. He was straightforward and uncomplicated. He wanted to settle down and get married soon and looked forward to raising kids. His dad wanted him working out in the field as a wage slave to learn all aspects of the business, but when his schooling was done, Josh would start working his way up in the company's main office. Nelson and Sons had one of the largest heating and cooling repair companies in the state.

I liked his gentle sense of humor, but even though he was fun to hang out with, I didn't feel any chemistry. When he drove me back to my car after a sound spanking at bowling, I was glad to give him a hug. I felt as comfortable with him as I would Mace or Cory. I stepped out of his embrace but kept my hands on his upper arms and squeezed lightly.

"I had a great time, Josh. You're easy to be around, and I'm sorry it took me so long to find the time to do it."

He smiled. "It's okay."

"Don't take this the wrong way—" his smile slipped, "but I'm not really in the market for a relationship right now, and I don't think we have that kind of connection, do you?"

He smiled again. "No, I guess we don't."

"What would you think about me setting you up with a friend of mine? You'd be perfect for each other."

He leaned against my car to stare down at me, a bemused expression on his face. "It seems like I should be offended somehow that you're trying to set me up with someone else at the end of our date. And yet I'm not."

"Don't be offended," I said. "I wouldn't set her up with just anybody. Do you remember that couple who was in the store the night you came in with the roses?"

I could see the tips of his ears redden in the parking lot lights, but he nodded.

"They're brother and sister. The girl, Courtney, is a good friend of mine, and I think you should meet her."

He hesitated. "This is weird."

I grinned. "I know. But trust me; you guys are a good fit."

He sighed. "All right. If she likes the idea, we might as well." His smile peeked out again. "If I remember right, she was pretty cute."

"You're remembering right. I'll call you soon with the details."

An hour later, I curled up with my laptop once more to reread my Urban Grit piece. I hadn't had a chance yet to check out the comments, and I was excited to see twelve waiting for me. Three were obviously from my family members, bless them. I read through the rest. Most of them said either, "Rad, I didn't even know about this company," which made me happy for Kirbi that she might get new customers, or "I love their stuff. Glad someone is writing about them." Only one comment near the end of the trail referred to the reporting itself, and in three little words it sent a tickle through my system that I hadn't felt in two hours with Josh. "You can write." That's all it said, but what got me was the initials on the comment: TG.

Tanner Graham.

* * *

Saturday, around lunchtime, I stood on the edge of a field at Warm Springs Park and wondered what to expect. The morning couldn't have gone any better if it had been hand delivered on special order from my very own fairy godmother. I had a story burning a hole in my brain, dying to fly out of my fingertips and into my laptop. But I had another assignment to get through first—my date with RJby25, also known as Rhys Jensen, a twenty-four-year-old accountant at a major firm in Salt Lake. It was the first time I had kind of, sort of, looked forward to a Lookup date, and it made me far more nervous than I had been on any of my other outings. Even Ginger's mockery that morning couldn't deter me.

"You're going out with a guy named Rice?" she demanded after accessing my account to look him up.

"It's pronounced *Reese*," I said, refusing to be baited while I sorted through my closet. She made up a little ditty about Pepper Rice while I debated what to wear and ignored her. Now, waiting for Rhys to show up, I couldn't get the stupid tune out of my head.

I checked out my outfit again, hoping it would be okay. I had on plain black, cropped, knit yoga pants and a berry-colored hoodie. I wore my semi-decent Adidas instead of my trashed running shoes, but I wasn't sure I had successfully struck the balance between sporty and cute. A minute later, I heard a hesitant "Pepper?" and looked up to find

Rhys approaching with a gym bag in one hand. He was better looking than his picture, and I could only hope I wasn't measurably worse than mine. His casual clothes made me feel better about my outfit.

After exchanging hellos, we stood staring at each other for an awkward moment, and my brain, panicking at the silence, shifted my mouth into overdrive. "So it's nice to meet you. Are my clothes okay? I've never played Ultimate Frisbee before, so I wasn't sure what to wear. And then I wasn't sure what the weather would do either. It's so uncooperative, right? I guess that's spring for you though." *Ack! Shut up, shut up!* But my mouth wouldn't listen. "I wonder if spring is unpredictable everywhere or if that's, like, a Utah thing. I have a cousin in Georgia who says half their year is like that, from October to May. She likes it though. I mean the living in Georgia part. I don't know what she thinks about the weather. I haven't really asked her. I'm not sure why not. I guess probably because conversations about the weather are kind of boring." *And yet you've just spent approximately a full minute having a one-sided conversation about it. Well done!*

Rhys looked slightly bewildered by my avalanche of words, but when he decided that I was done, he smiled. "I served my mission in North Carolina, so I know what she means. I could live there, except I like to snowboard, so I'd miss that."

I nodded in response, reluctant to open my mouth and let another river of words pour out unchecked.

He held up his duffel bag. "I brought lunch. Are you hungry?"

I nodded again but still didn't risk speaking. His bag had some sort of weird Mary Poppins property to it because he dug in it four or five different times to produce an unending stream of items, from a blanket for us to sit on all the way up to a lemon-roasted rotisserie chicken so warm I could see condensation beading in its plastic container. I'd put money down that Rhys was an Eagle Scout.

"Looks delicious," I said.

"Yeah, I have a real talent . . . for picking the best one in the display case," he said, smiling. Nice. Sense of humor still evident in person. Good sign.

I helped him spread the blanket out, and we ate and talked, but I stayed on the quiet side to avoid hysterical babbling. By the time we finished, several guys and a couple of girls had gathered on the opposite side of the field, all dressed in play clothes. A few Frisbees flew back and forth among them as they warmed up. I helped Rhys put the picnic supplies back in his Mary Poppins gym bag, and then we walked over to join the other players.

He introduced me as his friend, Pepper, who was new to the game. That met with lots of cheerful smiles. Rhys explained the rules, and then he offered me a tutorial on how to throw the disc. Turns out, you can't just fling it. There's a trick involving advanced geometry and angles. Despite his patience, I did poorly.

"Sorry," I said, after approximately my tenth failed attempt to get the disc to his friend Lance, who was standing a mere twenty yards away. My stupid nerves were sabotaging me.

"It's okay," Rhys said. "Relax. You're overthinking it."

Great. Could he tell I was nervous? That was embarrassing. And it made me more tense. My next throw went farther off course than any of the others. I blew out a sigh and jammed my fists in my hoodie pocket, staring at the disc as it rested ten yards to the left of Lance.

"Let me see if I can help you," Rhys said. Lance flicked the disc back to us in a fluid motion, and Rhys snagged it easily. He handed it to me, and then moving me like a store mannequin, he positioned my arms and feet. He stood behind me, rested one hand on my shoulder, and wrapped his other arm around me, following the length of my arm. His hand rested lightly on mine as I held the disc. I was too distracted by his nearness to even give him credit for his smooth move. To be honest, I don't think he was even trying to pull anything; I think he couldn't figure out how else to help me. Instead of snapping my wrist when I was supposed to, I was so distracted by his breath tickling my ear that my fingers clung to the Frisbee, and it didn't go anywhere at all.

Rhys stifled a laugh, and I blushed, mortified. "Sorry," I muttered. "I, um, thought that was a practice one." He kindly didn't point out that these were all "practice ones."

"Let's try it again," he said. This time, I let go when he gave my fingers a light squeeze and the disc sailed within ten feet of Lance, my closest effort by far. Rhys grinned when I whooped. "You're getting it. I'll help you with one more, okay?"

I nodded, and he took up his coaching stance, his hand once again on my own. When I snapped it this time, the disc flew to within two feet of Lance, who leaned a little to his left and plucked it from the air with no trouble. I whooped again and did a jump for joy, glad to redeem myself, but as I threw my hands in the air to celebrate, my elbow caught Rhys square in the face.

He groaned and dropped to the ground, and I whirled and crouched beside him as he held his hand over his left eye. I sucked in a sharp breath.

"Oh, my gosh! I'm so sorry! I'm so, so sorry! Are you okay? Is your eye okay?" I babbled, imagining the worst, sure I had somehow blinded him with my unfunny bone. It was karma for making fun of Brent's flailing elbows, I just knew it. "Can I get you anything? Do you want me to drive you to urgent care? Should I call someone for you?" I blathered some more, desperate to help.

Lance jogged over as soon as Rhys went down, but his only contribution was a sympathetic, "Dude."

Rhys didn't say anything for another minute, only pressed the heel of his hand into his eye and moaned some more. Finally, he looked up at me out of his uninjured eye. "This really hurts," he said. "I'm going to need some ice."

By this time, several of the other players surrounded us. One of the girls pushed forward to kneel by him. "I'm an RN," she said. "Can I look at it?"

Rhys hesitated and then pulled his hand away. I gasped at the massive welt forming over his eyeball where the point of my elbow caught him. The nurse tsked and said, "You definitely need ice. I think there's a convenience store two blocks over if someone wants to go."

A bunch of voices volunteered for the job, but I jumped to my feet. "It's the least I can do," I said. "I'll be right back." I sprinted for the car and sent up half-formed prayers for Rhys's eye on the way to the gas station. I tore into the parking lot, grabbed the largest soda cup I could find, filled it with ice, and threw two dollars on the counter as I raced back out, not bothering to wait for the change.

By the time I got back to the park, at least ten minutes had passed. Most of the players were tossing their discs around, and Rhys sat on the sideline, flanked by Lance and the nurse. He no longer held his eye, but it was a puffy slitted monstrosity resembling not so much an eye as it did a bulbous mushroom with an innie belly button where his pupil would be. I thrust the ice at him, and he took the cup, but all three of them stared at me, waiting. Realizing I didn't know what they were waiting for, the nurse sighed. "Is there something to put the ice in?"

I winced. "Uh, hold on." I ran back to the car and dug through the papers and litter scattered through it until I lucked out and found an empty plastic grocery bag. I hurried back and thrust it at the nurse gasping, "Here!" before I collapsed cross-legged on the grass in front of Rhys. Nurse Girl shook some of the ice into the bag and wound it closed to make a compress, then positioned it over her patient's eye and guided his hand to hold it. She looked like she enjoyed her ministrations more than if the patient were, oh, say, a cranky old lady or a testy middle-aged man. Well, who could blame her? Even with his puffy eye, Rhys was kind of delicious looking.

"I'm really sorry," I apologized again, anxious to make it right.

"I know," he said.

But he didn't say, "I understand," or, "I forgive you."

In fact, what he said next was, "This really hurts. I hope you don't mind if we end the afternoon early. I think I need to go home and take something and get a real ice pack."

He made like he was going to climb to his feet. Lance's hand shot out to help him up, and Nurse Girl supported him with a possessive arm around his back. She glared at me.

I scrambled up too. "Taking a painkiller or three sounds like a really good idea. Again, I am so, so sorry."

He nodded and made his way toward the parking lot opposite of where I had parked on the road. When I saw Lance pull out with Rhys in the passenger seat, I trudged back to The Zuke. I wanted to avoid the embarrassment of an instant mental replay on a continuous slow-motion loop, so I spent the drive home trying to pick an angle for the awesome story idea I'd sniffed out at the heritage festival. But instead, I kept coming back to the headline for my next column: This Date Will Self-Destruct in Five Minutes. I don't think it had even taken that long for me to chatter like a brainless idiot once Rhys showed up in person. By the time I checked into LDS Lookup again, I had a feeling his profile would have magically disappeared from the site.

I guess my parents had gotten this part wrong, at least. I was most definitely not ready to date. Not by a long shot.

Dear Marisol,

Thank you for trusting me to tell your story. You're incredible, and I'm going to make sure all of Salt Lake knows it. I don't know how someone rises from the ashes like you have, but every one of your scars tells a story, and that story ends with you standing victorious, even if you're too humble to see it that way.

I learned so much from being with you even for such a short time. Thank you for teaching me, sharing with me, and exercising extraordinary patience with my ignorance. We have to keep in touch. I need to know where life takes you because it can only be somewhere awesome. That's what awesome people like you deserve.

Sincerely,
Pepper Spicer

Chapter 13

On Sunday, I slipped into my seat beside Courtney and offered a smile, a real one, to Tanner, who sat next to her. He smiled back, and I turned my attention to singing the last verse of the opening hymn. I wondered what he was doing here with Courtney. He'd never visited our singles ward before, and suddenly he shows up? It gave Courtney's theory more weight.

In the quiet between the end of the hymn and the opening prayer, my stomach rumbled loudly. Courtney snickered, and I poked her. "Fast Sunday hazard," I hissed. It had been a long time since I'd fasted for something I really wanted. Usually, I did a fast and paid my fast offering, but I wasn't focused on anything specific in my prayers. Maybe I had to pray extra hard not to kill Ginger before my fast ended since we were both cranky on fast Sundays, but that was about it.

Today was different, though, so even though my stomach grumbled loudly a couple more times before the end of sacrament meeting, I didn't care. Now that I'd had a full day to process my experience at the heritage festival, the need to do justice to the story I found had muted the embarrassment I felt over the date debacle with Rhys. I'd still have to write the column up for the amusement of everyone else, but I didn't mind if it meant ingratiating myself with Ellie and getting the chance to run an article on my new hero, Marisol Pacheco, in the magazine. Today I woke up looking forward to my fast because I wanted clarity of mind when I wrote about her. I needed to do right by Marisol's story and still strike the balance that would appeal to the *Real Salt Lake* readers.

When sacrament meeting ended, Tanner leaned forward and rested his forearms on his knees so he could see past his sister to me.

"I'm surprised you're here," I said. "Running into you is becoming a habit." He wore charcoal gray pants and a deep navy shirt, a color that emphasized his gray eyes and dark hair. He dressed a little better every time I saw him.

"I overslept for my ward. I figured I might as well come to yours since I was coming down for dinner anyway," he said. "Noon makes so much more sense for a young adult ward than nine in the morning."

"True," I said and then didn't know what else to say. Courtney intervened.

"How did your dates go?" she asked. Tanner's eyebrow rose, maybe at the plural. Was it so ridiculous that multiple people might want to go out with me? I clamped down on my hunger crankiness and ignored his surprise.

"Fine," I said. "Except for the parts involving grievous bodily injury. That was bad."

"I can't wait to hear this," she said, grinning.

"There's something I can't wait to tell you, but it's not about the injury date. It's about the other one."

She looked intrigued. "Cool. What?"

I eyed the bishop's counselor who was herding people out of the chapel and toward Sunday School. "Let's grab a piece of couch, and I'll tell you." My invitation didn't include Tanner, but it didn't exclude him either, which is why he must have felt comfortable enough to join us when we moved to the foyer. I stared at him. He stared back. I shrugged and turned to Courtney, who sat between us.

"You know how I went out with that Josh guy on Friday night?" She nodded. "Turns out he's a pretty cool guy, but we didn't have any chemistry. However, I think you would like him." Courtney looked startled, but not nearly as startled as her brother. "Seriously," I said. "I asked him if he'd be interested in going out with you, and he said you were pretty cute and that it sounded like a good idea."

Tanner sat straight up and looked like he wanted to protest, but I glared at him, and he said nothing, probably because Courtney was already shaking her head. "That's sweet, but I don't think so," she said.

"Why not?" I asked. "Do you remember him?"

"Yes, but—"

"What? You said he was cute."

"Well, yeah. But that's when you were going on a date with him."

"So he's not cute now?"

"No, he is. I just—"

"Think you're not ready?" I asked, my tone gentle.

She hesitated and then nodded.

I studied her for a moment, assessing whether it was nerves or grief holding her back. I decided to trust my gut. "How will you know when you *are* ready unless you try? It's not a relationship. It's only a date."

She looked unconvinced, and I could tell Tanner wanted to break in. "You should go out with him," I said. "He's super mellow and easy to be around. And we can even do a double date so you'll be comfortable."

The crease between her eyebrows smoothed the tiniest bit. "Maybe, I guess. Who will you bring? Someone from Loo—"

I cut her off with a head shake. I didn't want Tanner to know I was on LDS Lookup because I didn't want to take the chance that he might figure out I was Indie Girl. It was one thing if everyone in my inner circle knew about it. It would humiliate me if Tanner discovered that I had been reduced to writing an Internet dating column. "I don't know who I'll bring," I hurried to say before Courtney revealed too much. "I'll figure it out by the time we set up a date."

Tanner spoke up. "I'll go."

Courtney and I both stared at him. "Where?" I asked.

"I'll go on this date."

"I didn't invite you," I protested. I turned to Courtney for help, sure she would hate the idea of her older brother tagging along, but relief showed on her face, and I sighed. "Would you rather double with Tanner and his date than me? It won't hurt my feelings if you do."

"No! I want you *both* there," she said. "You guys can go together, and then I'll have strength in numbers."

"But—"

Tanner cut off my protest. "Sounds fine. I don't like the idea of you going out with some stranger by yourself. When should we do this?"

I stared from one to the other, unsure how I had suddenly become committed to a date with Tanner, but they both stared back expectantly, Courtney's expression slightly doubtful. That clinched it for me. She wouldn't agree to go out with Josh any other way. If she wanted us along as a security blanket, then I could do that.

"I'll call Josh later, I guess. Maybe we'll set it up for this week, if that works."

Tanner shrugged, and Courtney nodded. "I guess so," she said with an unconvincing smile.

"Let's go to Sunday School," I said, hopping up.

"I'll meet you in there," she said. "I need a bathroom break."

Tanner followed me to class and took the seat next to me on the back row. My stomach gurgled again, and he smiled. "It's not funny," I said, barely louder than my stomach.

"Sure it is," he said. "Because it's happening to you."

That won him a reluctant smile.

"Your Urban Grit piece was good," he said. "Really good."

The compliment surprised me. It seemed out of character for him to have left a favorable comment on the website, much less give me one in person. But then again, what did I really know about his character? I'd been so put off by our interview that I'd formed all my assumptions about him based on that miserable fifteen minutes. He'd been slowly undoing that perception over the last two months with one small act after another. For once, my gut reaction wasn't to get defensive. I decided to take the compliment at face value.

"Thanks," I said. "I worked hard on it."

"It showed," he said. "How did you even hear about the company?"

I hesitated. "I'm still learning. Is this one of those cases where I'm not supposed to reveal my sources because I could get scooped?"

He shrugged. "Depends on what kind of journalist you want to be. Your mentor would probably advise against it."

"My mentor?"

"Ellie. Your boss?"

I resisted a scowl. "She's not my mentor."

He searched my expression like he could sense my scowl lurking between the words. "That's probably for the best," he said, his tone so neutral that I couldn't decide what to read from it.

I probed a little. "Did you ever work with her?"

"No. She was with the *Advocate* before she started the magazine."

"I know that, but didn't your paths ever cross while you were covering a story or something?"

His jaw hardened. "Sure," he said. "Our paths crossed."

His expression didn't invite further questions, so I dropped it. For the moment. But the mellow vibe between us had evaporated, and I wondered how to bring it back.

"I'm working on a new piece," I said.

He relaxed. "What's it about?"

"I went to the Latin Heritage Festival in Salt Lake yesterday, and I met this amazing girl, Marisol. I'm going to write about her."

"What's the angle?" he asked.

"I'm not sure yet," I admitted. "She's from Ciudad Juarez in Mexico. She had to leave last year because her brother got caught informing on one of the drug cartels to the DEA. At first, they harassed the family to make him quit. She used to sell her jewelry at a small shop in town, and they burned it down. She was in it and escaped with severe burns." The scars on the backs of her hands told the story in angry purple scrawls. It had sickened me to see them, not because they were ugly but because they told an ugly story of how evil people can be.

"Things escalated," I continued, as gripped in the retelling as I had been when she'd slowly unfolded the events that had led her to Salt Lake. "But her brother was determined to bring the local kingpin down. When he gave up some key details to the US government, the cousins hiding him betrayed him to protect themselves, and the cartel killed him. Marisol, her mother, and her little sister barely escaped a massacre in their neighborhood when the drug lord's foot soldiers shot up a community center and killed seventeen other people as a warning. Marisol and her family had been tipped off and were at home packing. They sneaked across the border and made their way to a distant cousin's home up here in West Valley. Now she's making and selling the most amazing jewelry to support her family, and I want to tell her story." The words poured out in a rush, and I took a deep breath to calm myself. It was hard not to get worked up over the injustice she had suffered and overcome.

Courtney appeared at the end of our row just then and made her way to us. The teacher welcomed the class, and I subsided. But interest glinted in Tanner's eyes, and I wanted his take on things. Quietly enough not to disturb the people around us, he leaned over and murmured, "I'm already distracted by your story. Want to go back out and talk about it?"

I nodded, thrilled that he wanted to talk to me. About the article, I mean. We climbed over Courtney's legs. She shot us a curious look but stayed put, and I followed Tanner to the foyer. We reclaimed the sofa, and he stretched his legs out in front of him and leaned back, staring into the distance without speaking. I studied the interesting planes and angles that made up his face. He was unarguably hot, and when he smiled, with his strong jaw and high cheekbones, he had an all-American quality to him. But now, as I looked at him with his brow furrowed and his eyes intense, I decided he was even hotter. Something about the concentration in his face as he puzzled out an approach to

Marisol's story made my insides flip, like maybe my spleen was doing a happy dance. I cleared my throat, although what I needed to do was clear my head. Or my spleen.

He glanced over. "Your audience is going to want to hear about the jewelry, right? Not the drug lord stuff?"

"Probably," I said. "But I want to work it in. She's sending a huge chunk of her profits home on a remittance to her grandmother, and I want people to understand why."

"But *Real Salt Lake* readers are going to be looking for something that tells them where to shop, eat, or dance next, right?"

"That's not all we're about," I said, bristling that he would reduce us to a simple trend magazine.

"Yes, it is," he said. "But you get major credit for trying to bring something else to it besides a sense of your own importance and an overrated value of your opinions."

I raised an eyebrow. "Is there a compliment buried in there?"

"What's the *Real Salt Lake* tag line? 'Hip, Hot, Happening'? That magazine thrives on opinion-driven stories written by people who have an overinflated sense of themselves and their ability to judge what's cool. In that sense, they've put together the right staff to write for their audience. The hipsters who read your magazine love nothing better than to feel like they're on the inside of an exclusive club with people who think exactly like they do."

My jaw dropped. How could he say such incredibly insulting things in such a reasonable tone of voice? Especially after he'd complimented my work on the Kirbi Dawn piece? I pushed up from the sofa, but he reached out and snared my wrist, holding me in place.

"You're the exception," he said. "Don't be mad."

I looked down at his hand on my wrist and wondered if the heat from it would brand me with finger-shaped marks, a permanent reminder of a guy I found fascinating and infuriating all at the same time. I relaxed, and he loosened his hold but didn't let go. "You should definitely write about Marisol. Just do it in a way that readers will want to buy her jewelry and then be able to feel like they're making a statement for social justice at the same time."

"I already knew that's where I needed to go with it," I said, reclaiming ownership of my wrist. His assessment of *Real Salt Lake* still stung. "I want even more . . . layers, I guess."

He stared off into the distance for another moment or two and then refocused. "Don't make Marisol the story," he said. "Make each piece she designs the story. Then your readers will stay interested in the style side of things—"

"But I get to unfold her story anyway as I tell about the jewelry," I finished for him, realizing exactly where he was going.

He nodded. "Yeah. That should do it."

"If you weren't already so annoying, I'd totally tell you how genius that is." I wasn't ready to forgive him yet, but there was no denying it was the perfect approach.

He tilted his head and regarded me with a half smile playing around his lips. "Don't worry about it. I already know."

I laughed, knowing he was poking fun at himself. I liked that he could do that. These few minutes on the couch with Tanner were a perfect mirror to reflect every interaction we'd had—equal parts frustrating and exhilarating. I braced for every encounter with him, expecting him to make me mad, which he did. And then at some point, he always surprised me with a glimpse at the Tanner beneath his brusque professional facade. There was the Tanner who made scathing remarks about his competition's publication, and there was the Tanner who hung out with his kid sister a couple of times a week because he worried about her. Tanner Graham, the enigma.

"So tell me again when this double date is going to be," he said.

"It's not a double date. It's Josh and Courtney's date, and you and I are tagging along."

"Whatever. When is it?"

"I have no idea," I said. "I have to call Josh."

Tanner didn't say anything for a moment; he watched me like he was trying to figure something out. "Are you sure he's going to be okay with substituting Courtney for you?"

"Yeah. No chemistry. He thinks she's cute."

"No chemistry," Tanner muttered, and in an absent-minded gesture, his hand closed around my wrist again. He was still staring off, and I wondered what was running through his mind and what it meant that he was touching me without thinking about it, like it was the most natural thing in the world.

"Yeah. No chemistry," I said, flexing my wrist.

Startled, he glanced down and let go. Then he smiled. "None."

I let the little bubble of . . . something settle between us. And finally, when the silence grew too fraught, I broke. And I broke it. "Thanks for the story help," I said. "I'm going to go find Courtney."

"I bet she's still in the same seat."

My cheeks grew pink as he poked a hole in my excuse for leaving. I didn't know what I was running away from, but the urgent need to break away and breathe fueled my escape. Breathe air that didn't have the light, spicy scent of him in it. Just breathe.

I slid off the couch and straightened my soft-gray, corduroy, A-line skirt, so my hands had something to do. "I'll call Courtney with the details for our . . ."

"Date," he finished. "It's called a date."

"I think it's more like babysitting. That's what you're doing, right?"

He shrugged and held my gaze. "Maybe."

I cleared my throat. "I'm going to go."

He smiled. After another awkward pause, I turned and fled to the cultural hall and my seat beside Courtney, where I took a deep breath because I finally could.

"Everything okay?" she whispered.

"Maybe." I smiled, surprising myself. "Maybe it is."

Dear Mr. Handy,

I truly appreciate you for hiring me almost a year ago, and I am thankful I've had a job during a time when so many other people are struggling to make ends meet.

Things change, I guess. Even when we don't expect them to. If we're lucky, we make our breaks. Or maybe we at least manage to go with the flow when the tides of change come.

Then again, some things never change, like the Rust Bucket. She's going to give up the ghost soon, and I don't think Austin will get the same service from Nelson and Sons that I do. You might want to consider a new freezer. Like, consider it really strongly.

Again, I want to sincerely thank you for the opportunity to earn a paycheck when a lot of others don't. I've learned more than I expected to, like approximately fifty ways to use vinegar and why yeast really does matter. Life, lessons, Mr. Handy. Life lessons.

Sincerely,
Pepper Spicer

Chapter 14

For eight months, I'd wallowed at the bottom of a rut I'd dug. After breaking up with Landon, I went into retreat mode, a reasonable thing to do given how long we'd been together and how much it hurt to realize he loved me because I was convenient. I'd never gone through a major breakup before, but if I'm supposed to believe books and movies, right around the time I should have emerged from my emotional hibernation, the media blitz for *The It Factor* hit, and I burrowed deeper. Landon was everywhere, especially in the Utah news because of his hometown roots. It was like death by paper cuts every time I heard a report or saw his face on TV or in the *Bee*, even though my dad generally tried to hide the Arts section when it ran a story on Landon.

For eight months, I lived in a routine of sameness. Get up, face the day in my Handy's Sandwich shirt, come home and sulk on my blog, and slowly pay off wedding debt. Wash, rinse, repeat. Given the sameness and the excruciating slowness that defined everything in my life, I was shocked to discover that life could move so fast it was like old-school Star Trek warp drive.

In the three months since I had taken my dad's challenge, everything had changed. It started when I sent out my first batch of résumés, but it blew up when my replay of the Rhys date hit. I knew something was up when I walked into the kitchen Tuesday morning to find Mace hunched over a plate of French toast, staring at my dad's laptop and chuckling, each laugh louder and longer than the one before it.

"Something good on YouTube?" I made my way to the fridge in search of tortillas. It was a breakfast burrito kind of morning.

"Nah," he said and laughed again. "Oh man. This is good."

"What is it?"

"Your column."

I couldn't contain my grin. "You like it?"

"Dang, Pepper. I forgot how funny you can be when you're not pouting."

I threw a potholder at him. "Thanks."

He pushed back from the table and brought his plate over to the sink. "Man. I wish I could tell my English teacher it's you writing this. She loves your column. I'd probably get an A just for being your brother."

"Your English teacher reads 'Single in the City'?" I asked. Ginger wandered in and edged me out for space in front of the crisper drawer, where I rummaged for a bell pepper.

"Everyone reads it. Duh."

Classic delivery of a compliment, Ginger-style.

Rosemary trailed in behind my mother, frowning as she tried to tug the stubborn strap of her Disney princess backpack over her shoulder. "I didn't tell anyone it's you!"

"Okay. Thanks," I said. She looked proud of herself. "Way to keep a secret."

"It's up today?" my mom asked.

"Yeah. It's a good one," Mace told her on his way back up the stairs.

"Wait for me," my dad said. He pulled up his chair next to my mom's and within seconds, the giggling started, growing into a full-blown guffaw after a minute.

"I don't know what to think about the fact that the column making the most fun of me is the one that makes you laugh the hardest," I grumbled, but I was pleased.

My dad didn't say anything for a moment, finishing the column with a few more laughs, and then he stood and walked over to hug me. "You should think that we love your sense of humor and we're so glad to see you able to laugh at yourself again."

He relaxed his bear hug and headed out for his office. "Well done, daughter!" he called over his shoulder.

"Mom?" I asked, wanting her input too.

"I was about to say I wish I had been there to see this, but honestly, the way you wrote it made me feel like I was." She tapped the screen. "'Fear enlarged Sir Hottie's remaining good eye until it eclipsed his bright-blue regulation Frisbee when he saw me coming at him again, even though I waved an Alaska-sized cup full of ice as a peace-offering.' Brilliant," she said.

A text dinged on my phone, and I snatched it from the counter. It was from Courtney and read, *HAHAHAHAHAHA*.

I scooped my burrito up and sat at the table to read the column while I ate. I could probably recite it word for word, but there was something about seeing it official with the Indie Girl byline and the graphic they used in place of my picture. It showed a girl with a fall of dark hair hiding all but the curve of her cheek and one downcast eye. It was mysterious and artsy. And a little misleading since my hair wasn't nearly long enough or well-behaved enough to drape that way. But I loved the slick production values on it and the way it said, "This is a real column written by a real writer."

In past weeks, I'd grown used to seeing reader comments on the date recaps show up toward the afternoon of the first day they were posted, hitting a peak of around fifty after a day or two and tapering off toward the end of the week. This morning, more than two dozen comments already waited for me. I read through them, delighted. They ranged from single word comments like, "Awesome!" to paragraph length responses from a couple people who shared their own horror stories. Even with the use of screen names, it was easy to tell that most of the commenters were women, but there were a few guys who chimed in. The tone from all five guys was of the good-natured "glad it wasn't me" variety. One joker added, "I'm not good-looking enough to make you nervous. Can we count this as meeting online? Then you could go out with me."

The house quieted as everyone left for school and work, and I savored the rest of my breakfast as I read each new comment that posted. This should go quite a ways in my negotiation with Ellie for something a little more full time and permanent, especially given the presence of three shiny new banner ads at the top of my column's page. Business must be looking up. I had thought long and hard over the last several days about how to approach Ellie. I'd gone so far as to e-mail Chantelle and ask her advice, counting on her dislike of Ellie to win her help. Chantelle confirmed that based on everything she was hearing, my column was the biggest thing to hit *Real Salt Lake*. "Use that to your advantage," she e-mailed back. "Ellie is using it to hers, and you deserve a slice of that pie."

When my phone rang an hour before I had to be at Handy's, I wasn't at all surprised to see Ellie's number. She had a hit on her hands, and we both knew it. I answered, curious about what approach she would take when I asked for a permanent position.

"I loved it," she said. "Great column."

"Thanks," I said.

"You should work this angle more in the future," she advised. "You struck a nerve today. Or maybe a funny bone."

It was time to test the waters. "About the future," I started.

"Yes?" she said, her tone guarded.

"How are we doing on the page clicks?"

She cleared her throat. "I think you'll be happy with your check. I'm pretty sure you're going to max out this week, so that means the full amount."

"That's great," I said. "But it seems like if the page gets even more views than that, it's more valuable than what I'm being paid."

"This is a new feature," she said. "It'll take more time to gauge the impact of your column on traffic and advertising."

"Why? It seems like it should be easy to figure out how many people are reading my stuff. It should also be fairly easy to ask advertisers what draws them to spend money with you, right?" The instinct that "Single in the City" had suddenly become a key selling point for Ellie emboldened me to pin her down.

"It doesn't work like that," she said, refusing to be pinned. "We need to watch trends and see what's happening over time."

Talking and saying nothing was a talent all its own, I decided. I tried a different strategy. "But if you're specifically talking up my column to get more ad dollars, then it's only fair that I get a bigger piece of the cut." It's not what I wanted, but I gambled on it getting me my real goal.

"That's not our agreement," she said. "The whole point of running your feature is to attract new advertisers. Your pay is based on what we projected to bring in. Now that we're bringing that in, if we pay you over what we discussed, we lose the margin of profitability that was the point of the whole column in the first place."

I figured that was likely the case, and a knot formed in my stomach over facing off with her, even though it was a calm discussion. Then I pictured myself hanging up the phone and putting on my worn-out Handy's shirt, and I couldn't take it. I hated the thought of spending one more day there than I had to. The last three months had taught me that I had some control over what was happening in my life, and if I made good choices, I might see good results. I took a breath, and then I took the plunge, reaching the point of my amateur negotiations.

"My work with my real byline gets a good response too," I said.

"It does," Ellie conceded. "But that's not what drives readers and advertisers to our site."

"I don't have access to all your sales data"—which was a growing problem—"but I think maybe people are starting to show up for music reviews. And the only reason we don't know whether they're showing up for my features is that I've only gotten to write one. But you were happy with that one, right?"

"I was," she said. "And you're welcome to turn in more freelance pieces. You're working on something now, aren't you?"

"Yeah, but it's hard because I have to work full time somewhere else, and that's kind of my point. Maybe you can't pay me more for the Indie Girl stuff, but I've shown that you're going to get your value back if you pay me to write full time on stories outside of the dating and music pieces. You could fold the checks you already write me for the column into my salary which, okay, is going to cost you more, but you're going to get way more writing out of me. And build more readers by keeping the 'Single in the City' column."

"What do you mean, 'keeping' the column?" she asked, her voice sharp.

This is where I had to step very, very carefully. This is where I wished I had gone to business school or studied something that taught me about real negotiations. Heck, I'd give anything to freeze time and cram in a marathon of *The Apprentice* before broaching my next argument to her, but it was now or never. I breathed deeply and tested how much leverage "Single in the City" really gave me. "I can't keep writing that column if it's not going to pay off career-wise," I said. "It's a huge emotional and time commitment, and there's a point where it doesn't make sense for me to do it anymore, especially since I do it anonymously. It's hard to use it to build my résumé."

Ellie was silent for a long moment, and the knot in my stomach compressed on itself, becoming denser and nearly painful while I waited to see what I had gained or lost with my thinly veiled threat. *Stay calm*, I admonished myself. *It's Ellie's steely nerves that make her so intimidating. Keep it together; keep it together.*

"If you quit writing the column, I can find someone else to write it," she said. "That's the beauty of the Indie Girl byline."

"I know you can replace me. Eventually. But that's the problem, right? You told me you were having a harder time than you'd expected until I came along. Are you going to lose a lot of buzz while you go looking for a replacement? And will you be able to find someone who can strike the same tone?"

She fell silent again, but I could practically hear her thoughts scrambling to organize themselves into a counterargument. For a full twenty seconds, she didn't say anything, so I took the kill shot. "Look, I'm not asking for a bunch of money without offering any return on investment. I'll write way more and go far above and beyond in earning my keep. But I can't keep up this pace with two jobs plus dates and concert reviews. I'm exhausted, and I can't quit Handy's unless you make me full time at the magazine."

"I have to think about this," she said. Most likely she had to think about whether she had a way around me.

"I understand," I said. "If you decide that we can make this work, I have an amazing feature about a local jewelry maker to hand in."

She exhaled, her exasperation evident. "You're playing hard ball, aren't you?"

"I'm trying to find a solution we can all live with," I countered. When I hung up after her vague, "I'll call you later," I dropped my head onto my arms and stared at the worn wooden table beneath them. Maybe I would pull this off and get full-time status. I told Ellie the truth when I said that the two jobs were taking their toll. It got harder each week to fit it all in. On the other hand, I might have totally ruined everything. Ellie might be able to line up another option for the "Single in the City" spot, and I would have zero leverage and no job. Except for sandwich making, which beckoned . . . I hoped for the very last time.

* * *

I yanked my phone out of my apron again near the end of my shift, wondering if maybe it had shut itself off or if I wasn't getting a signal. I hoped so. Otherwise, I had no other theories as to why I hadn't heard from Ellie yet. The power was on, and it showed full bars. I glanced over at Austin, the assistant I had hired the month before in the fond hope I could off-load my job to him when things got going with *Real Salt Lake*. Sadly for both of us, it looked like I might be staying put at Handy's and maybe even cutting back his hours so I could go back to forty hours a week. It stank.

I yelped when my phone vibrated with an incoming call, and Austin eyed me in concern. I checked the caller ID. Ellie. After a deep breath, I answered.

"We moved some things around," she said. "I'd like to offer you a full-time position."

"Yes!"

"Don't get too excited," she said. "It comes with conditions. You'll get the grunt stories. Features you write will be on your own time, and I won't pay extra for them anymore. Doing them will be up to you. And you're getting entry-level pay, so don't get excited about the money." She quoted a salary that beat Handy's by nearly five bucks an hour, a note of an apology in her voice.

I knew she was trying to dampen my excitement so I would decide it was smarter to stay at Handy's, but as my eye fell on the table in front of me, with its caked-on mustard smears, I didn't care. I didn't want to be here one second longer than I had to, and she was handing me my ticket out. And she had no idea she'd given me a huge raise. "Still yes!" I almost choked in my eagerness to accept.

"All right," she said. "I know you have to give notice, so we'll expect you to start in two weeks."

"No," I said. "I can start tomorrow." Austin would be glad to get the hours, and I could easily tweak the schedule to replace myself. I'd help Austin find an assistant for himself if he needed me to, but for all intents and purposes . . . I was free!

"Thank you so much, Ellie! You will *not* be sorry. I'm going to make you so glad you did this!"

"You'd better." She sighed.

Even that less-than-stellar "welcome to the team" couldn't tank my mood. I ended the call, stared at Austin, who had heard enough to figure out what had happened, and grinned.

"Congratulations!" I shouted. "You're promoted!"

He gave me a good-natured fist bump and waved his arm to encompass all of Handy's. "I can't believe it's finally mine," he said with an eye roll.

"I'd tell you that you deserve it, but you're too nice a guy for that. So I'll just say good luck."

"You too. I like your concert reviews. I'm sure your other writing will be great too."

"Thanks, Austin." I glanced up at the clock, noting that we had only a half hour before our part-timer came in to finish out the evening shift with him. "If you don't mind, I'm going to go write a letter to Mr. Handy."

"Do it," he said. "I can handle it out here." His smile acknowledged the temporary lull in customers.

I sat down at my desk and texted Courtney. *The mag's hiring me full time!!!!! Ellie just called!*

Fewer than two sentences into my resignation letter, I got a text back. *Whoo hoo! I'll pick you up at 7:30 to celebrate!*

I drafted the rest of the letter quickly but made sure the thanks to my soon-to-be-ex-boss was heartfelt. It might not have been my dream job, but Mr. Handy had given me my first opportunity to begin digging myself out of debt. It wasn't his fault I had grown to hate making sandwiches. And he was easy to work for, always staying out of my way.

As soon as I scrawled my signature, I stuffed the letter into an envelope and stuck it up near the register for the postman to pick up, knowing it would make my exit final. But it didn't make me nervous. I had gotten used to the idea of making my own luck over the last few weeks, and I felt really, really sure that I had made the right move. When I walked out to my car, I didn't look back.

I wouldn't be looking back anymore.

* * *

At seven-thirty on the dot, I yanked the door open and smiled but faltered when instead of finding Courtney on my doorstep, I found Tanner.

"Hi," I said because nothing else came to mind.

"Congratulations. Courtney told me you're going to be full time now."

"True story," I said, leaning slightly to the left to see if Courtney was waiting in the car.

"She's at my parents' house," he said. "She's trying to put a little thing together for you, and she wasn't done yet, so I told her I'd come get you."

"All right," I said. "Come in for a minute, and I'll go grab my sweater."

He stepped in and shut the door behind him. I panicked for a split second, trying to figure out what to do with him. Did I just leave him standing there? Should I—

"Who's this?" Ginger asked, strolling out from the living room.

"This is Tanner," I said. "Courtney's brother."

"Where's Courtney?" she asked.

"Never mind," I said. "Can you go grab my black cardigan off my bed?" There was no way I was leaving her alone with Tanner. She'd either practice her flirting or grill him with questions, and I didn't like either scenario.

"Fetch your own sweater," she said, not even looking at me. "I'm going to talk to Tanner."

"No, you're not," my mom said, coming out of the living room as well. "Go get Pepper's sweater."

Ginger grumbled but turned and stomped up the stairs, each muffled thud of her bare feet on the carpeted steps intended to communicate her displeasure. Hmm. Not very intimidating.

"You're Tanner?" my mom asked, and her voice gave no indication as to whether that was a good or bad thing. Tanner might not realize it, but Mama Bear had just shown up. I'd have to muzzle her for Tanner's safety.

"Yes," he said, holding his hand out for a handshake. She took it but still didn't smile.

"Tanner came to pick me up to celebrate my promotion," I said, sounding chipper to indicate that it was okay for him to be here.

She eyed me before relaxing enough to crack a smile. A very small smile. I hoped Tanner didn't blink, or he would have missed it.

"Grant!" she called to my dad, who was still in the living room. "Tanner's here!"

I tried not to wince. Tanner was going to infer that he was a major topic of conversation around here, what with all the knowing glances flying around. I didn't want Tanner to take it the wrong way. I mean, I wanted him to realize everyone knew his name because he didn't hire me for the *Bee*, not because I liked him or something.

Sorry, I mouthed to him. He smiled and gave me a slight nod, his eyes twinkling. My dad stepped into view and shot me a glance of concern. "*Tanner* is here?" he asked, although there was clearly a stranger of male persuasion standing right in front of him.

"Yes, Dad. This is Tanner." They shook hands, my dad's face not softening any more than my mom's had. "He came to pick me up to celebrate my promotion."

My dad's eyebrow shot up. "That's nice of you. It's great to see Pepper's talent recognized."

It was a not-so-veiled criticism, and I loved him for it, but when I heard Tanner choke down a laugh, I decided enough was enough. "Be nice to him, please. He was right not to hire me and has helped me a lot since then."

My mom and dad exchanged a look, and my mom gave my dad a slight nod. Years of experience helped me interpret the entire conversation that passed between them in those two seconds. My mom said, "Do we give this guy a chance?" and my dad said, "I will if you will," and my mom said, "Fine. I'll be nice because Pepper asked us to."

What Tanner heard was my mom asking him if he'd like to come in for some ice cream, but I put a hand on Tanner's arm to keep him in place. "Tanner's only here because Courtney asked him to come and get me. We better get going."

He placed his hand over mine and said, "Actually, she'd probably like a little more time to get things ready. I'd love some ice cream." I tried to tug my hand back, but he kept his grip. Rather than make a scene, I left it there.

"Great," my dad said. "Come on in."

They turned toward the kitchen, and I finally yanked my hand away so I could follow, shooting Tanner a what-are-you-doing look on the way. He grinned. My eye twitched in time to the flips my stomach executed. How annoying. Our kitchen wasn't nearly as upscale as his parents', but it had all the same welcome.

"Have a seat," my mom said, her tone now several degrees warmer. "I'll get the mint chip."

We each pulled out a chair, and my dad studied Tanner with a thoughtful expression that I knew meant he was doing some analyzing. "Excuse the mess," he said, referring to the stray pieces of popcorn and other baking ingredients still cluttering the countertop. "We threw together an impromptu celebration for Pepper too, and the only thing I could think of to make was popcorn balls."

"Good choice," Tanner said. "Did you sing 'Popcorn Popping'?"

"Of course," my dad said, sounding dignified. "Any proper celebration requires singing to go with the feasting."

I stared at him for a second before I burst out laughing. "To hear him, you'd never think he was doing the disco version less than an hour ago."

"His hip hop version is better," Ginger said, walking in with my cardigan. I took it from her and smiled in dismissal, but she ignored me and pulled up a chair.

"Hi, Tanner."

It sounded like she was purring. I thought about rescuing him for a minute but then decided it would be funnier if I didn't.

"Hi. You must be Ginger," he said. I was impressed that he remembered her name. I'd only mentioned it once.

"I am. What brings you over tonight?" she asked.

"Asked and answered," my mom said. "He's picking up Pepper for Courtney. Don't make him repeat himself, sweetie."

Ginger pouted. "Don't send me out of the room, and then I won't miss anything."

My mom brought over two bowls of ice cream and set them down in front of my dad and Tanner then went back for more.

"I don't want any, Mom. I have to watch my figure," Ginger said.

Watch her figure? It sounded like something my grandmother would say. Tanner looked nonplussed. There wasn't an appropriate way to respond to that, so he kept his mouth shut. Smart guy. My dad decided to rein Ginger in before she got too outrageous.

"Where's Rosemary?" he asked. "I can't believe she hasn't come in here yet."

"She's still watching *Beauty and the Beast*," Ginger said. "She won't go anywhere until it's over."

"You better make sure she's all right in there," my dad said.

"But—"

"No, really. Go check on her." His voice was polite but brooked no argument.

She huffed and went to find Rosemary. That would take care of her for a while.

My mom joined us with two more bowls of ice cream. "How goes it at the *Bee*?" she asked Tanner.

"It's good," he said. "There's always news somewhere."

"I've read your articles," she said. "You write well."

That surprised me. She'd never mentioned reading his articles before.

"Thank you," he said. "I love doing it."

"It shows," my dad said.

What? He was reading Tanner's stuff too? Man, between the three of us, we were well on our way to supporting the journalism career of my nemesis. Only I didn't feel much enmity toward him at the moment. The mint chocolate chip was mellowing me. Oh, who was I kidding? Spending time around Tanner was mellowing me. He was beginning to resemble a human. He was *maybe* even likable.

I listened as my dad and Tanner shot the breeze about sports, the season the Jazz were having, and whether BYU football had a shot in the fall. I took my time with my ice cream, listening but not adding much. I did most of the talking when I was around Tanner, and it was enlightening to sit back and observe. He had an easy way about him with my parents, relaxed but still respectful. He never jumped in on anyone else's sentences, waiting for them to finish before he spoke. He bore the ribbing from my mom, a University of Utah graduate, with good grace when she teased him about BYU's dismal football record against the U over the past few years.

With a straight face, he sighed and said, "I know. It's because the coach never puts me in."

This cracked both of my parents up. I liked that this pleased him, that he wanted to make them smile.

Even after the ice cream was gone, I didn't say anything unless asked a direct question. Finally, Ginger popped back in, fed up with her banishment, and Rosemary followed her. "More celebrating?" Rosemary asked in delight upon seeing our empty bowls.

"Yes," my mom said. "Pepper deserves it."

Rosemary walked up to Tanner and regarded him with a friendly tilt of her head, like a puppy might examine a stranger in her play yard. "Who are you?" she asked.

"I'm Tanner," he answered.

"Oh! Like Too Good Tanner?"

I winced at the nickname she'd obviously heard me give him in some of my older rants.

He smothered a smile. "Yes, I think that's me." He held out his hand for a shake, and she accepted it. "You must be Rosemary. Pleased to meet you."

Her delighted expression revealed how much she enjoyed this grownup ritual. "I like him way better than Landon," she said, a smile on her face.

My dad cleared his throat. "I believe you mentioned that Courtney is waiting. We shouldn't keep you."

My cheeks burned at the mention of Landon's name, but I appreciated my dad's save. I so wasn't in the mood for any questions about him. Tanner took the hint and pushed back from the table.

"Thanks for the ice cream, Sister Spicer. It was great," he said. He turned to me. "We should go see what Courtney is up to. You ready?"

I stood and pulled on my cardigan. "Ready."

I followed him out to the car, thanked him for opening my door, and waited while he fiddled with the dials on the dashboard, making sure I had no cold air blowing on me from the vents. When he pulled onto the street, I chose and discarded three different conversation starters before I settled on, "I'm surprised to see you here on a Tuesday night. Don't you usually come down on Thursday?"

He shrugged. "When Courtney texted me that you got a full-time slot, I wanted to join the celebration."

Startled, I sat up straight and stared at him. "You drove down here just because of this?"

He smiled out at the road. "Yeah."

I blew out a breath because I didn't know what to say and slumped back into my seat. "You make no sense."

His smile quirked a little wider. "Why not?"

"Until recently, I was under the impression that you hated me."

"And why would you think that?"

"You know. You were there."

He laughed. "Neither of us had our best moment at that interview . . . that happened three months ago, by the way. What else?"

I sighed. "I don't know. You don't say much to me when we hang out."

"*We* don't hang out. You and Courtney hang out, and I hang around."

"Same thing," I said.

"Not really. You guys do your thing, and if it doesn't put my Y chromosomes at risk, I tag along."

My confusion only deepened. "Why do it if you think it's lame?" I asked. "Courtney doesn't need a babysitter, and even if she did, I'm qualified to do it." I knew there was a bigger truth lurking, something that had more to do with Tanner and me, but it wouldn't gel. Or maybe I didn't want it to.

Or maybe I wanted to hear it from Tanner.

He said nothing, but he shifted slightly to slip his phone from his pocket and speed dial a number. I was learning not to rush him, so I waited. A moment later he said, "Would you care if we're late? Good. How about if we don't make it all?"

I heard a whoop, definitely Courtney's, through the phone. Tanner grinned and said, "See you later. Or possibly not."

"It was nice of you to ask *her*," I said, my arms crossed over my chest.

"Didn't want to worry her."

That was it. That was all he said. I pointed out the small flaw in his thoughtfulness. "You didn't ask *me*."

He sighed again, but it sounded amused rather than annoyed. "Pepper, would you mind if we skipped the celebration with Courtney and headed somewhere else to talk?"

I paused to make him squirm. I saw no evidence that I had succeeded, but I hoped I made him worry for at least a small moment. "That might be my least favorite phrase in English," I said.

He took his eyes off the road to shoot me a quick questioning glance, so I clarified.

"*We need to talk.* I hate that sentence." But I knew my voice carried no heat.

"That's not what I said," he pointed out. "We don't *need* to talk about anything. But I'd like to."

"Curiosity will kill me if I don't," I said.

He smiled. "If that's what it takes." He drove us slightly northwest, and soon the graceful shape of the Mount Timpanogos temple rose in front of us, looming larger by the minute.

I shot him a sharp glance. Was he kidding? He says he wants to talk, cancels my plans with his sister, and then drives me to the temple? My stomach clenched, and I fought the urge to press my hand against it and reveal my distress. *It didn't mean anything*, I argued. *He probably picked it because it's quiet.* But when I felt the distinct sensation of acid churning somewhere near my gut, I knew my brain hadn't sold my stomach on the argument. Well . . . maybe he wasn't going to the temple. Maybe there was a nearby park or something . . . but that hope faded as he turned onto the road that would take us straight there.

"Is this okay with you?" he asked, pulling into the temple parking lot.

Don't overreact, I repeated about two thousand times in my head before I mustered my calmest voice to say, "Sure."

He killed the engine and gave me a long, searching look. I tried not to show panic. A full minute must have passed as he stared at me earnestly, and I stayed frozen, a tragic smile on my face intended to communicate that I wasn't at all freaked out. Then I saw it—the tiniest twitch at the corner of his mouth. I narrowed my eyes, and I saw it again, only this time it was nearly a tremor.

"You rat!" I cuffed his arm, and he burst out laughing, the first time I'd ever heard him let loose without any hint of irony or detached amusement. I smacked him again.

"I'm sorry," he gasped, wiping at an eye. "But you looked so terrified at the idea of talking that I couldn't resist. Did you think I was going to propose?" And that set him off again, laughing so hard he clutched his side.

At first, I glared at him, my arms crossed and my jaw clenched. But then I realized how completely ridiculous the situation was, and a smile threatened to ruin my scowl. "It happens all the time, you know."

He subsided into a grin and turned to face me, resettling himself in his seat without the restriction of his seat belt. "What does?"

"Proposals. You can't be too careful when you're a prize like me."

He sobered. "I believe it. How many proposals do you figure you've gotten just in the last year?"

I paused to count. "Forty-seven."

He considered that with a nod. "I would have guessed more, to be honest."

"It's hard to be me."

He leaned his head against his headrest and smiled again. "I think it would be interesting to be you. It would be nice to have access to the way your brain works."

Taken aback, I stared at him. "I promise you, it's pretty boring."

"Nah," he said.

I waited for more, but that was it. I guess I should have learned from reading his articles every day that Tanner believed in the efficient use of words. Fine. "You wanted to talk? Talk," I said, with a sweep of my hand to suggest that the floor was his.

"Yeah." He paused like he was collecting his thoughts. "I'm not great at doublespeak, Pepper. I pretty much say what I mean."

"I've noticed."

"Then I'm going to be blunt, if that's okay."

"Um, sure?" What was going on here?

"This double date with Courtney and Josh. When is that going to happen?"

I shrugged. "Probably next week, if it works with everyone's schedule." It hadn't been at the top of my list since I had so many other things demanding my time, but quitting Handy's opened a bunch of slots in my schedule.

"I know you think I invited myself so I could babysit Courtney, but I didn't." He rustled a little in his seat, finally situating himself the exact same way he'd been sitting before, except for his head was no longer resting on the back of the seat, and his fingers drummed the console between us in a fast staccato. I doubted he realized he was doing it. His uneasiness fascinated me.

He cleared his throat. "I want that to be a real date."

There it was again, that efficiency with words.

No "I was thinking maybe . . ."

No "How would you feel about . . . ?"

I realized I was letting his delivery distract me from his message because no part of my brain could process that statement at the moment.

It wasn't a surprise, exactly. But I wasn't sure how I felt about it. Did I want to go on a "real" date with Tanner? I'd long gotten over the interview. And I'd had time over the last couple months to get a sense of him through his writing and watching him interact with his family. I'd progressed from feeling stressed the first time I'd seen him to not minding when he showed up to . . . looking forward to it, honestly. But this announcement. What did I think? What did I want? The drum of his fingers stopped, and I glanced up to find him watching me, his expression wary.

"Sometimes I think better if I'm busy," I said.

"Let's walk." He didn't sound annoyed. He climbed out of the car and came around to open my door. I stood and found myself with my nose nearly nestled at the base of his neck, the closest I'd ever been to him, and another spark leapt between us. He rested his hands on my shoulders, and a split second before I could panic about why, he shifted me to the side and shut my car door, his movements calm and deliberate. But I wasn't fooled. I caught the tiniest twitch of his lips again.

"You're trying to throw me off balance," I said.

"I was trying to help you keep your balance while I closed your door," he said.

"No, you weren't. Admit it. You wanted to freak me out a little."

"How?" he asked, amused.

Making me think you were going to kiss me. No way would I give him the satisfaction of saying it out loud. "You know."

"I know you're playing pot to my kettle. You're the one keeping me off balance."

I flushed, knowing it was true because I hadn't answered him. "I'm not doing it on purpose," I muttered.

"No," he agreed. "*This* would be on purpose." And he took a step forward, which caused me to take a step back, putting me right up against the car. My pulse accelerated.

"Big difference," I agreed, struggling to keep my voice even.

He leaned in until only a whisper separated our lips. "Off balance yet?"

I swallowed. "I would be, if the car weren't keeping me from falling over."

"Wouldn't want you to fall," he said.

"Falling would be bad," I said, and this time a whisper was the most I could force out of my throat. Every part of me was frozen, but not the icy kind of frozen. It was like the stillness of a photograph where you witness a perfect moment captured in time. In the same way that a scene changes in the instant the camera captures a shot, whether you notice the difference or not, everything changed between us too. But the change was in the tiny fraction of space that Tanner closed between us, when his mouth touched mine and the gentle brush of his lips drew a sigh from me I didn't know I was holding. He smiled against my mouth and then kissed me again. I clutched a fistful of his shirt because suddenly his Honda didn't offer nearly enough support.

His hands rose to rest against the car on either side of my head, and the kiss grew more intense, shifting from a mischievous hello to an exploration that buckled my knees beneath me. I tightened my hold on his shirt, the only anchor I had in the crazy flood trying to sweep me away. When he lifted his head, my hand slipped around to his bicep because I was still trying to find my balance, and he cupped my elbow to steady me. I'd have felt stupid, but I could see by the dazed look in his eyes that he might need the help as much as I needed it.

I drew one long breath and then another before I let go of his arm, regretfully, since it was a well-formed bicep, and straightened. He took a step back and shoved his hands in his pockets. Neither of us said anything for a moment.

I cleared my throat. "We were going to walk?"

He nodded, and we took the few steps to the sidewalk and several beyond that in silence.

"How's your thinker?" he asked after awhile.

"Muddled," I said.

"Is it such a hard question? You can feel free to answer with just a yes or no," he said, a note of humor in his tone.

"Remind me of the question again."

"What do you think about going on a real date?"

"I was afraid that was still the question," I said with a sigh.

"So that's a no?"

"Unfortunately, it's not a yes or no question."

I wanted to say yes. There were a lot of reasons to say no. But I still wanted to say yes—and that was a problem. His kiss—that crazy, knee-weakening kiss—begged for me to yell, "Yes, and more kissing, please!" I didn't, but it was close.

"I didn't realize you were an overthinker." He sounded relaxed, which surprised me. I'd be feeling foolish and defensive if our roles were reversed.

"I never used to be," I said. "I've always been a go-with-the-flow kind of girl. But life happens, and now I'm more of a once-burned-twice-shy kind of girl."

A handful of patrons carrying small suitcases wandered between the parking lot and the temple doors, but the grounds were empty of other visitors. We ambled along a little farther, now rounding the front entrance to the temple, and I peered at the edges of blossoms barely visible as they lay curled up for the night. Tanner's expression stayed thoughtful, and he didn't seem bent on trying to change my mind.

"Is this coming a little out of left field?" he asked.

"A little." On the one hand, he'd confirmed the chemistry I sensed between us. On the other, it surprised me that he would see us as a good fit, considering our rocky history.

"What do you think we should do?" he asked. "Be buddies and wave hello when we bump into each other at my parents' house?"

Wait. Was he withdrawing his date invitation? I might not be totally sure of our next step, but I definitely didn't like *that* idea.

"No," I said.

Look who was practicing efficiency with words now.

"No? You don't want to be buddies?" For the first time, he sounded confused.

"No."

I walked another couple steps before I realized he'd stopped, and I turned around to stare at him. He stood in the middle of the sidewalk with his hands in his pockets, looking exasperated but highly amused. "You're not making any sense," he said. "Is that no, you don't want to be buddies; no, you do want to be buddies; or no, you don't want to go out. Help, please."

I grinned. "It feels good to turn the tables. I should do this more often."

"And I still have no idea what you're rejecting me for."

I laughed. I couldn't help it. Between my nerves, the aftereffects of his kiss, and my own confusion, the laugh felt like the safety release on a pressure cooker blowing off a jet of steam.

"I'm not rejecting you. I'm rejecting being rejected."

"I take back everything I said. That was perfectly clear." He sounded like he was trying not to laugh.

"I ended a pretty intense relationship last year," I said. "I don't know that I'm ready to dive into another one."

He studied me, puzzled. "Who said anything about a relationship? I was talking about a date."

"But that's where dates lead," I said.

He started walking again. "Some dates do. And some don't. And if this one doesn't, it's not such a big deal, right?"

It was my turn to stop. "If this is not such a big deal, then why are we having a talk about it?" *And what was that kiss back there?!*

He hesitated for a long moment and then said, "You got me. This is a slightly more loaded situation than a casual date."

"Yeah."

"That doesn't mean it has to be a relationship," he said. "I'm not really in a market for one either."

I started walking again. "Then what's the point of a date? If neither of us is looking for a relationship, I'm not sure I get it."

"I guess it's so I can feel like making out with you is sanctioned if we're officially dating."

"Tanner!"

He laughed. "I'm kidding."

We reached the large circular planter in front of the temple, and I took a seat. He joined me, his shoulder grazing mine as he sat. "Pepper, honestly, I find this whole situation pretty confusing too. I'm not thrilled at the idea of a relationship, but I like the idea of spending more time with you. I'm willing to risk that turning into something more. It seems crazy to waste exploring this connection we have. Maybe it's my reporter's curiosity, but I want to pursue this thing between us just to figure out what it is."

I stared at my shoes, conflicted, a typical reaction to Tanner. Did I feel flattered and validated? Or did I feel insulted that he wanted to explore our connection out of a sense of curiosity? I tried to guess what my dad would say to me, imagining his voice in my head. It would probably sound something like, "People who take offense to things have usually been looking for an excuse to be offended." To be fair, that about summed up my dynamic with Tanner up to this point. If I didn't rely on being prickly to keep him at a safe arm's length, what would happen? Did I want to find out?

Well . . . yeah.

Dang it.

That still didn't make it a good idea. If I gave in to curiosity and got to know Tanner better, I would have to curb my attitude with him, big time.

But if I had another buffer between us, a built-in reason that a relationship between us couldn't fully develop, like say . . . a job writing a dating column, then . . . maybe that would be okay.

"I'll go on a date with you," I said.

"Thanks." Tanner's tone made me realize that I had sounded like I was doing him a favor.

"I'd love to go on a date with you," I amended, and he smiled. "But I'm emotionally unavailable for anything past casual dating. So basically, I'm a real prize."

He shrugged. "Like I said, right now I'd like to figure out what this connection is, period. I'm okay with taking it a day at a time. Or a date at a time."

I thought about it. It really did come down to curiosity for him, the need to explore an attraction he hadn't expected and didn't quite understand. For me, the idea of spending time with someone I knew I would enjoy sweetened the deal. Maybe hanging out with Tanner in a low-pressure situation would be the antidote I needed for all the high-stress LDS Lookup dates. If we both walked into the situation with our eyes open, I couldn't see the harm.

Unlike my relationship with Landon, where I'd acted on impulse and drifted wherever he'd nudged me, I'd approach this dating . . . thing . . . with Tanner from the opposite end of the spectrum. I'd use logic and resist any nudging. With a buffer like a new "Single in the City" date every week, there could be no danger of falling so far for him that I'd lose sight of my new goals. Which led me to my next dilemma. Should I say anything about the column or not? Did I owe him an explanation?

Yes. But it didn't mean I owed him details. With my new full-time job, I had every intention of uncovering the unique parts of Salt Lake that stayed below radar and building a following for my feature reporting to rival Indie Girl's. Then I'd be done with the column, and the whole thing would be irrelevant. But I still owed Tanner some kind of heads up.

"How casual is this?" I asked. "Is it casual, like we-can-date-other-people casual?"

This earned me a wary look. "Sure."

"Every single week? Whenever we want?"

"Every single week?" He laughed. "That sounds like a counterintuitive approach to avoiding a relationship."

Not if the relationship I'm trying to avoid is with you, I countered. In my head. Out loud I said, "I think it's a smart way to avoid getting stuck too much on one person."

"Whatever," he said, a smile playing around his lips. "But I retain the right to not go out every single week with someone else if I don't feel like it."

I mulled that over. "This conversation just reached ridiculous, didn't it?"

"Yep."

"Then let's sum up. I'm emotionally damaged, and you'd be smart to avoid a relationship with me at all costs."

"Check."

"And I will go on one futile date after another to avoid any kind of reality in my love life."

He rolled his eyes. "Check."

He wasn't taking me seriously, but at least I couldn't be accused of hiding anything. My conscience eased.

"Now for my condition," he said.

Wait, what? "You have conditions too?" I asked.

"One, yes."

"Now who's being demanding?"

He waited me out. Curiosity got the better of me. "All right," I said. "Name your terms."

"We reevaluate once a month, make sure this dating thing makes sense. If it isn't working for one of us, we both walk away, no big deal."

"Good idea."

In fact, it was a pretty clinical approach, but . . . so was mine. Who was I to complain about him building in his own back door when I'd already installed multiple exits?

"Then we have a deal."

"A deal? How business-y. I feel like we should shake on it."

"No handshake." Instead, he leaned over and brushed his lips against mine in a feather-light touch, and my eyes drifted close again. "There. Sealed with a kiss."

"Tanner?"

"Yeah?"

"No jokes about sealing in front of the temple. It makes my stomach hurt."

He laughed out loud. "It's okay. We're on the safe side of the doors."

"Let's keep it that way."

Dear Cory,

I hope Ukraine is still treating you well. Things here are pretty good. My job at Real Salt Lake is pretty fun most times. I'm hoping that after putting in a little more time learning the ropes there, I can move on to bigger things. Actually, just moving on from the dating column would be superfantastic. Fingers crossed.

Oh, and I should probably tell you before anyone else in this family gives you a wildly exaggerated version of events that I'm kind of dating someone on purpose and not for the stupid column. His name is Tanner, and he's pretty cool. But we're maybe only a half step past hanging out, so don't believe the picture Rosemary drew. (The one of me in a wedding dress holding Prince Charming's hand. The other one of Ginger with feathers in her hair is right on. It's a thing now, but I just saw a middle-aged woman at the grocery store with feathers in her hair, so don't worry. By the time you get home from your mission, that fad should be dead.)

Anyway, I just wanted to say thank you for breaking your arm that one time. I know I was super ticked when Mom and Dad got rid of the trampoline after that, but in hindsight, I'm pretty sure you saved me from death. Trampolines and I do not go together. You know how if you put two positive magnets together, they go shooting apart? Yeah, me and trampolines.

I love you, Elder Spicer. And I'm proud of what you're doing. Keep up the hard work!

Love,
Pepper

Chapter 15

I snapped a leather cuff around my wrist and took it right back off. Too biker chick-ish. I fingered a wooden bangle but didn't pick it up. Too hippie chick. A bracelet made of silver chain links? Maybe. I fastened it and shook my wrist to check the effect.

Courtney watched me from her perch on Strawberry Shortcake. "You have no reason to be nervous, you know. Can we make this about me for a minute?"

I turned from my dresser to face her and grinned. "Josh is going to take one look at you and breathe a sigh of relief that he dodged a bullet." In a few minutes, we'd be climbing into Courtney's Mazda and heading off to a trampoline center where two boys waited for us. Courtney, as cute as always in a striped purple T-shirt and denim capris, looked ready to jump out of her skin with nerves, so she was in the perfect frame of mind to take on trampolines.

I thought I looked calm, cool, and collected until she busted me. "It's stupid that I'm nervous, right?"

She smiled. "Kinda, yes. You've hung out with Tanner a million times."

I plopped down on my bed across from her. "I know. But not on a date. I don't know what to expect."

She pretended to think about it. "Hmm. Based on my observations, I'd say a bunch of stolen glances where you stare at each other longingly when you think the other one isn't looking, a lot of insults to hide your true feelings, and a crackly energy in the air between you two that will make everyone else uncomfortable. Because that's what usually happens."

"No, it isn't!"

She rolled her eyes. "It totally is." She leaned forward and took my wrist, unfastening the bracelet I'd just put on. "I think it's great. I'm so glad you guys are giving this dating thing a try. Tanner is different with you, and you're great for him. But you really need to tell him about Indie Girl."

I dropped my now-liberated wrist. "I can't. I would evaporate in a cloud of humiliation if he knew I was behind that." I hesitated. Courtney and I didn't spend a lot of time talking about the particulars of me and Tanner. "Don't get too caught up in this, okay? I like your brother, but we agreed to take it way easy." I wondered if I was reminding her or myself. "This isn't a thing. We've mainly just decided to call a truce."

"Then why are you nervous for tonight?" She laughed when I blushed.

"I hate you a little bit right now," I grumbled.

"You can't. I need serious moral support." The hint of panic in her eyes belied her joking tone.

I pushed thoughts of my impending first official date with Tanner aside and smiled at her. "I promise this is going to be a fun night. We picked an activity that will make everyone look like an idiot except for you; it's perfect." Courtney had years of gymnastic experience going into our trampoline date. I had urgent care on speed dial.

"What if Josh doesn't like me?" she asked.

"First of all, so what if he doesn't? You don't have to like him either. Secondly, he's totally going to like you. Your personalities are a great fit, and he thinks you're cute."

"But he asked you out first," she said.

"Yeah, because he saw me first. He's repented." I jumped up and grabbed her hand to pull her toward the mirror hanging on the closet door. "Look at us," I said, pointing to our reflection. "I look pretty good. You look *great*. Tanner and Josh are lucky guys, and of the two of them, Josh is the way luckier one. Trust me, he'll know it."

She took a deep breath. "Okay. We better get in the car before I chicken out completely."

Twenty minutes later, we pulled into the parking lot of Altitude Sports. I spotted Tanner's car, and my stomach flipped like it was already on a trampoline. But it didn't feel like nerves this time. It felt like . . . excitement. I squeezed Courtney's hand. "Just have fun. That's all this needs to be. If all else fails, you can entertain yourself by making fun of my face plants, but I really think you're going to like Josh."

She squeezed my hand back. "What if I do?" I saw pain flash in her eyes. "Maybe I would hate myself if I liked Josh."

I opened my mouth to reassure her that Alex would want her to be happy, but she rushed ahead of me with her thought. "What's worse is maybe I *won't* like him because I can't like anyone ever again. This was such a bad idea."

My knuckles hurt from the pressure of her hand. "Courtney, stop. You don't have to decide anything about the rest of your life based on a couple of hours on a goofy date. Look at it as a chance to get to know someone new. Focus on right now, this moment, and nothing else." I repeated the advice my dad had given me when I asked him how I could help Courtney through the night. "Don't try to extrapolate what it means for the future. Me, you, your brother, and some guy on a trampoline is just that: three people watching you be awesome at something the rest of us are going to look ridiculous doing. Have fun. Make fun of me. Make fun of Tanner. Maybe even make fun of Josh. I bet he can take it."

She let that sink in before nodding. "All right." She let go of my hand. "I think I'm okay now. Let's bounce."

I laughed at her pun and climbed out of the car, ready to face Tanner for the first time since he'd dropped me off and kissed me senseless after our talk at the temple. We'd e-mailed and texted back and forth all week, but I think all the funny messages from him were only making my butterflies worse. With every step I took toward the entrance, they fluttered more wildly. At the main door, I stopped, took a deep breath, and then pulled it open and stepped inside with Courtney on my heels.

Tanner and Josh sat next to each other on a bench just inside the door. As soon as he saw me, a huge grin broke over Tanner's face, and he stood up with his arms open. I walked into them, and he wrapped me in a hug that quieted the butterflies. I'd have stood there soaking up his warmth and the scent of his spicy aftershave indefinitely, but Josh cleared his throat, and I slipped out of Tanner's embrace to make introductions.

"Josh, I guess you've already talked to Tanner, so I don't need to introduce him, but this is his sister, Courtney."

"Hi," Courtney said, her voice sounding hesitant.

"Hi," he answered, an easy smile on his face. "I want to tell you up front that I'm not going to try to make a good impression because the second we get on the trampolines, I'm going to undo it. I'm surrendering my dignity right here and now."

"Uh, me too," Tanner said. "Please still be attracted to me when this is done."

Courtney burst out laughing, and I slid my hand into Tanner's. "I don't think you have anything to worry about there."

When Josh and Courtney rolled their eyes in unison, I knew the evening would shake out just fine.

An hour later, I laughed so hard I nearly cried as I watched Josh try to imitate Courtney's soaring acrobatics. When Courtney goaded Tanner into attempting a flip awhile later, he landed on his back instead of his feet, and I really did lose it as tears of laughter streamed down my face. I couldn't have escaped Tanner's flying tackle if I'd tried. Which I didn't.

Once he'd pinned me, I smiled up at him. "You win." He leaned down and stole a quick kiss before pulling me to my feet. "Yes, I do." He kept my hand in his and tugged on it to lead me on a gentle bounce over a few adjacent trampolines, each one taking us a little farther away from his sister and Josh.

"You don't want to play her bodyguard anymore?" I teased him.

He dropped another kiss on my head. "You're right. He's a good guy. And she's smiling. I thought it might be good to give them enough space for her to figure it out too."

I watched as Courtney took an extra high bounce and then clutched Josh's arm when she landed. He reached out to brace her against a fall.

"I think she knows," I said. "It may not go anywhere, but I think that for now, she's doing all right." Turning to face him, I squeezed his hand and smiled. As my words echoed in my head, I realized that I was speaking about me and Tanner too, and the only drop in my stomach came from Tanner's sudden bounce as it sent me soaring with a startled shriek of laughter. When I landed in a heap beside him, still laughing too hard to stand, he stared down at me with that insanely attractive half smile playing around his lips. "I guess I should have warned you that I meant to knock you off your feet."

I reached for a hand up and when he took mine, I yanked, and he landed beside me. "Careful. I'll take you down with me."

But Tanner didn't look as if he minded one bit.

Dear Denny,

Sorry for throwing stuff at you. I have two brothers, so you think I'd be better trained not to take the bait when you're teasing me. I really didn't mean to hit you . . . there. I'm learning I have ridiculously bad aim. It's like all the passing grades I ever got in PE have all been a lie.

Also, I owe you a big thank you. I'm so grateful you caught my post before it went up under the wrong byline. It would have been confusing for the readers to have Indie Girl profiling a local chef and Pepper Spicer reviewing her latest Lookup date. It would have been absolutely disastrous for me. Thanks for making that save.

You and Chantelle have made it totally worth coming to the office. Thanks for that too.

Sincerely,
Pepper

Chapter 16

The most surprising part of being in the *Real Salt Lake* office turned out to be how little I was there. On nights I had concert reviews, I got to come in much later. Basically, I needed to put in forty hours a week in whatever combination of field time and office time that it took to get the job done. The whole office was in flux like that. Marin, the other staff writer; Chantelle, and I darted in and out as we chased stories. The four ad girls were in only for snatches of time between appointments with potential advertisers, and Ellie was gone for long stretches, schmoozing or doing whatever it was she did. The only regular fixtures were Denny of Homestar Runner T-shirt fame, who generally looked like he was suffering as the lone male in an office full of women, and Janie, our receptionist and sometimes salesgirl.

Since there were rarely more than four of us in the office at once, I lacked a rapport with the other girls like the one I had with my sandwich makers whom I'd shared shifts with for hours on end. I didn't mind though. With everyone absorbed in their own tasks, I didn't feel guilty about the time I spent with my head down, working on my own assignments. Besides a weekly concert review and my Indie Girl duties, I covered the grunt stuff like Ellie warned me I would. I wrote short stories on local leaders and businesses, pieces intended to ingratiate the magazine to the community.

The business articles translated into an astonishing number of advertising dollars. I tried not to be cynical about that. My pragmatic side acknowledged that it was smart business for Ellie to order these write-ups, but I felt like Rosemary at her first soccer game, nipping at her coach's heels and hollering, "Put me in! Put me in!" Ellie had run the Marisol piece, and it had picked up a few comments, but the real results were in Marisol's business. She e-mailed to say she couldn't keep up with the orders, and she thanked me. Still, Chantelle and Marin got the human interest pieces, and Ellie assigned me the brainless stuff.

Even with running all over town and chasing down silly fluff stories, I carved out bits and pieces of time to work on projects I enjoyed, like my current side project, a story about a guy and his boutique vegetable business. He grew produce for high-end restaurants that paid top dollar for hard-to-find varieties of squashes and tomatoes. It didn't give me the soul-deep satisfaction I'd found in writing about Marisol, but it was turning into an interesting piece—when I had a chance to work on it.

I glared at my computer screen and wished I was typing about a radishlike plant called Mooli and not just another chef at yet another high-end local restaurant. Especially since I didn't get to go in-depth about at him all. Seriously, it was a two-hundred-word profile that didn't dig any deeper than asking him to name his favorite dessert. When my phone rang, I snatched it up, still enjoying the thrill it gave me to have my own phone at my own desk.

"Pepper Spicer." I had been an official full-time staffer for three weeks, but I was cycling through different inflections and phone greetings, trying to decide which one I liked best.

"Perky and professional?"

I smiled when I heard Tanner's voice and relaxed into my chair. It was past five, and besides Denny, I had the office to myself. "Did you like it?"

"You know my favorite greeting."

"Pepper Spicer," I said, growling into the phone in my best jaded New York–reporter voice.

"That's the one," he said, and I heard his smile. My own smile grew bigger, and I heard a snort from Denny.

I glanced up, and he mouthed, "Tanner?"

When I nodded, he rolled his eyes and headed for the break room.

"How's the city?" I asked Tanner the same thing every day, teasing him that he got to see and cover way more of Salt Lake than I did.

"Still there," he said. "I'm done with it for the day."

"You made your deadline already?"

"I just hit send," he said, sounding tired. "What about you?"

"I'm covering that punk band tonight," I reminded him. "I'm only halfway through my day."

"That's right," he said. "What are they called? Something really inspiring."

"Circling the Drain."

"Fail."

I laughed. "Maybe their music is better than their name."

"I hope so for your sake. You want to take a dinner break?"

"I'd love to." It was becoming a habit—dinner with Tanner. A really good habit.

"How does Chez Tanner sound?"

"Way better than my microwave dinner in the freezer." Dinner at Tanner's would trump almost anything, truthfully. His kitchen skills rocked. His mom had taught him well. "I'll be there in twenty minutes."

After we hung up, I dug through my purse for my compact to make sure my eyeliner hadn't migrated then touched up with a little bit of lip gloss. I had less time than ever to be high maintenance, but in a job where I had to be taken seriously as a professional, I'd learned appearances counted. Showing up places looking like a fresh-faced kid did *not* work in my favor. When I made the acquaintance of the Cover Girl section at the grocery store, Ginger cheered.

Denny walked out and caught me primping. He rolled his eyes before tossing his crumpled soda can into a wastebasket near the front door. "Dinner with your boyfriend?"

"He's not my boyfriend."

"Right," he said, settling in front of his monitor. "You talk multiple times a day, go out several times a week, you spend every Sunday with his family, and can't face him without your lip gloss intact. What was I thinking?"

"We don't go out," I said. "We hang out. And we've only been doing that for a few weeks."

"My bad again. You're right. Big difference. Why would I think he's your boyfriend? Especially when you're dating other guys every single week too."

Yeah, there was that. I wadded up a piece of paper and bounced it off of his head. I winced. "Sorry. I was trying to swish it in your trash can to intimidate you."

He grinned and went back to zipping through the murky digital underpinnings of the magazine's programming code.

I turned back to my fluff piece on Chef Tom, but it was too late. I had lost the tiny shred of interest I'd barely had in it before. First of all, Chef Tom was a dumb name. It didn't sound right. Chefs have names like Wolfgang Puck. How was I supposed to take "Tom" seriously? And

I definitely couldn't concentrate with Denny's teasing ringing in my ears. My conscience throbbed.

Even though Tanner and I still had a full week to go before we had our first agreed-upon DTR, I knew I was in trouble. The emotional wiggle room I thought my Indie Girl dates would buy me had evaporated after a week with him. Without even trying, he'd shut down all my defenses. The humor I'd often seen lurking in his expression over the previous two months proved irresistible up close and personal, and we spent a lot of time laughing and debating and drifting into comfortable silences that neither of us hurried to break. There was no defense against that except distance, and I wasn't willing to give up time with him. Not when there was so much to learn about the way his fascinating brain worked. Not when he made me feel like the cleverest girl that had ever been born. Not when Rosemary was already madly in love with him, and my mom had automatically set a place for him and Courtney at the dinner table every Thursday for three weeks in a row.

Not when every date with him ended in a kiss that curled my toes.

It made the Lookup dates so much worse. I'd gone back to looking for dates with no real romantic future, thinking it would keep things less complicated for everyone. It did in one sense: it made it clear to me that I wanted Tanner and no one else. Talk about the law of unintended consequences.

It also made me dread every new date. Not only did I spend most of the inevitably uncomfortable dates wishing I were with Tanner, but I also spent them feeling guilty because he didn't know about the whole "Single in the City" column. I wanted to tell him, and I knew it needed to be soon, but I hadn't found the right way to bring it up with him. What was I supposed to say? "So I'm really into you, but I have to date other guys every week for my job. Hope you don't mind."

I didn't know if it would be worse for him to not mind at all or to mind so much that it forced me to choose. I wasn't sure that I could walk away from the column without losing my job altogether, and I couldn't walk away from *Real Salt Lake* because I didn't have a Plan B.

My phone chimed with a text from Tanner. *I'm home. Come see me, woman.*

I sighed and leaned back to study the ceiling for a happy moment.

Denny groaned, and I groped on my desk for a projectile. I snatched up the clay paperweight Rosemary had made me in Brownies and chucked it at him. He didn't even duck, and it bounced off the wall a foot to the left of his head.

"You could at least pretend like you're scared," I said.

"It's only scary when you're aiming at something *near* me," he said. "You never hit what you're actually aiming at."

I laughed. "I need a break," I said. "Maybe dinner will improve my coordination. Watch out when I get back. Tanner's food is magical."

"Enough!" Denny said, bouncing out of his chair. "I cannot take the goopiness anymore."

I scanned my desk for more missiles and snagged a full water bottle from it. I winged it at Denny, intending to hit him square in the chest. Instead, it hit him lower. Significantly lower. Denny dropped to his knees with a hiss.

"I'm sorry, Denny! I'm so, so sorry!" I winced as his eyes crossed. "What can I do? Can I do anything for you? I'm so sorry!"

He waved toward the door, and a strangled version of his normal voice said, "Go. Go now."

I snatched my purse and laptop bag off my desk and babbled as I hurried to obey him. "Denny, I feel so bad! I'm so sorry."

He pushed himself back up and limped toward the break room, maybe for ice.

"Go eat!" he called.

Once I reached The Zuke, I dropped my stuff in the front seat, the only open space in the car. I'd procrastinated cleaning it all week, but I really needed to get rid of the borrowed rock-climbing gear that ate up all the room in the rear seat. The grimy harness and other assorted equipment Mace had lent me for my last Indie Girl date hadn't made it back into the house after I'd limped home from an exhausting date on Saturday with "Fly Outdoor Guy." He was not, in fact, "fly." A talkative braggy pants, yes. But not fly. The conversation had exhausted me more than the forty-five-foot wall we'd tackled.

I revved the engine, anxious to see Tanner again. Fifteen minutes and a few borderline yellow lights later, I knocked on Tanner's door. What was this crazy pull he had on me that made me rush across town for a chance to grab dinner with him when I had a million other things to do? And why didn't I care more about his ability to distract me? In the middle of these muddled thoughts, the door swung open, and Tanner stood there, looking rumpled and delicious in chinos and a deep purple button-down shirt.

"How was the mayor's office?" I asked as he pulled me into his arms.

He dropped a kiss on my head before answering. "Not as huggable as you," he said.

His roommate Tyler groaned and raised the volume on the Jazz game. The eruptions from the television crowd provided pleasant white noise while I watched from my perch at their breakfast counter as Tanner cooked up chicken fettuccine alfredo, my favorite. "Are you going to tell me your secret ingredient this time?" I asked.

"I told you, I pass my hand over it."

I rolled my eyes, and he grinned, turning back to the pan where the cream slowly heated for the sauce. "What did you work on this afternoon?" he asked.

I sighed and told him about the puff piece on Chef Tom. By the time I finished my litany of complaints on all the boring "snapshots" I'd had to sketch out for the local profiles, the fettuccine noodles were boiling.

"Anyway, it's not fair," I concluded.

Tanner nodded and pinched a noodle from the boiling mass, taking a small bite to test its consistency. I waited for him to offer his input when he finished chewing, but instead, he took another bite of noodle.

"Well?" I asked.

He responded with a crook of his eyebrows that said, "What?"

"It's totally not fair, right?" I prodded.

He finished chewing and swallowed then took a long swig of his ice water.

"Tanner!"

"It's totally fair," he said. "That's how this business works. This is the dues-paying I told you about way back when."

I grimaced and traced an amorphous doodle on the countertop. Tanner never pulled punches. I really liked that about him, even when I didn't like what he had to say. I tapped my invisible drawing a few times then smiled.

"You're right," I said. "I'm pretty lucky I got a full-time gig at all. Remind me of that next time I complain."

"Okay, but I'm also going to remind you that you told me to remind you."

"Sorry. Do I complain a lot?"

He smiled and gave a small shake of his head. "No. You don't." He grabbed a plate from a nearby cupboard and plopped fettuccine on it then ladled sauce on top before sliding the whole shebang in front of me.

"It smells insanely good," I said.

"It's my mom's special recipe. She'll teach it to you if you want."

I took a big bite and chewed, basking in the rush of happy endorphins that only heavenly pasta can unleash.

"I want," I said.

It would be my second cooking lesson from her. Tanner and I had spent one Saturday evening in the Graham's kitchen while his mom taught me how to roast a duck. His parents' house was becoming a second home.

"Did Courtney call you about Saturday?" he asked after downing a few bites of his own.

A small pit formed in my stomach. "No. What's up?"

"She and Josh want us to go up to Park City with them."

The pit yawned wider. "What time?" I asked, hoping against hope the answer would be that it was a dinner thing.

"I think they want to grab lunch and walk through the shops."

It was their third date. Josh's sense of humor put Courtney at ease, and I didn't know if they were the love match of the century, but Josh's low-key approach was the perfect fit for Courtney and her reentry into the single life. They liked each other's company, and they both seemed content to leave it at that for the moment.

It was a stark contrast to the headlong rush I found myself in with Tanner. Denny hadn't overstated the amount of time I was spending talking to Tanner . . . or hanging out with Tanner . . . or thinking about Tanner.

"Pepper? Saturday?"

I stared down at my fettuccine, not wanting to give my answer and mess up dinner.

He sighed. "You have a date."

"Yes," I said, hating that my voice already sounded defensive, but I sensed an argument developing. "But maybe I can fit in Park City. I'll check my phone."

Annoyance crossed Tanner's face. "I don't really want to be squeezed in around another date."

"I'm sorry," I said. "I'd much rather go out with you."

"Then cancel the other date."

A reasonable request—if my job weren't on the line. "I can't. It's complicated," I said. "But I want to do the Park City thing. Let me check my phone. It may work."

He grumbled a less-than-encouraging, "Fine."

I dug through my handbag until I realized I'd left my cell on the car charger.

"I'll get it," he said. "You finish your dinner."

I handed him my keys and dug back into my chicken alfredo. A yell from Tyler startled me, but he seemed happy about something in the game, so I ignored him and went back to my food. It was half gone when Tanner walked in a few minutes later and dropped my keys next to me. He took his seat again and pulled out his phone, holding it next to mine. He messed with his for half a minute before handing mine to me.

"Can you call my phone?" he asked.

"Uh, why?"

"I needed to reprogram mine. I had your name spelled wrong. Can you just call it?"

"You're acting weird," I said, but I pressed his speed-dial number. He was six, up from number nine two weeks before. Part of me wanted to put him in the one spot, but that felt so . . . serious.

After a short pause, his phone rang and a song I didn't recognize played instead of his usual ring tone. "What song is that?" I asked. "It sounds like the Beastie Boys."

"It is," he said. "It's called 'She's Crafty.'" He turned his phone around, and the caller ID, lit up brighter than Edwards Stadium on the Fourth of July, screamed "Indie Girl."

I dropped my phone. He let "She's Crafty" play a few seconds longer before he hit Ignore. "Anything you want to tell me?" he asked.

"I'm Indie Girl," I mumbled.

The sound on the TV suddenly died. Tyler's head popped up over the sofa. "*You're* Indie Girl? No way!" he said and laughed like it was the funniest thing he'd heard in days. "I can't believe I know Indie Girl!" He whipped out his cell phone. "I have to tell my sister. She'll flip."

I hopped up and ran over to snatch his phone away, dancing out of reach when he lunged to get it back. "You can't tell anyone, Tyler. It's a secret identity for a reason!"

He eyed his phone, which I dangled out of reach then groaned. "Dude, I totally feel for Jimmy Olson now. It's lame knowing someone's alter ego if you can't tell anyone."

I handed his phone back. "I don't even get superpowers," I said. "It makes for a boring story. Seriously, don't tell. Promise me."

He sighed. "I promise." He shoved his phone back in his pocket and unmuted the TV.

I reclaimed my stool next to Tanner and picked at a noodle on my plate.

"Um, so . . . surprise," I said, unsure of what he thought. He didn't look angry. More like frustrated. "I meant to bake you a cake when I announced it, and maybe have Rosemary pop out of it with a sign saying, 'Don't dump Pepper!' or something."

"I read that column every week. Why is it suddenly so obvious to me now?" he said.

I couldn't read anything from his tone. Stupid reporter impassivity.

"Because you saw the climbing gear in my backseat?" I joked. I knew that's how he'd made the connection. He didn't laugh. I sighed and tried again. "I started writing those columns because I was the only sucker Ellie could convince to do it, but I forced her to make me full time when the column took off. I have to do it, or I lose the chance to do other stuff. You know, like exciting fluff bits about chefs named Tom."

He didn't say anything. He took another bite of his food. He wasn't freaking out, but he wasn't looking at me either.

"Tanner? Your thoughts?"

"I don't know what you want me to say here, Pepper. In hindsight, you warned me. Good job." He pushed his plate away and turned to face me completely. "For every single argument I want to make, I can hear the counterargument in my head, and it seems pointless to bring it up." I noticed the volume drop even more on the game and suspected if I could see through the sofa, I would catch Tyler straining to eavesdrop.

"I understand. I think. But my dad says the first place you have to start is by talking. So maybe I'll be surprised by what you say, or maybe I'll react exactly like you expect, but I'd really appreciate knowing what you're thinking. Only maybe on a walk." I jerked my head toward the sofa.

"All right," he said. "Let's go."

We dropped our dishes in the sink and then headed outside to the manicured path that wound through his apartment complex. He kept his hands shoved in his pockets, and I wondered if it was because he didn't want to hold mine.

We passed two more buildings before he spoke. "I don't have any claim on you. I get it. I don't have the right to tell you that you can't date anyone else. But I'm not okay with it. So I don't know what to say, and I've already thought myself into sixteen different circles over this in ten minutes flat. That's where I'm at."

It wasn't much, but it was a start.

"Would it help if I said I don't like any of these guys?" I asked.

"I would have guessed that from the column," he said. He picked up one of the smooth landscaping pebbles lining the path and chucked it through the rails of the nearby fence. "I still can't believe I didn't put this all together faster. I'm an idiot."

"No, you're not. You're the smartest guy I know."

"It's not like there were a ton of choices," he continued, unappeased. "I assumed it was Ellie, but those columns are way more your voice." He dropped onto a bench that lined the path. I sat next to him, silent, trying to let him work it through and not rush in, trying to be the good listener my dad had taught me to be. I heard crickets and concentrated on the smell of the freshly cut grass that lingered in the mild June air. I tried not to fidget, but it was hard not to when all I wanted to do was yell, "I hate the stupid column! I'll give it up!"

But I needed it, and there wasn't any getting around that yet. How would I feel if Tanner asked me to drop it? It would be a huge step in our relationship if I did that for him. But it might be a step backward because, once again, I would be torpedoing my own career for the sake of a relationship. I wasn't willing to lose myself in Tanner like I had in Landon. If I lost myself, I had finally figured out, then I had none of me to offer anyway.

"The column is good," he said. "Really good. That should have been my second clue."

"Thanks," I said, but I really wanted to scream, *Quit talking about the writing! What does this mean for us?*

"Do you like writing it?" he asked.

"I hate it. I hate the dates. I hate writing about the guys. I spend the whole date trying to think of how I can make myself look like an idiot so I don't have to make fun of them. It's exhausting."

I could see in his face that he still felt conflicted.

"Just tell me how you're feeling," I said. "Don't worry about logic and fairness. Just say it."

He gave a short, pained laugh. "You're asking me to do something you never do."

"What do you mean?" I asked, stung.

"I mean, we spend all this time together. Do you know that I spend every spare minute I have with you? All of my single friends have been teasing me for weeks, wondering when they're going to meet you and if the announcements are in the mail. They think I've dropped off the end of the earth."

"You should Facebook more," I joked. It fell flat. Again.

"My point is, I've made you my priority over everything for every single second I'm not at work. That should say something. And even if my actions didn't speak loudly enough, I've said things here and there over the last week so my renegotiation next week wouldn't come as a shock. And you've shut me down every time. I have to guess how you feel about me and hope I'm right."

"Renegotiation?" I asked. "What does that mean?" I'd caught all his hints, but I usually ignored them or changed the subject. Two days before, he had invited me on a camping trip to Lake Powell in August with a big group of people, but I told him I couldn't predict my workload and that I would have to wait and see. The truth was that it thrilled me that he was thinking two months ahead, but it scared me too. At Ginger's graduation the previous week, she had introduced Tanner to her friends as my boyfriend, and neither of us had corrected her.

"*Renegotiation* means that I don't need another month or even another week to know what I want out of this relationship. And just when I'm about to bring up exclusivity, I find out that dating other guys is part of your job."

"It sounds awful when you put it that way," I said. I tried not to focus on the "exclusivity" thing.

"I don't mean it like that, but . . . it's not great." He sighed and jammed his fingers through his hair again. It was hopelessly mussed now. "Here's another thing I can't wrap my head around. Even before we started dating, was it fair to these guys for you to date them just for the column?"

It was the same question I'd been asked a dozen times by my family. My usual defense of picking guys who weren't looking for anything serious sounded weak now. Serious just happens sometimes, like it had with Tanner.

Yeah, I was admitting it. At least to myself. But since I couldn't quit the Indie Girl column, what did it say about me that I recognized my feelings for Tanner and knew I'd still be going on dates once a week with other guys for the foreseeable future anyway?

Not much, that's what.

When I didn't answer, Tanner sighed again. "You want to know how I feel? Completely frustrated. I figured you might go for being exclusive because it seemed like things were going so well between us. I hoped the dates were symbolic of your independence or something, and you wouldn't care about giving them up if you felt the same way I do." He kicked at a spot in the grass with the toe of his shoe. "Knowing it's for your job makes it worse, not better, because it means there's no end in sight."

"You're right," I said, my voice low as a couple walked by, their beagle straining on his leash in front of them. "I don't know how long it's going to be before Ellie lets me off the hook. The fact that the column brings in so much advertising is the only reason I got her to hire me full time. If I don't write the column, she has no reason to keep me on. And I *hate* making sandwiches."

"Do you hate making them more than you like me?" he asked, still studying the ground.

I stared at him, disappointed. I expected Tanner to be less than happy about the situation. That was fair. But did he understand that he was indirectly asking me if I would give up my job for him? It would be a lot to ask any guy to put up with me dating other people while in a relationship with him. But Tanner was never supposed to be a relationship. I'd been clear about that, and it had happened anyway, against my better sense and judgment. And when it became inevitable that I would have to tell him about Indie Girl, I guess I hoped that some magic solution would fall from the sky, like my feature articles would blow up so huge that Ellie would let me quit "Single in the City," and it would all be a moot point anyway.

"I don't know how I feel about you," I said. "This is all new. I'm still figuring this out."

He didn't say anything, instead focusing on the grass with the intensity he usually reserved for working out a story angle.

I slumped down on the bench and rested my head against the back of it, staring up at the cloudless sky. Dusk was still at least an hour away. "I know I want to move forward with my life and not backward. I know that I like this thing between us, but I don't know what it is or what I want it to be. Do you?" I heard the frustration in my voice, but I didn't try to mitigate it.

"Yes," he said. "I do."

I sat up and stared at him until he looked back at me. "You do." I phrased it as a statement—testing out how it sounded—and not as a question. I wasn't sure I wanted the answer yet.

"I want us to keep building a relationship, Pepper. I want to be with you all the time, and I think about you all the time when I'm not with you. I want to be enough for you."

"And you want me to quit going out on the Indie Girl dates. I do too. But I can't, or I'll lose my job."

That was just a plain fact. Ellie had made it the major sticking point in hiring me full time.

"A few minutes ago I might have asked if it was worth it to you. But it's obviously not. I hate the way that feels," he said. "And I can see by your face that you're upset I even brought it up, which is why I didn't want to do it." He shoved a hand through his hair again and then left it there, dropping his elbow to his knee and resuming his study of the grass framed by his feet.

"I have a question, then." My voice was soft because I knew I was about to ask a hard thing. "What if you accept my job for what it is, and us for what we are right now, and leave it at that for a while? I'm not asking you to be okay with it but maybe to let it ride. Why can't we just do that?"

He straightened and when he locked eyes with me, I could feel him searching inside me for something. An answer, a clue? I don't know. And then instead of speaking, he leaned over and kissed me. Like the first time he'd done it that night by his car three weeks before, I felt the electricity of it hum along every nerve ending, and I shivered despite the warmth of the early evening air. Tanner broke away and sat back.

"That's why I can't let it ride," he said, as if it were answer enough.

And it was.

But I had no idea what to do.

Dear Chantelle,

I don't know why you decided I was worth mentoring, but I'm soooooo glad you did. This has been a very uneven friendship, but I hope I can start pulling my weight soon. I would never have gotten this far if it weren't for your advice and insights, and I can't thank you enough for all of your help. In a school yard pick, I'd take you first every time.

Let me know what I can do to repay you, up to and including babysitting your kids, smuggling you some of my mom's famous fudge, or covering a story for you now and then when you'd rather spend time with your little ones.

Seriously. Thanks.
Pepper

Chapter 17

I trudged into the office Friday morning exhausted. I'd driven home past midnight from the Circling the Drain concert and then spent the next three hours replaying the scene on the bench with Tanner over and over again, trying to reconcile the war between logic and emotion that had overtaken all my higher order brain functions.

By six in the morning, I'd given up on my restless sleep and had crept down to the kitchen to tap out an uninspired review of the punk-lite show from the night before. They were every bit as bad as their name suggested, but I could only partly blame my apathy on the lame show; I owed a chunk of it to the distraction of watching my love life circle the drain too.

I was on the road by eight, and when I pushed open the door to the magazine office, Chantelle's face showed surprise.

"What are you doing here?" she asked.

I understood her confusion. Normally, I didn't have to come in until midmorning after covering a show. I rounded the desk where Janie sat and headed to my spot next to Chantelle. I dropped my laptop bag on the desk with a muffled thump and collapsed into my chair.

"You look terrible," she said.

"Thanks," I replied. "It takes a lot of effort to look this bad in the morning."

"I bet. How hard did you have to fight the urge to pick up a hair brush?"

That earned her a tired smile. "I was more focused on trying to achieve the largest under-eye bags I could," I said. "Do you think I could write an article on it and convince our readers they're 'the bag' of the season?"

"What really happened?" she asked, no longer teasing. I glanced around, not wanting to share the story with the whole office. Janie and the other salesgirl looked absorbed in their phone calls, Denny hadn't shown up yet, Marin wasn't at her desk, and there was no sign of the boss.

I asked just to be sure. "Where's Ellie?"

One of Chantelle's professionally shaped eyebrows quirked. "At a breakfast meeting with some finance guy. This is about Tanner?"

I'd learned fast not to mention him in front of Ellie. Their bad blood went both ways, it turned out. It was rooted in nothing more than professional competitiveness and the disdain each of them had for the way the other did their job, but it was far less stressful for me if I kept them out of each other's orbits. Tanner only came by when Ellie was out, and I didn't mention him in front of her if I could avoid it. I jerked my head in the direction of the break room, a question on my face.

Chantelle nodded and got up to follow me. While I stowed my leftover chicken alfredo in the decrepit fridge, she sat at the table and waited. I grabbed the seat opposite her and slumped into it. "Tanner found out I'm Indie Girl."

Up went her eyebrow again. "Yikes. It obviously didn't go over great."

I sighed. "Do relationships get easier after you're married?"

She laughed. "I'm not going to answer that on the grounds that I don't want to be the reason you stay single the rest of your life."

"I think that's the likely possibility right now. I can't imagine ever being ready for marriage."

"Weren't you almost ready last year?"

I stared at her in surprise. I hadn't discussed my dysfunctional dating history with anyone at the magazine. I almost never talked to anyone about it at all.

"Landon Scott, right?" she asked.

"How did you know that?"

"My niece," she said. "When she outgrew Justin Bieber, she moved on to a new obsession. Landon Scott fit the bill. It's amazing what an obsessed thirteen-year-old can do with a Google search. She recognized your name on the Marisol story and remembered you as Landon's almost-wife. She asked me about you a couple of weeks ago."

"Whoa." It freaked me out a little that I would turn up in a Google search. I'd Googled myself a few times and had never found a connection between me and Landon, so Chantelle's niece had dug deep. It also weirded me out to hear myself described as an "almost-wife." I really had been *this* close.

"It's true, then?" Chantelle asked.

"Yeah, it's true." There wasn't any point in denying it. I only kept it quiet because for a long time it hurt to think about it, and now . . . well, it didn't matter anymore. Another epiphany. Any more might cause a stroke.

"Sorry," Chantelle said. "I didn't mean to interrupt your story. I couldn't resist the urge to confirm my scoop." When she saw my face, she burst out laughing again. "Don't worry. I'm definitely not going to share it with anyone. I just like being in the know. I can keep a secret."

"Thanks," I said. "I've already dropped one bombshell on Tanner. I don't really want to hit him with another one just now. The last thing I need is some garbage about me and Landon all over the local gossip blogs."

"So you and Tanner are still talking? That's good, right?"

"I don't know if we're talking or not. I'm not even sure where we left things last night after he dropped me off." We'd walked back to his apartment in silence, nothing resolved. On the short walk out to my car, I tried a couple icebreakers, but Tanner clearly wasn't in the mood to talk, so that had ended in silence too. He'd stayed long enough to watch me get in The Zuke, so I guess it was a positive sign that he hadn't left me to any lurking muggers or serial killers, but other than that—radio silence. No cell phone or e-mail. Nothing.

"I'm guessing he doesn't love the idea of you dating other guys."

"Yeah. I mean, he knew I was doing that all along, but he didn't know why. He thought I was just playing the field and that I might be up for making things exclusive."

"Are you?" she asked.

"How can I be?" I dropped my head onto the table. My neck couldn't support a brain so full of conflicting thoughts and feelings anymore. "That's like asking me if I'm ready to give up my job because that's what dating him exclusively would mean."

Chantelle didn't argue. She knew the column was a big deal to Ellie. "I'd offer to take over 'Single in the City' for you, but my husband would get kind of mad. He doesn't like it if I leave him alone with the kids too long."

I laughed. "Thanks anyway."

"If your job weren't an issue, would you want to make it exclusive with Tanner?" she asked.

I stilled. The answer scared me. "Yes."

"You like him. A lot," Chantelle said.

I felt a tear well in one eye, so I sat up and dashed it away, sniffling. "Sorry. Lack of sleep makes me extra emotional."

Chantelle nodded. "Yeah, me too. But 'like' isn't enough for tears."

"I'm dealing with a little more than 'like' here," I confessed. It scared me to realize how quickly my feelings for Tanner had grown. They'd been sneaking up on me since way back at the first dinner at his parents' house, but all the time spent with him over the last three weeks had pushed my feelings to a whole new level.

"Would you really let a job cost you a chance at love?" she asked. "Would you let *Ellie* cost you a chance at love?"

"No. Not if I was sure it was what I wanted," I said.

"You're not sure?"

"I don't know," I wailed, exhaustion making it hard to think straight.

"Calm down!" Chantelle said.

"It never calms people down when you yell at them to calm down!"

"Okay, okay. Just . . . relax for a minute. Breathe or something," she urged me. After I took two deep breaths, she let out one of her own. "Wow. I guess it makes sense for you to be so wound up, but remind me to duck after every question."

"Sorry," I said. "I'm a mess."

"Anyone would be," she said. "Would you rather not talk about this?"

I considered that for a minute. "No, it's okay. We're on a roll. Might as well keep it going."

After a long, measured glance, she nodded. "Good. But you need a soda if we're going to continue." She hopped up, grabbed a Dr. Pepper from the fridge, and tossed it to me before sitting down. "Stop me if you're about to lose it again, but let me recap. You like Tanner. Maybe even more than like him. If you weren't writing 'Single in the City,' you'd be exclusively dating already. But your job depends on the column, and you're not ready to give up your job for Tanner."

I nodded, miserable. "I sound horrible and selfish when you put it that way."

"No, you don't," she said. "Has Tanner been running around professing his love for you?"

"No," I said.

"Then he can't ask you to lay everything on the line right now. Is that what he wants? For you to quit?"

"He wants us to see where this relationship is going. He understands that I can't quit the column. He doesn't like it, but he didn't ask me to make a choice," I said. "We kind of . . . stopped talking. There wasn't anything left to say." Tears threatened again, and I took a quick swig of soda to distract myself.

"If you had a way to get out of the column and still keep your job, would you take it?"

A quick yes jumped to my lips, but I caught myself and really considered the question. Without the column, I had no buffer left between Tanner and me. Did I still want one?

"Pepper?" Chantelle's concerned expression made me smile.

"Don't worry. I'm not the mayor of Crazy Town yet," I said. "Patheticville, maybe. But not Crazy Town."

"You're not pathetic," she said.

"Would you still think that if I told you that I need to talk to my daddy right now?" I asked.

"No. It's great that you have a good relationship. I can go do some writer-type stuff at my desk if you want to call him."

I nodded. "You won't be offended that I'm trading you for him?"

She smiled and walked out of the break room. I pulled my phone out of my jacket pocket and dialed his number.

"Everything okay?" he asked as soon as he picked up the phone.

"It's fine," I said. "I think. Except for the parts that aren't."

"What's going on, Pepper?" he asked, and I loved hearing the concern in his voice, the tone that said, "I'm totally focused on you, daughter."

"I had a bad night with Tanner."

"Sorry to hear that. What happened?"

I swear, talking to my dad is better for the soul than even the most magical chicken soup. "He found out that I'm Indie Girl," I said. "It didn't go well."

"Want to tell me the details?" he asked, his voice gentle.

With a hiccup that betrayed my tenuous grip on my emotions, I explained the whole evening to him, feeling better the closer I got to the end because I knew my dad would tell me what to do. I could breathe again without feeling a heavy weight on my chest.

When I finished, he was silent for a long moment. "What are you going to do?" he asked.

"I was hoping you would help me figure that out," I said. "Am I too old to be calling you and asking you for advice about boys?"

I could hear the smile in his voice when he answered. "Of course not," he said. "But are you old enough to accept things you might not want to hear?"

I paused. "No." Then I sighed. "Yes."

"Good girl," he said. "How much of your hesitation with Tanner is because of Landon? Are you still mourning that relationship?"

I thought about it. "No," I answered. "I've been figuring that out lately. Landon never would have been the right guy for me. We want different things, and no matter how much I loved him, in the end, it wouldn't have been enough."

"Pepper," he said, his tone gentle again, "how much did you really love him?"

The question caught me off guard. "A lot," I said.

"A lot," my dad repeated. He sounded thoughtful. "How do you know?"

Again, I had to grope my way toward an answer. "Because it took so long to get over him."

"Hmm. Let's try a different question. *Why* did you love him?"

I lifted the phone away to stare at it for a moment. These were not the loving words of encouragement I had called to hear. These were hard, uncomfortable questions. But he had warned me. I thought about the why. I had loved being with Landon because he'd made me feel like, for the first time, I wasn't flying under the radar like I had all the way through high school. He'd acted like my quirks were cool. I'd liked the way other people, especially other girls, had looked at us with a touch of envy when we were together. Each jealous look stroked my ego. I'd liked knowing that I always had someone to hang out with on the weekends, a permanent movie date, and a guaranteed kiss every Valentine's and New Year's. I'd liked being part of a couple, being a part of Landon-and-Pepper.

I explained all that to my dad as best I could and waited for his verdict. He asked another question instead.

"Why did Landon love you?"

"I don't know, Dad. Maybe he didn't. We'd be married if he had."

"Try to come up with an answer, Pepper."

I thought some more. The truth was, I'd spent many months after our engagement had fallen apart asking myself why he didn't love me enough. I hadn't focused much on why he had loved me in the first place. I'd assumed he didn't, or I wouldn't be heartbroken. I asked myself the question grudgingly. Why had Landon loved me?

"I made him laugh," I finally said. "He liked my style. He liked that I'm a good girl. He thought we were a good team."

"Good," my dad said. "Was it true? Were you a good team?"

"I don't know," I said. "I used to think so." I struggled to come up with an analogy. "We weren't a team like doubles tennis, where you both work equally hard and share the rewards. It was more like he was the star and I was his ball girl."

"Did that bother you?"

"Not then. Now it does." I dropped my forehead to the table and stared at the scuffed tile between my shoes. "When are you going to tell me what to do about Tanner?"

"I'm not," he said.

I bolted up. "But—"

"Because I'm not clear on what you want from him. I'm trying to figure that out. More importantly, I think you're trying to figure that out. So let's go there next. I have the same questions. You care about Tanner. Why?"

"Because he's a good man," I said. I didn't even have to think about it, and there was no point denying to my dad how invested I already was in Tanner. I wouldn't be near tears on the phone with him if I weren't. "He treats his family with respect, and he treats me with respect too; he works hard; he makes me laugh; I like his sense of adventure; he has integrity—"

I broke off when I heard my dad laughing. "What?" I demanded.

"Nothing. Continue."

"No. That was everything." Except it wasn't. I could have kept going.

"Obviously, Tanner cares about you, or your unwillingness to commit to him wouldn't bother him," he said.

"That could just be his ego," I said.

"Do you believe that?"

I sighed. "No." The truth was bittersweet.

"So Tanner cares about you. Why?"

"Honestly? I have no idea." He should have washed his hands of me a long time ago. Like right after our very first interview. Heaven knows I hadn't done much since then to impress him. And yet . . .

"All the things you mentioned that Landon loved about you were things that individually are fine, but taken together, they add up to something different. Can you see what it says about your relationship?"

I considered the question. My dad was pointing me toward a realization I'd made once before. "All the things Landon loved about me were things that reflected back on him," I said. "They were things that either made him feel better about himself or that were convenient for him." The convenience part still stung.

"You were never a typical girl, Pepper," my dad said, his voice so warm it felt like a hug. "I watched you struggle through high school to understand why you didn't get all the dates the other girls did and why no one ever noticed you. But you missed something key. They all noticed you. Especially the boys. But they didn't know what to do with you."

"Because I'm such a freak?"

He laughed. "Far from it. But you were different then, and you're different now. You don't jump on all the latest trends or do your hair like everyone else or even like a lot of the same things that other people do. Some people act different to make a point. They refuse to let people reject them, so they choose a lifestyle or persona that allows them to say, 'You're rejecting me because you can't handle what I like or how I look, not me personally.' You genuinely *are* different, but you've had a hard time embracing that because you're afraid it will separate you from other people. Instead of letting people love you for your true nature and allowing that to act as a natural filter to sift out the people who wouldn't really appreciate you, you buried yourself in a relationship with Landon because it signified acceptance."

Whoa. Deep thoughts for my sleep-deprived brain. I shook my head to clear it, trying to process my dad's words.

"Pepper?"

"I'm here."

"Am I overloading you?" he asked.

"No." I said. "Or . . . maybe a little bit."

"Everything I'm telling you is an opinion. It's a theory. Granted, it's backed by a lot of experience and a PhD, but it's still a theory."

I laughed. "I'd take your theories over anyone else's anytime."

"Then consider this," he said. "You buried yourself in your relationship with Landon because he swallowed you up in his identity, and that was far more comfortable for you than trying to be a cornflower in a field full of daisies."

"At least you didn't call me a pansy even if I was acting like one," I said.

He chuckled. "I think you figured it out on your own and fixed it. You're not with Landon anymore. You must have learned something. He's not a bad guy, but he was never the right guy for you. Which reminds me. You're avoiding my original question. Why does Tanner care about you?"

"I don't want to speak for him," I said, hedging. "He's never told me his reasons."

"You can guess. It's important for you to answer this question. If you feel silly giving me an answer out loud, you should at least consider it seriously for yourself. Will you do that? I think it will help clear up some of your confusion."

"I can do that. But I was hoping you would clear up all my confusion," I wheedled. "Just tell me how to fix things with Tanner."

"You have to decide what you want from all this first," he said. "If you figure that part out, then the rest will come to you. Call me if you need anything else though. I'm here for you."

"I know, Dad. That's why I love you." I ended the call and sat up straighter in my chair. I'd come into work much earlier than I'd needed to, and I wasn't getting much done. I needed to reboot my day, and I couldn't do that in the office. With new determination, I headed back to my desk and shoved my things back into my messenger bag, smiling in response to Chantelle's look of concern.

"I'm all right," I told her. "But I need to think. I'm going to head out for a while and clear my head."

"Sure. Maybe I'll catch you later."

I headed out the door and had just reached the stairs when she called my name.

"Pepper."

I stopped in surprise and waited for her to catch up.

"When I asked what you would do if you had the chance to get out of the column and still keep your job, it wasn't an idle question. I'm pretty sure I know how you can do it, but you might not like it. Let me know if you want to talk about it."

I studied her for a minute then nodded. "I will."

She smiled and headed back to the office. I tossed my stuff in the backseat of The Zuke and started it up, anxious to find a space to decompress. A few of the stray thoughts careening around my brain since the disastrous conversation with Tanner the night before were calming down and looking suspiciously like insights. I wanted to tackle them without any distractions so I could wrestle my way to an answer.

No more limbo. I'd lived in it for seven months after Landon. I couldn't go back to self-pity and stagnation.

My dad had prescribed me a whole year of thank you notes, but it had only taken four months for his cure to work. I was changing, and I needed to figure out what the new Pepper would do.

Dear Hailey,

I don't know how you feel about your job. Maybe it's not that fun working at Straws, or maybe being the counter girl at a café is just your cup of tea. Or coffee. Or milk. But if I had to guess, I'd say you probably like it because you're always cheerful and friendly to everyone who comes in.

I stopped in the other day for a cookie and a minute of peace and quiet on a day when I desperately needed it. I don't know if you've ever had a day where you feel so fragile that you're sure even a loud sound could break you. But it was one of those days. So I stepped in for some comfort food and thinking time, and you, with your kind smile and thoughtful "How are you?" helped me find both. Because instead of pretending not to notice when I teared up at your question, you asked again, like you really meant it.

I've managed a little restaurant like yours. I know it's hard to hang on to a positive outlook after a long morning shift of dealing with customers. But just know that sometimes your friendliness and courtesy go way beyond providing your customers with a pleasant café experience. You can actually lift a spirit. That's what you did for me. I owe you thanks for a peaceful hour of reprieve in an otherwise really cruddy morning.

Sincerely,
Pepper

Chapter 18

Forty-five minutes later, I perched on the flat top of a large boulder in Mill Creek Canyon, overlooking the idyllic canyon stream. Besides one jogger and two dog walkers, I had the place to myself. I soaked up the sun, letting the confusion and frustration of the previous night evaporate in its mellow heat. I could hear the hustle and jive of chipmunks hurrying about their business on the grassy banks, and soon even that sound blended into the soothing rush of the water over creek stones. With a silent prayer for a clear mind and heart, I lay back and stared at a cloud while I sorted through the facts.

Even though it was late morning, I still hadn't heard from Tanner. That hurt.

It hurt because I liked Tanner. A lot.

More than a lot.

I squeezed my eyes shut and took a deep breath.

"I'm in love with Tanner Graham."

Forcing myself to say it out loud prompted my heart to give an extra thump, but my head didn't explode. I took that as a good sign. I did a little internal poking around to see what kind of space the word *love* took up.

I felt bigger inside, in a good way, like when you wake up from a nap and the more you stretch, the better and more awake you feel.

So.

I love Tanner Graham? Yes. A witness of the truth tickled my mind. *Yes.*

And I love him for all the reasons I told my dad. His loyalty and kindness and integrity. His intelligence and humor and friendship. For the way he curls my toes when he kisses me.

Heck, for the way he curls my toes just by smiling.

Does Tanner love me?

He cares for me, definitely. He wants to take our relationship to the next level, to figure out what our future together holds. That says a lot.

Why does he care for me? That was the stumper my dad had asked me, and as stupid as I felt trying to answer the question, I took another deep breath, stared back up at the cloud, and answered it anyway.

Tanner likes my sense of humor. He likes my brain. He thinks I have talent. He likes how I treat my family. He likes talking over his days with me. He likes hearing what I think about pretty much everything. He likes my testimony. He likes kissing me. A lot.

I am in no way convenient to him. He's done his best to encourage my writing and support my goal of being a journalist.

So what's the problem?

I sighed and sat up. He had asked if I cared more about my job than him, and it had offended me. And that was stupid because I would die a little inside if I thought his job were more important than me. It was fair for him to hope that he mattered more than the magazine.

He hadn't even asked me to give it up. He understood that I was stuck with the column and risked losing my job if I dropped it. He didn't like it, but he hadn't asked me to drop it all for him. What he'd done was ask me to be honest about my feelings: did the magazine matter more than he did?

And I'd given him no answer at all. In the moment, I'd been too confused and defensive to come up with an answer, and then silence had fallen between us and had grown louder by the minute. At the moment, with my inert cell phone by my side, the silence was deafening.

I itched to snap up the phone and dial him, to bridge the gap. But I still hesitated.

Tanner wasn't Landon. And I had changed. Had I changed enough? Because if I hadn't, I'd end up swallowed up in Tanner before I realized it, deferring the dream I had for myself in order to make our relationship work. Tanner was worth sacrificing for, but if I lost me in all of it, we were doomed to fail.

My cell phone rang, and I snatched it up, relieved when I saw his name on the screen.

His hello was subdued.

"Did you get my messages?" I asked. "I think it was three voice mails, two texts, and an e-mail. I was going to sit outside on your doorstep this morning until you talked to me too, but then I decided to use that in case of an emergency." I winced, hoping my joke came off as funny, not pathetic.

"I got them," he said, sounding tired. "I'm sorry I didn't get back to you sooner. I've been trying to sort through everything."

"I've been doing the same," I said.

"Did you come up with anything yet?"

Yeah. I'm in love with you. No way was I saying that out loud. "I keep going in circles, to tell the truth. I'm not even sure where we left things last night."

"I know," he said. He was quiet for a minute. Or maybe even half that, but it felt like forever. "I guess I can only speak for me. This is where I'm at. I would never ask you to give up your job. But I can't handle you dating other guys. I've never thought of myself as the jealous type, but I can't take it. I just can't. Even knowing you don't want to be there with them doesn't make it better. It would take a much bigger guy than me to be okay with it, I think."

"I get it," I said. "I totally do. I wouldn't like it if you were dating a ton of other girls."

He sighed. "That's good to know, but this is where I get stuck. Asking you to quit the column is the same as asking you to give your job up, and I can't be that jerk. So I don't know where to go from there. We can't go forward as it is. There's no going back. And that's where I am. Kind of nowhere."

"I've never told you about my past relationship—as in singular. As in only one," I said, drawing my knees up and wrapping my free arm around them. "I was engaged. We broke up almost a year ago, and we'd been together for four years before that. I think I'm trying to sort through some of that baggage."

There was another long silence from him. When he spoke, I could hear surprise in his voice. "I figured your relationship aversion had to come from somewhere, but I had no idea it would be on that level."

"Does that freak you out?"

"I feel like when you're going down the stairs and you miss a step so you end up taking two and scaring yourself a little," he said.

"It gets worse," I admitted. "Do you want to hear it?"

"I guess I need to," he said.

"I was engaged to Landon Scott."

After a beat he said, "You're kidding."

"No. And I spent four years being so totally wrapped up in everything he did, all the goals he had for himself, all of his plans, that I didn't realize

I'd spent almost our entire relationship out of touch with *me*." I stood up and brushed my seat off then scooped up my bag and headed out the way I had come, depending once more on the movement to keep my mind clear. "I don't miss that relationship," I said. "I'm glad it ended. But I'm scared about getting lost in another relationship."

When that met another long silence, I gritted my teeth. I hated doing this over the phone. I wanted to be able to read his face, to watch his reactions. Instead, my overactive imagination read the worst into each of his pauses.

"I don't really know what to say," he confessed. "You're blowing my mind here. A four-year relationship? I'm worried *baggage* might be an understatement. How deep do those scars run, you know?" He was quiet again. "It almost doesn't matter. We could figure that out. But then, there's your job. I don't see an answer. I don't think I really have any moves here. This is kind of up to you, and that worries me because you have an easy choice to just keep your job. I wish I were okay with the Indie Girl thing. I'm not. And maybe that means I'll have to accept that I'm the whole reason this falls apart."

"But I—"

"I have to go," he said. His voice was tight and hard. "There's a call coming in from the city desk, and I need to take it."

"Okay," I whispered, not sure he even heard me before he hung up. What now?

I dialed Chantelle's number. "I need to hear your plan. It's gotta be a million percent better than the plan I don't have now."

* * *

"I can't do that." I stared at Chantelle, appalled. I had driven from Mill Creek Canyon to Straws, a local café with a big breakfast crowd that quieted around lunch. A few customers dotted the tables inside the restaurant, and we had one of the four outside tables to ourselves.

"You don't have to," she said. "I told you that you wouldn't like it. But it will work. You know it will." A half smile played around her lips at my stunned reaction.

"There is no way I'm contacting Landon for an interview," I said.

"He's a huge get," she said, using the term journalists reserved for the hot interviews they all tried to land. "Everyone has access to him at the press conferences, but with his popularity in Utah right now, whoever scores an exclusive with him is going to draw a major bump in readers.

Ellie will be able to sell a ton of advertising while the story generates hits, and you're going to be her golden child if you pull it off."

"There are a hundred problems with this plan," I said. "I don't know if I can get the interview, and even if I could, what if I put myself through all that and Ellie still doesn't let me drop the column?"

"That's why you don't agree to the interview unless she agrees to the trade. You'll do the exclusive with Landon, but she has to let you out of 'Single in the City.'"

"I doubt I can score the interview," I said. "It's a moot point."

"You guys haven't talked at all since you broke up?"

I shook my head. I'd been hurt and angry and not interested in letting Landon lure me back in as his unpaid assistant/merch girl/cheerleader. "I shut him out," I said. "I didn't want him getting in my head again."

"He wouldn't agree to an interview even out of curiosity? Would he really not talk to you?"

I hesitated.

She noticed and pounced on it. "He would! You know how to get past his gatekeepers, and you know he'll talk to you."

"I can get to him," I admitted. "But that doesn't mean he'd want to do the interview. Some people don't like being used."

She regarded me, her eyes shrewd and far older than her twenty-nine years. "He owes you," she said. "After what you've told me about how he treated you, he owes you big time. Maybe a subtle reminder of that will be enough to get him to agree to it."

I could read between the lines. "You're saying I should threaten him," I stated flatly. "I'd never air our dirty laundry. It would be an empty threat, and he'd know it."

"Look, obviously you don't have to do this. But for Ellie, scooping all the other papers and weeklies around here for an exclusive with Utah's biggest celebrity would be totally worth putting the column on hiatus until she can replace you. It's your choice."

I slumped in my chair and stared at a few granules of sugar left behind by whoever had occupied the table before us. I pressed my finger against them to lift them from the tabletop and then brushed them onto the floor. Chantelle watched me move them a few at a time, but by the third pass, she grew impatient.

"You know this is your way out," she said. "So I guess now it's a question of whether you're willing to deal with your ex to fix your job situation."

"No. I'm not."

Shrewd Chantelle reappeared. "Then are you willing to do it for Tanner? Because that's what it's going to take."

* * *

After our lunch powwow, Chantelle returned to the office, and I called Ellie to tell her I was going to track down some information before coming back. Then I girded my loins, but only figuratively because literally doing that in public would have brought a whole new kind of headache involving complaints to the police and lots of pointing and staring.

Fifteen minutes later, I pulled into the parking lot of the *Bee*. I passed Tanner's car, relieved that he was there and not out chasing a story of his own. I slid The Zuke into a space and pulled the key out of the ignition, drumming my fingers on the steering wheel while I girded some more. You know, figuratively. My gut told me that Chantelle's plan would work. I knew I could probably get the interview and that once I did, Ellie would make the deal: I'd get her a Landon Scott exclusive if she let me out of the column.

But the devil was in the details. When I broke off our engagement, Landon had texted, called, and e-mailed furiously for about two weeks. When I didn't respond, his efforts tapered off dramatically. He probably got so busy with his Hollywood whirlwind that he didn't have more than two weeks to invest in trying to save a relationship he'd been in for *four years*. That stung. Two weeks of effort. That was it. While I truly didn't want to talk to him, it would have been nice to know that I took longer than two weeks to forget. Maybe the girls flinging themselves at him every time he took the stage during *The It Factor* finals made it easier for him to move on.

In hindsight, the proportion made perfect sense. I struggled for a year to get over him. He was good to go in half a month. That sounded like an accurate reflection of our individual commitments to our relationship in the first place.

I so, *so* did not want to sit down with Landon for any reason.

I ran through the other options that had chased through my head since leaving Tanner the night before. I didn't have enough credibility yet to have a real shot at another magazine. I'd start even lower than my current feeble grip on the bottom rung of *Real Salt Lake*, and I'd have to pick up a second job again to keep up with my debt. I had a sinking feeling that the stress from the extra hours would lead to resentment of Tanner and cause problems for us. I could try picking up a different full-time job and write freelance articles on the side to build my résumé before I attempted to get on with another newspaper. This was the best option—if it weren't for the minor detail of the whole country being in a massive recession. Random full-time jobs in any industry weren't falling out of trees. If I quit *Real Salt Lake*, I had nowhere to land. I'd torched my safety net when I'd signed my resignation letter to Mr. Handy.

Then there was the whole issue of fear. I knew intellectually that Tanner didn't expect me to quit for him, but even if I chose to do it without any coercion from him, I was afraid I might resent him for that too. Intellect can't always override emotion. For me, it almost never can. Thinking through the options had left me with a handful of other really bad solutions.

And that led me back to Landon.

I hated the idea of contacting him. A job wasn't worth it. I'd date a thousand toad-faced guys with mother issues and gradually earn my way out of my column on the merits of my writing before I'd ever sit down to discuss even the weather with Landon.

But if in a bizarre twist of irony, he represented my only chance to find a solution to my impasse with Tanner, then . . .

I needed to believe facing Landon would be worth it. I took a deep breath, got out of the car, and headed into the *Bee*.

When I pushed open the lobby doors, despite my fervent prayer, Giggle Girl still sat there, her hair as shiny and perfect as it had been on my last visit four months before. She offered me a plastic smile when I approached the desk, but no recognition showed in her face. Maybe it's because I wasn't limping this time.

"I'm here to see Tanner Graham," I said.

Her smile grew brittle at its edges. "Is he expecting you?"

"Could you just let him know Pepper is here?"

The name jogged her memory, and her smile faded completely. "He's not conducting any interviews today."

I wasn't in the mood for this. She was the first and smallest in a long line of hurdles I was here to clear, and I wasn't investing my energy in her turf war.

"Call him," I said, not bothering to phrase it as a question.

She shot me a peeved glance before picking up her phone and angling her back toward me. She lowered her voice, but since only her desk separated us, I could still hear her, which was probably her intention.

"Tanner? Hi! Yeah, there's someone here requesting to see you . . . Yeah . . . remember that Pepper girl? The one who walked funny? She's back. Do you want me to tell her—oh. Are you sure?"

I offered her a winning smile when she turned around. I think it made her madder. "You can go up. His desk is—"

"I know where it is," I said, which was not true, but I'd figure it out rather than admit ignorance. When I opened the door at the top of the stairs, Tanner was leaning against the desk that sat in front of it, waiting for me. He straightened when he saw me and, with an elbow under my arm, guided me toward the same office we'd interviewed in. It wasn't the hug and "I'm glad you're here" I'd hoped for, but at least he had told Giggle Girl to send me up. It was something.

He ushered me into the nondescript room and repositioned the only two chairs so they were by each other instead of being separated by the desk. We sat.

"What's up?" he asked. He didn't sound upset. Just tired.

I stared at him for a full minute. Four months ago I had sat in this office, berating myself for not planning what I would say in my interview. Here I was again, berating myself for the exact same thing. I hadn't thought out a smooth way to say, "I was wondering if you love me and stuff." Coming to his workplace was idiotic too. Who does that?

Lovesick seventeen-year-olds—that's who.

Not grownups. At least, not emotionally stable, fully functioning ones.

I sighed. "When I got in my car and drove here and then parked and walked into your office building and then made the receptionist call you and then told myself that I was being brave, I was operating under the effects of sleep-deprivation. I'm an idiot." I braced myself on the chair arms to push myself up. "I'm sorry. I'll go. Can you call me later?" I was halfway out of my seat when he reached out and placed his hand on mine to keep me there.

"It's fine. Sit down. I wasn't getting anything done anyway." He took his hand back and shoved it through his hair. I could tell it was not the first time he had mussed his hair that day. Despite his crisp blue dress shirt and gray pants, he looked . . . rumpled.

I eased back in the chair, and unsure of what to do with my hands, I settled them in my lap, where they lay looking limp and useless. Or perhaps I was projecting . . . ?

Tanner's eyebrow lifted, which meant, "I'm waiting." It was one of his reporter mannerisms, where he did it unconsciously when his Spidey senses told him he wasn't hearing all of a story. He would quirk that eyebrow and wait patiently until he got the rest of it. It was a powerful eyebrow.

"The army should skip waterboarding and just turn your eyebrow loose on prisoners," I said.

"What?" he asked, looking startled.

"Nothing." I clasped my hands and studied them then decided that looked even stupider than before, so I put them back on my lap, naked and forlorn. I cleared my throat. "I've been thinking a lot about what you said last night, and I wanted to say that I heard you. I really heard you. But, um. I have some . . . questions."

He leaned back in his chair. "Shoot."

"You said that you wanted us to reevaluate our relationship and make it exclusive. Why?"

He considered the question for a minute. "I know I don't want to be with anyone else. Exclusive makes sense."

The correct answer would have been, "Because I'm madly in love with you and can't live without you. Let my love give you wings as you face down Ellie!"

However, I had not given him a copy of his script and couldn't be too upset that he didn't know his lines. "I don't want to be with anyone else" was a start. I'd cling to it like a lifeline while I threw myself a little farther off the cliff.

"Okay, exclusive makes sense," I said. "Why don't you want to be with anyone else?" The correct answer was, again, "I'm madly in love with you and can't live without you."

Tanner's answer sounded like, "We connect." Because that's what he said.

We connect. Another true but unsatisfying answer.

I took a deep breath. "I don't want to be with anyone else either, and I know that moving this relationship to the next level is totally up to me, but it's a little complicated at the moment."

His face relaxed slightly. "It's good to hear you say that."

"That it's complicated?"

He snorted. "When is complicated ever good? No, I mean it's good to hear you say that you don't want to be with anyone else."

I frowned at him, taken aback. "I told you that last night."

He shook his head. "No. You said you didn't want to go on the Indie Girl dates. You never said you didn't want to be with anyone else."

"Oh. Well, I don't."

We stared at each other in silence for a moment. Wasn't this where the heavens should part and a ray of light shine down to illuminate our new-found love? I saw no parting heavens, only the flicker of a fluorescent tube that needed changing. My stomach churned. I wanted him to proclaim his love so I could take the dive and set up the interview with Landon, knowing that despite the inevitable, horrible awkwardness of it, I would have Tanner waiting for me on the other side. But he wasn't declaring his love for me.

This was a very ill-conceived plan.

Sensing my frustration, he leaned forward with his elbows on his knees and caught my eye. "You're upset. Why?"

"This isn't how I thought this would go," I admitted. "I'm having a hard time aligning my expectation with reality."

Confusion played over his face. "What were you expecting?"

I fidgeted. "I don't know. A better sense of how you feel?"

His confusion gelled into an expression of disbelief. "Wait. You think I'm being vague about how I feel?"

"Well, yeah." I lifted my hands back to the chair arms and gripped them, preferring to give them something to do.

"Pepper, you ignored me for months. The only times you weren't ignoring me, you were either glaring at me or making fun of me. Then I talked you into going out with me, but you've gone on a date with someone else every single week we've been dating."

"But that was for work!"

"And I didn't know that until yesterday! I thought it was just another way for you to say, 'Friends with benefits is *great*.'" His emphasis was frustrated. "I have been trying to read you for months, and now you're dragging me away from my desk to ask me how I feel about you because you think *I've* been vague."

I shrank a little in my chair.

He sighed. "I think I'm way too exhausted to have this talk right now, and I can see a bunch of people out there trying to pretend like they're not lip reading this whole conversation."

I turned to catch about four heads in the newsroom whip around to their own desks. I scowled and turned back to Tanner.

"I'm sorry," I said. "I wasn't being very considerate in coming here. And I'm sorry I've been so hard to read. I haven't meant to be."

Up went the eyebrow. "You haven't?"

I sighed again. "All right. I guess I have. I need to get back to the magazine. Can we talk later?" He hesitated, and my heart sank. Or not even that. It deflated and left a heart-shaped hollow in its place.

"I don't know," he said. "I mean, yes, I want to talk. But at the moment, I have no idea what there is to say. I need sleep. And perspective. And to think, maybe. I don't know." He scrubbed his hand over his face. "Mainly, I need sleep. My brain is fried."

"I'm sorry," I said. "I know that's pretty much my fault." I stood up, and he followed. Just as the night before, I didn't really know what to say next. "So . . ."

"So." He captured my gaze and held it. "I don't know how long it will take me to think."

"I understand. I'll wait." Kind of. But with any luck, the plan hatching in my mind would cut down that wait time significantly. I didn't know what I was supposed to do next. Hugging Tanner in front of the entire newsroom was probably a bad idea, so I offered a little wave before slipping through the door to leave. I ignored all the curious glances on my way to the stairs, but I felt relief when I reached the first landing and the itchy feeling of having a dozen pairs of eyes trained on me faded. When I hit the exit into the lobby, Giggle Girl's head shot up, and she stared at me, her expression disapproving. I gave her my most cheerful smile and headed out. What was that saying? "Smile. It makes people wonder what you're up to." Let her wonder. I was definitely up to something.

* * *

This was going to be way harder than I'd thought, and I'd already thought it was going to be pretty hard.

I sat in The Zuke and stared at my phone, glad no one upstairs in the *Real Salt Lake* offices was likely to see me in a casual glance out of the office window. It would look pretty odd, me sitting in my car in front of work, not going anywhere.

The number staring back from my phone belonged to Landon's sister, Kylie. She had always liked me, and I knew she'd be glad to put me in touch with him. Too glad, maybe. I'd have to make sure she understood that I wanted to interview him, not reconcile, or she'd get her hopes up. My finger hovered over the call button. Once I set this all in motion, there was no turning back, and this was about so much more than seeing Landon face to face.

When I'd dropped in on Tanner earlier, I'd gone to him looking for a sign. Or more specifically, a declaration. I'd be ready to face Landon if Tanner were waiting with open arms and a huge "I love you."

Instead, Tanner was guarded, and it was my fault. I'd forced him to take that approach with me from the beginning, at first by refusing to acknowledge the attraction between us and then by keeping him at an emotional distance with my "dating other guys" excuse. To add insult to all that injury, even after admitting to him that I didn't like dating all those other guys, I wasn't ready to quit because I wouldn't give up my job for him.

Except Tanner didn't want me to give up my job.

It was fair that not knowing how to deal with the dates was eating him up, yet he still refused to put me in the position of choosing between him and my professional goals. That already made him the polar opposite of Landon, not to mention his quality of character in every way that counted.

I understood that not asking me to risk my job didn't mean he could accept me dating other people. I had grown to understand him so well in the last month, after hours of talking and laughing with him, that I knew the real issue wasn't even me dating other people. I knew Tanner would really struggle with the lack of transparency in what I was doing, both in terms of the audience I wrote for and the guys I dated and wrote about. It would gnaw at him if he tried to ignore it, and we'd end up at this impasse at some future point even if he tried to accept it.

I stared at Kylie's number and again thought about how much I had needed Tanner to profess his love for me before trying to take this next crazy step.

Yeah, I needed to hear it.

But I had never said it.

And I had never given Tanner a reason to think that I would welcome hearing it. He'd tried a dozen different ways to show me that he cared, and I had reciprocated by *deigning* to spend time with him and not much else.

A tear slipped out and rolled down my cheek as the full measure of my jerkiness settled on me. I had walked away from Landon because I had deserved to be treated better. Would Tanner walk away from me for the same reason?

I hit Call.

Dear Landon,

Thanks for agreeing to do the interview. It was hard for me to even ask. And thanks for talking stuff over with me. I had every intention of just coming in and asking the standard questions then getting out. I'm sorry I was so stubborn when you first brought all of our relationship issues up, but I guess we both needed closure. I thought I had it before, but I know I have it now. I judged you too harshly.

I wish you success and happiness, Landon. I really do. I'm glad now that things didn't work out for us, and it took me a really long time to understand and accept that, but I think we're both happier for it. I knew you were. It just took me awhile to realize that I am too.

Sincerely,
Pepper

P.S. I got the card. I almost sent it back, but I guess keeping it is part of growing up and moving on. So thanks for that. Good luck with everything, Landon. I hope you find what you're looking for.

Chapter 19

"Come in," I called, recognizing my mom's soft knock on my bedroom door.

"Everything okay?" she asked, eying the pile of clothes on the bed behind me.

"Yeah. I have a big interview today. I'm trying to figure out what to wear."

"Do you want some help?" She looked doubtful about her ability to step in for Ginger. My mother dresses in the classics. While she always looks neat and trim, there's no mistaking her for hip.

I smiled. "No, it's fine. I'll figure it out."

She hesitated then sighed. "I don't want to be nosy, but you're really distracted this morning. Is everything okay?"

I held a black sweater against me and studied the effect in the mirror. "Like I said, it's a big interview."

She didn't comment, just stood there waiting.

I turned to face her. "It's with Landon."

A gasp escaped her, and she strangled it but dropped onto my bed with an "Oof." She opened and closed her mouth a few times before settling on, "Wow."

"Yeah." I added the black sweater to the reject pile. Too plain. If looking good was the best revenge, I needed something stunning. I wanted something that said, "I'm totally over you, and aren't you wretched that you let me go?" I grabbed a satiny magenta blouse and wondered how it would look with skinny jeans. Would it strike the appropriate funky/awesome balance? No. It said, "I'm trying too hard." I stuck it back in the closet and grabbed something else.

"Pepper?"

"Yes?" I said, not turning around because I didn't want my mom to read too much into my expression.

"Are you okay with this interview?"

"Sure," I said. "It was my idea."

"Why?"

I turned around this time, a drapey knit top in a deep teal blue grasped in my hand. "Because it's time," I said. "I'm okay with him and our breakup. I've been okay with it since . . . well, for a while now."

"Since Tanner?" she asked, her eyes knowing.

I shrugged. "Yes. Since Tanner."

"How does he feel about you going to see Landon?"

I had no idea how he would feel if he knew. I hadn't talked to him in three days, trying to respect his request for time and space. They had been three miserable days, and my parents could tell something was up, but they didn't push me, and I was thankful. I was barely holding it together. Trying to discuss all the things that had gone wrong would have wrung me out completely. As it was, I had lost hours of sleep over it and a few pounds in a few days because food turned my stomach. Worse, on top of wondering how badly I'd damaged my chances with Tanner, I'd had this interview with Landon to stress me out. I might set a new world record for shortest length of time to develop a terminal case of stomach ulcers.

I tried to be like a duck, the way my high school public speaking teacher had described, frantically paddling beneath the surface but appearing unruffled on top. I knew I hadn't fooled my parents, but I hoped they weren't worrying about me too much. I thought about how to offer my mom an honest answer that wouldn't set her to fretting.

"It will be awkward to see Landon, but if I can nail this interview, it could be a major career stepping-stone for me," I said. "I'm focusing on the positive." And that included not telling her I hadn't told Tanner because we currently weren't talking.

"I can't believe the magazine is making you do this," she said. "Didn't you tell them about your history?"

"Mom, I told you it was my idea, and I meant it. Nobody at the magazine even knows I'm doing it, so don't get too mad at them," I said. It would be misplaced anger, considering that Ellie didn't even know I was doing the interview. "I love that you're concerned, Mom. But I promise that I'm going to be fine seeing Landon." It was trying to reconnect with Tanner that worried me sick.

Her torn expression told me she wanted to advise me against doing the interview anyway, but she was stronger than I expected, and she held her peace. She stood and leaned forward to finger the soft knit of the shirt I held. "For what it's worth, I love this color on you. You go from gorgeous to drop-dead gorgeous."

I smiled and held the shirt against my chest. "Then I guess I have a winner."

She slipped out the door with one last worried glance. I knew it was hard for her to drop it, but my parents had been working as hard to let me grow up as I'd been working on trying to grow up.

I pulled out a pair of black skinny pants and my favorite wide black belt to cinch the shirt in and flatter my waist. I unboxed a pair of black suede wedges with a peep toe that Courtney had talked me into buying, liking the four additional inches of height they added. I checked my reflection and breathed a sigh of relief. With the right accessories, this outfit would definitely work. I chose my funkiest necklace, a chunky piece by Marisol. Asymmetrical bits of polished glass and smaller pieces of hematite formed a pleasing jumble that complemented the teal of my shirt. She'd tried to give it to me for free after the article ran, but I insisted on paying. It was a small price to pay for being able to tell her amazing story, and watching her business explode was worth far more than even one of her insanely cool designs.

I added a leather cuff embellished with sculpted wire to my look and decided earrings would be overkill. I was already making a statement loud and clear. I hoped Landon would get the message: I am stylish, self-possessed, and doing fine without you. My hair had grown a few inches longer since I'd last seen him. I hadn't gotten it cut in six months, but Ginger had done a little trim job on it a couple of weeks before in our bathroom and had shown me how to make it cooperate by framing my face in fun wispy pieces, my dark hair contrasting well against my fair skin.

I was so ready to be through with this whole part of my plan. I calmed myself with a small prayer and conjured a mental picture of what it would look like if this paid off. It involved me smiling and happy because I was folded in Tanner's arms.

I could only hope. And drive.

Time to point The Zuke toward Salt Lake and see if fortune would favor the stupid today. I needed a little good luck.

* * *

Two hours later, I pulled into the parking lot of the E-Center and killed the engine. A detour by the *Real Salt Lake* office on the way to meet Landon bolstered my spirits. When I'd walked in to get my mini voice recorder, Denny had met me with a wolf whistle. One of the salesgirls glared at him.

He apologized. "Sorry. I didn't mean to objectify you."

I saw the twinkle in his eye and smiled. "Don't worry," I told him. "I only embrace the good parts of feminism. You can pay me a compliment anytime."

I'd grabbed the recorder, a purchase made with my first paycheck from the magazine, and then had surrendered to the inevitable and had taken off to interview Landon.

Now backstage at the arena, I gawked at the layout. I'd been interviewing bands in tiny dressing rooms and watching shows in small venues. This was Byzantine by comparison, with long hallways and multiple doors down each side. Every member of Ozomatli could have their own room backstage, that's how big it was.

Even without the guard who swept me with a security wand before leading me back, I could have figured out which dressing room was Landon's. A half dozen people buzzed around outside. The security guard waved me onward. I took a deep breath and strode to the door with all the confidence I could fake.

Inside, Landon sat in a tall canvas director's chair, surrounded by several more reporters, all of whom I recognized from covering other stories. Not only that, cameras from three different television stations recorded the whole thing. I stood back to get a sense of what was going on. Seeing them didn't bother me. An exclusive could mean either that a particular media outlet was granted the story a day before everyone else or that they held a press conference for multiple journalists but gave one particular paper or magazine more in-depth access. That was the situation here.

If anything, I had the advantage of studying Landon before he could do the same to me. I noted the changes a year had wrought. He was average height, a little under six feet, with a slender build, but he'd gained weight, and it was all muscle. His chest was a little broader, his shoulders more defined. In addition to the help of a personal trainer, he'd obviously gotten some professional teeth bleaching and a skilled hair stylist. His straight hair had more body than I'd ever seen in it and sported highlights so subtle that it could only be the work of a seriously expensive foil job.

I didn't have time to catalog any more of the differences his Hollywood glam team had unleashed because he caught sight of me, and a big smile broke over his face. The back of my throat burned, and I cleared it. For the first time in a year, for the first time since I'd broken up with him to find the me I had lost, I was about to confront the guy who had swallowed up four years of my life. I needed desperately to believe that I had changed enough not to be sucked in again by his undeniable charisma.

"Pepper!" he said. A slightly older women wearing a headset glanced up on hearing my name then stepped forward and addressed the other reporters.

"All right, ladies and gentlemen. Thank you for coming out to cover our concert today. Landon always loves talking to his hometown reporters and connecting to his fans through your newspapers. We'll look forward to your coverage tomorrow. If you'll follow me out to our hospitality suite, our tour manager will answer any other questions you have."

Veiled in her speech had been a deftly delivered warning: make sure your coverage is good, or you don't get access to Landon again.

Landon didn't say anything until the door closed behind the last reporter, and then his smile returned. He reached out his arms for a hug, and feeling awkward, I stepped into them.

"It is so good to see you," he said, and I think he sniffed my hair. I waited for the rush, the butterflies, the tingling. And I waited. And after a moment, I realized it wasn't coming. I breathed out in relief.

I stepped back. "You too. You look good." It was true. He looked buffed and polished and slightly unreal, but girls swooned for a reason.

"How have you been?" he asked.

"Oh, you know. Good." I fought the urge to shift from foot to foot. "I can't open a newspaper without seeing that you're doing great."

He grinned and waved me toward a leather sofa pushed up against one of the dressing room walls. "Have a seat," he said, leading me over. I did but made sure to keep a careful distance between us. "Speaking of newspapers, I can't believe you're a reporter now."

I smiled. "It's a magazine, Landon." It was so like him to be inattentive to the details.

"Cool. Like *City Weekly?*"

"No, that's still a newspaper. *Real Salt Lake* is an online magazine."

"Cool, cool." He fell silent for a moment and studied me. I returned his stare. Something about the way his laugh lines bunched slightly around his eyes clued me in that spray tanning was part of his new beauty regimen too. I had a momentary vision of anyone suggesting a spray tan to Tanner and smothered a smile at the image. Tanner wasn't a spray booth kind of guy.

"You look good," Landon said, turning up the charm. It was second nature to him. "I like this style you've got going on. It's different, but it's cool."

I refrained from an eye roll over the notion that he would even think I was interested in his opinion. Not that it wasn't good to hear he had noticed. It just bothered me that he would assume I cared. Even though I had agonized over today's outfit for an hour. Never mind that.

I cleared my throat again and reached into my bag for my mini recorder. "I know you have a show to do tonight so I guess we should get started."

"Slow down," he said. "I've got lots of time still." He rested his hand on my arm to stop my rummaging. I let my hand drop from my purse, mostly so I could remove my arm from his grip. His touch felt unfamiliar now.

"Thanks for agreeing to see me," I said. "And for doing this interview. I wasn't sure you'd be up for it."

He grinned again, and the dimple in his right cheek that slayed so many teenage girls flashed at me. "The curiosity factor was pretty strong. It's been a long time."

This time the fidgets got the best of me. I knew it was inevitable that we would stray into old relationship territory.

I tried for a neutral expression. "I hope you understand why I didn't return any of your calls or e-mails," I said. "Done is done, and I didn't see the point in rehashing things."

"I understand," he said, unperturbed. "If we had burned each other out by overanalyzing everything, we wouldn't be able to build a bridge between us now." He turned to face me more directly and drew his leg up on the sofa. It put him closer to me, like maybe he meant to physically "bridge" the gap between us. I stilled and wondered what to do if he encroached any farther. I couldn't risk antagonizing him until I had our interview in the bag. He didn't seem like he was going to try anything, but I had no idea why he'd even agreed to see me. It was as good a question to lead with as any, I supposed.

"What did you think when Kylie told you I wanted to interview you?"

"Once my manager made sure you were legit and weren't trying to trick me into an interview to do a hatchet job, I thought it was cool that you're a reporter now."

"Landon! You know I wouldn't do a hatchet job on you. If I wanted to burn you, I'd have been blabbing to the tabloids and ripping you left and right for months."

A shadow flickered in his eyes. "I've learned never to be surprised by what so-called friends will do when money or notoriety are on the line." He smiled, but it was faint. "Besides, you and I didn't end as friends, so I had every reason to be suspicious."

I swallowed. "I guess I am kind of using you. I only called Kylie so I could get this story."

"I know," he said. "But you're being up front about it, which is more than I can say for most of the people who hit me up." He rubbed his palm up and down his thigh, and I hoped it wasn't sweaty because I knew that the jeans he wore didn't come cheap. Ginger had saved three paychecks to buy a pair of the same brand not too long ago. "I guess, in a way, it's kind of karma," he said. "You using me, I mean. I used you long enough."

My mouth opened, but nothing came out. I stared at him, surprised. The last thing I'd expected from this Hollywood version of Landon was self-awareness and a near apology.

His grin returned when he glanced up from his jeans and caught my expression. "Yeah, I was a jerk. But if you print that, I'll have my manager force your editor to make you print a full retraction."

I mustered a smile, still shocked. I had expected to find Landon still as self-absorbed as ever. There were clear signs of his narcissism in his appearance, but it looked like the dark side of the celebrity experience had taught him some cynicism with a tiny dose of humility.

"This is already not the conversation I imagined us having," I said.

He laughed. "I'm sure you thought I'd ooze the plastic charm I've learned to turn on for my media interviews, and then you'd walk away more sure than ever that you were right to dump me." He propped his elbow on the sofa back and chewed on his thumbnail for a second. He did that when he was thinking hard. "You always could see right through me."

"No way," I said, almost snorting. "If I had, we never would have lasted four years."

He winced. "Fair enough," he said. "I hope I didn't treat you that badly though. We had some good times, right?"

I sighed. "No, you didn't treat me badly. You just didn't treat me well." For most of our relationship, everything had been about him. We went where he wanted, hung out with his friends, talked about his plans. And I let it all happen, so wrapped up in basking in his reflected glory that I didn't bother to assert myself. He never abused me, verbally or otherwise, but that wasn't the same as being treated well. When I realized it at the end, I knew I had to demand better. When I didn't get it, I walked.

"I know," he said and sighed. "Self-awareness is . . . uncomfortable. It's been a hard year. "

When my eyebrows shot up, he shook his head.

"I know. Poor little rich boy, right?" He shrugged. "What can I say? I'm cash rich and friend poor. I'm not going to cry you a river, but I lied when I said that curiosity was the reason I told my manager to book this interview."

"Then what's your real reason?" This conversation was so far off base from what I'd anticipated that I had no idea what to expect next.

"I want to apologize," he said. He sat up and looked me in the eye. "I can't afford to lose the few true friends I've had in my life. I didn't do right by you, and I'm sorry for it. Can you forgive me?"

It was a sincere apology, and for that reason, it tugged on my heartstrings. He wasn't trying to charm me. He had abandoned all of the usual tricks he employed to endear himself: the flashing dimple, the flirtatious grin, the touchy-feely thing he liked to do to make you feel special.

That's probably why it worked. "I did not see that coming."

He didn't say anything, just sat waiting, his expression hopeful.

A small laugh escaped me. "Leave it to you to even steal my anger. But I'm glad to give it up." When his face reflected confusion, I explained. "I spent months hurting, being mad at you for not thinking I was worth marrying."

"I always thought you were worth marrying!" he objected. "You broke it off!"

"Honestly, Landon. How many more times do you think you would have postponed the wedding because things weren't convenient? Would we even have been married right now?"

He hesitated then shook his head. "Probably not," he said.

It hurt to hear it, but only my pride. It was final proof that my heart was no longer invested in him.

"I know. And I knew it then. Then I started this new job and a new relationship. When the marketing blitz started for your tour here, I braced for the worst and found . . . well, that I didn't need to brace for anything. I was fine. So, yes, I accept your apology."

Annoyance tugged at the corners of his mouth. "You're in a new relationship now?"

"Yes."

"Is he good to you?"

"Very."

"Dang."

That made me laugh. "You can't tell me that you don't have a million girls dying to date you," I said.

"They want to date Landon Scott, *The It Factor* sensation," he said. "You dated me when I was just Landon. I miss that. I hoped maybe we could look at a new beginning. Wishful thinking, huh?"

It was funny. In all the mourning I'd done for our relationship, I had never once wished for us to get back together. And here he was, telling me it had been very much on his mind. But I had no stars in my eyes as I studied him now, and I offered him a shrug of my own.

"Yes," I said. "That would be wishful thinking."

"What about if this new guy weren't around?" he asked.

"To be honest, we kind of hit a wall a few days ago. I haven't heard from him, and I don't know if I will." When I saw interest spark in his eyes, I rushed to explain. "It doesn't matter though." His face fell. "Even if I weren't involved with anyone, you and I wouldn't work. You're still talking about being with me because of what I offer you, not because you're thinking about how we balance each other."

His head drooped in defeat. "I'm an idiot."

I scooted over and covered his hand with mine. "You're not. I can tell you've grown. I have too."

When I withdrew to a safer distance, he smiled again. "Actually, it's kind of nice to see how together you are."

"My only lingering side effect is paying off that stupid wedding," I joked.

He looked amazed. "No way," he said. "I can't believe you're still dealing with that. I'll have my accountant cut you a check today."

"No!" I said. "That wasn't a guilt trip. It's been a good lesson for me on the dangers of pride." When he looked confused, I sighed. "I'm handling it, and I'm going to keep handling it. When I've cleared the debt, I'll throw myself a 'welcome to adulthood' party. I don't need you to do anything for me. Really."

He looked torn. "I don't feel right about that. Please let me do something. I want in on the grownup club."

I was all for making amends, but I still resisted his charm. "We should probably just congratulate each other on being adults and toast with some root beer."

He perked up. "I have a minifridge full of it. It's the only thing I put in my contract rider."

"How unsurprising," I said. "Some things will never change."

He pushed himself up and sauntered over to the dorm fridge by the huge mirror in front of his makeup chair. "Look," he said, flinging the door open and pointing. "Would you like A&W or A&W?"

"A&W, please."

He grabbed two cans and returned to the couch. "I need to ask you another question."

I sighed and waved my minirecorder at him. "No, I need to ask *you* questions, remember? That's why I'm here."

"One more," he said. "Then we'll do this interview." He popped my soda open and handed it to me and then did the same to his, taking a long swig before resting it on the arm of the sofa. "Does your boyfriend balance you?"

"Yeah," I said. "Perfectly."

He nodded. "Lucky guy."

"I hope he still feels that way, but if I think about it much longer, my brain will cramp. Are you ready for my deeply considered and thoughtfully phrased questions? Because I have, like, one of those and then about forty of the regular kind."

He snorted. "What angle are you taking?"

"After listening to you, I want to focus on the downside of the celebrity experience. Do you trust me to do right by you if we go there?" I asked. "I definitely won't take the poor-little-rich-boy slant, but I do think it would be eye-opening for your fans who want their own fifteen minutes of fame to realize that your life isn't all limos and A-list parties."

He considered the question for a while. "I'm sure my manager will kill me, but yeah. Let's do it. I trust you."

With a smile, I pulled out my notebook and set the recorder on the table. "Spill it," I said. "Start with the best stuff first. Is it possible to get tired of screaming girls and red carpet premieres?"

"You have no idea," he said, and the heavy truth in his tone sent a little shiver up my spine.

This was going to be *good*. Maybe good enough to make "Single in the City" a tiny dot shrinking even smaller in my rearview mirror.

Dear Readers,

Thanks for all the love over the last few months. Being able to spill all the ridiculous details here every week gave me something to look forward to when the dates themselves didn't. Your comments and hilarious insights on each of my romantic misadventures made a grim situation bearable and transformed it into something fun.

How would I have ever dragged myself into the dating arena again without you guys to cheer me on? Only the fact that dozens of you admitted to infinitely worse dates helped me suit up for another round the very next week. Take, for example, the week when the Bachelor Reject scheduled two ladies at once—on purpose—so he could "compare and contrast." Luckily, the other girl, Abby, was totally cool, and we passed a fun evening sharing a running commentary on our date, and I made a new friend. (To clarify, it was her, not the Bachelor Reject.)

You know, experiences like this one don't usually dish out the lessons you're expecting when you first jump into them. That is definitely true with this dating gig. My LDS Lookup experiment failed miserably for me, but I have a confession: I never wanted it to succeed. I took on this column because I needed the job, but I was nursing a broken heart and had no interest in finding love. I went out of my way to accept dates with guys when I knew there was no potential, but for the record, I totally believe that online dating works for those who want it to. Many of my friends and family members are living out their happily-ever-afters because of sites like LDS Lookup. I turned down some great guys in order to protect my heart. I kept my dates to the guys who weren't looking for commitment, and I got what I was looking for.

That's one of the major lessons I learned from this whole experiment. Online dating and regular dating are the same in key ways. You find what you're looking for. Your payoff is proportionate to your intentions and your input. There are great guys out there. There are creepers. It's your average singles dance, just . . . online. It takes common sense and solid self-esteem to navigate either dating environment safely. I didn't approach this with a good-faith *effort, and I deserved every dating disaster I experienced. I didn't want love out of LDS Lookup, and I didn't find it.*

But the joke is on me, right? Because love found me anyway. I squared my shoulders and put my dukes up, but stupid Cupid delivered a knockout blow I couldn't duck. I'm dazed; my head is spinning; I desperately need someone in my corner to say I'm going to be okay, and yet . . .

I'm deliriously happy.

How clichéd is it to fall in love with your best friend's brother? But that's what I did. And that's me. A walking cliché.

I don't know if things will work out for me. I've made more wrong turns with this guy than I ever did in my "Single in the City" flops, but there is no way I can maintain the Lookup facade now. Not only is my heart not in it but now it belongs totally and utterly to someone else.

Don't worry, readers. "Single in the City" isn't going anywhere. Indie Girl is leaving but not leaving you in the lurch. Remember my partner-in-crime from the date with the Bachelor Reject, Abby? Through the magic of Facebook, we've become good friends, and I know you'll find her as funny and insightful as I do. She's ready to take over here, but with one major difference: she really is looking for love, so I hope you'll sit tight for the journey as she begins her adventure in this space next week.

Again, I can't thank you enough for the support, jokes, and advice you've offered me throughout the months of this crazy experiment. I am overwhelmed and humbled to have hundreds of strangers cheer me on and so often cheer me up. I wish for you only the best, like you've wished for me week after week. If you remember to, wish me luck just a little longer. I'll need it more than ever. I just shouted my love from the roof tops, and maybe only awkward silence will greet me . . . but here's hoping I get way more than I deserve from a seriously amazing guy.

Ciao, peeps. I can't say it's been real because it hasn't been at all—but it's about to be.

In the mean time, I wish you all love.

Sincerely,
Indie Girl

Chapter 20

I sat at my work desk and pushed Send, knowing it meant a countdown of mere minutes before Ellie would erupt when she got my e-mail. I settled in to wait by opening up my interview with Landon and reading through it. It was a great article, as good as anything I'd done at *Real Salt Lake* so far. Forging a new peace between us had allowed the interview to go to deep places, revealing things Landon had never admitted to in any interviews before. I knew he was allowing me that level of access partially out of a sense of penance for four years of neglect, but I think it also made him feel lighter to unburden himself as he talked about the traps and pitfalls of the celebrity life.

The Landon from a year ago would definitely have spent the whole time whining about his bad luck. The Landon on the dressing room sofa three days before had been far more reflective than I had ever known him to be. He recognized that he'd been incredibly blessed with success, but he was losing his illusions about the Hollywood fantasy and was groping his way toward moderation, a foreign principle in the culture of excess surrounding him.

Writing it had been cathartic, and it gelled into a story I knew had real dimension, something lacking in most media coverage of "pop-lite" stars like Landon. I worked nonstop over the weekend to shape the hour's worth of notes I had into a story that spoke the truth. It allowed me a glimpse into the good man Landon was becoming, but it didn't tempt me down the what-if path. That door was closed. I had moved on even if I hadn't heard from Tanner since early on Saturday. I had texted him to tell him I'd be eating Sunday dinner at home and that the coast was clear at his parents'. He responded with, "Thanks. Sorry I've gone dark. I'm trying to get to a good place with all of this. Still need space. I'll call you."

I would have texted him back with a promise that I was making everything better, but until I knew for sure that Ellie would go for it, I couldn't offer him anything concrete. I needed more than empty words to give him. I needed actions that spoke as loud as his had when he had patiently waited for me to take notice of him and when he'd carved out every spare minute, and even some he couldn't spare, to make time for me. Calling him to say "I'm not sure what to do either" wouldn't move us forward, so the next step was clear. Ellie *had* to take the bait. At any moment, I expected to hear her calling my name in anger, demanding to know what my latest "Single in the City" column was all about. If Ellie agreed to run Landon's story in exchange for printing my Indie Girl good-bye, the interview would make a huge splash in the Utah market. I was glad, not only because I was finally sure that Chantelle's crazy suggestion would work but because I knew that what I'd told Landon was true: the article would make a lot of Hollywood hopefuls think twice about the high price of fame.

I pulled out the card I'd stuck in my bottom desk drawer this morning. It had arrived in a padded envelope the day after our interview with a fat check from Landon inside, written for an amount nearly double the wedding debt I had left on my credit card. My mom and dad begged me to take their advice and keep the check, especially when Landon made it clear there were no strings attached. I reread the card again and smiled. *"Dear Pepper, it's a strange thing when a check like this becomes pretty much pocket change, but I'm only telling you the truth about that so you'll feel better about taking the cash. Compared to the high price I paid in losing you because of my own self-involvement, the money is nothing. Thanks for being open and honest with me yesterday. I tried to do the same in return, and I hope that you got what you needed for your article. Regardless of how you portray me, the money is yours. It is* totally *separate from the interview. I know I don't even have to say that, but I want to be clear. I trust your judgment to write your story however you want. Either way, I'll get what I deserve."*

The check was in my purse, ready to deposit. She didn't know it yet, but Ginger was about to take full possession of The Zuke while I paid off my credit card and used the remainder for a down payment on a boring, reliable used car. I wondered if I could muster a tear when I surrendered custody of the green Camry.

Nope.

"Pepper!"

I jumped. Chantelle's head shot up at Ellie's holler, and I shoved Landon's card back in my desk and spun my chair around. Ellie stared me down from her desk fifteen feet away, trying to pin me with her gaze.

"What is this?" She stabbed her finger at her screen.

"My 'Single in the City' column. What do you think?"

She flushed red and hopped up. "I think we'd better step back to the break room to discuss my opinion."

I swallowed and stood. Besides Chantelle, Denny and Janie were also in the office. They watched, frozen in surprise, as I trailed after Ellie. Chantelle whispered "Good luck," as I passed. Every step toward the break room felt like swimming through Jell-O, and I clung tighter to the only defense I had, the thin sheaf of papers in my hand.

When I rounded the corner, Ellie was waiting, standing at the table with her hands on her hips, her jaw clenched tight. She pointed at a chair. "Sit, please."

I sat.

"The agreement when I hired you full time was that you would keep up your Indie Girl gig. If you don't fulfill your end of the deal, then we no longer have one. Let me ask you again. What did you just send me?"

"It's exactly what it looks like. I'm quitting Indie Girl, but before you fire me, I think you should know that I'm pretty sure you're going to like the Plan B I've worked up." I set my papers on the desk and pushed the top one toward her, hoping she didn't notice the slight hand tremor as I did so.

She hesitated for a moment before snatching it up.

"What is it?" she asked, skimming it.

"It's a 2,500-word exclusive with Landon Scott."

She shot me a startled gaze. "You're joking."

"I'm not."

She reread the page and then held her hand out. "I need the rest of it."

I placed both palms on top of my little stack. "I can't give it to you."

Her eyebrow shot up. "You work for us. You can't publish this anywhere else."

That was the opening I'd hoped for. "No, you're right. I can't publish this anywhere else. But I also don't have to publish it here if I don't work here either."

She leaned across the table. "You are a schemer."

I didn't flinch. "I'm learning from the best."

She didn't react, but when she realized I wouldn't either, she took the seat opposite me. "So your terms are that I either let you out of 'Single in the City' or I lose the exclusive?"

I nodded. "That's the upshot."

She watched me, calculating how serious I was. "I'm not sure that the right to this exclusive offsets losing the column."

I slid the two bottom sheets from my pile and pushed them toward her. "You won't lose it. This is who I think should replace me. Do you remember the date with Bachelor Reject?"

Her lips twitched. That had been a pretty funny recap. "Yes."

"I've kept in touch with Abby, the other girl. She should take over, and she'll do a way better job because she's into it. You'll get the added bonus that in all probability, she'll fall in love and readers will follow her on that journey. I asked her to write up the last date she went on like it was a 'Single in the City' column. She's a great blogger, but I didn't know if she could write for the magazine. I think when you read through it, you'll see she nailed it."

Ellie took the pages and read through them. A minute or two later, she looked back up. "She can write," she acknowledged.

"She'll be great," I said.

"I'm not sure her finding a relationship will make good column fodder."

I shrugged. "Readers would have gotten tired of my schtick soon anyway. Do you really want to read about someone for a whole year that's such a loser she can never get a second date? I think it was already starting to wear thin. Abby will inject it with new life."

She considered that. "I'd have to pay her, plus your salary, instead of getting a two-fer."

I nodded. There was no way around that. "True, but this Landon Scott piece is going to drive major traffic to the magazine. You'll get thousands of readers who have never clicked through to us before, and you'll have the chance to convert them into subscribers. And as for me, I'm still willing to do the grunt work and pay my dues. I'm not going to go all diva and demand special assignments."

She snorted. "Not now anyway. I have no doubt you'll be trotting in soon with a new scheme to get yourself off of the grunt stories too."

I grinned. "Probably. But haven't I offered added value every time we've bargained?"

She drummed her fingers on the first page of the Landon article. "Yes," she conceded. "You have."

I figured it was now or never. "So . . . do we have a deal?"

She picked up the Landon article and glanced over it. "If the rest of the story is good, then yes. It's a deal."

I sat back and exhaled. "It's good. I promise."

"I'll see," she said and gestured for the rest of it. "I'll take that now. I have a few minutes between appointments this morning, and I'll look at it then."

"Thank you, Ellie."

She shook her head and then got up and walked out. "I'll tell Denny to run your last Indie Girl piece," she called over her shoulder.

Battling her exhausted me, but it was the only shot I had at making a relationship with Tanner work. I'd done everything I could, and I believed Tanner cared for me enough that it was going to pay off. Now I just had to sit back and wait to see if I knew him as well as I hoped.

When I walked back to my desk, Chantelle shot me a look that demanded to know if I was still okay. Ellie was rustling her stuff up and preparing to leave to do Ellie Stuff, so I flashed a subtle thumbs up at Chantelle. She nodded and went back to whatever she was working on.

"The column is live," Denny said, eyes glued to the screen.

Chantelle and Janie scrambled to click on it.

Ellie shook her head again and headed out with a terse, "See you after lunch."

I sat down and texted my parents to let them know that Indie Girl had checked in for her last hurrah. I noted the time on my monitor. Almost ten. When would Tanner see it? I was banking on his curiosity luring him to it in spite of our argument. I'd have read it if our roles were reversed.

Denny finished first. He swiveled to face me and sat back. "Whoa."

A moment later, Janie chimed in. "Yeah. Whoa."

Chantelle turned away from her computer. "You did it."

"I had to roll the dice," I said. "I hope this works."

Excitement glowed in Janie's face. "This is so cool! Did you send this to Tanner? What did he say?"

Denny and Chantelle both looked expectant.

"Nothing. Yet," I added when Janie's face fell. "I didn't send it to him, and since it just went up, I don't know if he's read it yet."

Denny shrugged. "He's an idiot if he doesn't come running."

I reddened. "Thanks."

Chantelle switched off her monitor and grabbed her purse. "I have to review the new exhibit at the Anders Gallery, but I expect to hear all the juicy details when I get back later."

"This is going to be awesome!" Janie said. "I'll be gone all afternoon, so I hope Tanner does something soon."

"Me too, Janie," I said. "Me too."

* * *

Janie was destined to leave disappointed. By noon, there had been no word from Tanner. Not an e-mail, call, or text. Nothing. The column itself generated a ton of feedback from readers. Dozens mourned my leaving. Even more people congratulated me on finding love. A handful wished me luck, realizing that I hadn't quit "Single in the City" for a sure thing. In fact, my romantic future looked less certain by the second.

Denny left to get a sandwich and offered to grab me one, but even if I weren't burnt out for the rest of my life on that particular food, I couldn't have eaten. The cold, hard knot in my stomach left no room for anything else. If it got any bigger it would push on my lungs and make breathing hard too. I refreshed the column's web page and scoured the comment trail. There was nothing there from Tanner either. No "I hear you" by TG. Nothing.

Courtney had texted an hour before. It was another "Whoohoo," which I took to mean she approved. But beyond begging me to tell Tanner about Indie Girl, she had made a point of staying out of our relationship. I didn't want to put her in the middle of it now by asking if she had heard from him.

I needed something else to do before I lost my mind obsessing over this. It was only my love life at stake. Certainly, I had more pressing things to get to, like Mooli.

I tried to immerse myself in the world of designer vegetables but gave up within a half hour, sure that I had never hated vegetables more than I did at that moment. Denny wandered back in and raised an eyebrow. I shook my head. No Tanner. I spent another hour aimlessly clicking through some of the local news feeds, trying to find inspiration for a new article. Despite my stern self-talk not to, I clicked through to the *Bee*. No articles from Tanner had posted that day. Slow news day, maybe?

By midafternoon, both Ellie and Chantelle, plus two of the ad reps, had made it back in. Chantelle didn't even wait for the door to close behind her before demanding, "Well?"

I shrugged. "Nothing."

She looked disappointed and dropped her stuff on her desk. "At least half your plan worked," she said.

I shot her a pointed glance not to bring that half of the plan up in front of Ellie. She nodded and turned to her monitor. I stared blankly at mine, trying to cheer myself with all the "Single in the City" comments bemoaning my departure, but it didn't help. If I didn't hear from Tanner, then the half of the plan that worked didn't really matter anyway.

In the comment trail, one troll had left a truly lovely gem. "Good luck to the loser who dates you. He must not know about all your flame outs here, or else he's too dumb to run the other way."

Nice. Tanner might be dumb enough to stick with me, even when I wasn't smart enough to see what I had when I had it, but at least he understood the function of the caps lock key.

Then again, maybe troll boy had it exactly right. Maybe Tanner had wised up and run as far away as possible.

The office stayed quiet, even though it was a fuller house than usual. My little black rain cloud must have expanded to include the rest of the staff. How nice of me to dampen the mood for everyone. What started as a day of promise and possible new beginnings had become a sad, sorry footnote in the wreck of my love life. I checked the time again. Two hours before everyone cleared out and I could quit pretending I was being productive. Two hours until I could drive home and collapse.

Two hours had never felt so long.

Ellie left first, off to a "meeting" with one of the magazine's "investors." Chantelle and I had decided that these meetings probably translated into shopping with a girlfriend or eating with a young, eligible male power broker at one of the downtown venture capital firms or law offices.

An IM alert popped up from Chantelle at the bottom of my screen. *Investment meeting with a shadowy Russian?*

It normally entertained me to trade IM guesses with Chantelle about what Ellie was really up to but not today. Today I struggled to wade through even the simplest tasks, and they grew harder as the day wore on without a word from Tanner. *I got nothing*, I typed back.

Chantelle left an hour later with a murmur of encouragement and a squeeze on my shoulder. The ad girls left by five, and Denny and I had the office to ourselves. Usually, it was the most productive time of the day for me, but I knew it was hopeless. I stood and looked down at my blouse, a gauzy lavender confection I had paired with a denim pencil skirt this morning when I woke up deluded that I would reunite with Tanner.

"I'm out," I said to Denny. "I'll see you tomorrow."

"Sorry," he said, and I knew he was apologizing that my roll of the dice had come up snake eyes.

I shuffled my laptop and a few loose papers into my bag and slung my purse over my shoulder. For the first time in a while, I found myself wishing again that I didn't share a room with Rosemary. I badly needed to burrow and ignore the world for the rest of the night, and then maybe, just maybe, I would find the energy to hatch a new plan to make things right with Tanner. The thought left me desolate though. Today's major plays had been the biggest and boldest new plan I could think of. I had hoped that by publicly quitting the column, I could say in words and actions that I was sorry and I was ready. There was no way to mistake the message. That left only one option.

He had rejected it.

I trudged downstairs to my car in the small strip mall parking lot and stopped short. A box sat on The Zuke. It was the size of a shoebox and wrapped in newspaper comics. I glanced around the parking lot, and then I saw him, leaning on his Honda at the other end of the lot.

"Open it," Tanner called.

Inside was a copy of the *Bee,* folded in half to fit the box and bound with a red ribbon tied in a slightly squashed bow. I lifted it out and untied it then opened the paper and spread it flat on The Zuke's hood. A huge block headline screamed "Tanner Graham Finds Love." Underneath it was a full color picture that Courtney had snapped on our trampoline double date. The rest of the paper was blank, but this had definitely been done on the *Bee's* printing press. I jerked up in surprise and stared at him, eyes wide with shock. Tanner smiled and pushed himself away from his car, in no hurry as he strolled toward me, hands in his pockets.

"Wha . . . how . . ." I stammered, trying to process everything.

"I know people," he said, reaching me and stopping a few feet away.

"But . . . you didn't call me." I was bewildered. Two minutes before, I had walked out of my office convinced that our relationship was on life support. Now Tanner stood there smiling like nothing was wrong. Which was great, except . . . "You made me wait all day!"

He laughed. "I had to wait until my buddy came on shift this afternoon to pull this together. Besides, you made me wait. For months."

"But we've only been dating for a few weeks."

"A few weeks is all it took me to fall in love with you," he said softly. "I've been feeling this way for months."

My jaw dropped. I stared at him for nearly a minute, attempting to form a response a few times and failing miserably. He reached over and, with the lightest touch of his index finger, pushed my jaw back up. Then he took a step closer and kissed me, his hand sliding through my hair and cupping the back of my head like he was making sure I wouldn't slip away.

I'd sampled a lot of kisses from Tanner over the last month. Hello kisses, good-bye kisses, just-because kisses, you-look-cute kisses, the-Jazz-just-scored kisses, I-hate-that-it's-time-to-go kisses. But this kiss . . .

It wasn't even on the same planet as those kisses.

This kiss staked his claim. And I returned it because I fiercely wanted him to be mine.

"You were saying?" he asked, taking a step back. I heard the hitch in his breathing.

"When did you know?"

He smiled. "I figured there might be potential when I figured out that you had left that thank you note for Courtney. I'd seen the feisty side of Pepper Spicer, and then, in that note to her, I realized what was underneath."

"What's that?" I asked, my voice barely audible over the hum of passing traffic.

"A woman with the biggest heart I'd ever seen, hiding behind jokes and insults."

I swallowed. "Was I really insulting?"

"I deserved it."

"No, you didn't!" I said. "You deserve so much better than what I've dished out over the last month." I took a deep breath. "I'm sorry."

"Forget it," he said. "I triple forgive you. But there's one thing that's killing me."

"What is it?"

He reached out and pulled me into his arms. "Please tell me you didn't quit the magazine for me," he said, his breath tickling my hair. "Please? Because I might kind of hate myself if you did."

There would be time enough later to explain that getting out of the column owed a lot to Landon. I had a feeling Tanner might write a thank you note of his own to Landon since the interview freed me from a stream of dates with strangers.

"I didn't," I said. "I know that's never what you wanted."

"No," he said, leaning back to take my face in his hands and dropping another soft kiss on my lips. "All I've wanted since you limped out of my life the first day I met you was to have you back in it. Does that scare you?"

I stood on tiptoe to return his kiss. "Not even a little bit. Thank you, Tanner Graham."

He smiled. "For what?"

"For being patient. I'll make it worth it."

"You've always been worth it," he said, punctuating his opinion with another kiss. He broke it off when a hoot from the balcony sounded, and we looked up to find Denny standing there, grinning and waving. He disappeared back into the office.

Tanner smiled down at me, tightening his hold. "Thank *you*."

"For what?"

"For being you. I love you, Pepper."

I squeezed back. "You'll do."

He leaned back to look at me, his eyes twinkling. "I'll do? I read your column this morning. You don't have any secrets anymore."

I wound my arms around his neck and pulled his lips down to meet mine again.

"I love when you go all investigative journalist on me," I said.

He captured me with another kiss that overloaded my senses so completely that I knew Tanner had just single-handedly rewired my central nervous system. I broke away to draw a breath and stare into the eyes that captured me like nothing had before.

"Here's an exclusive, Tanner Graham. I love you like crazy."

"My favorite kind of story," he said. "I already know how this one ends."

"How?"

"Happily ever after."

Dear Mom and Dad,

Thank you seems inadequate, but it's the only way I know how to tell you what's in my heart. There are a million things I could thank you for, like all your help with the wedding. Mom, the bridesmaid dresses came out beautifully. When Ginger wants to keep hers, you know it's true! And Dad, the chest you made is going to have a permanent place of honor in our new home. We'll keep our most precious things inside.

But thanking you for the gifts and the help is the easy part. Finding words for what you've given me beyond that . . . that's the impossible part. Thank you for loving me enough to challenge me to become better, grow bigger, and be more. Thank you for teaching me the most valuable lesson I've ever learned: the power of gratitude. You were right, Dad. A thankful heart has let me witness daily all the blessings in my life.

You two are the most amazing parents a daughter could hope for.

Love,
Pepper

About the Author

Melanie Bennett Jacobson is an avid reader, amateur cook, and champion shopper. She consumes astonishing amounts of chocolate, chick flicks, and romance novels. After meeting her husband online, she is now living happily in Southern California with her growing family and a series of doomed houseplants. Melanie is a former English teacher and a popular speaker who loves to laugh and make others laugh. In her down time (ha!), she writes romantic comedies for Covenant and maintains her humorous slice-of-life blog. She loves to hear from readers at www. melaniejacobson.net.